Marc W. Miller

MW01689141

MEGATRAVELLER™

IMPERIAL ENCYCLOPEDIA

Science-Fiction Role-Playing
in the Shattered Imperium

Edited by Gary L. Thomas and Joe D. Fugate, Sr.

GAME DESIGNERS' WORKSHOP

MegaTraveller is the current edition of the rules for the **Traveller** science-fiction role-playing system. **MegaTraveller** incorporates rules changes, revisions and additions which have been made over the years in order to maintain it as a leading state-of-the-art rules system.

The following is only a partial list of all of those who have been instrumental in making **Traveller**, and now **MegaTraveller**, the role-playing game system it is today.

Paul Aoki, John M. Astell, L. Ross Babcock, Bob Barger, Jolly R. Blackburn, Anders Blixt, Robert Bodine, Steven Brinich, Timothy B. Brown, Bobby Bryant, Dave Bryant, Roberto Camino, Rob Caswell, Winchell Chung, John W. Colbert, Kevin Connolly, William Connors, James Cumber, Jim Cunningham, Liz Danforth, David R. Deitrick, Ian Delaney, Marc Desmond, Keith Douglass, Steven P. Drevik, Ed Edwards, David Emigh, John M. Ford, Bryan Gibson, Gregg Giles, Trevor Graver, Jeffrey Groteboer, Leroy M. Guatney, John Harshman, Dan Hawthorne, David Heath, Jim Henley, Mike Jackson, Alexander Jamison, Stefan Jones, Chuck Kallenbach II, J. Andrew Keith, William H. Keith Jr, James B. King, John Lewis, Bob Liebman, L. Crede Lombard, John Marshal, Phil Masters, Jeffery May, Terrence R. McInnes, J. P. McManus, Bob McWilliams, Mike Metlay, Roger Moore, John M. Morrison, Stan Mullins, Nancy Parker, Robert Parker, Daniel Perez, Herb Petro, Daniel Perez, Donald Rapp, Peter Rasmussen, Robert Reese, Matt Renner, Marcus Rowland, James Schwar, Dave Sering, Craig Sheeley, Steve Sowards, Jerry Stoddard, Chris Struble, Mark P. Suszko, J. D. Webster, Jordan Weisman, Michael Wharton, Loren K. Wiseman, Erik Wilson.

And a special thanks to Bob Swarm.

Credits

Design....................Marc W. Miller
Additional Design....................Frank Chadwick, Joe D. Fugate Sr., Gary L. Thomas
Editing....................Gary L. Thomas and Joe D. Fugate Sr.
Contributions....................Loren Wiseman, J. Andrew Keith, John Harshman, Timothy B. Brown
Art Director....................Barbie Pratt
Sr. Graphic Designer....................Lauretta Oblinger
Graphic Designer....................Dana Reischauer
Cover Painting....................Steve Venters
Interior Illustrations....................Bryan Gibson, Tom Peters, Liz Danforth, Steve Crompton, William H. Keith, Rob Caswell, Tim Bradstreet
Text Manager....................Michelle Sturgeon

The following **Traveller** rules and supplement sets are incorporated (in part) in the *Imperial Encyclopedia:* **Traveller,** *Mercenary, High Guard, Scouts, Merchant Prince, The Spinward Marches, Citizens of the Imperium, Azhanti High Lightning, Striker, Traders and Gunboats, Library Data (A-M), Library Data (N-Z).*

MegaTraveller
Imperial Encyclopedia

ISBN 0-943580-48-X
3 4 5 6 7 8 9

Since 1973
GDW
PO Box 1646
Bloomington, IL 61702-1646

Table of Contents

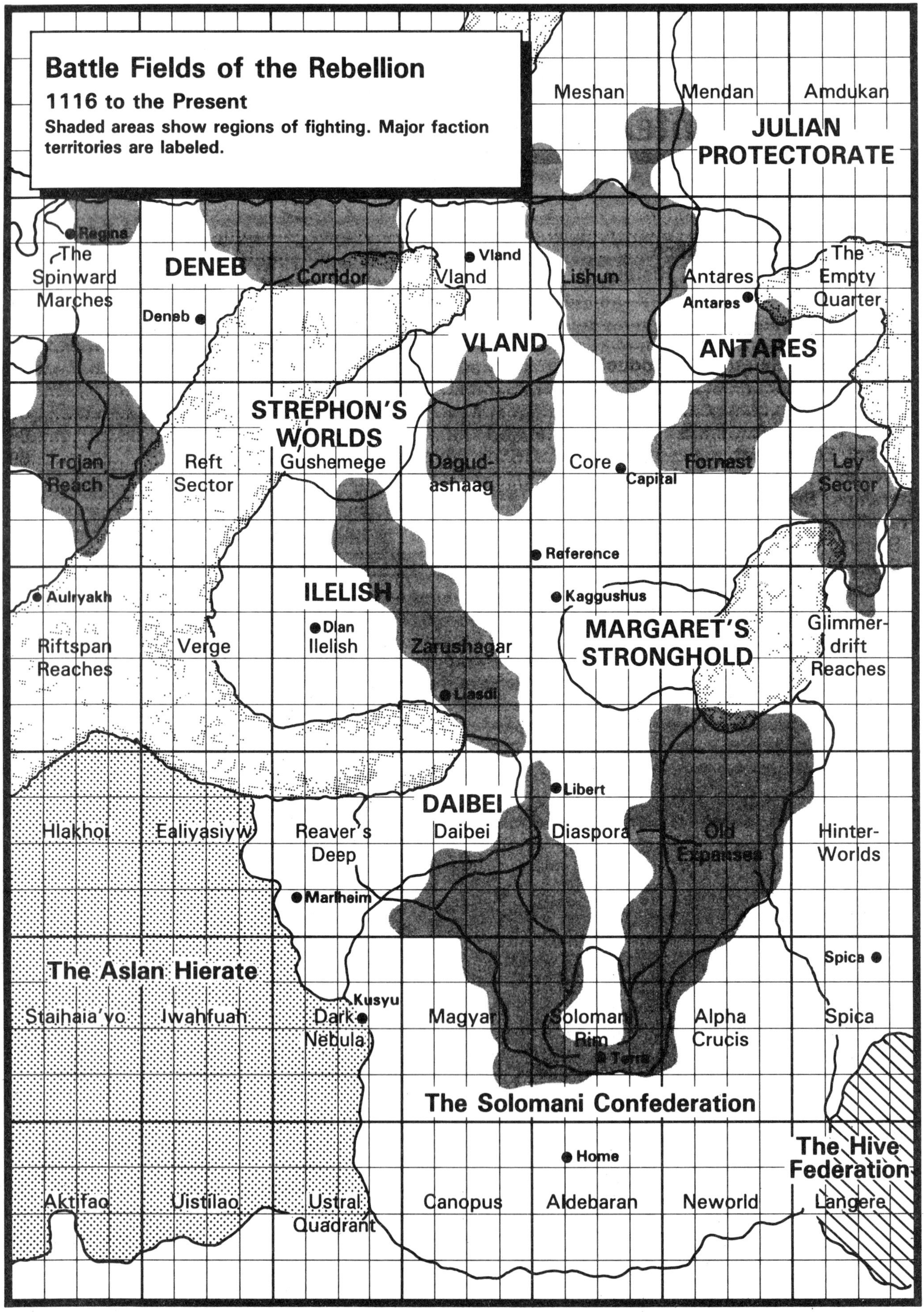

Battle Fields of the Rebellion

1116 to the Present

Shaded areas show regions of fighting. Major faction territories are labeled.

Dulinor I: Born in 1066 on Dlan/Ilelish, Archduke Dulinor Astrin Ilethian assumed the Iridium Throne of the Third Imperium in 1116.

Dulinor realized the Imperium would never regain its glory unless Strephon stepped down. In 1115, Dulinor asked Strephon to abdicate, but the emperor refused; the archduke realized that drastic measures were in order.

On 132-1116, Dulinor killed Strephon Alkhalikoi in personal combat, as required by custom, and ascended the throne as Dulinor I, Emperor of the Third Imperium.

The old regime has acted to impede Dulinor's accession to the Iridium Throne. Strephon's nephew, Lucan, has claimed the throne for himself without right. To enforce his will upon others, this pretender killed his own brother and prevented the Moot from confirming Dulinor's rightful status.

Because of the uncertainty fomented by Lucan and because his Navy interferes with free trade and communications, the Imperium must be united in its drive to crush Lucan.

—From the Library Data Service of the *Ilelish Interstellar Information Interchange.*

Dulinor: Born in 1066 on Dlan/Ilelish, Archduke Dulinor Astrin Ilethian assassinated Emperor Strephon thus reviving the "right of assassination" as a path to the throne.

Dulinor was appointed archduke to revitalize a region whose economy was faltering. While many criticized Strephon's choice, analysts agreed elevating an iconoclast promised to co-opt the man into the system.

On 132-1116, Dulinor struck, eliminating the Imperial heirs with three pistol shots, then fled to seed Imperium-wide rebellion. His brother, sector admiral of the Ilelish Fleet, formed the nucleus of the rebel navy.

The established succession procedures produced a legitimate heir, and Lucan assumed the throne. His first statement was an order to "crush Dulinor." Imperial forces have been mobilized to achieve just that end.

Because of the uncertainty fomented by Dulinor and because his navy interferes with free trade and communications, the Imperium must be united in its drive to crush Dulinor.

—From the Library Data Service of the *Imperial Data Network.*

MEGATRAVELLER

Information is controlled by those who provide it. The writers, even of encyclopedias, decide what is important and what is not. Their decisions determine what parts of history are available to the reader and what events will be lost in the mists of time.

This *Imperial Encyclopedia* is a compilation of information **Traveller** players can find illuminating and informative. Yet, taken literally, it can also be misleading and confusing. The information presented here can lead **Traveller** players on wide-ranging adventures to the ends of the Imperium and beyond. Truth is based on what the individuals believe. Two otherwise similar individuals can easily decide to support opposite sides in the struggle for the Imperium, and neither would be wrong in that decision.

A CHRONOLOGY OF THE IMPERIUM 1

This is a combined list of the important events in the histories of the major races in and around the Imperium. Equivalent dates are shown side-by-side from each race's dating system. Dates in the distant past (which are only approximations anyway) have been rounded off; otherwise, all dates are accurate to within one year.

Imperial	*Aslan*	*K'Kree*	*Vilani*	*Solomani*	*Zhodani*	*Event*
-500,000	-560,000	-400,000	380,000 PI	495,000 BC	-220,000	Ancient cities arise.
-400,000	-530,000	-325,000	300,000 PI	395,000 BC	-170,000	Ancients thrive. Humans transplanted.
-300,000	-340,000	-240,000	225,000PI	295,000 BC	-130,000	Final war (lasting 2000 yrs) destroys Ancients.
-200,000	-225,000	-160,000	150,000 PI	195,000 BC	-85,000	*Homo Zhdotlas* arises on Zhodane.
-75,000	-85,000	-55,000	55,000 PI	70,000 BC	-30,000	Droyne ascendance on several worlds.
-20,000	-20,000	-10,000	12,000 PI	15,000 BC	-6,000	Ancients' warbots on Vland finally run down.
-15,000	-15,000	-5,500	8,500PI	10,500 BC	-3,500	Rise of modern *Homo Sapiens*.
-11,000	-10,000	-2,300	5,300 PI	6,500 BC	-1,800	Flowering of Vilani culture.
-10,011	-9,042	-1,543	4,547 PI	5,493 BC	-1,446.1	First Vilani space explorations.
-9,900	-8,916	-1,450	4,462 PI	5,382 BC	-1,397.1	Scientific bases established in Vland system.
-9,400	-8,345	-1034	4,081 PI	4,882 BC	-1,176.1	Vilani sublight interstellar colonization.
-9,310	-8,243	-959	4,013 PI	4,792 BC	-1,136.1	Vilani discover non-Vilani human civilization.
-9,235	-8,157	-897	3,955 PI	4,717 BC	-1,103.1	Vilani discover Jump Drive.
-8,590	-7,421	-360	3,464 PI	4,072 BC	-817.3	Zhodani discover printing press.
-8,500	-7,319	-285	3,395 PI	3,982 BC	-778.1	Zhodani develop elementary psionics.
-7,980	-6,726	147	2,999 PI	3,462 BC	-548.1	First Zhodani space explorations.
-7,945	-6,686	176	2,972 PI	3,427 BC	-532.3	Plague on Zhodane.
-6,800	-5,380	1,129	2,099 PI	2,282 BC	-25.2	Zhodani recovery.
-6,731	-5,301	1,186	2,046 PI	2,213 BC	1.1	First Psionic Games. Zhodani calendar begins.
-6,200	-4,695	1,628	1,641 PI	1,682 BC	238.3	First Zhodani planetary missions.
-6,000	-4,467	1,795	1,489 PI	1,482 BC	327.1	First Zhodani sublight interstellar flights.
-5,823	-4,265	1,942	1,354 PI	1,305 BC	405.2	Zhodani Consulate established.
-5,430	-3,817	2,269	1,054 PI	912 BC	579.1	Vilani develop Jump-2 drive.
-5,415	-3,800	2,282	1,043 PI	897 BC	585.3	Zhodani discover Jump drive.
-5,400	-3,783	2,294	1,032 PI	882 BC	592.2	Start of Vilani Consolidation Wars.
-4,698	-2,982	2,879	496 PI	180 BC	902.3	Hivers develop inferior Jump drive.
-4,520	-2,779	3,027	361 PI	AD 1	981.2	Terran dating system begins.
-4,404	-2,646	3,123	272 PI	AD 114	1,032.3	Vega absorbed by Vilani.
-4,305	-2,534	3,206	197 PI	AD 213	1,076.2	K'kree unification of homeworld.
-4,212	-2,348	3,283	126 PI	AD 306	1,117.2	Hivers discover standard Jump drive.
-4,142	2,348	3,341	72 PI	AD 376	1,148.2	K'Kree discover Jump drive.
-4,045	-2,237	3,422	1 VI	AD 473	1,191.2	Consolidation Wars end; Ziru Sirka founded.
-4,000	-2,186	3,459	35 VI	AD 518	1,211.1	Vilani stop exploring. First Zhodani core mission.
-3,810	-1,969	3,618	180 VI	AD 708	1,295.1	Vargr discover Jump drive.
-3,500	-1,615	3,876	416 VI	AD 1018	1,432.2	First Imperium reaches greatest height.
-2,800	-817	4,458	950 VI	AD 1718	1,741.3	First Zhodani contact with Vargr.
-2,559	-542	4,659	1,133 VI	AD 1959	1,848.2	First Solomani space explorations.
-2,460	-429	4,741	1,209 VI	AD 2058	1,892.1	Solomani bases throughout solar system.
-2,431	-396	4,765	1,231 VI	AD 2087	1,904.3	Solomani discover Jump drive.
-2,424	-388	4,771	1,236 VI	AD 2094	1,908.1	Solomani visit Barnard's Star.
-2,422	-386	4,773	1,238 VI	AD 2096	1,908.3	First contact with Vilani.
-2,408	-370	4,784	1,249 VI	AD 2110	1,915.1	First Interstellar War ends.
-2,400	-360	4,791	1,255 VI	AD 2118	1,918.3	Vargr pillaging starts.
-2,398	-358	4,793	1,256 VI	AD 2120	1,919.2	Terran Confederation established.
-2,389	-348	4,800	1,263 VI	AD 2129	1,923.2	Terran Navy uses artificially intelligent robots.
-2,235	-172	4,928	1,380 VI	AD 2283	1,991.2	Nth Interstellar War starts.
-2,219	-154	4,942	1,393 VI	AD 2299	1,998.3	Nth Interstellar War ends.
-2,204	-137	4,954	1,404 VI	AD 2314	2,005.1	Terran Confederation ends; Rule of Man begins.
-2,190	-121	4,966	1,415 VI	AD 2328	2,011.2	Aslan First World War.
-2,160	-87	4,991	1,438 VI	AD 2358	2,024.3	Aslan Nuclear War.
-2,136	-59	5,011	1,456 VI	AD 2382	2,035.2	First Aslan space explorations.
-2,083	0	5,055	1,496 VI	AD 2435	2,058.3	Formation of the Tlaukhu. Aslan calendar begins.
-2,074	10	5,062	1,503 VI	AD 2444	2,062.3	Fleeing Vilani colonize Trojan Reaches.
-2,045	43	5,087	1,525 VI	AD 2473	2,075.2	First contact between K'Kree and Hivers.
-2,038	51	5,092	1,531 VI	AD 2480	2,078.3	K'Kree occupy several Hiver worlds.
-2,029	62	5,100	1,537 VI	AD 2489	2,082.3	Hiver-K'Kree War begins.
-2,023	69	5,105	1,542 VI	AD 2495	2,085.2	Hive Federation established. Navy built.
-2,018	74	5,109	1,546 VI	AD 2500	2,087.2	Hiver manipulations of K'Kree worlds start.
-2,013	80	5,113	1,550 VI	AD 2505	2,089.3	Hiver-K'Kree War ends.
-2,000	95	5,124	1,560 VI	AD 2518	2,095.2	First Zhodani contact with Vilani traders.
-1,999	96	5,125	1,560 VI	AD 2519	2,095.3	Aslan develop Jump drive.
-1,980	118	5,141	1575 VI	AD 2538	2,104.2	First Aslan contact with humans.
-1,802	321	5,289	1711 VI	AD 2716	2,183.1	First human contact with Hivers.
-1,776	350	5,310	1730 VI	AD 2742	2,194.2	Collapse of Rule of Man. Long Night begins.
-1,700	437	5,374	1788 VI	AD 2818	2,228.1	Vargr pillaging ends.
-1,690	448	5,382	1796 VI	AD 2828	2,232.2	Terran Mercantile Community established.
-1,658	485	5,409	1820 VI	AD 2860	2,246.3	Sack of Gashilean. Vargr Enclaves settled.
-1,526	635	5,519	1921 VI	AD 2992	2,305.1	Interstellar trade ceases. Long Night deepens.
-1,511	653	5,531	1932 VI	AD 3007	2,311.3	Solomani Traders contact Darrians.
-1,118	1,101	5,858	2232 VI	AD 3400	2,485.2	First Aslan Border War begins.
-1,110	1,110	5,865	2238 VI	AD 3408	2,488.3	Old Earth Union created.
-1,044	1,185	5,920	2288 VI	AD 3474	2,518.1	Aslan first cross Great Rift.
-1,000	1,235	5,956	2322 VI	AD 3518	2,537.2	Zhondani Consulate reaches present size.

A CHRONOLOGY OF THE IMPERIUM 2

Imperial	*Aslan*	*K'Kree*	*Vilani*	*Solomani*	*Zhodani*	*Event*
-924	1,322	6,020	2380 VI	AD 3594	2,571.1	Darrians reach TL 16. Sun destabilizes.
-650	1,635	6,248	2589 VI	AD 3868	2,692.2	Sylean Federation established.
-630	1,658	6,264	2604 VI	AD 3888	2,701.1	Island sectors colonized.
-399	1,921	6,457	2780 VI	AD 4119	2,803.1	Sword World colonization begins.
-200	2,148	6,622	2932 VI	AD 4318	2,891.1	First human contact with K'Kree.
-186	2,164	6,634	2943 VI	AD 4332	2,897.2	First Sword World confederation.
-110	2,251	6,697	3,001 VI	AD 4408	2,931.1	Shudusham Concords.
-30	2,342	6,764	3,062 VI	AD 4488	2,966.2	Cleon's Campaign begins.
0	2,376	6,788	3,084 VI	AD 4518	2,979.3	Third Imperium established. Imperial dating system begins.
50	2,433	6,830	3,123 VI	AD 4568	3,001.3	First Zhodani contact with Imperial traders.
60	2,445	6,839	3,130 VI	AD 4578	3,006.1	Colonization of Spinward Marches begins.
76	2,463	6,852	3,142 VI	AD 4594	3,013.1	Pacification Campaigns begin.
114	2,506	6,884	3,171 VI	AD 4632	3,030.1	Solomani Hypothesis proposed.
120	2,513	6,889	3,176 VI	AD 4638	3,032.3	Pacification Campaigns end.
148	2,545	6,912	3,197 VI	AD 4666	3,045.1	Scouts recontact Darrians.
210	2,616	6,963	3,245 VI	AD 4728	3,072.2	Vargr Campaigns begin.
348	2,773	7,078	3,350 VI	AD 4866	3,133.2	Vargr Corridor campaigns end.
380	2,810	7,105	3,374 VI	AD 4898	3,147.3	Peace of Ftahalr. Imperial-Aslan border established.
404	2,837	7,125	3,392 VI	AD 4922	3,158.1	First Shudusham Robotics Conference.
420	2,855	7,138	3,405 VI	AD 4938	3,165.2	First Survey of Imperium completed.
426	2,862	7,143	3,409 VI	AD 4944	3,168.1	Easter Concordat absorbed into Imperium.
461	2,902	7,172	3,436 VI	AD 4979	3,183.2	First Aslan contact with Zhodani.
475	2,918	7,184	3,447 VI	AD 4993	3,189.3	Empress Nicholle assassinated.
489	2,934	7,196	3,457 VI	AD 5007	3,195.3	Hive capital moved to Glea.
500	2,947	7,205	3,466 VI	AD 5018	3,200.3	Imperial explorations into Zhodani territory.
588	3,047	7,278	3,533 VI	AD 5106	3,239.2	Terra incorporated into Imperium.
589	3,048	7,279	3,533 VI	AD 5107	3,240.1	First Frontier War starts.
604	3,065	7,291	3,545 VI	AD 5122	3,246.3	First Frontier War ends. Beginning of Civil War.
606	3,067	7,293	3,546 VI	AD 5124	3,247.2	Plankwell murders Empress Jacqueline I.
615	3,078	7,301	3,553 VI	AD 5133	3,251.2	Second Frontier War begins.
620	3,083	7,305	3,557 VI	AD 5138	3,253.3	Second Frontier War ends.
622	3,086	7,306	3,559 VI	AD 5140	3,254.3	End of Civil War.
624	3,088	7,308	3,560 VI	AD 5142	3,255.2	Xboat system established.
679	3,151	7,354	3,602 VI	AD 5197	3,279.3	Solomani power broken at court.
704	3,179	7,375	3,621 VI	AD 5222	3,290.3	Solomani Autonomous Region created.
718	3,195	7,386	3,632 VI	AD 5236	3,297.1	Xboat system covers entire Imperium.
750	3,232	7,413	3,656 VI	AD 5268	3,311.1	Seventh Zhodani core expedition.
799	3,288	7,454	3,694 VI	AD 5317	3,332.3	Crisis of '99.
800	3,289	7,454	3,694 VI	AD 5318	3,333.2	Psionics Suppressions begin.
826	3,318	7,476	3,714 VI	AD 5344	3,344.3	Psionics Suppressions end.
852	3,348	7,498	3,734 VI	AD 5370	3,356.2	Current Sword Worlds government established.
871	3,370	7,514	3,748 VI	AD 5389	3,364.3	Solomani Confederation established.
940	3,448	7,571	3,801 VI	AD 5458	3,395.1	Confederation friction with the Imperium.
950	3,460	7,579	3,809 VI	AD 5468	3,399.3	Solomani reintegrated into Imperium.
979	3,493	7,603	3,831 VI	AD 5497	3,412.2	Start of Third Frontier War.
986	3,501	7,609	3,836 VI	AD 5504	3,415.2	End of Third Frontier War.
990	3,505	7,613	3,839 VI	AD 5508	3,417.2	Solomani Rim War begins.
998	3,515	7,619	3,845 VI	AD 5516	3,420.3	Imperial advance to core of Solomani Sphere.
1002	3,519	7,623	3,848 VI	AD 5520	3,422.3	Siege of Terra. End of Solomani Rim War.
1005	3,523	7,625	3,851 VI	AD 5523	3,424.1	Solomani Home Guard created.
1040	3,563	7,654	3,877 VI	AD 5558	3,439.2	Destruction of Phoenix project begins.
1045	3,568	7,658	3,881 VI	AD 5563	3,441.3	Destruction of Phoenix project ends.
1065	3,591	7,675	3,896 VI	AD 5583	3,450.2	Second Survey of the Imperium completed.
1082	3,610	7,689	3,909 VI	AD 5600	3,458.1	False War (Fourth Frontier War) begins.
1084	3,613	7,691	3,911 VI	AD 5602	3,458.3	False War (Fourth Frontier War) ends.
1107	3,639	7,710	3,928 VI	AD 5625	3,469.1	Fifth Frontier War starts.
1110	3,642	7,713	3,931 VI	AD 5628	3,470.2	Fifth Frontier War ends.
1116	3,649	7,717	3,935 VI	AD 5634	3,473.1	Strephon murdered. Imperial Moot dissolved.
1117	3,650	7,718	3,936 VI	AD 5635	3,473.3	Struggle for succession produces chaos.

The Emperors' List

The 1500-year period of interstellar anarchy known as the Long Night ended about a thousand years ago with the establishment of the Third Imperium. The traditions of the First Imperium and the Second Imperium (the Rule of Man) remained even after centuries of disorganization, and it was only natural for a new interstellar empire to draw on its predecessors for precedent and for stability.

In a thirty-year campaign which molded public opinion at the same time that battle starships were convincing local governments, Cleon Zhunastu committed a family industrial base and a firm foundation of industrial support to the creation of an empire that would rival the glories of past ages. He succeeded in forming a government that controlled, with velvet-gloved fist, nearly a hundred subsectors: the Third Imperium.

In the 1119 years since the assumption of Cleon I, the Emperors' List has been a convenient reference for the events in the growth and the development of the Imperium. The relationship of dates and emperors serves as a mnemonic device and lends color to the data.

ASCENDING THE THRONE

There is only one legitimate means to ascend to the iridium throne: by confirmation of the Moot, that governing body composed of all nobles (baron and above) of the Imperium. In the absence of an emperor, the Moot is the validating body for the new emperor. The Moot has the power to examine the qualifications and credentials of any apparent heirs, and it makes the final decision confirming or rejecting them.

Under very exceptional circumstances, two other methods of ascendancy have been invoked by various emperors. The first of these methods, the right of assassination, was introduced by the Moot in 245 to deal with Cleon the Mad, a legitimate emperor who became insane after his confirmation by the Moot. Cleon refused to abdicate and personally shot and killed those who asked him to do so. Faced with this problem, the Moot decided in high session to depose Cleon. Porfiria was chosen as Cleon's successor, and under the guidance of the Moot she exercised the right of assassination by killing Cleon and ascending to the throne.

The other method of gaining Imperial power is that used by countless usurpers in the past, which was attempted by the current usurper Dulinor. Acting without the all-important consent of the Moot, these interlopers have taken the government into their own hands by heinous acts of violence against the person of the proper ruler. While there are cases in Imperial history in which these usurpers have later been confirmed by the action of the Moot, such cases are rare, and the periods of time in which such actions took place have been marked by political turmoil and needless civil strife for loyal citizens of the Imperium.

EMPERORS BEFORE THE CIVIL WAR

Cleon I: First of the Zhunastu Dynasty and first emperor of the Imperium. Born in -57, proclaimed hereditary emperor for life by the Moot in the first year of the Imperium. Died in 53. Built the Grand Palace of Cleon, which still stands today in the Imperial Park and is a much visited monument.

Cleon II: Only issue of Cleon I; also known as Cleon the Weak. Born in 21, proclaimed emperor by the Moot in 53, abdicated in 54. In point of fact, a recent study indicates that the term weak may be an unfair description of Cleon II. Apparently unsuited to devious palace politics but still recognizing the need to consolidate the power of the fledgling Imperium, Cleon abdicated in favor of his brilliant chancellor, Artemsus Lentuli. Still vitally concerned with the welfare of his former realm, Cleon spent the rest of his long, active, colorful, and, from all accounts, happy, life on the frontier as a self-appointed (and extremely effective) one-man fire brigade.

Artemsus: First of the Lentuli Dynasty. Born in -17, proclaimed emperor by the Moot in 54, died in 166 at the age of 183, demonstrating the natural longevity of the Lentuli line. Artemsus established the domains and instituted the Pacification Campaigns (76 to 120) to bring the historical territories of the First and Second Imperia into the Third Imperium.

The Solomani Hypothesis (that the humans of the galaxy are all descended from one genetic stock, spread by some ancient race for reasons unknown; and that the source of that stock was Terra of Sol) was proposed in 114 and received immediate, although somewhat disinterested, acceptance.

Martin I: Eldest son of Artemsus. Born in 12, proclaimed emperor by the Moot in 166, died in 195. Martin had an elder sister, but she did not pursue a career in government. Martin's reach exceeded his grasp as he attempted to add the coreward Makhidkarun territories (the sectors of Meshan, Mendan, and Amdukan) into the Imperium. These three sectors united under Julian, fought the Julian War (175 to 191), and maintained their independence.

Martin II: Oldest issue of Martin I. Born in 53, proclaimed emperor by the Moot in 195, died in 244 without issue. He built the Grand Palace of Martin II, which was destroyed in 620 after a brief siege by the forces of Marava. Martin II, recognizing the growing importance of the frontier sectors of Deneb and the Spinward Marches, began the Vargr Campaigns (220 to 348) to clear the routes connecting them to the main territories of the Imperium.

Cleon III: In the dynastic crisis caused by the death of Martin II without direct issue, Cleon Zhunastu, great-great-great-grandson of Cleon II by direct first issue, appeared to be the most legitimate claimant to the throne. Born in 201, proclaimed emperor by the Moot in 244, assassinated in 245. Known also as Cleon the Mad, it appears that while his claim to the throne was flawless, he was not. His behavior in office (he resolved disagreements within his cabinet by shooting vocal opponents) soon convinced surviving members of the government that he was a homicidal maniac, and a decision to dispose of him was made and implemented in short order. The decision to depose a ruling emperor was not made lightly, but was agreed upon not only by those nobles closest to the emperor himself, but also by a secret meeting of the Moot, which ordered Cleon's assassination. Porfiria was chosen by lot as Cleon's heir, and succession was accomplished by the right of assassination.

Porfiria: Fourth in the reestablished Lentuli Dynasty, Porfiria was the oldest issue of the grandnephew of Martin II. Born in 201, proclaimed empress by the Moot in 245, died in 326. Porfiria actively pursued the Vargr Campaigns, and it was during her reign that they were essentially completed.

Anguistus: Oldest issue of Porfiria. Born in 246, proclaimed emperor by the Moot in 326, died in 365.

Martin III: Second issue of Anguistus (a preceding infant died in childhood). Born in 289, proclaimed emperor by the Moot in 365, died in an air/raft accident in 456 at the age of 167, having outlived his only issue. In memory of this deceased son, the title Martin IV was never used by an emperor.

It fell to Martin III to crush the Ilelish Revolt (418 to 435) and its challenge to Imperial authority.

Martin V: Grandson of Martin III; oldest issue of Martin IV. Born in 357, proclaimed emperor by the Moot in 456, died in 457.

Nicholle: Oldest issue of Martin V. Born in 401, proclaimed empress by the Moot in 457, murdered in 475.

Cleon IV: Generally believed to be responsible for the murder of Empress Nicholle and her immediate family, Cleon IV was a distant relation in the Zhunastu Dynasty and based his claims to legitimacy on that. This interloper was the first of the nondynastic emperors and kept the Moot at bay by threats of violence against its members. Born in 423, proclaimed emperor by the blackmailed Moot in 475, assassinated in 555.

Jerome: Ascended the throne by Moot election. Born in 525, proclaimed emperor by the Moot in 555, assassinated in 582.

Jaqueline I: Ascended the throne by right of Moot election. Born in 561, proclaimed empress by the Moot in 582, assassinated in 606. During the reign of Jaqueline, extensive expansion of the Rimward Fringe of the Imperium took place, which was due primarily to her economic policies which depended on cost-effectiveness. Terra of Sol was reintegrated into the Imperium in 588.

EMPERORS OF THE FLAG

Olav: First of the Emperors of the Flag. Olav hault-Plankwell, as Grand Admiral of the Marches, defeated the massive incursion of the Out-World Coalition in the First Frontier War (589 to 604). Upon return to the Imperial Core, Olav personally murdered the Empress Jaqueline I and proclaimed himself emperor by so-called right of fleet control. Born in 532, self-proclaimed emperor in 606, killed in battle in 609.

Ramon I: As Olav's chief of staff, Ramon was able to convince large portions of the fleet to attempt an overthrow of Olav. In the Battle of Tricanus 5 (609), Ramon's forces were apparently defeated, but Olav's flagship was destroyed with all hands in a final closing action. Born 560, proclaimed emperor by right of Moot election in 609, murdered in 609.

Constantus: Born 562, self-proclaimed emperor by supposed right of assassination without support of Moot in 609, killed in battle in 610.

Nicolai: Defeated the forces of Constantus in the Battle of Rakakaka (610). Born in 559, proclaimed emperor by the Moot in 610, murdered in 612.

George: Born in 558, self-proclaimed emperor by right of assassination without Moot support in 612, murdered in 613.

Numerous emperors of uncertain status and unlikely heritage ruled fragments of the Imperial Core from 613 to 615. None held a sufficient balance of power to be judged truly emperor, none were supported by the Moot, and the Home Worlds had formed a temporarily autonomous state. Nevertheless, no break in the Imperium is judged to have taken place as the Imperial bureaucracy continued to function without interruption.

In 615, Cleon V was finally proclaimed emperor by a close vote in the Moot, reestablishing a proper dynastic succession. Only a few years later, at the instigation of radical nobles in the Moot, Joseph attacked Cleon in battle and killed him. He was proclaimed emperor by the Moot, again by a very close vote, and many nobles refused to swear allegiance to him. Over the next four years a number of men and women sat on the

iridium throne, some with the support of the Moot and some without it. Because of the lack of popular Moot support for certain emperors and empresses, their successors were in some instances able to garner Moot support even after murdering the previous ruler. The same Moot could elect one man emperor and then later the same year elect his murderer as the new emperor. These were not proud times for the Third Imperium.

A proper line was not permanently reestablished by the Moot until the time of Arbellatra in 629.

Cleon V: Born in 565, proclaimed emperor by the Moot in 615 after the resubjugation of the Home Worlds, killed in battle in 618.

Joseph: Born in 581, proclaimed emperor by the Moot in 618 after defeating Cleon V in the Battle of Markatch (618), killed in battle the same year.

Donald: Born in 579, self-proclaimed emperor without the support of the Moot after the defeat of Joseph in the Battle of Arakoine (618), murdered in 618.

Emdiri: Born in 571, self-proclaimed empress by supposed right of assassination without support of Moot in 618, murdered in 619.

Catharine: Born in 582, proclaimed empress by the Moot in 619, murdered in 619.

Ramon II: Born in 566, proclaimed emperor by the Moot in 619, killed in battle in 619.

Jaqueline II: Born in 569, proclaimed empress by the Moot after defeating Ramon II in the Battle of the Nivzhine Belt (619), killed in battle in 619.

Usuti: Born in 558, proclaimed emperor by the Moot after defeating Jaqueline II in the Second Battle of Araloine (619), killed in battle in 620.

Marava: Born in 551, proclaimed empress by the Moot after defeating Usuti in the Third Battle of Araloine (620), killed in battle in 620. Destroyed the Grand Palace of Martin II.

Ivan: Born in 580, named emperor by the Moot after defeat of Marava in the Battle of Sulgami (620), killed in battle in 621.

Martin VI: Born in 597, proclaimed emperor by the Moot after the defeat of Ivan in the First Battle of Zhimaway (621), murdered in 621.

Gustus: Born in 581, proclaimed emperor by the Moot in 621, killed in battle in 622.

Arbellatra: First of the Alkhalikoi Dynasty (and occasionally considered to be the 18th of the Emperors of the Flag). Born in 587, served as Grand Admiral of the Marches and led the defeat of the Out-World Coalition in the Second Frontier War (615 to 620). Arbellatra returned to the Imperial Core and defeated the remnants of the Central Fleet under Gustus in the Second Battle of Zhimaway (622). Proclaimed regent by the Moot in 622 pending the location of a suitable surviving heir to the throne. Proclaimed empress by the Moot in 629. Died in 666. Built the Grand Imperial Palace, a magnificent sphere one kilometer in diameter, which floated one-half a kilometer above the landscape of the Imperial Park on Capital.

Zhakirov: Oldest issue of Arbellatra. Born in 624, proclaimed emperor by the Moot in 666. Zhakirov's marriage to Antiama in 679 marked and cemented an alliance between the Alkhalikoi Dynasty and the business interests of the Imperial Core; it broke the power of the Solomani interests at court and ultimately led to the Solomani Rim War (990 to 1002). Died in 688.

Margaret I: Oldest Issue of Zhakirov. Born in 684, proclaimed empress by the Moot in 688, died in a tunnel collapse without issue in 736. Margaret established the Solomani Autonomous Region in 704. Built the Consortium Trinary, three companion spheres near the Imperial Palace, in 729 to celebrate the hundredth birthday of the structure.

Paulo I: Second issue of Zhakirov. Born in 684, proclaimed emperor in 736, died of natural causes in 767. Built Paulo's Annex, a companion structure to the Imperial Palace, in 740.

Tomutov I: Oldest issue of Paulo I. Born in 712, proclaimed emperor by the Moot in 767, abdicated in 768, died in 801. Built Tomutov's Palace, a companion structure to the Imperial Palace, from his own funds after his abdication. This floating sphere is used as a residence for important visitors to the Imperial Palace.

Paula II: Oldest issue of Tomutov I. Paula II is perhaps best known for her steady hand at the helm during the Psionic Suppressions of 800 to 826. Born in 752, proclaimed empress by the Moot in 768, died in 836.

Tomutova II: Third issue of Paula II (preceding heirs died before ascending the throne). Born in 782, proclaimed empress by the Moot in 836, died in 908.

Margaret II: Oldest issue of Tomutova II. Born in 824, proclaimed empress by the Moot in 908, died in 945.

Styryx: Oldest issue of Tomolin (oldest issue of Margaret II, born in 901, died in 944). Born in 920, proclaimed emperor by the Moot in 945, abdicated in 989 in the repercussions following the mismanaged Third Frontier War (979 to 986).

Gavin: Oldest surviving issue of Styryx. To Gavin fell the management of the Solomani Rim War (990 to 1002), already set into motion by his father. Born in 946, proclaimed emperor by the Moot in 989, died in 1031.

Paulo III: Oldest issue of Gavin. Born in 981, proclaimed emperor by the Moot in 1031, died in 1071.

Strephon: Oldest surviving issue of Paulo III. Born in 1049, proclaimed emperor by the Moot in 1071, murdered in 1116.

During Strephon's reign, the Fourth Frontier War (1082 to 1084) erupted; his delegation of war powers to Norris, Duke of Regina, is credited with bringing a speedy end to a conflict that otherwise would have been hampered by the long delays in communication between Capital and the front. Norris later became the conquering hero of the Fifth Frontier War, and in partial recognition of this, one of Strephon's last official acts was the appointment of Norris as Archduke of the Domain of Deneb, which consists of the sectors of Deneb, the Spinward Marches, Trojan Reach, and Reft Sector.

SUCCESSORS TO STREPHON

The Moot has been unable to decide upon a proper successor, but claimants and pretenders have come forward.

Dulinor I: Also known as Dulinor the Usurper. Born in 1066, Strephon's murderer proclaimed himself emperor by the so-called right of assassination and then fled with his black-garbed troops to his home world of Dlan/Ilelish. Dulinor, who had convinced Strephon that he was one of his closest friends, was appointed Archduke of Ilelish in 1104, an action opposed by most nobility. Dulinor's murder of the Yerlyaruiwo Aslan ambassador blamed for Aslan *Ihatei* incursions into Imperial territory.

Lucan: The nephew of Strephon by his sister Lydia, Lucan has already proclaimed himself as emperor; however, in his first act, he dissolved the Moot for one year, so his claim has not had the opportunity to be officially verified. The Moot, for its part, disputes his dissolution of their body, but for security reasons, the Moot has not been able to safely meet and conduct Imperial business. Some detractors accuse Lucan of the murder of his older brother Varian, who was killed in fighting in the Imperial Palace shortly after the murder of Strephon by Dulinor.

Margaret: The great-granddaughter of Gavin by third issue, Margaret is seen by many nobles as an easy and legitimate alternative to Lucan, although her lineage is not as direct to Strephon.

The "Real" Strephon: Appearing in Usdiki/Gushemege in 1117 and claiming that his double was the one killed in the Imperial Palace, the so-called "Real" Strephon has many adherents, who support his claim by pointing out Emperor Strephon's known interests in genetic and robotic methods for duplication of a human.

Archduke Norris of Deneb: Supported by many nobles in the Moot, Norris is highly respected for his very competent handling of the Fifth Frontier War and for his ability since Strephon's murder to keep intact an important border region of the Imperium. Because it would have been easy for Norris to declare independence for his territories, particularly since the so-called Restored Vilani Empire region now falls between the Domain of Deneb and the Imperial Core, Norris's loyalty and fidelity to the Imperium have attracted support for him from nobles.

Archduke Brzk of Antares: As the pinnacle of power in the Domain of Antares, Archduke Brzk of Antares has received attention for his handling of the disorder during the Rebellion. He considered himself a candidate for the throne until 1118, when he decided the Moot would never ratify a nonhuman as emperor.

NOTES ON WORLD GENERATION

The purpose of the world generation sequence is to aid the imagination. Even the most imaginative individual soon loses brilliance in the face of creating hundreds of individual worlds.

The procedure substitutes die rolls for random imagination, allowing you to use that information to determine specific world data. Imagination may be required to explain a tech level 4 civilization in an asteroid belt or a high population world with a participating democracy for a government.

Additional notes about world generation are given below:

Size: Any main world with size 0 is an asteroid belt. The code *S* refers to a small planet or satellite with a diameter less than 800 kilometers.

Small worlds are treated as size 0. They range in size from 200 to 700 kilometers in diameter (1D + 1 times 100 kilometers).

Rings: Planets may have rings occupying orbits around them. The size code *R* is used to specify a ring that occupies an orbit around a world. The individual components of a ring are usually small particles often less than 500 mm in diameter.

Rings have little practical use, and they rarely have bases or settlements located on them. In most cases, the UPP will be a series of zeroes following the *R* code. However, in exceptional circumstances, you may choose to establish a small population (probably consisting mainly of miners, prospectors, or scientific researchers) in the ring.

The generation tables assume that a world is a naturally occurring solid matter sphere. Alternatives to this condition are extremely rare, and they tend to have very high tech levels. These alternitives include those listed as follows:

Rosettes (Tech Level 21): Three or more equal masses (such as worlds) which are set at the points of an equilateral polygon. The correct equal angular velocities about their center of mass will result in a stable orbital configuration; no central star is required. Rosettes never occur naturally.

Ringworlds (Tech Level 25): An incredibly strong band may be set rotating about a central star, which results in existance of a ringworld. Ringworlds use centrifugal force to provide a simulation of gravity. A ringworld at the distance of Earth's orbit and with a width of 1.6 million kilometers has a usable surface area of approximately three million Earths.

Sphereworlds (Tech Level 27): Using materials similar to those in a ringworld and adding gravity generators where necessary for strength and comfort, a spherical shell could be used to enclose a star. Such a shell would then trap all stellar radiation for use by the civilization. With a radius of about 93 million miles, the internal surface area would equal approximately one billion Earths.

Nobles

The Third Imperium is not a democracy. Social Standing indicates not only the lifestyle and peer group for a citizen of the Imperium, but also the social weight an individual can throw around when he wants something done. High strength or intelligence is an advantage; high social standing is a similar advantage. But while noble status does accord an individual a special place in the Imperium, it also obliges certain responsibilities to prevent abuses of this power.

Since Strephon's death and the subsequent division of the Imperium, nobles in some areas have fallen on hard times, and certain Imperial subjects have refused to recognize the authority of the nobility. In most regions, however, the peerage continues on as it has for centuries, with an organized hierarchy of nobles constituting the upward chain leading from an ordinary Imperial citizen to the emperor on Capital.

THE IMPERIAL NOBILITY

The Imperial nobility is a narrow class of persons at the upper strata of society who hold, either personally or through their family line, noble rank from the emperor. Noble rank is a mark of high social status for citizens and serves two purposes: it rewards individuals for significant achievements, and it provides social station for the political leaders within the government. All but the highest noble ranks (count, duke, archduke) can be awarded in recognition of achievement or preeminence in a field of endeavor.

The nobility includes within it a subset called the peerage, which consists of all nobles except knights and baronets. Except in extraordinary situations, to hold a high office in the Imperial bureaucracy a person must be a peer (although, on the other hand, not all peers hold office).

Collectively, the peerage constitutes the Moot, the Imperial government's only deliberative body. Technically, the Moot is supreme in the Imperium, but its power is extremely limited. In practice, its deliberations are advisory to the emperor, and he is wise to heed them. The Moot has only one power: to dissolve the Imperium. When this power is brought to bear, it compels compromise between opposing factions. The Moot also has the power to confirm emperors and other nobles to their posts.

Nobility is usually hereditary. Once confirmed by the Moot, a title continues to be passed down to succeeding generations. Titles need not pass through the first born (although this is the accepted practice), and individuals with several titles may divide them among their children as they see fit. An individual who is a member of a close family with noble rank is usually considered a member of the nobility even though that individual may not personally hold a title.

Nobility is acquired through letters patent (patents of nobility) issued by the emperor. Traditionally, appointments are published in the Holiday List (appearing on the first day of each new year) and in the Birthday List (appearing on the emperor's birthday). Additional patents of nobility for political purposes or special occasions are published when necessary.

All nobility is part of the feudal system of Imperial government. Nobles, upon receiving their patent or upon confirming their inheritance when coming of age, swear continuing loyalty to the Imperium, to the emperor, and to the emperor's successors. Failure to do so can void the patent for the generation or even permanently.

Noble rank can be revoked by the emperor, personally or through the Moot. Reasons for such revocation are treason, murder, kidnapping, and extortion as well as other felonies. Incompetence can also be a reason for revocation of a title. Occasionally, a noble rank will not be confirmed upon inheritance (the emperor has this option, as does the Moot and the holder). The rank may then go to another member of the same family or lie dormant for the generation. Furthermore, the emperor has the option of appointing a new family to hold the noble rank, displacing the former line.

All noble ranks within the peerage come from the emperor. The ability to create knights and baronets, however, is shared with the archdukes of the Imperium. The archdukes, within their domains, have an authority to create knights and baronets that it subject to disapproval only by the emperor. The purpose of these knighthoods (and baronetcies) is to allow the archdukes to create supporters and retainers for their own purposes rather than to depend on the emperor to do so. The noble ranks created are not members of the Moot.

TYPES OF NOBLES

Nobles in the Third Imperium can be divided into three types: honor (achievement), rank (position), and high (service). In the Imperium, an individual is noble by having a patent from the proper authority, which confers nobility upon him.

In general, a noble's status is lower when he leaves his "sphere of influence." On "average" Imperial worlds, having normal technology and ordinary Vilani-Solomani-Imperial cultural influences, this reduction will be small but noticeable when the noble leaves his "sphere of influence." (A noble's sphere of influence is the environment in which he is acknowledged and which he affects accordingly.)

Honor Nobles: Honor nobles (also known as achievement

or award nobles) receive patents from the emperor for "heroism in the military, success in civil or commercial enterprise, or innovation and discovery in the sciences." Only patents for knights, baronets, barons, and marquis may be issued for achievement; patents for counts and other high ranks are too important to be given as mere rewards.

Each year on Holiday, the first day of the new year, a list of new patents is published on Capital. From this tradition comes the term "holiday noble," which refers derisively to nobles serving no real administrative function in the Imperium. Notwithstanding, honor nobles are the real celebrities of the Imperium; their noble rank is a recognition of an already important status within the community.

Honor nobles' achievements are deemed important enough to warrant attention from the emperor or an archduke. Sphere of influence for such a noble extends as far as the achievement of the noble is considered significant. Note that the measurement of this sphere of influence is not necessarily a physical distance.

For example, one knighted for a discovery in gravitics might have status among other physicists all over the Imperium while having no real fame among musicians or businessmen. Honor nobles sometimes travel on the interstellar "lecture and cocktail circuit"; remuneration for public speaking can provide a valuable income.

Rank Nobles: Patents for rank nobility are given because of a citizen's position, and all noble classes are eligible for such a patent. Members of the rank nobility belong to one of two subtypes.

Local Nobility: The first subtype comprises the "local nobility," who make up the majority of those titled within the Imperium. These nobles serve as Imperial representatives in systems that have a government somehow not conducive to administration by high nobility. These representatives occupy "specific governmental offices" and are equivalent in social standing to barons and knights.

Patents for rank nobles are typically hereditary and remain with families of local leaders from generation to generation. Essentially, the sphere of influence of local rank nobles encompasses one star system. Although such nobles often have little power outside their local sphere of influence, they may be recognized by other local nobles. Note that nobles of this type are members of the peerage, albeit of low precedence.

Administrators: The second subtype of rank noble comprises citizens who hold Imperial office. Often, these nobles are administrators of worlds or territories with no formal Imperial representation. Because the title is tied to a position, these patents are not hereditary. Here, a noble's sphere of influence includes operational territories or influence among others within a specialized field. These patents often include a generous letter of pension to keep the noble comfortable after a career of long and faithful service.

Patents for rank nobles are awarded as needed, generally upon assumption of duties. Patents may be revoked or transferred at the conclusion of duties, but use of the noble title is still allowed.

High Nobles: The high nobility is the smallest segment of the peerage, consisting of people belonging to old and powerful families entrenched in the Imperial system for generations. Because of this, these nobles are the most powerful, but they are hampered by the responsibilities of office.

The rare titles of the high nobility are given for "political support in office, victory in the military, or contributions or economic assistance from the commercial sector" beyond any reasonable expectation. Patents are hereditary (upon confirmation of the Moot) and almost always include a fief or feudal estate granted by a letter of enfeoffment.

These nobles directly administer Imperial territories and are personal representatives of the emperor. Members of the high nobility are trained from birth to lead, and they have enormous

personal power to sustain the awesome responsibility of holding together an interstellar community. When successors to title cannot fulfill their duties, supporters or the noble family can take (often drastic) steps to see responsibilities fulfilled.

In addition to Imperial title and enfeoffment, the high noble frequently holds titles of lesser precedence, which may include other local titles. A high noble's sphere of influence is essentially the area administered by his local peerage.

The high peers have precedence in the peerage and thus are the most powerful of the nobility. Even their barons are immensely powerful. They have almost direct control of entire economies. High nobles spend large amounts of time and resources developing their territories because they realize that, in the end, it is the successful management of populations that ensure continuity of the Imperium.

PROTOCOLS

The peerage regulates itself through standard codes of behavior known as protocols, which exist at multiple levels. At the Imperial level there is standardization, but within local peerages one can find a wide diversity in protocols to accommodate variant cultures and their traditions (including alien ones).

At best, violation of the protocols is a breach of taste and ethics; at worst, it may be cause for patent review, which could lead to a recommendation that a patent be revoked. Recommendations from local peerages carry much weight with the emperor.

Protocols aside, nobles have few obligations in terms of provision for each other, notwithstanding the payment of taxes, attendance of summits, and settlement of disputes that fall within each other's jurisdictions. Members of the peerage are largely autonomous and have few restrictions on their activities, especially if they are in a backwater.

In most cases, the intelligent noble will follow the local dictates of a peer simply out of respect and courtesy.

NOBLES AND THE LAW

The rights nobles have under local law is of major concern. Nobles are subject to all the Imperial laws any other citizen is. Local laws may be another matter.

Where a noble is not acting under the auspices of a peer's local laws or of the protocols, he is accorded the rights of any Imperial citizen. With regard to personal safety, he is allowed (applying to retinue and bodyguards) to "bear arms" to his content, as long as he is armed (with respect to any peers in mind) discreetly.

Bearing arms in the presence of a superior may be a serious breach of protocol. On the other hand, cultural influences (as in the case of Archduke Dulinor and his Dlani heritage) within a peerage might dictate that a noble must bear arms in the presence of another peer. Failure to do so could be a form of disrespect, as serious a breach as bearing weapons when inappropriate.

Additional privileges might include the ability to set and revoke local laws and trade policies. Preferential (or occasionally free) starship passage is another noble privilege offered by some lines. Nobles may accept diplomatic gifts from neighbors, whether Imperial or alien; they may also call for Imperial justice or trial by peers. Certain rank nobles may be able to mete out Imperial justice or grant pardons. As the ultimate Imperial power, a noble might even carry an Imperial Warrant.

NOBLE RANKS

The lowest noble rank is knight; the highest is emperor (although the emperor and his family are not members of the Moot and in fact are prohibited from entering the Moot Spire on Capital unless invited by the body).

Several aspects of rank are governed by strict protocol, including title (the formal reference to the person in print or by reference), style (the method of addressing the individual personality), and precedence (the relative seniority of the individual among others). In addition, customary perquisjtes for each noble rank vary widely.

The noble title includes the allowed prefixes (such as Sir) and suffixes (such as "of Yori") to a name and the order in which they are presented.

The noble style dictates the manner in which a noble is addressed and includes such honorifics as "Your Grace" or "Your Majesty."

Precedence is accorded strictly on the basis of government position, with seniority determined by following date of patent. The date of noble rank is taken from the date of confirmation when an inherited rank is assumed.

Knight: The lowest of noble ranks is knight, which is awarded by the emperor or an archduke as an honorific rank in recognition of achievement or service: as such, a knighthood is coveted by nonnobles and is seen as more attainable than membership in the peerage. A knighthood entitles the recipient to use the prefix Sir (some females prefer Dame, but such usage is obsolete) before the name and to suffix the initials of the order of knighthood after the name.

Knights are not members of the peerage and are thus not subject to all protocols. Knights instead belong to orders of knighthood and are awarded privileges according to the order. Each order has its own code (some lax, some stringent), and member knights are expected to abide by these codes. (In cases where a member of the peerage also holds title to an order of knighthood, he is expected to abide by both the protocol and the code of his order, and conflicts in behavior are resolved in favor of the protocol.)

Several dozen orders of knighthood exist within the Imperium. Some are restricted to specific classes of individuals, such as members of the Imperial Family, racial Aslan, racial Vargr, or other special groups. Others are awarded for specific achievement or service or for holding specific positions within the government. Still others are broadly based orders into which most new knights are inducted.

The most common orders of knighthood in the Imperium are the Order of the Emperor's Guard, established in 52 and originally limited to the Emperor's personal retainers but now of wide and diverse membership, and the Order of Starship and Crown, established in 17. More exclusive orders have also been established: the Order of Hlyuea (established to honor loyal Aslan citizens), the Order of Gvadakoung (established to honor loyal Vargr citizens), and the Honorable Order of the Arrow, (established to recognize interstellar explorers). The domains each have orders named for them: the Order of Antares, the Order of Vland, the Order of Sylea, the Order of Sol, the Order of the Gateway, and the Order of Deneb. Of these, the Order of Sylea is administered by the Emperor himself (as *de facto* Archduke of Sylea); the Order of Deneb has only recently been used, as Norris is the first Archduke of Deneb to be named.

An individual accorded a knighthood for service may receive a fief of land on a single world, generally not more than 10 square kilometers.

Members of the peerage generally consider knights "separate but equal" members of the nobility, and it is considered a breach of protocol for a member of the peerage to treat a knight with disrespect.

Baronet: Intermediate between the first and second level of noble rank is the baronet. Baronet is a special form of baron awarded by an archduke of one of the domains of the Imperium. Baronets rank below barons in seniority and precedence. Although the emperor can create baronets (either as emperor or in his capacity as Archduke of Sylea), in practice they are created only by the archdukes. Baronets do not generally receive fiefs of land.

A baronetcy entitles the individual to use the prefix Baronet before one's name.

Baron: The second level of noble rank is the baron, the lowest level accorded membership in the peerage. Barons are referred to in several different styles, which include the use of prefixes to the surname (such as von, haut, or hault) and the title Baron (or Baroness for females). An individual accorded a barony for service may receive a fief of land on a single world, generally not more than 100 square kilometers. When a barony includes a fief, then the title is generally followed by the fief's name (such as Baron Solvenos).

Marquis: The third level of noble rank is the marquis. A marquis is associated with a single world (generally a large and important one with a good starport). The title consists of the world name after the title, as in the Marquis of Aramis (or, alternatively, the Marquis Aramis). An individual accorded a marquisate may receive a fief of land on a single world, generally not more than 1000 square kilometers.

Count: The fourth level of noble rank is the count, who is associated with two or three worlds within a subsector. Counts are referred to by their title followed by the individual's surname or by the name of one of the worlds within the county. An individual accorded a county may receive a fief of land on a single world, generally not more than 10,000 square kilometers.

Duke: The fifth level of noble rank is the duke, who is associated with a subsector or sector. The noble is referred to by the title followed by "of" and the subsector or sector name. The power of the duke depends on circumstances and the situation within the sector, but generally one duke within a sector rises to power and comes to be the sector duke, who is the ruler of that sector. An individual accorded a duchy may receive a fief of land on a single world, generally not more than 100,000 square kilometers.

Archduke: Each of the six original Imperial domains has an archduke exercising overall control and acting as an intermediary between the Emperor and the other levels of nobility (except for the Domain of Sylea, where the emperor is the archduke). Such nobles are referred to by the title archduke followed by the title of the domain, such as Archduke of Deneb. An archdukedom includes a fief consisting of an entire world, generally retained as a private reserve.

Emperor: Above the range of noble ranks is the emperor and the Imperial family. The emperor is the ultimate object of thousands of oaths of loyalty and fealty.

FIEFS

Patents of nobility, especially for service, may include fiefs of land. Fiefs are granted in a Letter of Enfeoffment separate from the patent of nobility. Fiefs are granted to the individual at the discretion of the emperor and remain the latter's possessions. However, the fief conveys the right to use the land, to rent or lease it out, and to collect income from it. The fief is a convenient method for the emperor to reward certain nobles.

The size of the fief depends upon how great an income the emperor wishes to award a noble and upon the location of the fief itself. A knight with a fief consisting of several hundred square kilometers of sparsely settled wilderness and one with a single hectare of the business district of a city can be considered to hold equal fiefs.

Hereditary nobles have often had the fief in their family for generations, and they have built it up in value and income potential. Some sites at Capital generate considerable income each year. Other fiefs have been administered with great care to ensure that the territory be not only valuable but also tastefully used. Still others have been exploited ruthlessly in mining or industrial pursuits. Completely separate from fiefs, a noble may own land obtained from other sources (inheritance, purchase, and so forth). These lands remain the property of their owner even if his title is revoked, and can they be disposed of separately from fiefs.

THE NOBILITY LISTS

The Holiday List is published on Holiday, the first day of the new year, and covers achievement. The Birthday List is on the Emperor's Birthday (Lucan's is day 301) and covers service. Continuing awards for position may be given any time.

RESPONSIBILITIES OF NOBLES

Honor and rank nobles are expected to conform to social conventions. Those of Cogri are blinded upon ascendency in recollection of when actions of the hereditary nobility caused hundreds of citizens blinded by the intense rays of their sun.

A culture may be prejudiced against technologies like bionics, robots, regeneration, or other medical treatments. They may have to use breath masks or wear eye patches, or use exotic technical solutions, such as powered grav chairs equipped with life support. Most nobles have the resources to purchase these devices. The Marquis of Inthe, when not in zero-G areas, must wear a delicate powered exoskeleton to counter his frail bone structure (reportedly due to inbreeding).

The upper crust of the Imperium is also expected to avoid psionics: the emperor will not publicly admit a psionic noble.

Sociocultural or religious traditions may hamper a noble. Certain lifestyles or careers may be deemed "inappropriate." A high or rank noble may not be able to travel far because of a required presence for some type of ceremony or event.

Library Data

"Library Data" is a general term used to describe the information available from a typical ship's computer using its library program. In the past, library data had as its source a vast communication network paralleling that of the Xboat system that once operated throughout the united Imperium. An entire series of "hubs" amassed and organized vast quantities of data and send it out to each other. At each hub the entire collection of information could be compiled and redistributed to private customers, including starships, hotels, universities, fixed-location libraries, and hand computer services.

In the divided Imperium, library data services have diminished much as the Xboat routes have. In various areas, reliable service can still be found—sometimes taken over by a commercial firm, sometimes taken over by a local governmental body. The farther that a message or data must travel, however, the more tenuous is its consistency. And Xboat messages have difficulty travelling across borders or are sometimes lost to marauding pirates. Library data likewise is sporadic and intermittent in its arrival, which causes much of its information to have lost its up-to-the-minute flavor.

In addition, the library data "network" (pretending for the moment that the system still exists as intact as it once was) has lost contact with many of its original sources of data. Researchers, historians, and journalists often fail nowadays to submit timely reports of their discoveries. Embarrassing gaps exist in many library data entries today, and severe overgeneralization has resulted in misinformation occasionally being published as apparent fact.

SMART

One of the areas of the Imperium that was first to lose its accurate library data was the area "behind the claw," Trojan Reach, the Spinward Marches, and Deneb, but thanks to the quick action of Archduke Norris of Deneb, the library data service for the region was reestablished and made as accurate and efficient as it had been under the united Imperium.

SMART, the Spinward Marches Archive Retrieval Team, was selected from historians working at the region's colleges and universities. Under the direction of Eura Regnis of the Regina Center for Research, the team set to work in 1117 to restore library data service throughout the archduke's domain. Norris's mandate for this group's work has been instrumental in insuring that the Imperium, once reunited, will be able to build upon the scientific and historical legacy of its predecessors.

Regnis and her colleagues accomplished their task in only two short years, and in 1119, SMART Library Data, LIC opened its doors as a semiprivate company, guided by a board appointed by the archduke. The library data in this book was generated by one of the SMART system's computers; it was automatically summarized to provide the highlights of a number of interesting topics.

Within this summary, the reader can find historical information on the Third Imperium and the events that led up to the divided Imperium today. Information on all the major races of the Imperium and its surrounding environs is also here, complete with updates of alien activities since Strephon's untimely death. The most important minor races are summarized in this volume, too.

Several in-depth summary supplements round out the information here, giving background information on the united Imperium, its worlds, its emperors, and its nobility; the megacorporations and major merchant lines doing business in the Imperium; the activities and organization of the Imperial Interstellar Scout Service; and a special report on recent military technology and its use by the Imperial Navy in reuniting our worlds and punishing the usurper Dulinor.

While the SMART library data is as complete as humanly possible, it must be understood that a number of mitigating circumstances have interfered with this collection. Since the revolt of Vland Sector and its neighbors, the SMART researchers were unable to establish a reliable communications link between the Spinward Marches and some of the larger fixed libraries, such as the AAB on Vland and the Imperial Library on Capital. Despite this incapability, SMART Library Data is proud of the successes it has had in producing a work that should help all loyal Imperial citizens strive toward the establishment of the united Imperium and the coronation of its rightful emperor.

A

AAB: The Argushiigi Admegulasha Bilanidin, which in Vilani means literally the "Vilani Repository of All Knowledge," is a major scientific institution located on the world of Vland. The extensive AAB facilities include a vast museum, a library, and several research centers and publishing houses. Not only does the AAB collect samples, specimens, and recorded materials from all over explored space, it also publishes an abridged 15 holocrystal encyclopedia set of its extensive data files. Known simply as "The Encyclopedia," the set contains the equivalent of 7500 extensively illustrated volumes, yet it can easily fit into a large pocket.

Amber Zone: Travellers' Aid Society classification for a nation, world, or system which presents a need for caution in dealings and activity. The amber code may indicate chaos, upheaval, or xenophobia in local business, politics, society, or culture, or it may be applied for other reasons. Travellers should exercise caution.

Until recently, the Imperial Travellers' Aid Society considered all worlds within the Imperium safe unless specifically noted otherwise. With the recent fragmentation of the Imperium, the travel zone classification of worlds has been relegated to local branches of the Society.

The Domain of Deneb branch of TAS has classified worlds outside its borders as amber zones. Travellers are advised to exercise caution, especially in areas bordering Aslan space, Corridor Sector, the Vargr Extents, and the Solomani Rim.

See also Red Zone, Travel Zone.

Ancients: Highly intelligent race which gained prominence approximately 300,000 years ago.

Most of what is known about the Ancients has been gleaned from archeological excavations of Ancient sites: the remains of cities, bases, outposts, and settlements of the Ancients. Scientific dating techniques have established that a "Final War" spanning a 2000-year period destroyed virtually all of the Ancients at that time.

The influence of the Ancients is broadly felt in the universe. Humans from Terra were transported to many worlds by the Ancients; their descendants became the Vilani and the Zhodani, as well as the 46 known minor human races. The Vargr have been shown (through genetic testing) to be descendants of genetically manipulated Terran canines (apparently, the canine stock was acquired at the same time the humans were taken from Terra). Ancient artifacts which have been discovered show a very high tech level and an equally high degree of sophistication; such artifacts often reveal new, previously undiscovered or unexploited technologies.

The Ancients were responsible for several major features within the region now occupied by the Imperium. Their warfare resulted in the large proportion of asteroid belts throughout explored space. There is evidence they created the multiworld rosette ar Tireen (Knaeleng 2910, in the Vargr extents). Scattered empty cities (most severely damaged by battle) stand as evidence of their wars; most, however, are restricted areas under investigation by the Imperium and not open to the public. One notable exception is the world Antiquity (Corridor 0816). The Antiquity Ancients site is open to tourists; its fascinating museum displays many wondrous and mystifying artifacts, many of which are still in working condition.

See also Antiquity, Humaniti, Solomani Hypothesis, Vargr.

Andory (Spinward Marches 0236 C695735-9): Prime candidate for Droyne homeworld. Discovered in 802 and placed under interdiction (red travel zone) by Imperial Interstellar Scout Service.

See also Droyne.

Anglic: The official language of the Third Imperium. A distant descendent of Terran English, Anglic was the language of the Rule of Man (−2294 to −1776). Anglic remained a common interstellar language for trade and commerce during the Long Night. Its widespread use on the original worlds of the Third Imperium made it the natural language when the Imperium was established.

On many worlds, Anglic is only a second language used for system traffic control, commercial operations, and interstellar communications. Anglic is sometimes called Galanglic (for Galactic Anglic).

The Imperium has not been able to prevent the emergence of a wide variety of Anglic dialects. Interstellar communications, holocrystals, and recordings help to spread a uniform pronunciation of Anglic throughout the entire Imperium. Within the Imperium, any Anglic speaker can understand almost any other, but isolated communities on worlds with little contact with the interstellar trade lanes shift their speech patterns to form dialects. In addition, broad areas within the Imperium have established their own pronunciation patterns; accepted dialects include Rim (which includes Terra), Core (the central region of the Imperium), Riftian (the spinward frontiers), and Transform (the Antares region).

Antares: Trailing region of the Third Imperium. The name Antares is applied to a variety of places at the trailing fringe of the Imperium. Antares is a domain of the Imperium, a sector within that domain, and the capital of that sector.

Antares, League of: The League of Antares (although it does not include the Antares system) is an autonomous region within the Imperium. The worlds were originally pressed into the Imperium in 89 during the Antarean Pacification Campaign. The worlds were occupied by the Julian Protectorate during the Julian War. When regained for the Imperium at the end of that war, the peace terms included a mandate that the League of Antares be given limited autonomy for control of trade, commerce, and internal affairs.

The autonomy of the League of Antares served as a model for the later establishment of the Solomani Autonomous Region.

Ansing Expedition: Famous exploration of the accessible reaches of the gas giant Annikkittar in the Pretoria system in 870 to 884. Extensive use of specially designed exploration vessels, protective environment suits, and high technology

equipment allowed the Ansing Foundation of Vland to extensively map and explore the upper reaches of the gas giant's atmosphere.

Antebellum: Literally, before the war. General historical term referring to the period within the Imperium before the Civil War, specifically 210 to 604.

The antebellum period was characterized by expansion of the Imperium with large-scale colonization efforts, integration of numerous regions into Imperial society, and an overall mood of growth and exploration. With the end of the antebellum period, the Imperium turned more attention inward and devoted resources to internal development and consolidation.

Antiquity (Corridor/Ian 0806 A223420-C): One of the best preserved Ancient sites in existence. Discovered in 385, the site is unique in that many parts of it are still operational. The biggest problem faced by researchers has been figuring out what things did and how they worked. Many items are still a mystery.

Artifact: Any manufactured object. The term artifact is commonly used to refer to any object, item, or group of related items produced by the Ancients.

Aslan: The Aslan are a race of intelligent beings with an established interstellar empire spinward and rimward of the Imperium; in addition, large numbers have settled within the Imperium.

Aslan stand roughly human-sized, averaging 2.0 meters in height and weighing about 100 kg. They are descended from four-limbed, upright, bipedal carnivore/pouncer stock originally adapted to a solitary arboreal existence.

The earliest Terran explorers saw in them a vague resemblance to the Terran lion, and they have been described (by Terrans) as lion-like ever since, although there is very little true similarity. The derivation of the word Aslan is unknown. There are two sexes, male and female. The most notable external difference is the increased size and mane of the former. Females outnumber males by 3:1.

Aslan have a single highly specialized dewclaw under each thumb which folds back jacknife fashion into a horny covering in the base of the thumb and palm.

A vast Aslan-dominated empire (the Aslan Hierate) lies far to rimward, but Aslan themselves have ranged well beyond its borders, with many settling within the Imperium and attaining full status as citizens. As citizens, they subordinate themselves to Imperial authority, although they have remained culturally separated from human society. Aslan serve in the Imperial armed forces; they achieve nobility; they pay taxes; they run businesses.

Aslan Society: The Aslan are a warrior race, proud, noble, and devoted to those in authority above them. An individual Aslan is usually a member of a family of from 2 to 12 individuals under a patriarchal leader. Several families will combine into a pride with one family dominant. A number of prides form a clan, again with a top pride. Aside from military organizations and the ruling council (within the Hierate), the clan is the highest social-political organization among the Aslan.

A deep-seated territorial instinct causes the Aslan to have an inordinate (from a human standpoint) concern with land. For male Aslan, owning land is a major goal in life. An Aslan's stature is determined by the amount of land he (or her husband) controls, or by the amount of land owned by any higher lord the Aslan may be vassal to. The lowest classes of Aslan are landless, and provide the farmers, laborers, craftsmen, and factory workers. A holder of a large territory will often grant authority over it to vassals (usually sons, brothers, or male relatives by marriage) who administer the land in his name.

The sexes have very different roles in Aslan society. Males (in all but the lowest classes) are concerned mostly with military operations, acquisition of territory, and political affairs. Females are concerned with trade, industry, and the accumulation of knowledge. Upper class males have little conception of money and are literally incapable of functioning in a technological society without aid, so they are thus seldom encountered without the supervision of a wife, mother, or other female relative or employer.

For instance, a typical Aslan mercenary unit will be organized by a wealthy married female, who will then assign its operation, for a share of the proceeds, to an unmarried female relative. The battle commander and most of the troops will be unmarried males (many of them also relatives) hired with the promise of land grants (and the opportunity to gain honor and reputation in combat); however, staff, operations, supply, and intelligence officers will generally be female.

The extremely deadly nature of any combat between Aslan has led to a rigid, ritualized pattern of behavior designed to reduce conflict. Aslan are very polite, and while most have learned to be patient with non-Aslan, accidental fights still occur. Disputes between individuals are handled by the patriarchs; disputes between families are handled by the pride leader; disputes between prides are handled by the clan leader.

Aslan Calendar: The Aslan calendar is based on the period of Kuzu (the Aslan homeworld) around Tyeyo, its star. The Aslan ftahea (year) is 319.98 standard days in length.

See also Aslan Border Wars, Aslan Hierate, Kuzu.

Aslan Border Wars (−1118 to 380): Series of conflicts between various Aslan clans and human systems as the Aslan expanded toward already settled human territory. The Aslan achieved jump drive late (-1999) and proceeded to expand into the available territory in their region of space. Contacts along their trailing border necessarily resulted in friction with the human systems in that region.

Because the Long Night was already well under way by the time the Aslan encountered humans, there was no central human government to resist Aslan attacks. Since there was no united Aslan authority either, the sides were fairly matched, and numerous small wars erupted between Aslan clans and human splinter states, with alliances among the various powers constantly forming and dissolving.

The border between human and Aslan space remained relatively constant, with a few systems changing hands after each war. At this time some clans also launched raids into the interior of the former Imperial domains, where they conquered and settled worlds as much as 40 parsecs beyond the border.

Once the Third Imperium expanded into the region (circa 200), its superior organization and technology gradually put an end to the Aslan threat. The final treaties, known as the Peace of Ftahalr, were negotiated with all the major clans. They established a buffer zone about 30 parsecs wide between the Imperial border and the region of Aslan control. There has been no war since then (380), although the Solomani have violated portions of the zone and incorporated it into their boundaries.

See also Aslan, Aslan Hierate.

Aslan Hierate: Interstellar, multisector government of the many Aslan clans. Aslan society centers on the clan. Within the Hierate, the family structure of the Aslan and the governmental structure are the same. The highest governmental functions are performed by a council of twenty-nine clan leaders chosen from amongst the most powerful clans.

"The 29" (as they are called) have quasireligious status and represent the essential unity of the Aslan race. To be chosen one of the "the 29" is the highest honor to which any Aslan can aspire. The 29 meet continuously on Kuzu to adjudicate interclan disputes and decide matters of group policy. No member of the 29 speaks for the Hierate as a whole, nor does the whole 29.

There are no Hierate military forces; each clan has its own, and they rarely act in concert with those of other clans. The Hierate itself can call upon military forces only insofar as the clans themselves agree to provide such forces. Even the minor forces conveying the 29's decisions are actually under the control of individual clan leaders.

Dulinor the Usurper shot and killed the Aslan ambassador from the Yerlyaruiwo clan at the same time he murdered the late emperor; this sparked Aslan reprisals in the rimward border of Trojan Reach Sector and the Solomani Rim. Officially, however, these scattered border hostilities do not constitute a state of war between the divided Imperium and the Aslan Hierate.

See also Aslan, Aslan Border Wars, Kuzu.

Assassination, Right of: The first Third Imperium emperor to be shot by his successor was Cleon II, also known as Cleon the Mad. Selected by lot in a secret meeting of the High Moot, Porifia shot Cleon II in his council chambers in 245. Porifia was subsequently proclaimed empress by Moot confirmation.

During the Civil War period, several usurpers attempted to claim the throne by the right of assassination—few succeeded.

Although the right of assassination has fallen into disuse, it is generally agreed that for the method to be a valid route to the iridium throne, certain precedents must be followed: 1) the assassin must be a high noble; 2) the assassin must kill the emperor by his own hand in the presence of witnesses; 3) the Moot must approve of the new emperor, just as with any successor.

Thus, the reason for the assassination must be well founded, or Moot confirmation will likely be denied. Moot confirmation can make all the difference—depending on what the Moot says, the assassin could be hailed as a courageous hero or prosecuted as a seditious murderer.

The attempt by the usurper Dulinor, Archduke of Ilelish, to claim the throne via Strephon's assassination is not seen by most loyal Imperial citizens as a legitimate claim to the throne. The Moot has not yet had an opportunity to decide on the matter.

Astrography: The science of mapping interstellar space. Basic to any science of mapping is a coordinate system. The scientific system used by the Imperium is based on rings of longitude, rays of latitude, and parsecs. By convention, rays of latitude and rings of longitude are measured from a starting point at Reference/Capital, the world where the data from the First and Second Imperial Grand Surveys are stored.

This mapping system is highly Imperio-centric, and other systems are used by other peoples and races outside the Imperium. This system has gained wide acceptance, however, among Imperium dominated client-states, human and otherwise. This mapping system breaks down and is prone to error beyond certain limits. It does serve admirably for a band approximately 400 parsecs wide at a longitude of 10,000 parsecs, which is a region precisely centered on the Imperium.

In ordinary discourse, a world is referred to by its name, sector, and subsector. For example, the homeworld of Archduke Norris is Regina (Spinward Marches/Regina): that is, the world Regina in Regina Subsector in Spinward Marches Sector.

B

Barracks Emperors: Collective term describing the succession of emperors springing from military backgrounds (and usually seizing the throne by force) during the Civil War.

See Emperors of the Flag.

"Behind the Claw:" A slang term used by inhabitants of the Spinward Marches, Deneb, and Trojan Reach Sectors to refer to these areas. The term derives from a supposed resemblance between a claw and the Great Rift, as seen on maps of the Imperium. Inhabitants of this region feel a certain pride in this designation, and it is used to imply that they share a camaraderie and common interest. The name was once used as the title of a popular news magazine with a circulation area encompassing the three sectors named above. The term is rarely used by inhabitants of other areas of the Imperium.

The entire area "behind the claw" is now part of the Domain of Deneb.

Belt Mining: The process of extracting useful minerals and other substances from asteroids. Asteroids fall into three basic categories, each of which is different in nature and value.

Nickel-iron asteroids are reasonably dense, high-grade sources of metal of most value to the manufacturing industry; large asteroids can be sold to local shipbuilding concerns as planetoid starship hulls.

Carbonaceous asteroids are the most common planetoids and have the lowest value of all asteroids in most marketplaces. These stony chunks have the most value in systems where space colonies and large stations can make use of the variety of the useful elements—carbon, hydrogen, oxygen, and so on—that can be extracted from them.

Ice chunks are made up of various frozen volatiles, including methane, water, and the like. These "dirty snowballs" are a source of hydrogen fuel and hence support an entire specialty of "ice miners" who seek them out. In systems where gas giants cannot be used for one reason or another, a starport or space station may pay reasonably good money for ice chunks, though they will never make a belter rich.

None of these three categories of asteroid is particularly valuable, and few belters ever made a fortune strictly from discovering and mining any of these. In point of fact, there are other things to be found. Many asteroids, most particularly nickel-iron rocks, contain varying amounts of the valuable minerals, platinum, iridium, and so forth, and sometimes radioactives. Occasionally an asteroid will be discovered with an unusual configuration that makes it valuable for scientific or even aesthetic purposes. And, finally, there are artifacts, which take in the entire gamut from the flotsam of a week-old wreck to a trove left by the Ancients, and which vary in value accordingly.

Belter: Strictly speaking, one who practices the profession of asteroid prospector and miner, usually working alone or with a small number of partners. Loosely, any resident of an asteroid belt (including citizens of civilized belts such as Glisten, some of whom have never been in a spaceship).

Bilstein Yards: The Bilstein company of Glisten (Spinward Marches/Glisten) has achieved a high reputation for specialist starships of nonstreamlined types. Though constructing on a small scale compared to builders like Ling Standard, Bilstein vessels are sought after due to their attention to customers' special requirements.

Bilstein is the main supplier of private yachts to the March nobility, and this provides the bulk of their output. Occasionally, however, a class of vessels such as the Leviathan merchant cruisers are turned out, and several powered planetoid types have also been constructed.

Since Strephon's murder, Bilstein has begun retooling its lines to produce a series of planetoid warships to defend the Domain of Deneb from outside intruders.

Brzk: Archduke of Antares. Brzk's great- (to the eighth) grandfather, Admiral Soegz, was a loyal supporter of Arbellatra in the final years of the Civil War.

C

Capital (Core/Capital 2118 A586A98-F): Central world of the Imperium and seat of government since its founding. Situated in the center of the Imperium, Capital's astrographical position has proven of prime importance as a communications hub, a cultural center, and an industrial focus.

Under the divided Imperium, with no emperor officially proclaimed by action of the Moot, Capital is a head without a brain, and the separate domains of the Imperium have been forced to fend for themselves under the independent leadership of their local archdukes. Once the current political turmoil has settled down and the Imperium is reunited, Capital will again take its place as the centerpiece of human civilization.

Centaurs: Common name applied to the K'kree, because of their resemblance to mythical Terran creatures.

See K'kree.

Chirper: Semi-intelligent minor race native to many worlds in and outside the Imperium.

Chirpers are omnivore/gatherers in the 25 kg class. Living in small groups with limited social organization, they gather fruits and berries, supplementing their diets with occasional small animals, which they catch and kill with crude tools.

Chirper intelligence is at the low end of the scale and ranges from a few points above animal levels to a few points below the average for humans.

Chirpers are named for the sharp bird-like chirp which characterizes their speech.

Chirpers are recognized by Imperial authorities as intelligent, and as such, they enjoy the protections and responsibilities of intelligent species within the Imperium. Most chirpers live in established reservations with only limited interchange with humans.

Church of the Chosen Ones: A fanatical Vargr sect which believes that the Ancients not only "invented" the Vargr race by genetic manipulation of Terran carnivores, but that the Ancients also returned to the Vargr several times and improved the race to the point that it could take its rightful place as the leader of this part of the galaxy. Some Church members even believe that the Ancients will return again to bring this about. The Church has waned in influence since its founding 200 years ago, but it still has followers on many worlds.

Ciencia Iphegenia (1088 to 1116): Grand Princess of the Imperium, daughter of Emperor Strephon and Empress Iolanthe. As heir to the Iridium throne, Grand Princess Iphegenia was educated from birth to eventually assume the mantle of authority for the Imperium. Her early fascination with the sciences prompted an extensive interest in the Imperial Interstellar Scout Service, which considered her its patron.

The Grand Princess died in the assassination attack of the usurper Dulinor in 1116.

Civil War (604 to 622): Fought between various factions within the Imperium for control of the bureaucracy. It had its origin in the strain on communications within the Imperium caused by the long lag times dictated by the very size of the Imperium. To cite one cause, however, would be simplistic. The diverse backgrounds of the many constituents of the Imperium had its effects, as did rivalry for power by major naval and military commanders and a lessening in the Imperium's expansionist tendencies.

The spark which started the Civil War came from the First Frontier War (589 to 604) in the Spinward Marches. Communication lags and a lack of preparedness forced the Marches to conduct most of the war on its own with little additional help or support from the Imperium. Grand Admiral of the Marches Olav hault-Plankwell forced the war to an end and found solid support for a new government. Marching on Capital with his war fleet, he forced an audience with Empress Jacqueline I, supposedly for recognition of his war effort. In the course of the meeting in 606, he personally murdered the Empress, and then proclaimed himself Emperor by right of fleet control. The ensuing power struggle lasted through 18 years and 18 emperors.

The fighting in the Civil War was of two varieties: fringe battles for power bases, and central battles for power in the Core. The fringe battles were fought throughout the Imperium as rival factions recruited forces. Once any power block built up enough strength to make a victory seem possible, the forces were moved to the Core and used to either seize power or to wrest it away from someone else.

But there was also a cheaper, easier route open to many. The dynastic crisis of 244 had produced a precedent for the assassination of the emperor if he or she overstepped the bounds of legitimate activity. The concept was introduced to legitimize the elimination of Cleon the Mad and was never intended for any other purpose. Nevertheless, in the turmoil of the Civil War, assassination was introduced and accepted, at least by those utilizing the technique, as a way of promoting a succession in government.

The line of Emperors during the Civil War came mostly from naval officers, and they are collectively called the Emperors of the Flag. Of these eighteen, seven were assassinated, ten were killed in battle, and one survived—Arbellatra.

During the course of the Civil War, the Outworld Coalition (of Zhodani and Vargr) saw that their defeat in the First Frontier War at the hands of Olav need not be permanent. They attacked again in the Second Frontier War (615 to 620). Their defeat in that war had greater effects than they would know. Grand Admiral Arbellatra managed the meager forces of the Imperium against the Coalition and managed to force a second defeat.

Arbellatra's strategy after the war was (like Olav) to march on the Capital and seize power. She, however, did not make the mistake of seizing the throne. Instead, she defeated the putative emperor and then took possession of power, holding it in trust for a rightful successor. She held the post of regent for seven years while a search for a member of Jacqueline's family could be found to take the throne.

In the stability that followed with her as regent, she made an impression on the Moot and succeeded in establishing a broad power base. Ultimately, the Moot approached her to take the throne herself, an end which was probably in her mind all along.

With the end of the two Frontier Wars and the Civil War, the Imperium entered a period of renewed expansion and consolidation. The express boat system was established to enhance government, commercial, and private communications; the Solomani influence in the Imperium was lessened and replaced with a more cosmopolitan policy; renewed efforts at interior development of existing Imperial territories provided a new focus for the nobles of the Moot.

See also Emperors' List, First Frontier War, Moot, Outworld Coalition, Second Frontier War.

Client State: An independent political unit which has elected (or had forced upon it) the patronage of a larger political unit. This relationship is generally mutually beneficial and is essentially commercial in nature. That is, the political or defensive ties which may be part of any patron-client relationship are ultimately intended to promote trade between the two.

Confederation: Group of independent states, worlds, or systems united for specified purposes while generally retaining more freedom of action than the members of a federation. Also a league or alliance (especially of princes, nations, states, worlds, or systems).

Corridor: Imperial sector containing 267 systems dramatically split by the Great Rift; 69 systems lie rimward of the Rift and 149 systems form the coreward third of the sector. Corridor is named for its role connecting old, well-established Vland Sector with the frontier sectors Deneb and the Spinward Marches. The name Corridor dates from about 140 and has displaced the old Vilani name (Eneri, rough translation: "star salad") for the sector. Corridor today is disputed territory, which lies between the so-called Restored Vilani Empire and the loyal Domain of Deneb.

Coyns: Of the rare artifacts recovered from Ancient sites, the most common are coyns, small disk of metal engraved with various symbols. Their specific purpose is unknown. It may be that the objects served as money, jewelry, psionic focuses, or for some other unknown purpose.

Original coyns have been found in various precious metals such as gold, silver, platinum, iridium, monadium, and even uranium. Sets range in size from six to thirty-eight pieces and are considered desirable to museums throughout the Imperium. Each coyn has a scrap value of Cr400 (if gold); to a museum, the value is closer to Cr4000.

Copies of sets of coyns are made of aluminum, lead, or zinc and are more frequently encountered from unscrupulous merchants or traders. Such fake coyns have a value of about Cr20 each.

Crisis of '99: Albert Croale, in his book *Almost Disaster*, presents a hypothesis that the Third Frontier War (979 to 986) occurred two centuries too late. After reviewing the progress

of events in the spinward reaches of the Imperium from the antebellum period to the late seventh century, Croale then analyzes the rise of the Psionics Institutes, their growing public acceptance, and their spreading power. Finally, he presents that a straight projection of events would predict a resurgence of the Outworld Coalition, increased hostilities, and finally, a Third Frontier War.

Instead, his hypothesis as stated in his book indicates that the Psionics Suppressions (800 to 826 and beyond) were a massive manipulation of the population of the Imperium, a form of psychohistory, intended to eliminate the power of the Institutes. Preparations were ongoing for war, and the Imperium made representations of strength (in 799) to the Coalition. It backed down.

But, the psychohistory project went wrong and resulted in widespread rejection of psionics as a whole within the Imperium to the point that even the government had difficulty in using the science of psionics for its official purposes.

Currency, Imperial: The basic unit of legal tender in the Imperium is the Imperial credit. Individual worlds may issue their own currencies, and those currencies may or may not be acceptable on other worlds. Similarly, corporations and megacorporations may issue scrip, and its acceptance outside of the corporate environment is a matter of conjecture. But Imperial credits are accepted everywhere in the Imperium and in many locations outside of it.

Imperial credits are almost impossible to counterfeit because of their unique method of manufacture. Plastic fibers are combined under high temperature and pressure and extruded as a rectangular bundle of great length. The different colored fibers form the pattern of the bill. It is not printed on but actually made a part of the structure of the note. The bundle is sliced to paper thinness, and a 14-digit alphanumeric (letter/number combination) is added for uniqueness. Credit bills are issued in 10, 20, 50, 100, 500, 1000, and 10,000 credit denominations. Plastic coins, manufactured in a similar manner in various shapes, are issued in quarter, half, one, and five credit denominations.

Imperial credits can be bulky in large enough quantities. Bills measure 75 millimeters × 125 millimeters; 1000 bills stand 50 millimeters high and weigh 500 grams.

Imperial credits are still legal tender in the Domain of Deneb; their acceptance in other areas of the divided Imperium varies widely.

D

Darmine: Cultural region in the Zarushagar sector. Darmine had a separate but submerged cultural identity within the First Imperium and happily threw off that domination when the First Imperium fell. Allowed to flourish by the Rule of Man, the community of worlds survived the Long Night with little harm.

Darmine was the major focus of the Ilelish Pacification Campaign (76 to 120).

Darrian Confederation: Group of worlds in the Darrian subsector settled by humans from Darrian (Spinward Marches/Darrian 0627 A463955-G) during the period -1137 to -927. The current capital is Mire (Spinward Marches/Darrian 0527 A665A95-B).

The Darrian Confederation contains 18 worlds within the same subsector and has a population of 17.19 billion. Darrians are humans who developed independently on Darrian. Some Solomani blood is evident from Solomani traders who encountered Darrian in -1511 and provided them with sufficient technology to explore their subsector.

See Humans.

The Darrian Confederation is a client state of the Imperium. It has had long-standing conflicts with the Sword Worlds.

Since Strephon's murder, the Darrians have reaffirmed their loyalty to the Imperium through Archduke Norris of the Domain of Deneb.

Deneb: Imperial sector containing 385 systems lying beyond the Great Rift; named for the sector's brightest star, Deneb.

Deneb sector was fragmentarily settled by both Vilani and Vargr during the latter years of the First Imperium, but major development of the sector only took place after Third Imperium Scout Service explorations located major resource worlds in quantity. Industrial worlds that exploited those resources soon created trade routes and commercial ties that linked the Imperial core with the Spinward Marches.

Deneb sector is primarily Imperial. The Imperial border runs just within the coreward edge of the sector, and scattered Vargr systems (as well as non-aligned systems and client states) lie beyond the border.

Deneb is part of the Domain of Deneb, a region loyal to the Imperium under the leadership of Archduke Norris. The sector is on red alert on its coreward border and is ready to defend against alien insurgents from the Vargr Extents. Its trailing border abuts the so-called Restored Vilani Empire, a rebellious sector containing Vland; occasional hostilities have been reported.

Digest Touring Award: Outstanding journalism award offered every seven years by the Travellers' Digest magazine (a popular magazine with a wide circulation in the spinward sectors of the Imperium, available on either plastic vellum or electronic media).

The recipient, who must be a professional journalist living and working "behind the claw," is given honorary membership in the Traveller's Aid Society (worth one million credits); he or she is then expected to travel through the region during the tenure of the award and to submit a feature article about his or her latest journey once every thirteen weeks. The intent of the Digest with this award is to "promote understanding of the cultural diversity within the Imperium." The most recent winner of the award, in 1114 is Silenia Stensen, a well known journalism professor from the Torri Institute on Trin (Spinward Marches/Trin's Veil).

Directions, Galactic: North, south, east, and west are insufficient terms for referring to directions within the galaxy. Instead, the following conventions have achieved widespread acceptance when referring to direction:

Toward the galactic core (toward Capital from Terra) is coreward; away from it, in the direction of the rim, is rimward. In the direction in which the galaxy is rotating (toward the Spinward Marches from Vland) is spinward, and the other direction is trailing.

These directions are in widespread use in describing Imperial features and businesses. For example, the Spinward Marches is a sector at the extreme spinward fringe of the Imperium;

Rimward Lines is an important interstellar transport company.

Finally, within the Imperium, the term coreward is also used to indicate the direction of Capital, the Imperial core. There is some potential for confusion if the term is accepted out of context.

Domain: Group of four sectors within the Imperium under the general control and direction of an Archduke.

Droyne: Intelligent major race inhabiting scattered worlds within an area slightly larger than the region of the current Third Imperium. The Droyne are a small race derived from winged herbivorous gatherers. They vary in size depending on caste but generally stand one meter tall (large workers and warriors can be larger than humans). The history of their evolution remains a puzzle because their home world is not known with certainty.

Droyne society is divided into rigid castes determined when an individual reaches adolescence. The six castes of the Droyne all serve different functions within Droyne society. Although identical at the time of caste selection, caste members develop pronounced physical and mental differences by maturity. Different genetic programs are awakened by differences in diet and environment among the various castes. Young leaders, for instance, experience a nearly 30 percent increase in brain size in the first year after casting; drones develop sexual organs; and so on. The following are descriptions and definitions of the castes:

Worker: Manual labor and mundane ordinary activity are the province of the worker. Workers are not too smart and are temperamentally suited to contentment with ordinary labor and subservient tasks.

Warrior: Trained for combat and possessing comparatively well developed muscles and reflexes, the warrior is the security troop, the soldier, the marine, and the policeman of the Droyne culture. They are common in frontier bases, and less numerous in civilized areas.

Drone: Drones have a variety of purposes in Droyne society. They perform a reproductive role which makes them both fathers and mothers to Droyne young, and they have a role in the ceremonies which determine caste for maturing young. In addition, drones comprise a sort of middle management caste, which is responsible for many of the routine functions in business, trade, and administration.

Technician: This caste is the science-oriented portion of Droyne society and is concerned with both research and practical implementation of technology.

Sport: Although the caste system of the Droyne is rather rigid, the sport is the deliberately accepted exception to caste structure. Sports are special individuals who cross caste lines to become individual scouts, messengers, representatives, hunters, prospectors, and to take other occupations that require individual initiative or separation from Droyne society for long periods of time. A sport is the most encountered Droyne away from a Droyne world.

Leader: Leaders are required to manage and direct society. They are ultimately responsible for everything that the Droyne as a whole do.

Society: There is little individual freedom in Droyne society, and as a result, society and government join into one concept. Workers work. Leaders lead. All of society is dedicated to continuing the existence that provides all members with food, shelter, and the other amenities that make life enjoyable. In addition, there is little discord in Droyne society when things are running smoothly, as each member of society has its own function to perform. Only when disaster happens is the group forced to strain.

A typical Droyne group consist of a variety of Droyne from the different castes. There will be many workers, few drones and leaders, and technicians and warriors based on current needs. Each group will also have several sports, although they may not be present; instead they may be occupied with their own solitary tasks.

This is not to say that Droyne are mindless. Leaders are quite capable and responsible; warriors have strategic and tactical senses; technicians are inventive and clever. But all accept the central group as a part of their lives and work for its benefit above their own.

Dulinor: Archduke of Ilelish. Assassin of Emperor Strephon (in 1116) and pretender to the Iridium Throne.

E

Emperors of the Flag: During the Civil War period (604 to 622), the Imperium was in the hands of a series of naval officers of flag (admiral) rank. These eighteen emperors achieved the throne through assassination, fleet action, political maneuvers, and general mayhem. The year 619 particularly saw six emperors serve on the throne, none of them for more than three months.

The succession of Emperors of the Flag began with the seizure of the throne by Olav hault-Plankwell in 604, which precipitated the Civil War. It ended with the naming of Arbellatra regent of the Imperium by the Moot in 622.

See also Civil War.

Empire: Group of independent states, duchies, nations, tribes, worlds, or systems under supreme rule of an emperor.

Express Boats: Rapid communication ships which are designed to make optimum use of jump technology in communicating information within the Imperium. Because the Imperium is so large, ordinary communication must depend on ships travelling along established trade routes, making Regina nearly 4 years out from the Imperial Core.

The express boat (abbreviated Xboat) system, established originally in 624 and expanded to cover the entire Imperium by 718, cuts this communication time by nearly 75 percent. Selected locations along major trade routes are established as sites for express stations, which are orbital facilities which service and refuel the Xboats on their communications runs.

As an Xboat arrives in a system, it beams its recorded data to the express station, which then retransmits it to an Xboat standing by for a jump outsystem. Time between jumps is almost always less than four hours and has been recorded at under seven minutes, making the speed of communication nearly the speed of jump (since Xboats carry jump-4 drives, speeds near four parsecs per week). In practice, this speed is somewhat reduced by the fact that trade routes do not follow straight lines and that not all jumps are made at jump-4. Nonetheless, the system achieves approximately jump-2.6 per week.

F

False War (1082 to 1084): The short, fourth war in the series of Frontier Wars between the Third Imperium and the Zhodani Consulate.

See Fourth Frontier War.

Federation: Group of states, worlds, or systems, each internally independent, joined into a union to which has been surrendered certain rights and responsibilities, most generally to do with foreign affairs.

Fifth Frontier War (1107 to 1110): Latest in the series of continuing wars between the Zhodani and the Imperium. Following several years of unrest and provocation, Zhodani forces attacked across the Imperial borders while previously placed guerrillas on selected Imperial worlds began uprisings. Vargr and Sword World forces allied with the Zhodani also participated in the attacks.

The armistice, signed in 1110, resulted in the loss of no worlds to the hostiles and returned to the status quo.

First Frontier War (589 to 604): The first of the modern border clashes between the Imperium and the Zhodani, which sparked the beginning of a continuing antipathy between the two major lines of humanity.

With the conclusion of the war, Olav hault-Plankwell returned to the Imperial core with his war fleet and took the reins of government, dispatching Empress Jacqueline and thus beginning the Civil War and the reign of its Barracks Emperors.

First Imperium (-4045 to -2204): The first major interstellar civilization, politically and culturally dominated by humans originating on Vland. The jump drive was discovered on Vland in -9235. Immediately the Vilani discovered a number of interfertile and technologically primitive human races on worlds within 60 parsecs. These were gradually brought to a high-technology state with Vilani help and assimilated into a loose interstellar community bound by trade and common culture.

Eventually, the client races themselves explored beyond the local sphere, contacting and trading with still more races. These new races gained their technology without being assimilated into Vilani culture; the resulting increased friction eventually resulted in a series of wars beginning in about -5400.

In response to the threat, Vland began tightening its control of its trade sphere, and finally organizing it into a centralized state in -5273. This marked the beginnings of the First Imperium, although there was as yet no emperor. During the thousand year period of the Consolidation Wars, Vland conquered and absorbed its enemies until there were no longer any civilized states on its borders (except for a portion of the Vargr Extents, isolated from the Imperium by the Great Rift).

The last war ended in -4045, and the Vilani declared the establishment of an interstellar empire to govern all Vilani territory. Known as the Grand Empire of Stars or Ziru Sirka, Vilani dating begins at this point. With no exterior threats, the Ziru Sirka lasted for nearly 1200 years; at its height, which was attained soon after the end of the wars, the First Imperium contained 27 sectors and over 15,000 worlds.

However, the cost of maintaining centralized control over this vast expanse was cultural rigidity; exploration had ceased with the beginning of the wars; now scientific research slowed to a halt, and the beginnings of a hereditary caste system began to emerge. Civilization was in decline.

As long as there was no exterior threat, the Grand Empire was safe; but gradually, despite all efforts, technology leaked across the borders. New interstellar states arose, and the Imperium could no longer afford to absorb them. Gradually, the Imperium lost territory along its coreward and trailing marches. Then, in -2422, the Imperium was contacted along its rimward border by the Terrans, who had recently emerged into space. Terran expansionism led to a series of interstellar wars, which ultimately resulted in Terran conquest of the Imperium in -2204 and the founding of the Rule of Man.

First Interstellar War (-2408 to -2400): The first military engagement between the Vilani of the First Imperium, and the Solomani of the Terran Confederation. This began an on-again, off-again series of wars between the two major human races, which ended in the defeat of the Imperium and the beginning of ascendence of the Solomani.

See Nth Interstellar War.

Fourth Frontier War (1082 to 1084): Also known as the False War. Short, inconclusive war fought primarily in Jewell Subsector between the Imperium and the Zhodani Consulate. The war was in the Spinward Marches with initial assaults by the Zhodani against Jewell and Regina Subsectors stalled at the borders. Its final battle, the Battle of Two Suns, 1084, was waged in the vicinity of Yres and Menorb and resulted in Imperial victory. The armistice was signed before instructions for the conduct of the war were received from the capital.

G

Galanglic: Primary language of the Third Imperium.

See Anglic.

Gas Giant: A large planet with an extensive atmosphere of hydrogen and hydrogen compounds. Starships fuel themselves by diving into this atmosphere and skimming hydrogen from this atmosphere. Jupiter, in the Sol system, is an example of a gas giant.

General Shipyards: The largest starship manufacturer in Regina Subsector with yards at Regina, Efate, and Pixie. Originally a military contractor, General no longer produces ships for military use; instead it concentrates on the more lucrative commercial market. The yard at Regina is capable of producing ships up to 5000 tons, while the subsidiary yards at Pixie and Efate are limited to 600 tons per ship, and devote most of their attention to annual maintenances.

Rumors of late indicate that General may be involved in negotiating a renewed series of military shipbuilding contracts.

Glea (Centrax/Glea 2609 A667800-F): Main coordinating center of the Hive Federation since 410. Center of the Glean Cluster, an unusually rich grouping of 16 Hiver-habitable worlds which are mutually accessible by jump-1 shipping.

Good War/Bad War: The terms "good war" and "bad war" are expressions used by mercenaries to differentiate between small-scale actions within the Imperium and full-scale wars between the Imperium and outside forces.

Small scale actions are viewed as good because the Imperial rules of war are in effect, and a unit knows that it will not be subject to nuclear weapons. Good wars are usually short and not particularly bloody. A unit in a tight spot need merely surrender and activate its repatriation bonds to be removed from combatant status. Even antiguerilla actions are good, under this classification, because of the fact that although most guerillas usually observe no restraint with captured government forces, captured mercenaries can usually be ransomed to serve as a source of income.

A war is bad when no such controls are in effect, and a mercenary unit will be subject to the full horrors of war. Mercenary units are understandably reluctant to accept bad war contracts, but they may be forced into them, especially when near the border areas adjoining two or more factions of the divided Imperium.

Grand Prince: Imperial titular designation of the heir to the Iridium Throne. Under Imperial custom, the eldest son or daughter of the Emperor becomes heir to the throne at the age of 12. Elaborate ceremonies confer the title of Grand Prince (or Grand Princess) on the heir and proclaim the information to the Imperium.

Great Rift: Broad expanse of space with a very low density of stars lying spinward of the main region of the Third Imperium. The Great Rift is a pronounced impediment to interstellar travel, and it constrains jumps through Corridor sector to the Spinward Marches.

The Great Rift is one of many astrographic terrain features which have provided long-term security for the Third Imperium. By its very nature, the Great Rift has made outside incursions difficult, which has made the interior of the Imperium a secure population center.

Guaran (Ricenden/Guaran 0827 A565800-F): Homeworld of the Hivers. Guaran has no special political importance, although it attracts millions of tourists annually from all over the Federation.

H

Hiver: Intelligent major race with a large federation trailing the Imperium. Hivers average 1.5 meters from ground to top of upraised head and weigh about 150 kg. Descended from omnivore gatherer/scavenger stock, they are the most alien of the major races. Hivers exhibit a modified six-fold radial symmetry; the body has a calcareous internal skeleton consisting of a series of rings supporting the limbs and a fused carapace protecting the brain and internal organs.

The head is a modification of one of the limbs and contains six eyestalks and six manipulative tentacles, plus paired infrared sensor organs. The other five limbs are identical (except for slight modifications of the hand opposite the head) and are used as arms and legs indiscriminately. Each limb ends in a six-fingered radial hand. Fingers are very flexible and have muscular suction cups on the lower surface about halfway to the tips. Hiver arms and hands are generally weaker than a human's but are very tough and difficult to injure.

The mouth (digestive opening) is on the lower surface of the body. There is no sound-producing organ, but hivers do have three ears placed around the neck near the head.

Hivers have only one sex. Reproductive cells are exchanged each time that hivers meet, using the modified rear hand (the process has been termed by humans "shaking hands"). The cells are kept in a reproductive pouch on the lower body surface where they conjugate and exchange genetic material. Once every forty days or so, a cell will develop into a larva, which then drops from the parent's body.

Hive planets are mostly wilderness, and the larva enter the wilds, where most are killed. After about a year, survivors return to civilization, where they are welcomed into any nest and begin their education as citizens. Parental instinct in hivers is very strong, and the young are adopted by the entire nest. (Note that this instinct applies only to the year-old returnees; Hivers have no concern for the younger larvae, and in fact they consider them minor pests.)

Hiver language is a combination of arm/tentacle waving and physical contact. The written language is ideographic and is used as a standard language among the races of the Hive

Federation. Hivers talking among themselves use all three aspects of language (gesture, touch, and writing) at once, a process capable of great subtlety and sophistication, but unintelligible to the outsider.

Hivers are unique among major races in that they had a complex culture before becoming sentient. Originally, they lived in the tunnels and built-up mounds of a large (1000kg) burrowing animal. In exchange for shelter, they gave food. They farmed fungus and foraged outside for decaying vegetation and dead animals as a source of food for the fungus.

Burrowers were allowed to graze in the farm tunnels. Hivers ate the fungus and whatever fresh food they could find outside. Intelligence arose as the outside environment changed, forcing the foraging parties to travel farther to discover new sources of food and fertilizer; foragers advanced from simple scavenging and gathering efforts to complex cooperative efforts of hunting and trapping live game.

Today, fungus remains the staple of the Hiver diet; fungus growing is a highly developed art. Most buildings retain the beehive shape and large underground tunnel complexes of the original burrowers, but they are constructed by machines; the burrowers (known as snohl) are now reduced to the secondary function of keeping the tunnels clean. Hiver attachment to them is essentially nonrational; they just feel more comfortable with snohl around.

Society: Hive society is highly individualistic. The term "Hive" results from an early human misconception which stems from the appearance of the Hivers' building and tunnel complexes. Nests contain from five to five hundred individuals, who are usually centered around some common endeavor.

While one hundred is an average size for a nest (and was the size in precivilized times), larger groups may come together for some civilized purpose such as large manufacturing companies or universities. Small nests are usually spaceship crews or isolated research parties. A young hiver will spend his first fifteen years in his home nest; thereafter, nest changes may take place as often as a modern human might change jobs.

Because of the nature of their reproduction, hivers never experienced the population pressures so important to human history. The population of the homeworld is now only a few hundred million, only ten times greater than it was in prehistoric times. Predators control the young; when the adult survival rate rises, thus increasing the numbers of young produced, the predator population increases proportionately and the balance is maintained. Space colonization arose not from pressure but from curiosity, with which Hivers are amply endowed.

The Hivers have colonized only those planets with climates most pleasant to themselves; if the planet has no predators that like to eat Hiver larvae, they are imported. Because of the high birth rate, a colony will rapidly fill up to its maximum population level of a few hundred million and will then stabilize. Hivers like planets of size 6 or less, with thin or standard atmospheres and unvarying climates. Hiver enclaves, for commercial or scientific purposes, are found on worlds of more extreme characteristics.

Hive industry and business excels at communications technology and robot construction. Major exports include artificial and computer languages, translators, and sophisticated electronic hardware of all types. Hiver mathematical systems are much in demand for their power and elegance.

Hive Federation: Human term for the loose interstellar community dominated by the Hivers; Hive Confederation is also sometimes used. The Hivers have only one culture and one language; the Hiver genotype (with individual variations similar in degree to differences between individual humans of the same race) is also constant.

The Federation government (if such a term is at all applicable) is mostly concerned with maintaining the uniformity of the Hiver culture and species. This is accomplished by frequent reproductive embassies from one planet to another. Members of many different nests will shake hands with everyone nearby in a sort of farewell party and will then board a large embassy ship bound for a far-off world. Once there, they will meet with as many people as possible, shaking hands and exchanging news, art, gossip, scientific information, political views, and so on for about a year. They will then return home for another year-long round of parties, discussions, and handshaking.

Most disputes among communities are handled in these embassies; others, considered too urgent or transient to wait for an embassy, are settled by judges. There is a considerable body of Hiver common law and custom, and a judge is a person who has spent years in study of the law; judges' decisions are not necessarily binding and are open to compromise, but they carry a great weight of custom.

The discovery of alien races and their integration into society required a slightly more formal organization, which grew out of the coordinating body which schedules embassies. Two additional bodies were established: the Federation Navy and a development agency.

The Hiver parental instinct was aroused by the discovery of numerous intelligent species less fortunate than themselves, and work began immediately to lift the "children" to civilization. An early experience with an aggressive race led to the establishment of a system of quarantined worlds, denied entry to (or knowledge of) interstellar society.

Covert operations are in progress on quarantine worlds to modify overly aggressive cultures into acceptable members of the Federation, and several quarantined planets have been opened since the beginning of the program. So far, no quarantined race is close to achieving interstellar travel on its own; public debate continues on what to do in such a case.

The navy is the main instrument of military force. Hivers came late to the concept of war and are more comfortable with high-tech, long-range oriented violence; they dislike the personal approach of ground combat.

When ground forces are absolutely needed, other races of the Federation generally supply the troops. Federation armed forces are essentially a deterrent force and are seldom used as an instrument of policy.

Other races of the Federation are equal partners in society, although the structure of society is Hiver-generated, and those races able to adapt best to a Hiver way of life and customs have been most successful. All races participate in the embassies, although in a modified form.

Some associated species retain strong internal governments or police forces to regulate the aggressive tendencies of their members, but whatever solution is reached, all Federation member societies are nonaggressive.

Most worlds of the Federation have communities of several species; races inhabit the worlds they find most pleasant.

Holiday Year: The year zero in the history of the Third Imperium, established by Cleon I to commemorate the establishment of the Imperium. Technically an aspect of calendar reform, the use of the year zero provides a central date point for counting years back into the Long Night and forward into the future of the Imperium.

The actual advantages of a holiday year are slight: centuries begin in the hundredth numbered year instead of the first numbered year, and the number of years between any two dates can be determined by subtraction.

More importantly at the time, the holiday year was used as part of the public relations campaigns which were impressing the authority of the Imperium upon local governments. The minor requirement of changing to the new calendar was used to determine cooperation by those governments.

Humaniti (former spelling Humanity): Collective name for human races, including Solomani, Vilani, Zhodani and others.

See Humans.

Humans: Intelligent major race dominating the Imperium and several additional interstellar communities. Humans stand approximately 1.8 meters in height and weigh about 100 kg. Descended from omnivore gatherers, humans developed intelligence in response to shifting climatological factors.

The most unusual aspect of humaniti is the fact that humans are present on many different worlds and stand at various levels of development on those worlds. The Solomani Hypothesis states that Humans evolved on Terra (Solomani Rim/Sol) and were scattered to many different worlds by the Ancients for reasons currently unknown. The result is that many different, parallel human races exist and coexist throughout known space.

The three most widespread human races are the Solomani (humans from Terra), the Vilani (humans from Vland), and the Zhodani (humans from Zhodane).

See also Ancients, Humaniti, Solomani Hypothesis, Solomani, Vilani, Zhodani.

I

Imperial Calendar: Calendar established at the creation of the Third Imperium as a universal calendar reform. Dates count from the founding of the Imperium, the year "zero." Dates before zero are negative, dates after are positive. For example, Terra discovered jump drive in -2431. The Imperium was founded in zero. Emperor Strephon was assassinated in 1116.

The year is divided into 365 standard days, which are grouped into 52 weeks of seven days each. The lengths of days and weeks is a legacy of Terran domination during the second Imperium. Days are numbered consecutively, beginning with one. The first day of the year is a holiday and is not part of any week. For example, the first day (Holiday) of the year 1116 is 001-1116. The emperor was assassinated on 132-1116. The last day of the year is 365-1116.

Imperial Edict 97: This executive order is the enabling act for the use of Imperial warrants. Unusually obscure for such a wide ranging and powerful edict, it is nonetheless on file at all Imperial installations. The edict text runs to 34 pages, much of it pure legalese; when distilled down, it proves very direct; it assists the holder of an Imperial warrant with all the power you can bring to bear.

Only the emperor has the power to issue these warrants.

A similar edict (Imperial Edict 3097) provides limited power to the Archdukes of the Imperium to issue similar warrants, although they are limited in their duration and territory.

Imperial Research Station: The worlds of the Imperium manifest a wide range of technological levels. The third Imperium has always allowed its member worlds a wide degree of latitude, and it meddles very little in local affairs. With communication limited to the same speed as transportation, a single offworld query can involve weeks, months, or even years before a reply is received. In addition, the cost of offworld transportation (in both time and money) tends to limit the interchange of information, the shipment of experimental prototypes, and other such activities that are basic to the dissemination of scientific knowledge.

Most worlds have found that simply purchasing advanced technology from a neighboring world is impractical. Not only is such high technology expensive, putting it to any cost-effective use requires that the technology be understood.

Consider: as useful as Tech Level 8 solid-state chip circuits are, they cannot be used on a large scale without the knowledge of electronics or the ability to provide supporting circuits (power circuits, circuit boards, and so on), which further implies a knowledge of photo processing, and even crystal culture. In the final analysis, attempting to jump to a higher Tech Level without passing through any of the intervening Tech Levels just doesn't work: one must pass through the lower stages of technological development on the way to higher Tech Levels.

Regardless of what the individual member worlds do, there are also certain large-scale interests in the Imperium which back research projects. Such research is generally privately

backed (such as under contract by multiworld corporations), or it is sometimes performed in established Imperial Research Stations.

Private Research: On a scale as vast as the Imperium, it is often cheaper to duplicate research rather than search out and contract for technology elsewhere in the Imperium. However, trade between worlds tends to introduce new knowledge and technology to those who do not yet have it. If a certain offworld item proves useful, local companies may try to achieve the same technology with the goal of entering into local manufacture. Local manufacture has the advantage of taking into account local preferences, as well as providing local employment. It also avoids potential problems with licensing agreements and arrangements.

Imperial Research: The Imperium finances research into a variety of areas. Sometimes this is an attempt to duplicate technology observed or reported in neighboring cultures and not yet within the ability of the best known science in the Imperium. Other times, the research is an area of interest expressed by some Imperial body (such as spinal mount weapons research performed by the Imperial Navy).

Imperial research stations may be located on worlds which need a boost to the local economy or in remote systems far from the potential disturbance of Imperial politics. Many different stations may be located in several systems of the same region, and many different areas of knowledge may be under investigation at one time.

In general, however, one station is constructed for one purpose, and it continues in a single area of knowledge for its entire span of usefulness. Its size, personnel roster, power plant capacity, and even visibility profile are dependent on its area of investigation.

Imperial backed research may delve into many areas. Some examples include black hole research (both large-scale and mini-black hole investigation), instantaneous transmitter development (so far proving impossible), antimatter containment, new weapon development (such as disintegrator beams), black globe development, deep planetary scanning, psychohistory, mass population behavior prediction, genetic transformation of living organisms, self-aware robots and starships, stasis and time travel, personal shields, memory transfer, and total rejuvenation.

The Divided Imperium: The divided Imperium is having varying effects on Imperial research stations. Some stations continue as if nothing has happened, others have been directed (under new authority) to change the focus of their research, still others have been either shut down or sacked by the local authorities for anything of value to the defense of the local realm.

Imperial Rules of War: To mitigate most of the potentially disastrous aspects of armed conflict, the "rules of war" evolved as an accumulation of unwritten concepts, which were established on a case-by-case basis. The rules of war were never officially codified, both to prevent them being seen as an Imperial endorsement of war and to keep formal precedent from preventing Imperial intervention whenever the Imperium deemed it necessary.

The main aim of the rules was maintaining the economic and military well-being of the realm. They gave the Imperium the right to intervene only when local military action threatened this well-being. The primary causes of instability, as viewed by Imperial analysts, have been long-term economic dislocation and excessive extraplanetary influence:

A. Long-term social or economic dislocation is suffered when a region loses its ability to carry on at its prewar level of economic activity.

B. Excessive extraplanetary influence is even more vague. Historically, the Imperium has tolerated the use of force as a necessary outlet for built-up political and social pressures. In such cases, a short war is deemed preferable to continuing tension, sabotage, political agitation, etc. However, attempts by extraplanetary forces, such as offworld governments or large commercial interests, to seize control of a world's affairs are beyond the scope of the "safety valve" rationale.

"Assistance" is tolerated so long as it is deemed appropriate to the level of legitimate interest in the affairs of the world held by the extraplanetary organization. For example, the Imperium has often tolerated the provision by megacorporations of training cadre, arms, equipment, etc., on a limited scale, and even of training fully equipped striker units to local governments. However, when it has appeared that the primary burden for the conduct of the war has been carried by an extraplanetary power, the Imperium has intervened, claiming the power is using the misfortune of a local dispute as a pretext for aggression.

Unlike the above rules, one prohibition is clear and firm throughout the Imperium: use or possession of nuclear weapons, if discovered, and regardless of size or type.

After Strephon's assassination, the Imperium's rules of war policy has taken a thorough beating. Many high level Imperial officials have abused the provisions of the extraplanetary influence concept, largely because of their growing distrust in the motives of their peers elsewhere in the Imperial government.

However, some Imperial officials view the current state of affairs in the Imperium as a valid application of the rules of war. In their view, the current wide-scale struggle was inevitable: it is simply a larger scale version of the "necessary outlet for built-up political and social pressures," a key concept in the rules of war. Thus they believe "a short war is deemed preferable to continuing tension, sabotage, and political agitation."

Imperial Stationery: The Imperial family has reserved (both by custom and by law) a distinctive design for its personal stationery. Well-known throughout the Imperium through its use for routine messages and for Imperial appointments, the form is cream-colored and embossed with the Imperial Sunburst in gold. Both physical and electronic versions of the stationery are used.

Because it is used for Imperial appointments (even when issued in blank for offices in the marches) all Imperial officials are familiar with the design and can readily tell physical forgeries from the real thing. Electronic versions are data-encrypted with a special code lock and require a special hardware key to be unlocked, thus making even electronic forgeries difficult.

Imperial Sunburst: The symbol of the Third Imperium established by Cleon (the first emperor) when the empire was proclaimed. Images show him standing before the original banner with a golden yellow sunburst against a black background, representing Capital's type G star against dark space.

In 247, the Eliyoh (a nonhuman minor race) joined the Imperium. To that race the symbology was unimpressive. The Eliyoh vision centered in the far infrared, which resulted in distinction between the official colors of black and yellow being impossible. So the Empress Porfiria declared that the symbol would have no official color.

The original banner in the Imperial throne room is still black with a yellow sunburst. The Imperial Interstellar Scout Service uses a red sunburst; the Imperial Navy, yellow; the Imperial Army, black; the Imperial Marines, maroon.

Imperial Warrant: Instrument of power issued by Imperial dukes, archdukes, or the emperor. A warrant is a written or electronic document on Imperial stationery provided to trusted agents of the Imperium as a method of bypassing the bureaucracy.

Typically, a warrant is provided to an individual who uses the power it provides to accomplish some mission of interest to the issuing official. Missions may include establishment of colonies in areas requiring development, the assumption of military command in the midst of a crisis, and the unilateral establishment of new noble lines to administer provinces which have suffered from war or economic collapse.

For example, the late emperor Strephon sometimes exercised his power through agents rather than directly through the bureaucracy of the Imperium. These instances were rare, although there is reason to believe that such agents are more numerous than it appears. The Imperial warrant would contain a statement similar to the example below:

"Capital. The bearer of this warrant is acting for the good of the Imperium and the Emperor. Extend him every assistance. Strephon."

See also Imperial Edict 97.

Interdiction: The Imperial practice of interdiction of worlds within the boundaries of the Imperium had long been a source of contention between liberal and conservative factions in the government. Interdictions must be approved by a member of the Imperial family, but generally such approval is given in response to a request from an interested service, which is almost always the Scouts or the Navy.

It is generally held that the Scouts recommend interdiction to shield a young or sensitive culture from the interference that trade and commerce will bring.

The Navy is held to be more vindictive in its recommendations, for they use interdiction to punish local governments or to hide its own mistakes.

In the current turmoil of the divided Imperium, various regions are reclassifying some indicted worlds as open and some previously open worlds as interdicted. The Domain of Deneb, however, is honoring all Imperial interdicted worlds as before.

Interdicted worlds are awarded travel zone red ratings by the Travellers' Aid Society.

See also Red Zone.

Iolanthe (1052 to 1079): Empress of the Imperium. Iolanthe, the daughter of the senior duke of Gushemege sector, and member of a prominent Vilani noble family, married Strephon in 1079. Her primary avocation is the preservation of developing cultures within the Imperium. She was murdered, along with her husband the emperor and her daughter the grand princess, in Dulinor's assassination attack of 1116.

Iridium Throne: The symbol of the continuing line of emperors of the Third Imperium. The physical throne was originally an iridium construction on which the emperor sat. Over time, the term has come to represent not only the emperor's throne, but the office of the emperor himself.

J

Jump Dimming: The transitions to and from jumpspace are momentous occasions during an interstellar trip. Following an old Vilani superstition, the pilot of a ship customarily dims the ship's interior and exterior lights before going into jump. Historically, this custom derived from the need for most of the ship's power to be diverted into the computer and jump drive systems, so that the jump drive could be guided into creating the jump field properly. Zhodani and Solomani pilots do not follow this tradition of "jump dimming."

Lights on a ship are typically dimmed for a period of about two minutes; the lights are brought back up to full strength as soon as the ship is in jumpspace.

Jumpspace: The basic concept of interstellar travel: that of an alternate space. Theoretically, jumpspaces are alternate spaces, each only dimly understood from the standpoint of our own universe. Jump is defined as the movement of matter from one point in space (called normal space) to another point in normal space by travelling through an alternate space (called jumpspace). The benefit of jump is that the time required is relatively invariant—about one week. If the distance travelled is greater than can be covered in one week in normal space, then a gain has been made. Jumpspace makes possible enormous gains.

Entering jump is possible anywhere, but perturbations due to gravity make it safest to begin a jump at least 100 diameters

out from a large massive body such as a world or star. Ships are naturally precipitated out of jumpspace before they get too deep into a gravity field.

Normal jumps take 168 hours (plus or minus 10 percent) to complete, regardless of the distance travelled.

Sometimes a jump goes wrong. Catastrophic failures (called misjumps) can destroy the ship and its crew. Other failures can destroy a drive or send a ship in the wrong direction. Some misjumps reduce a jump-6 to a mere jump-1, or convert a jump-1 into jump-10, 20, or higher.

K

Kedzudh, Commonality of: Loose interstellar government in the Vargr Extents. The Commonality dates from 1044, when several world governments joined together in an attempt to suppress piracy. The Commonality government has limited powers of taxation; government institutions include a small navy/police force and a university. Individual worlds conduct their own interior and exterior relations.

Kirur (Ruupiin/Thirty 1315 B863A03-F): Homeworld and capital of the Two Thousand Worlds—the interstellar empire of the K'kree. The planet's oceans are extremely shallow and the world exhibits almost no volcanic activity, which is very unusual for a world of its size. Kirur has one large continent, which was conquered in prehistoric times by the current ruling clan; Kirur is one of the most politically stable planets known.

K'kree: The K'kree (once called Centaurs by humans) are among the most massive of the major races and are the only one of the major races to be descended from herbivores. An adult K'kree stands about 1.5 meters at the shoulder and between 2.0 and 2.4 meters tall when standing erect. Weight averages 550 kg. They are bilaterally symmetrical, hexapedal, and homeothermic. They bear some resemblance to the centaurs of ancient Terran myth, a trait noted by the earliest human explorers.

The arrangement of the manipulative organ (or hand) on the front limb is one of their most interesting features. Complex or cartilaginous tubes permit the fingers of the K'kree hand to telescope up out of the way when the hand is used as a weapon. Fully extended, the fingers are mutually opposable to each other and to the "thumb" which is in reality an extension of the ulna. The K'kree hand is very flexible but somewhat weaker in grasping power than the human hand.

The K'kree are covered with a short gray or black fur and with a dense black mane covering the head and neck and upper back of both sexes. Unlike Terran mammals, the young are fed partially digested, regurgitated food instead of milk. Males average 15 percent to 20 percent larger than females.

K'kree are extremely conservative in all aspects of their culture. Ceremonial military units (such as bodyguards) are armed with equipment which K'kree military technology outdated centuries ago, and (aside from modifications made necessary by the discovery of spaceflight) K'kree government has not changed significantly in centuries.

Because of their origins as plains-dwelling herd animals, the K'kree are claustrophobes; they cannot stand to be enclosed. K'kree cities are clumps of low, broad, buildings; the interior is never more than one story in height, which allows the sky to be visible. Internal building divisions are achieved with curtains or tapestries.

K'kree are extremely gregarious. They are never found alone, and will quickly sicken and die if removed from other K'kree for any length of time. Receiving a trade or diplomatic delegation from the K'kree means entertaining the entire family (one or more wives, servants, scribes, assistants, etc.) of the merchant or the ambassador. The K'kree word for "my" refers to a possession of an individual's herd, not to that of an individual. Privacy and individuality are exotic and little understood concepts for the K'kree.

Society: K'kree society is divided into castes. The system is a remnant of ancient times which no longer fits K'kree culture perfectly, but the K'kree stick with it because it is traditional. There are hundreds of castes, but the distinctions are too faint for non-K'kree to understand. For simplicity, castes can be divided into three general groupings: noble, merchant, and servant. It is possible for a family to rise in caste, but this is a rare occurrence.

The lowest caste, the servants, has come to include farmers, factory workers, and unskilled laborers as well as servants for all classes.

The next higher caste, the merchants, includes most skilled workers, scientists, engineers, technicians, scribes, and government administrators, as well as merchants and businessmen.

Nobles are the governmental officials (the Krurruna and others), the high military officers, diplomats, and heads of trade and manufacturing concerns. Nobles are usually garbed in much more ornate fashion than the lower castes.

Every male K'kree must serve a term in the military upon coming of age. Warriors are drawn from all castes; rank in the military is determined by the caste of origin (nobles enter the service as general officer trainees, merchants as lower officers and noncommissioned officers, etc.). Upon completing the required term of service, a warrior returns to his original caste and position. Warriors are the only K'kree permitted to bear weapons, and they are further distinguished by their peculiar flared and horned helmets. They serve as soldiers, police, firefighters, and bodyguards for diplomatic and mercantile expeditions.

Female K'kree are casteless, and take on the caste of their father or husband. Females have no position in government or society other than the rearing of young.

Government: The basis of K'kree government is rooted in the traditional herd system. The basic unit of government is the herd, which consists of thousands of individuals of all sexes, castes, and ages led by krurruna (literally: bosses) under a single steppelord.

In recent times, most herds have been assigned specific geographic areas (several may be assigned to a city or a single herd may be assigned millions of hectares of farmland). A number of herds are governed by a single "lord of steppelords" (usually the ruler of a planet); and the K'kree race as a whole is ruled by a "Steppelord of the 2000 Worlds."

K'kree Calendar: The K'kree calendar is based on the period of Kirur (the K'kree homeworld) around Gzang, its star. The K'kree Pim!bigr (year) is 439.56 standard days in length.

See also Kirur, Two Thousand Worlds.

Kuzu (Dark Nebula/Kilrai' 1919 A876986-E): Homeworld of the Aslan race and capital of the Aslan Hierate.

L

Lair (Provence/Grnouf 2402 A8859B9-F): "Homeworld" and capital of the Vargr Extents. Lair has never been accorded any particular status in the hearts and minds of the Vargr race, unlike worlds like Terra, Vland, Zhodane, Kuzu, or Kirur. Lair was only recently united; several sections of the planet boasted independence until only a few years ago—which is unusual for the homeworld of a major interstellar race.

Lancia: Cultural region in the Gushemege sector of the Third Imperium. The area was extensively ravaged during the Vilani Pacification Campaigns, and afterwards resettled from the Vland sector under an special program sponsored by Makhidkarun.

Lanthanum: A rare earth element, the first of the inner transition metals. Vital to the construction of the inner coils of interstellar jump drive units.

Lesser Rift: Broad expanse of space with a very low density of stars trailing the main region of the Third Imperium. This rift is a pronounced impediment to interstellar travel, for it constrains jumps through the Empty Quarter. The Lesser Rift is lesser only when compared to the larger, more prominent Great Rift spinward of the Imperium.

The Lesser Rift, like the Great Rift, has provided long-term security for the Third Imperium by constraining access to the Imperium's borders.

Llellewyloly: Sophont race native to Junidy (Spinward Marches/Aramis 3202 B434ABD-9). Llellewyloly have five multijointed limbs which function as hands and feet interchangeably; main sensory organs are also located on the limbs. The spherical central body is covered with long, coarse hair. Many body features are adaptations to the extreme temperature variations of Junidy's day.

Llellewyloly have a complex society with many dimensions of social precedence; the same individual may be entitled to high status in one situation and low status in another, and to make an error concerning propriety is a serious matter.

Loeskalth: Minor human race from Gushemege sector; known only from ancient First Imperium records. During the early stages of the First Imperium the Loeskalth culture absorbed a great deal of science and technology indirectly from the Vilani and founded a small empire which embraced, at its height, most of their home subsector.

About 5400 years ago, the Vilani consolidation destroyed the Loeskalth Empire and absorbed the civilization into the mainstream of Vilani culture. An aggressive and warlike race, the Loeskalth resisted but were ultimately overwhelmed.

M

Main: A grouping of systems forming a chain of worlds all reachable by jump-1. This grouping provides a sort of "corridor" allowing jump-1 capable ships to travel to any world along the chain without ever exceeding jump-1.

Many such groupings of worlds exist in the Imperium. Prominent examples include the Spinward Main in the Spinward Marches, the Vilani Main centered in the Vland Sector, The Sylean Main in Core Sector, and the Antares Main originating in the Antares sector.

Major Race: An arbitrary distinction based on the achievement of a specific intelligent race. A race which achieves interstellar travel (jump drive) through its own efforts is classed major; one which does not is classed minor.

To date, generally accepted major races include Humaniti (Zhodani, Solomani, and Vilani, but not other examples), Aslan, the Hive, K'kree, Vargr, Ancients, and Droyne.

The Suerrat (a human race) are considered minor because their achievement of interstellar travel utilized generation ships. Similarly, the Geonee were originally thought to be a major race, but their development of jump drive was based on recovered Ancient artifacts rather than on true racial efforts. The Geonee dispute this prevailing opinion and hold the (generally unshared) view that they are of major standing.

The Droyne have been demonstrated to be major, for they have developed jump drive as far back as -7000. At present, however, they do not build or use jump drives, and remain voluntarily sequestered in their scattered systems to spinward.

Mercenary: The remote centralized government of the Imperium is possessed of great industrial and technological might, but it is also unable, due to the sheer distances and travel times involved, to exert total control everywhere within its starspanning realm.

Extensive home rule provisions allow planetary governments to choose their own forms of government, raise and maintain their own armed forces for local security, pass and enforce laws governing local conduct, and regulate (within limits) commerce. Defense has been a cooperative effort of local indigenous forces, which is stiffened by Imperial naval bases manned by extremely sophisticated forces.

Conflicting local interests have often settled their differences by force of arms, with Imperial forces looking quietly the other way, unable to intervene en masse. Imperial forces have been able to operate as a police force so as to not jeopardize their

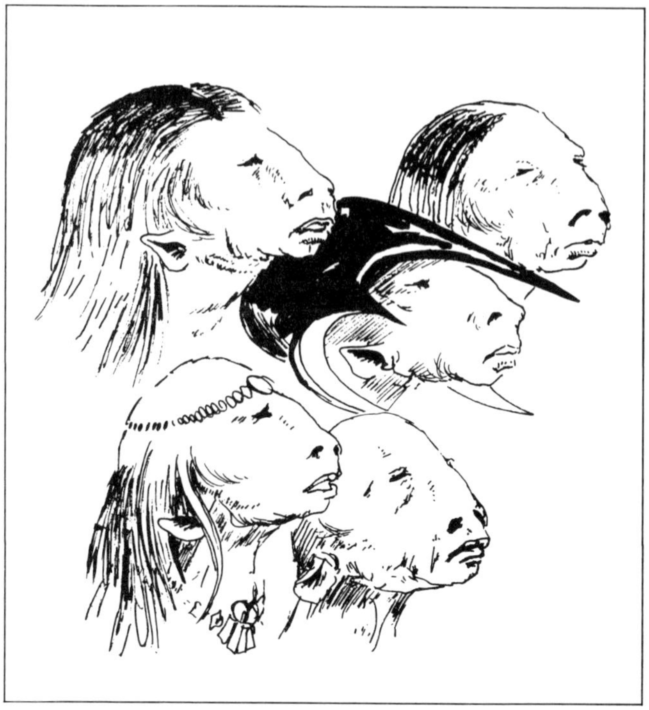

primary mission of defense of the realm. Only when local conflicts threaten either the security or the economy of an area have Imperial forces taken an active hand, and then with overwhelming speed and force.

In this environment, the soldier for hire has found active employment. The tolerance exhibited by the forces of the Imperium have made the hired military force a practical matter. Imperial policy has allowed the marketplace to provide military force to those who can afford it; one line of thought has been that a hired military can be more effectively controlled if it gets out of hand, as opposed to nationalistic or politically motivated military forces.

The united Imperium stood ready to enforce its own standards; things have changed in the uncertain climate of the divided Imperium, however. The basic restrictions against improper scales of force are no longer observed, and weapons such as poison gas or nuclear devices are being used by belligerents. Matters have gotten out of hand as each archduke has done what he though was best for the defense of his local realm. Imperial forces have attempted to intervene, but the wide-scale nature of the turmoil has diluted their effect and even turned Imperial forces against each other in border areas.

Minor Race: An intelligent race which has not achieved jump drive through its own efforts. For most races, this classification is appropriate. Many are contacted before they have reached a technological level capable of even considering jump drive, thus permanently prejudicing their potential.

Indeed, the shock of such classification, and the realization that this classification pervades interstellar society, is sufficient to relegate a race to a permanent role as shopkeepers and accountants. Some slump, while others violently resist the classification. The fact that the categorization is informal and arbitrary, and tends to elevate those already in power has made resistance difficult, if not impossible.

Moot: The Imperial government's only deliberative body. It has few powers and even more rarely exercises them. In theory, the Moot includes all Imperial nobles of baronial or higher status, but most nobles do not find it convenient to travel to Capital, and so many of those seated hold proxy votes. Large blocks of these votes can be wielded by a single influential noble.

Technically, the Moot is supreme in the Imperium, but its power is extremely limited. In practice, its deliberations are advisory to the emperor, and he is wise to heed them. The Moot has only one power: to dissolve the Imperium. When this power is brought to bear, it compels compromise between opposing factions.

When an emperor dies, abdicates, or otherwise becomes unfit for office, the Moot becomes important as the validating body for the new emperor. It has the power to examine the qualifications and credentials of the heir apparent and, in unusual situations, to reject him.

The Moot holds its sessions in the Moot Spire, which, at 1.75 kilometers high, is the tallest building on Capital. By tradition, the Spire is the only building allowed to tower above the Imperial Palace, which is 4.25 kilometers away. Elevators with gravitic compensators can speed visitors from the bottom to the top in 18 seconds. At the top of the Spire is the High Moot, where select committees hold the most private deliberations.

In the resulting turmoil after Strephon's assassination, Prince Lucan ordered the the Moot dissolved for a year in an effort to prevent any infiltrators from convincing the Moot to approve the usurper Dulinor's claim to the throne.

Monadium: Inpenetrable bluish-gray metal used as the basic construction material by the Ancients at the site on Antiquity (Corridor/Ian 0816). It has defeated all efforts to determine its exact composition; some experts believe it contains titanium. Even modern tech level 15 plasma and fusion weapons have been unable to penetrate it.

N

Naval Base: Port facility for the support, maintenance, repair, and refit of naval vessels. Planetary surface facilities are generally provided for vessels of 1000 tons or less; orbital facilities handle larger ships.

A naval base has several distinct parts to it; each part helps in the accomplishment of the overall mission of the base. The typical naval base is composed of an orbital berthing area, a surface berthing area, a maintenance section, and an administrative headquarters.

Berthing areas provide locations for ships to lay over, for a day or for months. All berthing areas include provisions for refueling from storage tanks or fuel lighters.

Maintenance sections at naval bases vary from base to base. Where such a section would be redundant to the local starport shipyard, it is small, and repairs or alterations are carried out under contract by the local facility. Where adequate facilities do not exist, the naval base itself may have a large maintenance section capable of extensive repairs and refits. Maintenance is performed on the ships on the world surface or in orbit as necessary.

The administrative headquarters handles the day-to-day operations of the base, as well as its paperwork (including the allocation of funds, distribution of personnel, and disbursement of maintenance and repair contracts).

The naval base is not a tactical unit. It has no battle forces of its own, and it does not exert control even over local system defense boats (which are under a separate command). The naval base is responsible for supporting the fleet and keeping it in optimum condition for its combat missions.

Naval Depot: Depots serve as focuses for naval efforts: supplying a fleet's every need, providing construction and repair facilities, and producing and testing experimental ship prototypes. A depot generally occupies an entire system. Facilities, material, and personnel are extensive enough to repair and resupply a large fraction of the fleet at any time. A depot may be isolated from outside contact for years at a time without serious setbacks. As depots cover large parts of a system, there is no distinction between orbital and surface berthing.

In peacetime, the main function of a depot is the design and testing of ships. A large staff of naval architects (the cream of the area) and construction personnel is maintained at every depot.

In wartime, depots serve as repair and resupply centers for the fleet. In emergencies, the depot's construction yards are sometimes pressed into service for production of military ships.

Since a depot is obviously a very sensitive installation, security is tight. An extensive array of both entry and exit codes are employed to ensure no unauthorized vessels enter or leave the system. Contingents of marines and system defense boats are stationed throughout the system, and they are constantly ready for action.

There is usually no more than one naval depot per sector. Depots are placed in systems where they will be close enough to the expected action to be useful, but far enough back to insure that they will not be captured.

Nobility: The foundation of interstellar government within the Imperium. The Imperium depends on nobles ranging from knights to archdukes to carry the chain of authority and the mantle of responsibility from the Emperor to the people.

Nth Interstellar War: Any one of an indeterminate number of interstellar wars fought between the Terran Confederation and the First Imperium during the Period -2408 and -2219.

The First Interstellar War (-2408 to -2400) marked the initial clash between Terra and Vland. The peace that concluded the hostilities was both uneasy and short. The second through seventh wars were marked by seesaw exchanges of territory, mostly confined to the Dingir and Sol subsectors. These initial wars were fought, on the Vilani side, with only the forces available to the Vilani provincial governor; the central government was preoccupied with other problems. This was fortunate for the Terrans, as Vilani power, even at this late date, was sufficient to crush the Terrans in short order had it been applied.

The Eighth War finally broke open the frontier and ended in the first major Terran victory. Finally, the Grand Imperium took notice, and dispatched major fleet elements to the area, but the time for action had passed. Terran invention of the jump-3 drive made the Ninth War a crushing victory for Terra and forced the Vilani to relinquish most of the Solomani Rim. Thereafter, the Terrans were almost constantly on the offensive.

In the centuries after the conclusion of the wars, no consensus could be reached in the academic community as to when the later conflicts began or ended; all were interrupted several times by armistices, cease fires, or shaky periods of peace (indeed, a new war would often break out along the front lines before the existence of a peace treaty could be communicated to the respective capitals).

Periods of warfare are lumped together or split apart depending on the historian's individual point of view, and a single war to one historian can be identified as two or more wars by others. The situation is complicated by the fact that records for some of the years in question are sketchy. To clarify matters, an accommodation was arrived at which simply labels all interstellar wars after the Ninth with the indeterminate variable N. Proper usage calls for the war to be defined with the actual years being discussed. Many history texts use this system to refer to all the wars except the first.

The Nth Interstellar War (-2235 to -2219) ended the series when the Vilani Grand Imperium collapsed, as much from its own weight, age, and decadence as from Terran victories. The Terrans moved quickly to occupy the remaining Vilani territory.

See First Imperium, First Interstellar War, Rule of Man.

O

Octagon Society: Established in 342, the Octagon Society was the first major distressed spacefarer assistance operation to appear in the Spinward Marches. The group thrived on public contributions and on some tax revenues for 150 years; then it collapsed in the late 400s when scandals emerged over the quality of shelter construction and the disposition of certain funds.

Society shelters were generally of an octagonal shape. Large hostels were established on major worlds, while smaller weather shelters were placed on frontier or unsettled worlds. The characteristic octagon-shaped buildings are still visible on various worlds, although none are still in use as shelters for distressed spacefarers.

The Octagon Society was dissolved in 499, and its assets were sold at auction.

Oort Cloud: A spherical shell around most stars containing numerous small bodies of cometary material. A typical Oort cloud is about 0.5 to 1 light year from its primary and has an aggregate mass about that of Terra; density is thus extremely low. The main constituents of cometary bodies are ice and dust ("dirty snowballs"). Bodies in the Oort cloud are occasionally perturbed by collisions or by the influence of nearby stars into orbits which pass near the star; these form the visible comets. The Oort cloud is named after its discoverer, Terran astronomer Jan Oort.

Outworld Coalition: Traditional name for the belligerent groups allied against the Imperium during the First and Second Frontier Wars. Commonly applied to any alliance of powers threatening the Spinward Marches and Imperial territories spinward of the Great Rift.

The original Outworld Coalition was formed in the early 500s at the instigation of the Zhodani Consulate. Vargr allegiances vacillated, but memories of the Imperial campaigns against certain Vargr states in the Corridor swayed some into membership. Zhodane, as the major partner, contributed military aid and assistance (such as technicians and advisors). While some

Vargr governments contributed personnel and naval units, other Vargr remained neutral or sided with the Imperium.

The initial history of the coalition was one of continuing struggle for organization, as the Zhodani were continually occupied in establishing Vargr governments, and then maintaining them in power. The intent was for the Vargr to raid the coreward edge of the Spinward Marches, especially Regina and Aramis subsectors, while the major thrust from Zhodane took Cronor and Jewell subsectors. The Vargr portions of the offensive failed dismally. Furthermore, the failure resulted in a collapse of the coalition.

The internal Imperial upheavals (the Civil War) which followed the First Frontier War (it was just called the Frontier War then) exposed a continuing weakness in the Imperium, and the Outworld Coalition reformed after a hiatus of five years. At the appropriate moment, the reformed Coalition again attacked the Marches, this time taking portions of Jewell subsector. Although the Vargr again failed to take any territory permanently, their performance as a whole was considerably improved.

Traditionally, frontier wars in the Spinward Marches have involved coalitions of Zhodani and certain Vargr states. The Sword Worlds have also joined the coalition at times.

P

Pacification Campaigns (76-120): A series of economic, diplomatic, and military operations directed at forcing membership in the Imperium upon those worlds which resisted the initial efforts to annex them.

Although the campaigns were predominantly economic and diplomatic in nature, the Imperium was not averse to using force when peaceful methods failed. Imperial battlefleets and ground forces rarely failed when brought to bear.

By 120, the pacification campaigns ended, and the initial phase of the Imperium's growth came to a close.

Four specific Pacification Campaigns were undertaken, each by an archduke of the Imperium. The Vilani Pacification Campaign was targeted at portions of Dagudashaag and Gushemege sectors. The Ilelish Pacification Campaign was aimed at the Darmine region. The Antarean Pacification Campaign hit much of Lishun sector. The Sylean Pacification Campaign operated in Delphi and Fornast sectors.

Peerage: The hierarchy of nobles within the Imperium.

Phoenix Project: Reported plot by Solomani guerrillas on Terra to destroy Imperial forces occupying Terra. Imperial intelligence reported penetration of the project command in 1045, with subsequent compromise of its basic plans and dismantling of its structure.

The Phoenix Project was supposedly born in the final years of the Solomani Rim War (990 to 1002) as Solomani leaders saw the possibility of their defeat and the loss of the homeworld to the invading Imperials. The project was said to have consisted of two distinct parts: prepositioned caches of military goods to supply the coming uprising and a continuing program for the training of guerrillas.

The caches were concealed in many different places on Terra in areas calculated to preclude accidental discovery over the years. Each cache contained large quantities of munitions, weapons, vehicles, and medical supplies, all of varying technological levels so as to be of use regardless of the technical knowledge of the users. Each cache was hidden with its location entrusted to a single local family. These families were to form the core of the guerrilla forces when the rising was to take place.

A massive Imperial counter-guerrilla effort in 1040 to 1045 was directed at the discovery and destruction of the caches and the arrest of the families entrusted with their secrets.

Persistent rumors of two additional aspects of the project—Lambda (a codeword to trigger the uprising) and Omega (the reinforcement of the uprising by offworld Solomani)—have been dismissed as baseless by Imperial officials.

Many historians believe that the extent of the plot was greatly exaggerated by Imperial authorities, and hold that it was little more than an extreme example of wishful thinking on the part of the Solomani leadership. At any rate, the Phoenix Project no longer threatens the security of the Imperium, if indeed it ever did.

Postal Union: A Group of political units associated to a greater or lesser degree for the purpose of communication among citizens, businesses, and governmental units.

Nearly all star systems are members of one postal union or another. Governments cooperate along their borders in order to allow the efficient flow of communications between them. Members of a postal union forward mail through their territories (subject, of course, to local security needs, acts of war, and so on) to the proper addresses. On the average, communication is at the speed of the fastest available transportation, which means about three or four parsecs per week.

Psionics: The criminal use of mental powers for the manipulation of matter and energy and for communication. It has been demonstrated that minds (human or nonhuman, conscious or unconscious, intelligent or unintelligent) contain some capacity to operate without apparent use of physical facilities. For an individual to seek out such training is a criminal act.

Until circa -1000, psionics was little studied in most regions except on a disorganized level (parapsychology, the occult, spiritualism, and so on). It was known and practiced among the Zhodani and by some minor races, but it was by no means widespread.

However, during the Long Night, many races, (human and others) turned introspective. As a result, many finally began to engage in serious research in psionics, which revealed much about the empirical nature of the phenomenon, although the principles involved were, and remain, little understood.

However, even though it assumed scientific validity, psionics remained a backwater science until about 650, when it underwent a tremendous burst of popularity. Psionics within the Imperium reached its peak in the latter half of the 700s. In the 790s, however, the crest of popular opinion broke with the revelation of scandals within the Psionics Institutes; the result was the psionics suppressions (800 to 826), which shifted public opinion away from support of psionics.

Psionics Institute: Any clandestine organization devoted to the illegal training of individuals in the use of psionics talents. Active Imperial campaigns to eradicate the Institute have been pursued for over 200 years.

Organizations of this nature have existed since before the advent of space travel, but they attained prominence only during the Long Night, when reproducible scientific discoveries made psionics a teachable, learnable science.

In the Imperial antebellum period, psionics institutes were rare, and they were formed only on a few scattered worlds which, for one reason or another, had an unusually high rate of psionic talents appearing, or which encouraged psionics for social, political, or commercial reasons. In the years after the Civil War, institutes were organized on most high population worlds within the Imperium.

Psionics institute is a generic name; each such institution was independently organized and maintained. Institutes were generally supported by that portion of the population which had psionic talents; since that portion was small, they were viable only on high population worlds (approximately one billion or more).

During the psionics suppressions, the institutes' charters were revoked, and talented individuals were persecuted. In some cases, the individuals fled to assume new identities on other worlds; in others, whole families emigrated to the Zhodani Consulate or to other places beyond the frontiers of the Imperium.

Following the psionics suppressions, there were theoretically no psionics institutes remaining. In practice, however, illegal underground institutes are rumored to still remain on many worlds.

Psionic Suppressions (800 to 826): Between 772 and 798, a series of financial, ethical, and moral scandals within the Psionic Institutes of the Imperium shifted public opinion against the Institutes. At the same time, it became clear that a good number of the Institutes were under the control of the Zhodani Consulate. In 800, the Imperium moved against the institutes by canceling their charters, jailing their leaders, and passing laws restricting the teaching or practice of psionics. Many institute figures went underground to espouse their cause in a type of guerrilla war.

The Psionic Suppressions had a profound influence on Imperial opinion. Over the course of 26 years, the Suppressions equated psionics with the Zhodani and established in the average Imperial citizen a distaste for both that continues to the present day. The average citizen will admit to a general dislike of psionics, and if pressed, will usually state that psionics violates a person's right of mental privacy.

Psychohistory: The science of historical prediction and macrosocial manipulation. The main thesis of psychohistory is that the actions of trillions of individuals take on a fluidity and predictability which can be compared to that of molecules in a gas. The very size of the population being dealt with factors out individual peculiarities and allows the prediction of its behavior. With the ability to predict the reaction of a population to a particular stimulus comes the ability to manipulate that population, psychohistorians reason.

Psychohistory began as a combination of public relations/advertising techniques and behaviorial science, and although its techniques have been put on a more rigorous footing, the basic principles are still not well understood. A number of minor experiments have confirmed the general validity of the science, but it was also shown to be too expensive to be of any practical utility. Research continues at a small number of Imperial universities.

R

Rachele Society: Secret Vilani supremacist group founded on Pretoria/Pretoria by Zid Rachele in 992. Genocidal policies favored by the group culminated in the attempted takeover of the Pretorian government in 1010. An attempt at nuclear blackmail backfired when 26,000 people (including 1,900 Rachelean commandos) were killed by a nuclear explosion after the Society seized Imperial Scout facilities on Saki (Deneb/Pretoria). Zid Rachele disappeared in 1015 after escaping from the prison world Exile in Usani Subsector (Deneb/Usani 1928).

In 1103, Zid Rachele and the Rachele Society surfaced again in Lishun in a brief power play at the Dynam Naval Depot (Lishun/Masionia 1219). Rachele and his followers attempted the theft of several mothballed naval warships but were quickly defeated. Zid Rachele's vessel was destroyed in the battle.

Rachelean Revolts (1010-1011): Major uprising on Pretoria (Deneb/Pretoria) fomented by the Rachele Society, which resulted in martial law under the Imperial Navy since that time. The Imperium as a rule does not interfere with local politics, but their intervention was forced when a Scout base on Saki (Deneb/Pretoria) was destroyed by nuclear weapons.

See Rachele Society.

Ramshackle Empire: Common term used during the Long Night to refer to the Rule of Man, also known as the Second Imperium. As the successor to the First Imperium, the Rule of Man took over the territories (and the problems) of its predecessor. Pro-Second Imperium histories contend that the Rule of Man delayed the inevitable collapse. Pro-First Imperium histories claim that the First Imperium was stagnant, but stable, and that the Ramshackle Empire actually precipitated the Long Night by looting subject worlds and promoting Terran superiority.

See Rule of Man.

Red Zone: The Traveller's Aid Society travel zone classification for a nation, world, or system which is dangerous to travellers. In general, the imposition of a red zone classification indicates the location is quarantined, interdicted by higher authority, or at war.

Quarantine indicates that a dangerous disease is present, and the danger of war is self-explanatory, but interdiction requires further discussion. Interstellar governments often find it necessary to restrict access to worlds or systems for political or military reasons, and they do so by publishing interdictions.

Enforcement of interdiction varies with the reason for the restriction. Interdiction may be imposed on a world if it is a military base or other sensitive installation, for the private reservations belonging to powerful families desiring seclusion, for developing societies which the government has elected to allow to evolve in isolation, or for valuable resource areas being saved for later development or exploitation.

Repatriation Bond: A document guaranteeing passage of an individual to a specified location upon completion of contract work or upon suspension of contract work for any reason. Repatriation bonds are guarantees given as inducements to workers who might otherwise be wary of leaving their own worlds with no assurances that they could return. They are most commonly used by mercenary units.

Repatriation bonds are usually administered by a large financial institution which holds the necessary funds in escrow.

Rule of Man (-2204 to -1776): A short-lived interstellar empire formed after the conquest of the Vilani Imperium by the Terrans. The conquered territories were under military rule from -2219 to -2204. Vilani military forces were incorporated into the Terran forces. Terran naval officers took over key posts in the Vilani bureaucracy (which was otherwise retained intact).

In -2204, the Terran Secretariat attempted to transfer control directly to Terra and to incorporate the conquered regions into the Terran Confederation. The commander in chief of the Terran Navy, Admiral Hiroshi Estigarribia, realized that the Confederation government could not possibly control the vast territories of the Vilani Imperium. He proclaimed himself Regent of the Vilani Imperium, and Protector of Terra, so both states were now united in the Rule of Man. Nearly all the fleet sided with Estigarribia both because it was composed largely of colonials, who were under-represented under the Terran Confederation government, and because of Estigarribia's careful preparation. The Confederation was dissolved without significant resistance.

The Terran fleet headquarters on Dingir became the capital of the Rule of Man. The bureaucratic center of the Imperium remained on Vland, although arrangements were undertaken to gradually transfer it elsewhere.

Upon Estigarribia's death, he was succeeded by his chief of staff, who crowned himself Emperor Hiroshi II. Estigarribia, even though he did not actually assume the crown, is therefore known to history as Emperor Hiroshi I.

Hiroshi II transferred all functions of government from both Vland and Dingir to a more centrally located world, renamed bilingually Hub/Ershur. This world was to remain the capital of the Rule of Man for the next four hundred years.

During the Rule of Man, large numbers of humans from Terra and its oldest colonies emigrated throughout the Imperium. People of Terran ancestry or culture (many of them assimilated Vilani) assumed positions of power on most worlds and became industrialists and administrators.

The problems of sheer size and scientific stagnation, which had brought about the fall of the Vilani Imperium, continued to plague the Rule of Man. The Vilani had coped with the problems of ruling a large empire by a rigid caste system with all citizens rooted permanently in their places, but this system could last only as long as there was no significant external threat. The Terrans did away with this system but were not able to replace it with a new social order. The destruction of the caste system swept away the foundations of society. Key industries fell apart as their workers became free to move elsewhere.

The -1776 date for the end of the Rule of Man is arbitrary, and it notes the financial collapse of the central government, which occurred when the Treasury at Hub/Ershur refused to honor a monetary issue of the branch treasury at Antares. The resulting lack of confidence within monetary circles marked the end of large-scale interstellar trade and of effective governmental power within the Rule of Man. Although the Imperium did not completely fall apart for many years, the Rule of Man had effectively ceased to exist as a viable interstellar community, and the period known as Twilight had begun.

The Third Imperium refers to the Rule of Man as the Second Imperium, which emphasizes its own roots in the Solomani-dominated Second Imperium and the Vilani-dominated First Imperium. Anti-Solomani elements emphasize the failure of the Solomani-dominated Ramshackle Empire.

Rule of Terra: Solomani terrorist group active in selected regions of Solomani/Imperial border. Violently anti-Imperial even by the standards of most Solomani political groups, the Rule of Terra seeks to force the return of all "rightful Terran property" to Solomani hands through assassination and other acts of violence.

The organization, although interstellar in scope, was apparently not a very strong organization in the beginning; some of its claimed attacks have proven to be accidents, while others were the work of different dissident individuals or organizations.

The Rule of Terra's acts, although not its goals, have been disavowed by many other Solomani groups, including the Confederation government; in return, the Rule of Terra has attacked even Solomani populations, by stating that "all who do not contribute to the Manifest Destiny of the Race are not worthy to be part of the Race."

Since the death of Strephon and the resulting Solomani incursions into the rimward reaches of the Imperium, the Rule of Terra organization has apparently mushroomed in popularity. The group has claimed responsibility for many terrorist acts along the current Solomani/Imperium border.

S

Scout Base: Port facility for the support, maintenance, and repair of scout vessels. The Imperial Interstellar Scout Service maintains a variety of scout bases scattered throughout the Imperium, with installations tending to be on less well-developed worlds with starports type D or C. Scout bases tend to be surface installations equipped with basic facilities for fueling and for minor maintenance activities oriented toward ships of 1000 tons or less.

Scout bases are positioned in systems more out of the way than are naval bases for a reason. The scout bases serve as a source of ships carrying dispatches from the well-travelled Xboat lanes to more remote worlds.

Scout bases also have other responsibilities, and most have an administrative responsibility in addition to the maintenance and refueling of scout ships. Within a subsector, one base will hold responsibility for cartography in the subsector, another will be responsible for technical developments, and still another for contact or liaison activities. The scout base is more extensive than an Xboat station, but less comprehensive than a way station.

See Way Station, Xboat Station.

Second Frontier War (615 to 620): Fought between the Outworld Coalition and the Imperium during the period of the barracks emperors. Arbellatra (587 to 666) was named Grand Admiral of the Marches by Cleon V and led the combined local and Imperial forces to defeat the Coalition, and then he proceeded to reestablish the central Imperial authority.

Second Imperium: The successor to the First Imperium, established by the Terran Confederation Navy to rule the territories conquered from the Vilani Empire by Terra.

See Rule of Man.

Sector: Mapping unit in astrography equal to sixteen subsectors. Average density 500 to 650 worlds per sector.

Sectors are named, and several synonyms are in common use, including march (or marches), region, reach (or reaches), quadrant, and matrix. The Spinward Marches, for example, is a sector.

As a rough means of comparing size (and as of 1115), the sector counts of the large interstellar states and areas of settlement are: the Imperium: 27; the Aslan Hierate: 18; the Hive Federation: 17; the Two Thousand Worlds: 14; the Vargr Extents: 14; the Zhodani Consulate: 13; the Solomani Confederation: 11.

Shudusham Concords: Agreement signed by twelve worlds of the Sylean Federation at Shudusham (Core/Capital) in -110 which dealt with weaponry carried by robots. The Concords have no legal force now, of course, but many worlds have adopted similar or identical standards using the Concords as a template, and most robots produced commercially in the Imperium are designed with these restrictions in mind.

Signal GK: Abbreviation for Gashimeku Kaalariin, Vilani for "vessel in distress. The code signal GK originated on Vland as a distress signal in maritime and aviation activity, and it was one of the standard communications codes of the Vilani Imperium. When the Second Imperium succeeded it, signal GK was retained as a distress code co-equal with the Terran SOS and Mayday signals.

The Imperial Navigation Act of 103 requires all vessels, whether military or civilian, to respond to the GK, SOS, or Mayday signals, provided such response does not endanger the ship and crew of the responding vessel.

Six Races: Traditional term for the intelligent races which dominate this region of the galaxy. It appears independently in Aslan, Vargr, and K'kree literature.

There is some disagreement as to the meaning of the term and the identity of the races involved. Most commentators agree that all of the six races must be major races; the candidates are Aslan, Droyne, Hive, K'kree, Solomani, Vargr, Vilani, and Zhodani. Various racially based hypotheses have emerged, but none has gained ascendancy.

Soegz: Admiral Soegz was a loyal supporter of Arbellatra in the final years of the Civil War, and he was elevated to archduke of Antares by her decree, which incidentally and simultaneously ordered the execution of the previous archduke for the treason of not supporting her.

Soegz, a Vargr and a subordinate admiral under Arbellatra, commanded a task force during the fleet actions of the Second Frontier War and late in the Civil War.

Solomani: Strictly, a member of that human race which developed on Terra from the original human stock *(H. sapiens)*. The term Solomani is often used to refer to members of the Solomani race (or, more palatably to some, to members of the human race of Solomani descent) or to members of the Solomani political movement. Its original meaning is obscure, but the word seems to have originally meant either "men of Sol" or "sole men."

After the Solomani developed jump drives in -2431, Solomani humans scattered to the stars in several waves. Early colonization efforts first settled the worlds closest to Terra; the later conquest of the First Imperium and the establishment of the Rule of Man sent more Solomani humans out primarily to occupy the former Vilani controlled regions.

Solomani Autonomous Region: Area within the Imperium granted self-government through a charter from Empress Margaret I in 704. The charter granted control of the region of space within a radius of 50 parsecs of Terra (hence the name Solomani Sphere) to a Solomani governing body, which was given broad powers of authority.

For two hundred years, the Imperium effectively ignored the region and concentrated instead on its coreward frontiers.

By 940, Solomani oppression of nonhuman (and non-

Solomani) worlds forced Empress Margaret II to revoke the region's charter. After years of diplomatic actions proved fruitless, it was decided to forcibly reintegrate the region into the Imperium. Naturally, the Solomani resisted, and the Solomani Rim War (990 to 1002) began.

Solomani Confederation: In 871, the government of the Solomani Autonomous Region reorganized itself as the Solomani Confederation in an attempt to strengthen its claims to the heritage of the old Terran Confederation. Although tantamount to a declaration of independence, the reorganization was officially ignored by the government of the Imperium until the increasingly belligerent and extremist policies of the Solomani caused many border worlds under Solomani rule to petition the Imperium for redress.

The branches of the Solomani Confederation's government took the names of the government of the Terran Confederation, but the present institutions have little resemblance to those of the past. The chief governing body of the Solomani Confederation is the Secretariat. The Secretariat is presided over by the Secretary General, who is elected from its membership. The Secretary General is the chief administrative officer of the Solomani government, and while the office holds great power, it is fully accountable to the Secretariat.

Representatives to the Secretariat are appointed by the governments of the individual districts. The number of representatives each district may appoint is determined according to that district's contribution to the Solomani economy.

A district typically consists of a single world, but low population worlds or depressed areas are combined into multiworld districts. In the case of a district such as this, an election is held to determine the representative from that district. These, however, are not elections in the normal sense; the governments vote, rather than the populace. Each government of such a district is allocated votes (again, according to its economic importance), which are used to elect a representative for that district.

All government officeholders and officials must be members of the official party, the Solomani Movement. Although once waning in power and influence, the party is gaining in popularity as a result of successful Solomani incursions on the Imperium's rimward border. Still, the real power in the Confederation is held by the government and its factions.

Because of the greater degree of local autonomy that exists in the Solomani Confederation, interworld factionalism exists to a much greater degree than had been allowed in the Imperium. Coalitions of worlds exist outside the normal government channels which sometimes equal them in importance within a given region.

For example, the Near Bootes cluster, in the Capella subsector, dominates large portions of the adjacent subsectors both economically and politically. Bootean mercantile interests have traditionally favored peaceful trade with the Imperium, and their influence has been held to be largely responsible for many peace negotiations between the Imperium and the Solomani Confederation.

Another example of this factionalism is the ongoing trade war (in Solomani Rim/Kukulcan) between Kukulcan and the coalition of Thetis and Laputa. The war has been causing severe damage to the economy of Kukulcan, but the Thetis-Laputa coalition has thus far been able to muster enough power to prevent effective intervention by the Confederation government.

Solomani Hypothesis: When the Solomani discovered jump drive in -2431, they also discovered that more than a dozen human races had already colonized the worlds surrounding Earth. At the time, there was no satisfactory explanation for the more than 40 genetically identical human races.

The Solomani Hypothesis, first proposed by Magis Sergei haut-Devroe (64 to 141), theorized that all of the many widely scattered human races of the galaxy originated on Terra, and he thought that they were transported to their current homeworlds by an alien race (called the Ancients) for purposes which even today remain unclear. The approximate date of the scattering has been established as -300,000.

When Terra was incorporated in the Imperium in 588, a small historical mission verified much of haut-Devroe's work. The hypothesis was already generally accepted by the majority of the human population in the Imperium.

More than 40 known human races have been located (and several more of them failed to adapt to their new worlds and are now extinct); only three of these human races have reached widespread prominence: they are the Vilani, the Zhodani, and the Solomani.

Most other human races accept the hypothesis but lend it no special importance. The hypothesis is used by the Solomani Movement as a basis for its claims of Solomani racial superiority.

Solomani Movement: An organization devoted to the doctrine that humans of Solomani descent are superior to all others and are most fit to rule the galaxy.

Solomani Rim War (990 to 1002): War between the Third Imperium and the Solomani Confederation during which a large portion of the Solomani Rim sector was returned to Imperial control.

Hoping to profit from Imperial preoccupation with the Third Frontier War and the disorganization which followed upon the abdication of Styryx in 989, the Solomani reasserted their control over the complete Solomani Sphere, including those portions reabsorbed into the Imperium (see Solomani Autonomous Region). The Imperium declared war in 990.

The initial phase of the war went very well for the Solomani. Although the Imperium maintained sizable fleets along the border, they were inferior in strength to the massed naval elements of the Solomani Confederation. In most areas, the Solomani regained the border worlds lost to the Imperium in the last half century and even occupied a number of worlds that had never been part of the Solomani Sphere.

However, Solomani fortunes were checked in 993 when a large invasion force attempted to regain the worlds in the Old Expanses sector; it encountered near-fanatical resistance and was repulsed with heavy losses.

The period from 993 to 998 was one of stalemate. The Solomani abandoned their plans for further expansion in order to rebuild their forces. However, their policy of inflexibly defending every border world was a constant drain on their resources, and the Solomani were not able to regain the initiative. By 998, the Imperial Navy had achieved strategic dominance as the greater industrial base of the Imperium made its power felt.

The last phase of the war, 998 to 1002, consisted of a near-continual advance by Imperial forces into the heart of the Solomani Sphere. The basic Imperial strategy was to attack along two parallel axes of advance, with lesser task forces spreading out to create a huge pocket of Solomani Territory.

Although the Solomani occasionally achieved a tactical success against a task force (such as in the Battle of Kagukhasaggan in early 1002), they were unable to halt the main advances. With the liberation of the Vegan district in 1001, the Imperium gained the secure base envisioned in the reign of Styryx. The loss of the Vegan district prompted the Solomani to embark on a desperate gamble. Recalling the time when the outnumbered Terran Confederation was able to defeat the Vilani Imperium, the Solomani consolidated their remaining naval forces into a single fleet and struck at the Imperial fleet that was advancing out of the Vegan district.

At the Battle of Dingir, in early 1002, the Solomani Grand Fleet was scattered and substantially destroyed. The remnants of the Solomani fleet fell back deeper into the Sphere, and the Imperial forces firmly established themselves in Terra's own subsector.

The Imperial high command decided that Terra would have to be invaded in order to end forever all claims of Solomani superiority and thus the use of Terra as a rallying standard elsewhere in the Sphere. In order to invade Terra, a sizable fraction of the Imperial forces in the Solomani Sphere were assembled into an assault force, which effectively ended the pursuit of the defeated Solomani fleet. The invasion began in the second quarter of 1002, and the hard-fought campaign lasted until nearly the end of the year.

In the end, the Imperium conquered the planet. However, the battle for Terra had consumed so much of the Imperial military's resources that the Imperial high command felt they lacked sufficient strength to resume their advance into the rest of the Solomani Sphere. Accordingly, they negotiated a temporary armistice with the Solomani military commanders, who were glad to gain a respite to regroup their remaining forces. The war ended on this basis as both the Imperial and Solomani civilian governments, who were concerned with the strain placed on their economies by the protracted war, informally agreed to extend the armistice indefinitely.

Although scholars have debated the wisdom of invading Terra, some claim that the battle was a marginal if not a pyrrhic victory for the Imperium. The general consensus has been that the war as a whole was a victory for the Imperium. A substantial amount of the Solomani Sphere was reabsorbed by the Imperium, and a vigorous Vegan Autonomous District was set up to oversee Imperial interests along the new border.

However, much of this territory has been lost once again to the Solomani because of the turmoil following Strephon's assassination.

Solomani Security: Secret police force maintained in service to the Solomani Confederation for the purpose of maintaining state secrets, conducting espionage, and implementing political policies of the government.

Solomani Security maintains both a network of contacts which provide information from outside the Confederation and a network of informants which provide information within the Confederation. Solomani Security agents themselves are highly trained individuals capable of conducting espionage and sabotage.

Solomani Sphere: The territory governed by the Solomani as the Solomani Autonomous Region.

See Solomani Autonomous Region.

Sophont: A generalized term for an intelligent life form.

Sophontology: The study of intelligent life forms. Subsidiary branches of this science include: cultural sophontology, the comparative study of sophont societies; physical sophontology, the study of the genetic and physiological makeup of intelligent life; and developmental sophontology, the study of the various means by which life forms evolve intelligence.

Spinward Marches: The Imperium's farthest frontier sector, containing 437 star systems divided along a coreward/rimward line by the Imperial border. The region is dominated by two major powers: the Imperial Spinward Marches sector and the frontier provinces of the Zhodani Consulate. In the independent territory between the two powers lie four small territories: the Federation of Arden, the Sword Worlds Confederation, the Border Worlds (a splinter state cut from the Sword Worlds during the Fifth Frontier War), and the Darrian Confederation. Each follows its own diplomatic line designed to maintain independence from both the Zhodani and the Imperium.

The Spinward Marches has been settled since the 400s and is still a frontier sector. High-tech worlds are scattered among empty, fallow worlds; there is potential for exploration, exploitation, and development for centuries to come.

Starport: Establishment for the landing, servicing, refueling, and control of starships. Starports range in quality from A (the best and most extensive) to E (the worst, little more than a spot of cleared ground).

Starports generally have two components: a surface facility and an orbital facility. The surface facility includes cargo handling installations, a landing field, control towers, and other

necessary areas. Surface starport components are frequently called Down (as in Credo Down Starport on Regina). Orbital facilities are present (usually in stationary orbit above the surface component) to enable handling of unstreamlined ships and to allow construction of heavy craft in orbit. The orbital component is often called Orbital (as in Credo Orbital Starport).

Type D and E starports have no extensive orbital facilities, but they usually have navigational satellites or similar equipment. Nonstreamlined ships at these starports must be serviced by shuttles. Starports, being the primary point at which starships interact with a system, are usually the location for shipyards and additional bases, such as scout bases, naval bases or other military installations.

Strephon (1049-1116): Forty-third emperor of the Imperium; eldest son of Emperor Paulo III (981-1071). Born 1049. Coronation 1071. UPP 768ABF. Murdered by Dulinor in 1116.

Subsector: Mapping unit in astrography. Average density: 30 to 40 worlds per subsector.

Subsectors are noted within a sector by their position using the first sixteen letters of the alphabet (A-P). In addition, they are named and may be called by a variety of synonyms for subsector, including province, cluster, or district. Imperial convention is to assign numbers to districts (for example, District 268) which are under Imperial protection because they are pending integration into the Imperium.

Superheavy Elements: Although elements heavier than uranium are increasingly unstable and radioactive (with half-lives measured in fractions of a second), quantum theory predicts an "island of stability," consisting of the elements with atomic numbers 114 to 122, which have half-lives measured in the millions of years. These superheavy elements, also called eka-metals or island metals, are generated in small amounts in supernova explosions. Only a few grams have ever been discovered in nature, which is just enough for scientists to determine that superheavies would be immensely valuable to industry if a source could be found.

Survey, First (published 420): The first comprehensive astrographic and demographic survey of the Imperium, which was performed by the Imperial Interstellar Scout Service. More than a hundred years in the making, its publication in 420 made available the Imperium's records on its component worlds for public use.

Survey, Second (published 1065): The second comprehensive survey of the Imperium, which was performed by the Scout Service, and which updated the long obsolete and incomplete data in the First Survey. The Second Survey was seventy years in compilation, went to greater lengths than the first survey, and included more world data as well as more complete astrographic data. In addition, the expansion of the Imperium since 420 had added many new worlds that had to be included.

Sword Worlds Confederation: A loose confederation of worlds in the Spinward Marches, spinward of Imperial space and coreward of the Darrians. The first settlement in the region was on Gram in -399.

By circa -200 the settlement of the area was largely complete, and the first interstellar government in the region, the Sacnoth Dominate, was formed in -186. Consisting of the twenty worlds settled up to that point, the Dominate lasted until -102, when it was fractured by rebellion into several smaller states.

During the ensuing centuries, various Sword World governments rose and fell; they sometimes coalesced all the worlds under a single world's domination and sometimes splintered into several small states. Contact with Imperial traders in 73 brought increased trade and had a stabilizing influence on the region, but this stability was short-lived.

The First Frontier War brought a desire for cooperation among the various squabbling worlds, and the end of the war saw the formation of the first unified confederation in centuries, which was centered on Sacnoth and which was referred to as the Second Dominate. As a result of the Outworld Coalition's victory, the Sword Worlds annexed Terant 340, Torment, Trifuge, and Cunnonic, which are all in the Darrian subsector.

The Second Dominate held power until 698, when it was overthrown by a coalition headed by Gram. The Gram Coalition ruled until 788, when a short war with the Darrian Confederation resulted in the loss of the four worlds gained during the First Frontier War.

Public outrage at the mishandling of the war caused the subsequent fall of the Gram government. The replacement for the Gram Coalition was the Trilateral Alliance, a decentralized organization headed by Narsil, Sacnoth, and Durendal. The Alliance broke up in 848 due in large part to the inherent weakness of its organization, and an interregnum of essentially independent worlds lasted until Gram reasserted its influence (helped substantially by Zhodani money and advisors, rumor has it) in 852. This government has remained in control down to the present.

The government allows almost complete local autonomy. Individual worlds maintain separate military forces, pass their own laws, and completely regulate their own internal affairs. The Confederation government regulates interworld trade, handles diplomatic relations with outside powers, and adjudicates interworld disputes.

In peacetime, the Confederation government maintains a pool of high-ranking military officers (selected from the military forces of all worlds) who are trained in large unit command and staff operations.

During time of war, all military forces are confederalized and placed under a single unified command. For ground forces, divisions will be commanded by generals from the individual worlds, corps, and higher organizations by Confederation officers. The component forces of a division will be from the same world whenever possible. For naval forces, individual ships are under the command of local officers, squadrons, or higher organizations under Confederation officers.

Sylean Federation (-650 to 0): Large interstellar federation which served as the basis for the Third Imperium.

Established on Sylea in -650, the Federation grew slowly, absorbing several surrounding worlds and increasing trade and interaction between worlds.

By -30, the real power in the Federation was an industrial consortium headed by Cleon Zhunastu. Cleon, a Solomani noble of great vision, used his family industrial base and the support of other families (obtained by the persuasiveness of his personality) to obtain behind-the-scenes control of the Federation government and to begin an active campaign to increase the number of worlds under its control.

After 30 years of economic and diplomatic maneuvering (and

occasional military action), Cleon had increased the size of the Federation and extended its control to the edge of what is now Core sector. Cleon envisioned a territory larger than a single sector, however, and concluded that the tightly controlled, highly centralized nature of the government of the Sylean Federation was not suitable for a large, starspanning empire.

Cleon decided the Federation had served its purpose, and he began plans for a more suitable form of interstellar government, which would allow greater local autonomy but maintain cohesion over large distances. In addition, to restore the past glories of the Rule of Man (and therefore lay claim to all former territories of the First and Second Imperiums), Cleon proposed to revive the Imperium.

This was made possible by the fact that in the closing years of the period known as Twilight, one of the last claimants to the throne of the Rule of Man had made Sylea his capital. Cleon traced the legitimacy of the Sylean Federation backwards through this emperor to the Rule of Man and (since the Rule of Man claimed to be the lawful successor to the Vilani Imperium) to the First Imperium as well.

In the 651st year of the Sylean Federation, the Grand Senate of the Federation "persuaded" Cleon to accept the Imperial crown. That year he was crowned First Emperor of the Third Imperium, and he proclaimed the 651st year of the Sylean Federation to be the Year Zero of the Third Imperium.

System: A star and its family of planets and satellites. The term *system* denotes a major world and its associated star, plus any other planets, satellites, asteroids, and other bodies.

System Defense Boat: A nonstarship specifically intended for defensive operations inside a star system. It was developed on the principle that a nonstarship (because of the increased armament made possible by its lack of jump drives) can normally defeat a starship of equal tonnage. SDBs are typically stationed at the vital points of a system (the gas giants, the asteroid belt, the major world, and so on), and they attack invading vessels according to one or more predetermined plans.

System defense boats range in size from 100 to 5000 tons and are constructed at all tech levels from eight to 15. There are hundreds of different types, which depend upon the specific mission for which they are designed.

T

Terra (Solomani Rim/Sol 1827 A867A69-F): Earth. Origin world of the genetic stock from which all races of Humaniti descended, former capital of the Terran Confederation, former capital of the Old Earth Union, and former capital of the Solomani Autonomous Region. The word *Terran* (used in the past to refer to an inhabitant of this world or to a citizen of the Terran Confederation) is derived from the name of this world.

Terran Confederation (-2398 to -2204): Interstellar government consisting of Terra and its colony worlds. The Terran Confederation has its roots in the formation of the United Nations Space Coordination Agency (UNSCA) in -2499. In addition to handling mundane responsibilities that helped avoid conflict, UNSCA soon became a clearing house for space operations.

One of UNSCA's natural directions was research. In 2087, UNSCA researchers in the system's asteroid belt who were looking for better drives to transport ores discovered jump drive. The first jump drives were used only in the solar system—they were too weak to be used for interstellar travel. In 2096, for various reasons, the first interstellar jump expedition travelled to Barnard's Star rather than Alpha Centauri.

Upon their return in 2097, the expedition members were hurried into a hushed meeting with UNSCA. The expedition had encountered alien intelligent life—humans no less! The expedition members had encountered a Vilani prospecting outpost, an outpost on the very fringe of a vast, advanced empire controlled by alien humans. It came as quite a shock to the Terrans that many of the worlds only a few parsecs away were already claimed. Politicians echoed the popular sentiment that it was unfair for alien humans from several hundred light-years away to claim worlds near Terra. Individual nations began expanding their armed forces and building starships.

Over the course of the next three decades, UNSCA and the United Nations transformed itself into a true world government, which administered the defense of Terra against the Vilani Empire. Terran colonies formed on other worlds were granted membership into the United Nations. In -2400, the UN officially changed its name to the United Worlds. Two years later, the name was changed again to the Terran Confederation. Modern historians, for simplicity, use this term exclusively.

The Terran Confederation fought a series of interstellar wars with the Vilani Imperium over the period -2408 to -2219. These wars ultimately resulted in the fall of the Vilani Grand Imperium. The Confederation was dissolved in -2204 upon the proclamation of the Rule of Man to replace the Vilani Imperium.

See also Rule of Man, Nth Interstellar War, and Solomani.

Third Frontier War (979 to 986): The long period of uneasy peace between the Imperium and the Zhodani Consulate erupted into war in 979 with simultaneous blows by the Zhodani in the Querion and Jewell subsectors. Imperial reaction was deficient, and the hostilities continued for nearly six years with little to show for it. The armistice finally signed in 986 gave each side little, and it brought about the abdication of Emperor

Terran Confederation Symbol

Styryx in 989.

Third Imperium (0 to present): Also called The Imperium. Founded in 0 by Cleon Zhunastu from the Sylean Federation in what is now Core sector. The Imperium grew swiftly during the pacification campaigns and more slowly thereafter until stability was reached in the 600's, by which time the Imperium had absorbed much of the territory of the First and Second Imperiums.

Government Structure: The Imperium can be best thought of as a form of feudal confederation. Member worlds of the Imperium agree to pay taxes and obey a few fundamental laws which the Imperium promulgates, known as the High Laws. In return, the Imperium agrees to patrol the space between the worlds, to protect interstellar trade, to encourage travel and commerce, and to arbitrate diplomatic relations between worlds. Beyond this, individual worlds are left to their own devices so long as they acknowledge the power of the Imperium to rule the space between the stars.

Imperial power is present on member worlds in the form of consulates, bureaucratic offices, and bases. Sometimes, larger enclaves of Imperial power are placed where they can enhance the emperor's strength.

The Imperium's territory is divided into sectors, which are in turn divided into subsectors and systems. Groups of sectors, called domains, have been created above the sector level.

During the Pacification Campaigns, Emperor Artemsus divided space into six regions, labeled them domains, and appointed an archduke over each of them. To each archduke, he assigned the continuing pacification of the domain's many systems and their integration into the Imperium. The domains were: Sylea (Core, Fornast, Massilia, Delphi), Vland (Corridor, Vland, Gushemege, Dagudashag), Gateway (Ley, Glimmerdrift Reaches, Gateway, Crucis Margin), Ilelish (Ilelish, Zarushagar, Reaver's Deep, Daibei), Antares (Lishun, Antares, Mendan, Amdukan), and Sol (Dispora, Old Expanses, Solomani Rim, Alpha Crucis). Most of the domains were never totally absorbed into the Imperium.

In 589, during the First Frontier War, a seventh domain was established: Deneb (Spinward Marches, Deneb, Trojan Reach, Reft). The intent was to appoint an archduke to be responsible for their supervision. However, the Civil War broke out before an archduke was appointed.

Following the civil war, the emperors expressed concern about individuals with powers equaling their own, so they moved to lessen the power of the archdukes in the Imperial government. Because of this, no archduke of Deneb was never appointed. As a result, the domains came to have little practical significance. Each archduke did retain the power to create knights and baronets.

In the years after the Fourth Frontier War, and after the problems it presented from lags in communication, Emperor Strephon felt a strengthened archduke position could enable the Imperium to more quickly respond in defending the realm. Against the protests and opposition of some prominent members of the Moot, Strephon reestablished the domain as a level in the bureaucracy of the Imperial Navy and returned to the Domain the ability to collect taxes. Still later, Strephon gave the archdukes the ability to legislate and enforce the desires of the emperor on the local level. One of Strephon's last acts before his murder was to finally appoint an archduke of the Domain of Deneb: Archduke Norris.

The Divided Imperium: With the assassination of emperor Strephon and all immediate heirs to the throne in 1116, the resulting turmoil has caused some confusion as to who will succeed Strephon to the throne. Thus, at the moment, factionalism in the Third Imperium is at an all-time high.

Even with the uncertainty of the current moment, the Third Imperium still stands. The archdukes are instituting local stopgap measures until such time as a strong central government can be reestablished.

See also Sylean Federation.

Thoengling Empire: Large, centralized state in the Vargr Extents. The thoengling Empire is one of the most stable of the Vargr states and has existed in its current form since 792. The Emperor, who has great governmental authority, is chosen for life by vote of an elected assembly; by law, no member of his family may succeed him. Sons and daughters of the higher nobility are brought up at the Imperial court, where every effort is made to inculcate personal loyalty to the Emperor.

The Thoengling Empire has become a major trading partner of the Imperium and generally supports Imperial interests in the Vargr Extents.

Trade Routes: Routes which jump-capable starships travel between major worlds and which connect vital suppliers with essential markets, important government worlds with high population worlds, and strategic resources with exploiting industry. Trade routes are a natural outgrowth of economic and market pressures. When a market is no longer profitable, the trade routes bypass it.

The trade routes are typically the territory of the Imperium's largest trading companies. They maintain fleets of commercial transports and merchants who serve these tradeworlds, and they reap large profits in doing so.

But the trade routes directly serve fewer than a tenth of the worlds of the Imperium. The other 90 percent of the Imperium's worlds are served by feeder lines, tramp freighters, and free traders. These smaller companies and unscheduled ships carry passengers and cargo between worlds off the main trade routes.

Travel Zone: Standard form of classification for worlds in terms of relative danger. As a service to spacefarers, the Traveller's Aid Society publishes travel zone classifications which indicate the degree of danger a world presents to visitors. Standard classifications are green (no danger), amber (caution advised), and red (severe danger).

See also Amber Zone, Red Zone.

Trojan Points: In a gravitational system composed of a small body orbiting a much larger one (such as a planet and star or a moon and planet), there are two stable points lying in the small body's orbit 60 degrees ahead and behind it, and thus equidistant from the small and large bodies. These are called Trojan points (also LaGrangian points, which are abbreviated as L4 and L5).

The Trojan points of a gas giant near an asteroid belt commonly collect a cluster of asteroids. The name comes from the first such cluster discovered by Terrans at Jupiter in the Sol system; the asteroids were named after mythical heros of the Trojan War.

Twilight (-1776 to -1526): The failure of the Rule of Man triggered the collapse of most interstellar civilization. While interstellar travel and commerce continued, it was at a greatly reduced rate, and the many worlds of the Imperium turned in on themselves. The period of collapse is termed Twilight, and it lasted for two and a half centuries.

Modern historians consider Twilight to have begun in -1776 when the treasury on Hub/Ershur refused to acknowledge a monetary issue of the branch treasury at Antares, which triggered a financial collapse and the destruction of large-scale trade within the Imperium.

The end of Twilight is commonly accepted as the year -1526, when the last governmental body claiming to be the Rule of Man ceased to exist.

Twilight's Peak: Legendary or apocryphal story of lost starfarers on an unknown world who discovered fantastic structures and devices while surviving a terrifying winter. Phrased as an epic poem of execrable quality, the story is most notable only in that it is based on this fact: a task force was lost in the time period specified, and it has not been recovered or accounted for.

Two Thousand Worlds: Most common name in the Imperium for the region of space ruled by the K'kree. "Two thousand worlds" is a literal translation of the K'kree T't'tkahk Xeng Kirr. The same words can also be rendered idiomatically as "universe." In times past, the words meant "night sky," for roughly two thousand stars can be seen from one hemisphere of Kirur, the K'kree homeworld. The name should not be taken to mean that there are exactly 2000 worlds in the K'kree empire.

The K'kree government is highly conservative. The current dynasty ruling the Two Thousand Worlds has been in power since prehistoric times, and the form of the government has remained unchanged except for a few minor modifications made necessary by the problems inherent in governing an interstellar empire.

K'kree expansion into space progressed very slowly after the discovery of the jump drive in -4142. The conservative nature of society and the technical limitations placed upon spaceflight by that society (K'Kree spaceships must be very large, for example) combined to inhibit early exploration and colonization.

The discovery of other sophonts caused a xenophobic reaction in K'kree society. The realization that intelligent carnivores might exist somewhere in space sparked the K'kree obsession to convert the universe to herbivorism. This obsession stimulated the growth of the Two Thousand Worlds to its present size and still dominates K'kree culture. Local cultures are tolerated and other aspects of K'kree society are not heavily enforced, but all races within the Two Thousand Worlds are herbivorous.

K'kree contact with the Hive Federation was soon followed by the Hiver-K'kree war of -2029 to -2013. The military technology of the K'kree proved superior in the first stages of the war. The war ended due to nonmilitary considerations, however, when the Hive Federation demonstrated a plan to radically alter the K'kree social order through the use of psychohistorical techniques and threatened to implement it. The K'kree withdrew to the antebellum borders, and the border between the two states has remained stable to this day.

The K'Kree Empire eventually stopped in its expansion. Increasing problems of administration over interstellar distances and contact with other starfaring races (such as Hivers and humaniti) have stabilized the Two Thousand Worlds at its present size.

V

Vargr: Intelligent major race derived from Ancient genetic manipulations of Terran carnivore/chaser stock, which apparently dates from approximately the same time that humaniti was scattered to the stars.

Inhabiting a region rimward of the Imperium, the Vargr were a puzzle to xenologists. The biochemistry and genetic makeup are almost identical with a number of terrestrial animals, but they differ radically from most of the flora and fauna indigenous to Lair, which is the purported Vargr home world.

Researches during the early years of the Third Imperium concluded them to be the result of genetic manipulation of transplanted Terran animals of the family *Canidae*, which is almost certainly of genus *Canis*. The obvious conclusion, supported by archeological evidence, is that the race known as the Ancients was responsible.

The typical Vargr is about 1.6 meters in height and weighs approximately 60 kilograms. They are upright, bipedal carnivores, with rear limbs digitigrade and hands very similar in size and appearance to those of a human, although there are significant internal differences. They have approximately the same physical parameters as humans and are able to use the same equipment without modification or additional instruction.

On the average their reactions are slightly faster than those of the typical human, but individuals vary widely. The Vargr senses of smell and sight are superior to those of humans.

Government: There is no central Vargr government; indeed, there is no governmental type that can be said to be "typically Vargr." Every conceivable form of governmental organization

can be found somewhere in the Vargr Extents. The only cohesive force in the Extents is a fierce racial pride which causes a slight tendency towards racial cooperation.

The higher the level of the Vargr government, the more unstable it becomes because of the difficulty of obtaining consent of all Vargr involved.

Vargr in the Imperium: While only a few planets populated completely by Vargr exist within the Imperium, there are millions of Vargr citizens of loyal subject planets. Additionally, Vargr adventurers, criminals, mercenaries and traders can be found throughout the coreward reaches of the Imperium.

Society: The key elements shaping Vargr societies are a very strong centrifugal force resulting from an emphasis on consensus and informal lines of authority, and an equally strong centripetal force resulting from a deeply ingrained family-clantribe-nation loyalty.

Centralized authority is extremely limited at the upper levels of Vargr society, and action is based on broad coalitional concerns, with a constant splitting and rejoining of dissident factions. Traditionally, this has made it very difficult for more centralized and organized societies such as the Imperium to deal on a meaningful basis with what passes for Vargr states.

The Vargr have little respect for formal authority, and what respect they might have decreases as that authority becomes more remote. Vargr tend to respect informal authority figures more, and they obey superiors who are better known to them.

The Vargr have an intensive racial pride, and they are easily insulted. They are prone to enter into fights without regard to possible consequences. Vargr social organization is difficult to characterize in Terran terms, but it can be most closely compared to the Dakota Sioux of North America in the 1800s AD, if the analogy is not pressed too far.

Even among the most stable Vargr governments, a highly charismatic leader can attract followers for almost anything. The neighbors of the Vargr are constantly the subject of impromptu raids and scattered piracy by bands of Vargr (totally without government sanction, of course) who have been talked into a raid, a battle, or a war by a charismatic leader.

Vargr Campaigns (220 to 348): The series of wars, encounters, conflicts, and disputes between the Imperium and the various Vargr states in Vland, Corridor, and Deneb sectors along the coreward edge of the Imperium.

As the Imperium expanded, it initially recruited worlds which were former members of the Second and First Imperium. As its borders reached still farther, the Imperial expansion met already established Vargr states of varying sizes. The Imperium struggled for over a century to secure its territory against the Vargr; the inevitable series of conflicts which resulted are collectively called the Vargr campaigns.

Vargr Extents: The territory dominated by Vargr governments. The term Vargr Extents refers to those sectors with major Vargr populations. Extents are situated roughly coreward of the Imperium and especially coreward of the Spinward Marches, Deneb, Corridor, and Vland sectors.

Vegan: An intelligent race originating on Muan Gwi (Solomani Rim/Vega 1717 A456A86-F) and inhabiting the Vegan Autonomous District; they are named by humans after the bright star near their homeworld.

General: Vegans are upright, bipedal, and bilaterally symmetrical, and they average 2.2 meters in height. They are bisexual, homeothermic oxygen breathers with an average lifespan of over 200 years. Because of their low-gravity origin, they are physically quite weak and are unable to live on high gravity worlds.

The head serves both as braincase and as sensory appendage. Auditory organs are located in the collar-like structure around the neck. Despite external appearances to the contrary, Vegans have two eyes located inside the hood-like fleshy structure which dominates the head.

The paired eyes are covered by a transparent eyelid-like structure, which acts as a polarized light filter. This structure protects the eyes from glare, like built-in sunglasses, and also serves to keep windblown dust out of the eyes. This filter can be retracted when not needed. The eyes themselves are large and pick up radiation well into the infrared portion of the spectrum, an adaptation to Muan Gwi's small red sun. Since the skull is fixed solidly in place, a Vegan cannot turn its head, but the fleshy hood containing the eyes can turn through a large arc.

The mouth is a vertical slit in the upper thoracic region with paired breathing/vocal slits on either side of it. Two mandibles are located inside the upper chest, and they grind food between their opposing sets of teeth.

Where the forearm and hand would be on a human, Vegans have three tentacles, which serve them as manipulative organs. Their legs end in broad, splayed feet, which prevent them from sinking into the soft sand.

The urogenital opening is a vertical slit located ventrally in the lower abdomen. There are no external differences between sexes.

Vegans have a number of adaptations to the arid dry region of Muan Gwi where they developed. Their tall, thin bodies are designed for maximum radiation of heat. The torso is covered with a thick integument, whose convoluted surface is richly supplied with blood vessels.

By increasing or decreasing the supply of blood to the integument, heat radiation from the torso can be regulated to optimum effect (more during the day, less at night). This arrangement obviates the necessity for sweating and its consequent water loss. All orifices of the body can be sealed to prevent unnecessary moisture loss.

History: The Vegans received the jump drive about -6000 from Vilani-influenced traders, and they colonized several nearby worlds before being absorbed by the First Imperium in -4404. They were severely restricted under Vilani rule, as were all races who resisted being integrated into the rigid Vilani culture. Because of this, they welcomed Terran victory in the Interstellar Wars and the advent of the Rule of Man.

The Vegan Polity prospered under the Rule of Man and survived the Long Night largely intact. However, with the advent of the Third Imperium, the Vegan area was broken into individual planetary states in accord with Imperial policy; nonhumans were treated as full citizens but, in order to cement Imperial authority, no multiworld governmental units were allowed.

Under the Solomani, the Vegans were again restricted. Human colonies were founded on many Vegan worlds to maintain Solomani influence there, and Solomani governors were installed on all Vegan worlds. After the Solomani Rim War, the present Vegan Autonomous District was formed as a counterweight to the Solomani.

Society: Vegan society is divided into hundreds of different tuhuir, which might be roughly translated as culture, philosophy, or tao. Each tuhuir has its own customs and traditions and its own interpretation of the proper way to live. The civil service which governs the Vegan District is a tuhuir which oversees and mediates among all the other tuhuir. Although rare, heretical and rebellious tuhuir do exist.

Archeology shows that the tuhuir were once separate societies and each were associated with a particular geographic location, like countries on ancient Earth. Now, however, they are mixed together in complex patterns.

Tuhuir are not hereditary; when a Vegan nears sexual maturity, he or she enters a period of search, which may last for many years. Eventually, the individual chooses a tuhuir; once made, the choice is for life. In practice, about 50 percent of all Vegans enter the tuhuir of their parents (the exact percentage varies with each tuhuir); about 0.5 percent find that they enjoy the search as a way of life and never join a tuhuir.

Vegan Autonomous District: After the pyrrhic victory over the Solomani at Terra in 1002, the Imperium found that it could not completely conquer and absorb the rest of the Solomani Sphere. The Imperial high command decided to create the Vegan Autonomous District to act as a counterweight to the remnants of the Solomani Confederation. The Vegans have complete internal control over their district, but free passage is guaranteed for Imperial citizens and goods.

Although many factors have contributed to the present peace and stability along the Solomani Rim, it cannot be denied that the creation of the Vegan Autonomous District has achieved its original purpose.

The worlds of the Vegan Autonomous District are under a single, centralized government. State power is contained in a civil service and is chosen and promoted by competitive examinations.

Vilani: Human major race (*H. sapiens*) which developed on Vland from human stock placed there by the Ancients.

History: The world of Vland, while possessed of a hospitable environment, boasted an alien ecology based on its own independently evolved biology, a biology that produced proteins, sugars, and amino acids that were difficult for humans to digest and metabolize. The humans just could not use local plant and animal life for food.

One of the oldest occupations in Vilani society is that of shugilii (which translates roughly as miller). The shugilii was a person who could transform raw food into edible food through special aging and chemical treatment. The shugilii task was more akin to shaman or witch doctor than of that cook. Since virtually no food on Vland was edible without some treatment, shugiliis were powerful members of society.

The alienness of Vland was reciprocal: humans were unsuitable as food for predators, parasites died because humans provided no nutrition, bacteria could not infect the human system, and even viruses were unable to invade and take over human cells. Consequently, the primitive human society found no need for medically oriented shaman. Vilani medical understanding was very slow to develop because of this.

Vilani legends are full of accounts of the wars of the gods, terrible destruction, and occasional intervention in human affairs by the gods. Legends exist of early explorers who found lands with great living stone-metal gods possessed of immense magical powers. Modern archeologists now believe these "gods" were actually great robot warriors and juggernauts used by the Ancients in the final war. Apparently, the last of these machines finally ran down around -20,000.

Society: Early Vilani society was dominated by three groups: the shugiliis, the aristocrats, and the merchants. Aristocrats were the natural leaders of society, the shugiliis were the all important food processors, and the merchants controlled trade.

With the flowering of Vilani society (circa -11,000) and its attendant industrial revolution, each of these three forces gained power rather than lost it; each participated in the creation of the industrialized wealth of Vland.

In -9235 the Vilani made their ultimate breakthrough—one that would assure their ascendance for the next 6000 years. A research team working on the fringes of the Vland system created the first working prototype jump drive and demonstrated its effects.

The Vilani found intelligent lifeforms on other worlds within 60 parsecs of Vland. None of the races had progressed enough to have begun interstellar travel. The Vilani found it easy to dominate these less technically advanced races. The Vilani were able to impose Vilani culture and law on these other races among the stars. However, the Vilani conquerings were not militaristic in nature, but rather were economic subjection.

As their sphere of influence was expanding, the Vilani found it difficult to maintain control across such great distances with jump-1 as their maximum rate of travel and communication. At the same time, each of the three power classes of Vilani society found itself threatened by the forces around it.

Three bureaux were established, each independent of the other two, and each assigned a territory among the stars for

which it was responsible. Each of the three bureaux was effectively identical, but they initially espoused different philosophies, which were based on their origins. The bureaux maintained their own governments within their territories.

Sharurshid, originating with the merchant class, emphasized interstellar trade. Makhidkarun, originating with the aristocracy, emphasized interstellar government. Naasirka, originating with the shugiliis, floundered after it found that it could not control food supplies on most of the worlds it dealt with, but it ultimately became a broad-line organization which emphasized energy, transport, and luxury goods.

In -5430, the Vilani finally discovered jump-2. No other race had jump-2, and the Vilani maintained a sole monopoly on jump-2 by jealously guarding its secrets from all subject races. Beginning in -5400, a series of wars to subjugate the resisting fringe cultures was waged. This period of consolidation wars lasted until -4045.

Grand Empire of Stars: In -4045, the ruling Vilani council, the Igsiirdi, declared the Grand Empire of the Stars, or in the Vilani tongue, the Ziru Sirka. The Vilani calendar starts from this date.

At first, the Empire had no emperor. Within 10 years, the chairman of the Igsiirdi (elected for life by the council) was the Ishimkarun—the Shadow Emperor—ruled through published proclamations, but never appeared in public. In -3610, the Shadow Emperor became the Emperor of the Stars, who was the absolute monarch of the Empire. Successors were elected from the Igsiirdi upon the death of the old emperor.

For nearly 1,200 years the Grand Empire of the Stars kept the peace among its star-spanning population. However, the empire insisted on cultural rigidity. Exploration was stopped by -4000. Scientific research was controlled and then stopped altogether by -3800.

The beginning of the end of Vilani domination, however, was signalled by the contact with the Terrans in -2422. By -2408 the Terrans and the Vilani were at war; by -2219 the Terrans had surpassed the Vilani technologically and were marching through the cities of Vland as conquerors, and the Grand Empire of the Stars was at an end.

Currently, Vilani is a cultural rather than a racial or national labeling, and it is applied to those within the Imperium who retain some of the old ways. Dialects of the old High Vilani language survive in certain places, along with a few fragments of Vilani culture, such as musical forms and other fine arts. Certain of the old Vilani noble families have maintained more of the old culture, particularly the families who control the Vilani megacorporations.

Vilani Calendar: The Vilani calendar is based on the period of Vland (the Vilani homeworld) around Urakkalan, its star. The Vilani Gurkala (year) is 478.72 standard days in length.

See also Vland, First Imperium.

Vland (Vland/Vland 1717 A967A9A-F): Homeworld of the Vilani, former capital of the Vilani Imperium, current capital of the Vland sector, and current capital of the so-called Restored Vilani Empire or Ziru Sirka. Vland has been a major trade and cultural center for the core/spinward regions of the Imperium.

W

War: Major violent conflict between nations, megacorporations, or races.

See Good War/Bad War, Imperial Rules of War.

Way Station: Link in the express boat network. The way station is a large (for the Scout Service) base devoted to the overhaul and refit of express boats at points in their journeys. During a normal tour of duty, an express boat will jump from system to system, and occasionally change pilots, but steadily work its way farther and farther down the line.

At each stop (Xboat station), the Xboat is routinely checked, refuelled, reprovisioned, and sometimes recrewed. Ultimately, however, the Xboat must undergo maintenance and possible repair after the rigors of its mission. The way station performs this function.

Way stations have stocks of scout-oriented repair and maintenance equipment, as well as trained staffs of service personnel. They are the equivalent of naval bases, although they are capable of servicing only smaller tonnage ships (10,000 tons and less) due to the size and orientation of their facilities.

X

Xboat: See Express Boat.

Xboat Station: Facility for handling Xboats at a star system. At each system served by the Xboat network, an express boat station is maintained to handle the message traffic and to manage incoming and outgoing Xboats.

Usually located near the edge of a star system, the station picks up messages beamed to it by incoming Xboats and relays the data to the local world for delivery. Messages destined for worlds farther down the line are transmitted to a waiting Xboat which then jumps for the next world in the network.

The Xboat station contains receiving and retransmission equipment; refueling and support facilities for the local staff and waiting crew are also provided. The Xboat station maintains a local office on the system's major world for the acceptance of Xboat messages, as well as to handle delivery of the messages to addresses on the world.

Y

Year Zero: The base year of the Imperial calendar and the founding year of the Third Imperium. By selecting a base year numbered zero (instead of the generally selected year 1), the Imperial dating system became a standard number line extending forwards and backwards in time.

Years before the founding of the Imperium become simple negative numbers, and the differences between dates before and after the founding of the Imperium could be determined by subtraction.

Z

Zhdant (Zhdant 2719 A6547C8-F): Capital of the Zhodani Consulate homeworld of the Zhodani people. Unlike the capitals of other empires, Zhdant is largely divided into the estates of the members of the ruling Zhodani council, which makes the world's population unusually low. Zhdant is often spelled "Zhodane" in Anglic texts.

Zhodani: Human major race *(H. sapiens)* inhabiting the Zhodani Consulate, a region far spinward of the Imperium.

The Zhodani are a branch of humaniti similar in most respects to other human races. In general, they tend to be taller than Solomani or Vilani and lithe of build. Their most important difference is the acceptance and use of psionics.

Society: Zhodani society is divided into three classes: nobles, intendants, and proles. Nobles are the enfranchised ruling class, and they receive psionic training from childhood. Intendants are managers and administrators of society, and they also receive early psionic training. Proles constitute the masses, they are forbidden the use of psionics and do not receive training.

Within this rigid class system, there are two opportunities for promotion to a higher class. All prole children are tested for psionic potential, and those showing high scores are taken from their families and adopted into the intendant class. Intendants are rewarded for great diligence, service to the state, or victory in the psionic games through the granting of noble titles.

The presence of psionics in the hands of those in power means that many aspects of society work at high efficiency. Psychology, behavioral science, communications science, and education are more refined and exact than in other societies. Educational methods are finely tuned and capable of teaching concepts rapidly and accurately. Mental deviance or criminal tendencies can be detected early and corrected with facility.

Zhodani society is generally a happy one. Individuals are members of a functioning whole, and each makes a contribution to its success. The relative lack of upward mobility for the proles is offset by the possibility for their children to move upwards if they have the proper potential. The burden of responsibility imposed on the intendants is lightened by the ever-present possibility of reward through elevation to the noble classes. The nobles themselves temper their burden of authority with comfort derived from their station in life.

Morality: The Zhodani have a general distaste for other human races which do not practice psionics. Effective indoctrination and the ever-present possibility that one's mind is being read have removed dishonesty and deviance as common features of society. The Tavrchedl' (Thought Police) are a special branch of the government who are charged with maintaining right thought in the population.

Imperial citizens have a strong distaste for the Zhodani. Because the Zhodani practice psionics, an Imperial cannot be sure that a Zhodani is not invading his mental privacy at any time. Imperials feel exposed and uncomfortable when they are knowingly in the presence of Zhodani.

Because of their psionic abilities, the Zhodani have the most effective authoritarian rule in history. Imperial citizens, who are used to a great degree of local autonomy, fear Zhodani conquest because of the loss of freedom it would entail.

Government: The Zhodani consulate is a participatory democracy in which only nobles are allowed to vote. Executive and judicial functions are the responsibility of a series of councils of varying sizes. Each council elects one of its number as executive officer and a number of its members as delegates to the next higher council.

A city, for example, will elect several of its council members to be representatives to the world council. The process continues upward through several layers of councils to the overall Grand Council of the Zhodani. Nominally, each member of a council serves for one olympiad (three Zhodani years), but in practice, each councilor serves until his replacement arrives and replaces him officially, or until word of his reelection to another term is received. Oftentimes, the district from which a councilor is elected will have only his relatives as voters, and his reelection is virtually assured.

Standard practice (when possible) calls for Zhodani councils to submit important questions to a plebiscite of those affected. The principle can be suspended where immediate action is required, but the official ordering the action stands responsible to the voters and must justify his actions as soon as possible.

Supreme executive power is vested in three consuls; one is elected each year for a term of one olympiad by and from the members of the Grand Council. No consul may be elected twice in succession, and retired consuls become life members of the Grand Council.

History: The Zhodani date their empire from the traditional date of the first organized use of psionics on Zhodane, -6731 Imperial, the year of the first olympiad. They achieved jump drive about 1300 years later, in -5415 Imperial.

The expansion of the Zhodani was gradual and uneventful. Although some states on the fringe resisted absorption into the Consulate, most were annexed peacefully. The Zhodani first came into conflict with the Third Imperium in the 500s, which started the First Frontier War in a dispute over present and future limits to settlement in the Spinward Marches area. Frontier wars over the next 600 years have failed to resolve the basic differences between the two empires.

Zhodani Calendar: The Zhodani calendar is based on the period of Zhdant (the Zhodani homeworld) around Pliebr, its star. The Zhodani Chten (year) is 275.19 standard days in length. Zhodani dating uses three Chten called the Thequzdij (olympiad). A Zhodani date is written as: Olympiad.Year; for example, 3173.1 is the first year of the 3,173rd olympiad.

See also Zhdant.

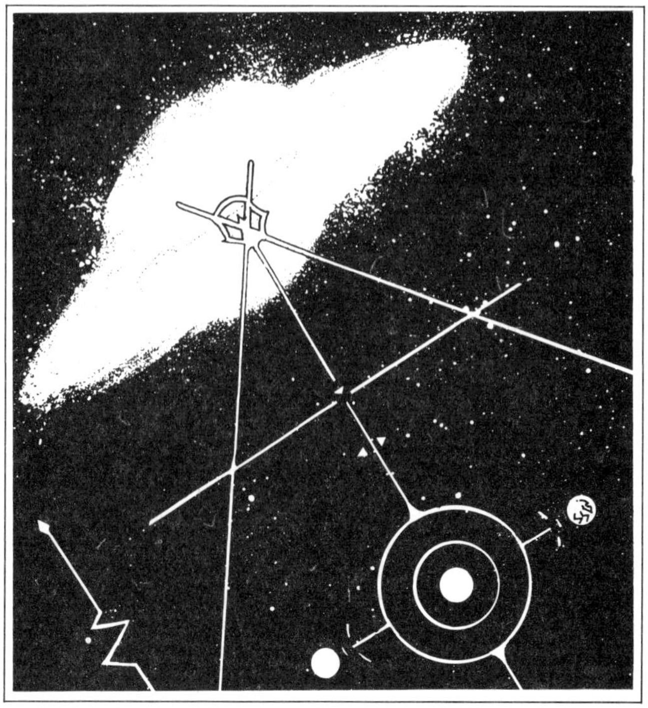

Library Data: Referee's Introduction

As explained in the general introduction to the Library Data, the material in this book was computer-generated from library data prepared by a team of pro-Imperial citizens working under the direction of Archduke Norris of the Spinward Marches. This means, of course, that the library data is necessarily biased or incomplete in certain ways, and characters who fail to realize this might be dealing themselves trouble.

The chief and strongest bias of the book is directed toward Archduke Norris, who approaches the wisdom and goodness of sainthood in the eyes of Eura Regnis and her team of researchers. Norris's role in recent events is mentioned with high praise in several entries in the library data, including his own entry, which is overly long even in its computer-summarized version.

Another of the most obvious biases in the book is its strong slant toward the reachievement of one united Imperium. The archduke supports this, and the library data entries are unabashed in their nostalgic remembrance of the "good old days" of the united Imperium and its in disdain for the day-to-day difficulties of life under the divided Imperium.

The library data also suffers from overgeneralization, as would any summarized report of such a wealth of information.

A

Ancients: What exactly is the secret of the Ancients? The Ancient "race" started with one individual specimen, a Droyne who found himself to have remarkable mental and psionic powers. This individual, who calls himself "Grandfather," is still alive today, hiding out in his own private "pocket universe."

Grandfather was an incredible specimen of an otherwise fairly ordinary intelligent race. His psionic powers enabled him to regenerate any damage, including that leading to normal aging, which rendered him virtually immortal. His mental prowess, on the other hand, fueled a burning curiosity for anything and everything that he could learn.

He started researching but realized that he needed competent assistants. He tried to fulfill this need in three different ways. The first method was that of procreation: Grandfather sired 20 children, each of whom had 20 children of their own who were all nearly as intelligent as Grandfather. With 420 offspring, Grandfather decided he had enough and stopped.

His second method was to experiment with other species of life. In his attempt to find good help, he carried humans from Terra to many other worlds in this part of the galaxy. He and his descendants also experimented with Terran canine stock, and genetically created intelligence in the race now known as the Vargr.

Last, Grandfather created a number of different models of superintelligent robots to assist him in his research. Only this last method proved successful, with living beings proving to be unreliable.

Grandfather assigned research projects to each of his children and grandchildren, and progress was rapid, with many new discoveries made by the teams of scientists on their various worlds. Grandfather, basking in the light of this success, decided to take a vacation, and travelled about Droyne space seeing all that there was to see.

When he finished with this vacation, he decided to explore the remaining frontiers of existence. He called all of his children to come and help him, but they had started on their own projects and were too busy to show up.

Grandfather started his work anyway, but he soon found that his children's experiments interfered with his own. His decision to have children long ago was an error, he realized, and now he must rectify it. He began a campaign to eliminate all of his offspring.

Naturally, the children found out about his campaign and resisted. The war of Grandfather against his children was a long and complicated one. Initially, his opponents did not understand that he meant to totally eliminate them; later, they adopted his tactics of total destruction.

The war went on for two thousand years. Staggering weapons were called into use, including planet-busters, nova-triggers, bombardment with asteroids, and such ordinary weapons as tailored plagues, poison gas, and thermonuclear devices.

By the end of the war, Grandfather had beaten all of the opposing factions and destroyed all of his children (he kept careful count). The galaxy was somewhat the worse for wear; it had many new asteroid belts and quite a few ravaged worlds.

Grandfather determined that he would in the future limit himself to more easily-controlled assistants. He improved on the robots he had built before and constructed a corps of robots and androids to help him in his experiments. Then, he pinched off a pocket universe around his base world and retreated from the larger universe to pursue his studies unhindered by the concerns of the larger universe.

Who in the Imperium today knows these facts? No one knows them all, but there are a few scattered sophontologists who have come to the conclusion that the Droyne are the modern-day descendants of the Ancients, and they are somehow not as intelligent as the earlier race. The fact that the "Ancients" still exist is not known by anyone.

See also Chirpers, Church of the Chosen Ones, Coyns, Droyne, Solomani Hypothesis, Vargr.

Aslan: The Aslan ambassador from the Yerlyaruiwo clan was shot and killed by Archduke Dulinor at the same time that Strephon was assassinated. While apparently an accident brought about by the rapid events in the room, it is unfortunate that many Aslan have taken this act as provocation calling for retaliation. At the same time, the shattered Imperium is not as able to defend its borders as it once was. Aslan *ihatei* (second sons, who do not inherit) have invaded the Imperial regions "behind the claw" and the Solomani Sphere in order to gain land, which is the determining element for an Aslan's social stature.

Assassination, Right of: The right of assassination is certainly a legitimate means of ascending to the throne, despite the implications of the SMART library data entry. Dulinor acted entirely properly, as was his right as an archduke. Was the killing justified? Was Strephon leading the Imperium down the path to destruction? Was Dulinor capable of turning events around and restoring the Imperium to its prior glory? Who knows?

C

Chirper: Chirpers are immature Droyne who have not been casted. If Droyne do not caste, they continue development, though very slowly. Sexual differences emerge, but casteless Droyne remain small and semi-intelligent and continue to resemble immature Droyne. Those Droyne groups which have lost the ability to caste (these are fairly common) live as primitives. Chirpers are also psionic, so they are impossible to catch. A chirper may occasionally befriend a human.

Church of the Chosen Ones: Much to the Church's dismay, its teachings are incorrect. Grandfather was not trying to create a perfect race, but rather a race of servants, and in this he failed miserably. Since that time, Grandfather has taken no interest whatsoever in any actions of the Vargr.

See also Ancients.

Coyns: Coyns are used in the Droyne casting ceremony, which is among the best known and most important of all Droyne rituals. Researchers were long baffled by the apparently random draw of coyns, under the direction of a leader and several drones, which ended in the choice of a caste for an immature individual. Recent research, though, has proven that the coyns that are drawn are used as focuses for concentration. The leader and drones use psionics to open the young Droyne's mind and awaken the appropriate genetic programming latent within its makeup. It has even been suggested that the draw of the caste coyn is not so random as it may appear to outsiders and that it may be selected by clairvoyance or telekinesis to match the potential discovered while probing the young candidate's mind.

Periodically, the coyns are also consulted in a ceremony which determines whether or not an individual can continue to serve his commune. The coyns are believed to reveal the future of an individual—a task or voyage, a battle, and so forth—and they are hence ritually consulted on a variety of matters. What has been frequently dismissed as "random fortune-telling" has proven to be surprisingly accurate in many instances. This has been explained as everything from coincidence to luck to some form of precognitive ability, but the truth remains unknown even to the Droyne. Certainly they believe strongly in the validity of their rituals; the coyns dictate not only life, but death as well, for in most circumstances the failure of an individual to pass the favorable scrutiny of the coyns in a Ceremony of Continuation leads to a self-willed voluntary death, using psionic self-awareness to painlessly turn off both the body and the mind.

See also Ancients, Chirpers, Droyne.

D

Droyne: See also Ancients, Chirpers, Coyns.

Express Boats: Though current technology in the Imperium allows jump-6 travel, the standard means of ferrying information, the Xboats, travel only at jump-4. Publicly, the Imperium writes this discrepancy off by sighting the high cost of building new ships and the fact that many frontier routes simply do not need jump-6 service. True, the cost of jump-6 is high enough to make a universal jump-6 Xboat network inefficient. But the Imperial government also knows the power of information and maintains a variety of naval couriers which can make jump-6. Knowing vital facts before they become general knowledge is essential to a well-run bureaucracy.

H

Hive Federation: The Hive Federation is one of the few alien governments which has not made an attempt to attack the divided Imperium. Trade between the Imperium and the Hivers has slowed down, however.

I

Imperial Rules of War: While the Imperial Rules of War strictly forbid the use of nuclear weapons by local combatants, the Imperium does retain the right to use such weapons itself.

Imperial Stationery: Notice in the Library Data entry the

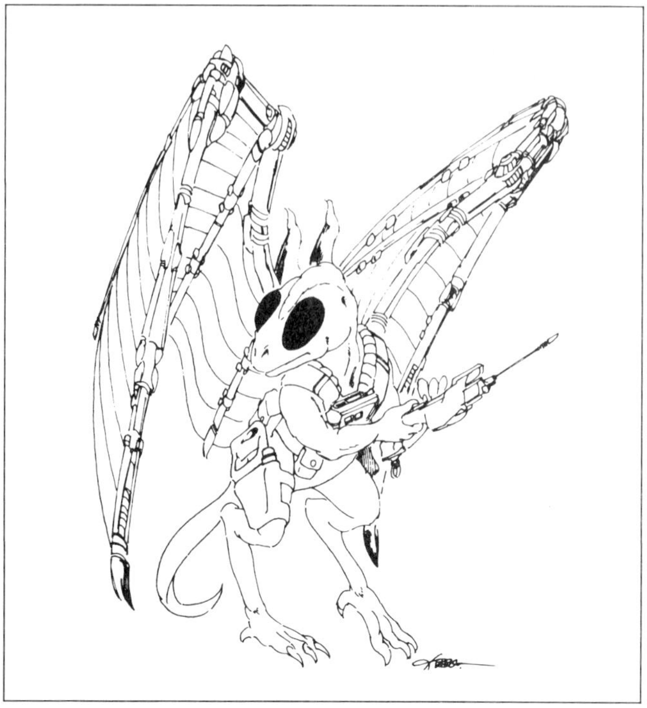

following phrase: "because it is used for Imperial appointments (even when issued in blank for offices in the marches)." In fact, Norris was never officially appointed by Strephon to be Archduke of the Domain of Deneb. True, he might have done so, if he had lived, but he didn't. Norris used the advance notice he had in learning of Strephon's death to fill in his own appointment.

See also Express Boats.

Imperiallines: An interstellar shipping corporation serving worlds off of the main trade routes of the Spinward Marches. Most class C starports in the Marches are served by Imperiallines.

Referee: Imperiallines is wholly owned by the Imperial family through a devious line of shareholders. Although it engages in real trade, the company's primary purpose is to provide a covert transport and courier system for the Imperial government. Imperiallines uses two outwardly identical ship types: type TI, capable of jump-2, and the secret type TJ, capable of jump-6.

K

K'kree: The K'kree, like the Hivers rimward of them, are not attacking the Imperium since the death of Strephon. The most likely reason for this apparent restraint is the vast distance between Imperial space and the Two Thousand Worlds, as well as the presence of client states and minor races between the two civilizations.

M

Moot, The: The Moot is not as important as the SMART library data entry implies. While the Moot does confirm emperors and high noble appointments, it did not act to confirm those emperors who ascended by the right of assassination. Is Dulinor, then, the proper emperor of the divided Imperium? Imperial law is somewhat fuzzy on this point, and there exists in the Imperium no body which has the actual power to decide the question. The answer will come *de facto* rather than *de jure*; that is, if Dulinor succeeds in reconsolidating the shattered Imperium, history may recognize him as a legitimate emperor.

If not....

P

Phoenix Project: While there were in fact caches of goods hidden to supply an uprising, this preparation was never as complete as some military theorists believed. What's more, much as squirrels do with acorns, the Phoenix leaders seem to have completely lost track of some of these caches over the years. While most of these would today be obsolete and decayed, there does exist the possibility of a valuable discovery.

Psionics Institute: Officially, all 65 of the Imperial Psionics Institutes were closed in 800 when the Psionic Suppressions hit. In fact, two of these (on Regina and Terra) continued to operate secretly under the auspices of the Imperial government. Today, almost all of the original institutes have been secretly reestablished by their partisans, and dozens of additional institutes have been formed since on other worlds. The Imperial Navy also conducts secret research on psionics at several locations, including a laboratory on Vanejen (Spinward Marches 3119).

Psionic Suppressions: In the latter half of the 700s, high Imperial figures (including the Office of the Emperor and the Intelligence Agency) became convinced that the approximately 60 percent of the psionics institutes within the region spinward of the Corridor sector were being financed, at least in part, by Zhodani money. Indeed, there is a natural affinity between the institutes and the Zhodani (with their long-standing history of psionics study and training). The Zhodani were believed by many at that time to be laying the groundwork for a "fifth column" to operate in Imperial space during a war planned to break out between 810 and 820. The Imperium moved to combat this.

Evidence of scandal was uncovered (or perhaps it was merely fabricated) and released with careful attention to public opinion. Simultaneously, high level officials at the sector and subsector levels were apprised of the true situation, and both the Zhodani and the Vargr states were informed (through private channels) that the Imperium knew of the upcoming war and was prepared for it. War was averted, but the suppressions succeeded far better than even the Imperium had envisioned. Public opinion swung widely against psionics and became solidified in the form of strong local laws and customs against psionics. The suppression campaign continued for 26 years before its formal halt. Many small, local campaigns have occurred since.

The cancellation of the charters of the various psionics institutes effectively removed them from the community. They have continued to exist at all only because psionics gives such an important advantage to those who have it against enforcement officials.

Sixty-five psionics institutes held Imperial charters in 800. The suppression orders issued by Paula II, which appeared over a period of 10 years, first "suppressed" the various charters, rendering them temporarily suspended and then revoked them at a later date. Sixty-five suppression orders were issued, numbers 2 through 66 (SO 1 was a general order to the realm concerning the issue), followed by 65 orders for revocation (SO67 to SO131). Of these, actual records indicate that SO 83 and SO **96** were themselves revoked by orders published elsewhere. The result is that a cursory examination of the SO files will reveal all Imperial charters of psionics institutes to have been revoked; in actuality, two institutes retained their charters under the auspices of the Ministry of Defense.

One institute, however, even now remains at its original site, at Terra (Sol 0207). The revocation order was cancelled in 1014. Another institute, which was originally sited at Regina, has now been reestablished at Wypoc (Lanth 0401), but it retains a low level recruiting establishment as part of the Navy base at Regina.

Both Imperial-chartered Psionics Institutes are under military control, and are engaged in psionics research. Their existence is of the utmost secrecy.

See also Psychohistory.

Psychohistory: The general information in the library data entry is not entirely correct. The reason large-scale psychohistory experiments are no longer conducted is due to the unpredictable results achieved by the only sizable experiment to date, which was conducted as a part of the psionics suppressions. The unforeseen results of this experiment were so far-reaching that Imperial scientists concluded that their knowledge of the principles involved was woefully inadequate and that further study was required. Imperial research into psychohistory is undertaken at a small number of research stations and is carried out under the strictest of controls.

See also Psionics Suppressions.

R

Rachele Society: Zid Rachele died a few years after escaping from Exile, but his partisans "recreated" him with the help of a pseudoreality computer simulation. By recreating the personality of this nefarious figure, they were able to continue their racist activities, which culminated in 1103 with the failed attempt to raid the Dynam Depot. Presuming that a copy of the Rachelean software was made before its loss at Dynam, a recreated "Zid Rachele" could still surface yet again.

S

Six Races: See also Chirpers.

Solomani Hypothesis: The Solomani Hypothesis as mentioned in the SMART library data is on the whole correct, although a little incomplete.

See also Ancients.

Solomani Security: Secret police force maintained in service to the Solomani Confederation. The purpose of the Solomani secret police force is to maintain state secrets, conduct espionage, and implement political policies of the government.

Solomani Security maintains both a network of contacts which provide information from outside the Confederation, and a network of informants which provide information within the Confederation. Solomani Security agents themselves are highly trained individuals capable of conducting espionage and sabotage.

Strephon (1049-1116): In one sense, Strephon tied his own noose by reinstating the power of the archdukes after a long lapse in such power. A better leader might have recognized the signs of Dulinor's dissatisfaction and also might have foreseen the drastic plans that transpired with the emperor's sudden death.

See also Third Imperium.

T

Travel Zone: Since the breakup of the Imperium, the Travellers' Aid Society is not as efficient as it once was in classifying areas. While many worlds are amber or red zones, there are probably many more that should be now but aren't.

Twilight's Peak: The epic poem in fact describes the accidental discovery of an Ancient site on Fulacin (Spinward Marches 2613).

V

Vargr: See also Ancients, Church of the Chosen Ones.

W

War, Imperial Rules of: See Imperial Rules of War.

Z

Zhdant (Zhdant 2719 A6547C8-F): As is the case with all the homeworlds of human races, Zhdant is an Ancient site. In historic times, in addition to being the home of the Zhodani, Zhdant was also the home of a large population of chirpers. From this population of chirpers the Zhodani were able to learn their first few lessons in the previously unknown skill of psionics. All of the chirpers which made their home on Zhdant, as well as a population of them on Viepchakl, Zhdant's moon, were killed accidentally by a plague left over from the Ancient's Final War.

Zhodani: Surprisingly enough to those Imperial citizens living "behind the claw," the Zhodani have not taken any advantage of the weakened state of the divided Imperium by attacking.

The anti-Zhodani slant of the SMART library data does not bear objective consideration. In fact, in quite a few respects, Zhodani society is somewhat superior to that of other human cultures.

For example, one of the foremost values of the Zhodani society is the basic honesty that pervades everything there. Trust is an implicit assumption. Locks are extremely rare, and when locks are used, they are more likely to be safety devices to protect children than bars against theft. Walls protect individuals and items from the elements rather than from intruders. Laws deal more with appropriate action than with crimes.

Zhodani society also helps direct individuals to the most productive and satisfying pursuits available to them. Psionically based techniques are available to help each person understand his or her needs and motivations, and place each individual where his or her ability and aptitude can contribute most to personal well-being, as well as to the community as a whole.

Equipment

The vast number of physical objects in the universe and the variation in their potential costs and values defy classification; it is impossible to note and define them all. The objects in this listing are presented as indications of common qualities and values.

Each object's description is followed by its technological level, volume, weight, and price in credits. The technological level indicates local technology required to manufacture an item with the capabilities listed. Volume is given in liters, weight is given in kilograms, and price is in credits. An item with negligible weight or size can be carried or worn without difficulty.

This section may be considered a shopping list for travellers. When they originally outfit themselves for an adventure, each character may purchase or acquire items from this list in preparation for action or mishap. This list does not include weaponry or vehicles, and for the most part all items are generally available for purchase without difficulty on worlds with a sufficient technology level (on other worlds, they may be available as imports at higher prices).

Objects are in alphabetical order, generally by the basic noun used to describe the object. For example, infrared goggles, light intensifier goggles, and sun goggles can all be found in the *G*s under "goggles."

A

Airlock, Portable: An inflatable, portable chamber that can be attached to the vacuum side of a bulkhead, entered, and pressurized, which allows a hole to be cut into a pressurized area without depressurization. It includes a patch held in place by pressure which seals the hole when the airlock is depressurized. Size: 500cm by 20cm by 200cm (deflated, 2000 liters), 1.5 meters by 1.5 meters by 2 meters (inflated, 4500 liters); deflated volume includes a pressurized air cylinder and an automatic pump.

TL	*Vol*	*Weight*	*Price*
9	2000 liters	6 kg	Cr1000

Air Tanks: A complete set of compressed oxygen tanks which allows independent breathing in smoke, dust, gas, or exotic atmosphere (type A and special situations). Refill: Cr10.

TL	*Vol*	*Weight*	*Price*	*Duration (hrs)*
5	5 liters	2.5 kg	Cr500	2
12	4 liters	2.0 kg	Cr400	4
14	1 liter	0.5 kg	Cr200	12

Air Tanks, Underwater: Equivalent to oxygen tanks but designed for use underwater. Tanks include regulator and breathing connections. Two tanks last 4 hours and weigh 5 kg. Refill: Cr20.

TL	*Vol*	*Weight*	*Price*	*Duration (hrs)*
5	5 liters	2.5 kg	Cr800	2

Atmosphere Tester: A solid-state device with read-outs indicating the atmospheric percentages of elements present. In addition, a red light glows if the atmosphere is not breathable, and a green light glows if the atmosphere is breathable.

TL	*Vol*	*Weight*	*Price*
7	2 liters	1 kg	Cr150

Attache Case: An aluminum and magnesium carrying case similar to that used by technicians to carry precision instruments.

TL	*Vol*	*Weight*	*Price*
7	2 liters	1 kg	Cr75

Axe, Ice: An ice axe is frequently useful in making climbs in snow and ice.

TL	*Vol*	*Weight*	*Price*
3	3 liters	1.5 kg	Cr25

B

Backpack: Backpacks increase a character's carrying capacity.

TL	*Vol*	*Weight*	*Price*
3	40 liters	3 kg	Cr45

Ball, Rescue: Standard on all Imperial military vessels and on most private ships as well. When folded, the rescue ball is a cylinder 5 cm in diameter and 10 cm long. When deployed, it forms a sphere one meter in diameter which contains air sufficient to last one person for two hours. In the event of explosive decompression or other loss of air, a rescue ball allows an individual not in possession of a vacc suit to survive until aid arrives. The user pulls a lanyard, climbs inside and seals the zip closure. The ball is made of a metal-coated plastic film for ease of location by radar and contains a bottle of compressed air, a first aid kit, and a transparent window through which the occupant may observe conditions outside the ball. Rescue balls provide some protection from stellar radiation and corrosive and insidious atmospheres for five to seven hours.

TL	Vol	Weight	Price
7	1 liter	5 kg	Cr150

Base, Advanced: Modular pressurized quarters for 6 persons, with airlock and atmosphere recirculating system. Can be carried in the hold of a starship.

TL	Vol	Weight	Price
8	72 kliters	6000 kg	Cr50,000

Battle Computer: Man-portable battle-coordination system, capable of collating intelligence estimates, providing approximations of enemy forces, and of suggesting tactics. It can be linked to unattended ground sensors to increase its potential, and can provide visual displays overlaid on maps when combined with a map box. When linked to a communicator, it can direct laser/maser-communication beams to ground or orbital stations, it and can automatically switch to secondary beam paths if primaries become unavailable.

TL	Vol	Weight	Price
9	28 liters	15 kg	Cr10,000

Beacon, Emergency: A combination long-range communicator and signal transponder, the commlink beacon is a very sophisticated emergency signaling device. The internal transponder monitors common emergency search-and-rescue channels (one at a time). When traffic is picked up on this channel, the device simultaneously emits a shrill warning tone to alert users to the possibility that help is at hand and transmits a coded distress signal. Some more expensive models have provision for a taped, auto-repeat distress call, instead of the automatic code signal. In either event, the commlink beacon serves as a means of establishing contact when there is any search being mounted within 500 kilometers, and then it serves to continue communications after that initial contact. The transponder operates for 30 days.

TL	Vol	Weight	Price
9	2 liters	1 kg	Cr750

Binoculars: Allows improved vision at greater distances than would unaided eyes. Weighs 1 kg.

TL	Vol	Weight	Price
3	2 liters	1 kg	Cr75

Binoculars, Electronic: Vision aid providing electronic enhancement of images. Electronic binoculars feature light enhancement and range-finding capabilities. Comes in an over-the-shoulder carrying case; a sling is also provided for separate carrying.

TL	Vol	Weight	Price
8	2 liters	2 kg	Cr750

Binoculars, Image Converter: Most night-vision devices and electronic sights either are sensitive to infrared (heat) radiation or use light intensifiers to detect their targets. Both have minor disadvantages: IR images can be camouflaged by insulation and LI requires background light to amplify. In addition, the user can only see as far as the unaided eye.

Commercially available at Tech Level 10, the image converter is sensitive to both infrared and visible light. It picks up both heat images and visible-light pictures. The converter can intensify these images, making night-vision possible, as well as magnify them up to 20 ×. Both functions are completely adjustable, but high intensification will cut contrast drastically, making the resulting images unclear. Automatic polarizers cut in if the image is bright enough to blind. A laser rangefinder is also included.

In infrared mode, personnel may be detected up to 3 km away, and vehicles at 6 km. In visible-light mode, personnel may be detected at 5 km and vehicles at 10 km. Note that physical concealment does not necessarily mean that a target is undetectable. The rangefinder is effective out to 7 km, making it useful for infantry or hunting use only.

Special hardware/software packages are available for hand computers that expand the capabilities of the image converter. When hooked up to a computer using a graphics package, the image converter can be tied into a map box (allowing others to see what the user sees), and electronic "photographs" can be stored in the computer's memory. Another package allows the computer to calculate the speed of a target relative to the user.

Physically, the image converter is similar to a set of binoculars. Power packs are mounted inside the converter casing and average one week of constant use.

TL	Vol	Weight	Price
10	1 liter	1.25 kg	Cr12,000

Binoculars, PRIS: The portable radiation imaging system

(PRIS) has many more capabilities than binoculars from any previous Tech Level. The PRIS can be set to observe images in the spectral range from infrared to gamma rays. (The PRIS will not detect radio waves.) The front surface of the PRIS is transparent to all radiation; just behind it is a series of lenses tailored to various specific bands. Besides this, a tight beam laser rangefinder gives an accurate reading on the target within sight up to about 20 km, depending on conditions, with the range displayed as a digital readout in the viewfinder. The PRIS also has a built-in clock and limited memory, so the rangefinder can determine the velocity of the object being viewed by comparing its distance from the observer over time.

The unit can be calibrated to a standard self-precessing gyrocompass, in which case the bearing of the direction viewed will be digitally displayed in the corner of the viewfinder. The magnification strength of the PRIS is adjustable up to 225×. A built-in flywheel for gyro-stabilization insures a steady field of view at all magnifications.

Besides its obvious uses in the field, the PRIS also finds itself used in a variety of industrial and engineering applications. Its infrared images can be color-coded to show the ambient temperatures of objects in the viewfinder. A PRIS can therefore be found near every jump drive, to be used by engineers looking for "hot spots" on the drive housing. In other areas of a ship, the PRIS can detect problems in electrical circuits, again by finding an area of higher temperature.

TL	*Vol*	*Weight*	*Price*
12	3 liters	2 kg	Cr3500

Boots, Climbing: Sturdy hiking boots worn for long excursions. A well-chosen climbing boot is valuable in reducing the wearer's rate of fatigue.

TL	*Vol*	*Weight*	*Price*
3	3 liters	1.5 kg	Cr50

Bugs and Detectors: Bugs are near-microscopic, difficult to detect monitoring devices, which enable an individual to hear conversations or to record them for later monitoring. Typically, a bug array is packaged as a small rod containing fifty implantable bugs, together with a bug detector. Placed by touching the rod to a wall joint, light switch, or some other feature of a room, implanted bugs are not recoverable, but they can be destroyed. Bugs send a constant signal to a central monitor. Bugs, once placed, are impossible to detect without a bug detector. A detector is calibrated to detect the signals of bugs and to note their location. A bug detector can be set on one of three settings: Detect, Smother, or Destroy. "Detect" merely indicates the presence and location of a bug. "Smother" prevents a bug from sensing conversations, but allows the bug to remain active. "Destroy" actually destroys the bug which has been detected.

TL	*Vol*	*Weight*	*Price*
15	1 liter	1 kg	Cr1000

Bullhorn: A device which amplifies faint sounds, enabling a voice to carry to very long range.

TL	*Vol*	*Weight*	*Price*
5	3 liters	0.5 kg	Cr120

C

Cabin, Prefabricated: Modular unpressurized quarters for 6 persons. 2 by 6 by 6 meters. Can be carried in the hold of a starship.

TL	*Vol*	*Weight*	*Price*
6	72,000 liters	4000 kg	Cr10,000

Cable: Fine flexible plasteel cable, capable of supporting 250 kilograms. Available in 50 meter coils.

TL	*Vol*	*Weight*	*Price*
9	1 liter	3 kg	Cr100

Calculator, Hand: Provides basic mathematical calculations.

TL	*Vol*	*Weight*	*Price*
7	0.25 liters	0.10 kg	Cr10

Camera: See Recorder, Image.

Carpentry Tool Set: Includes basic tools necessary to cut, shape, and build with wood. Woodworking may include construction and repair of shelters, buildings, or furniture.

TL	*Vol*	*Weight*	*Price*
2	30 liters	25 kg	Cr300

Charges, Breaching: Breaching charges are shaped charges of plastic explosive designed to blow man-sized holes in walls. The charge is the size of a thick notebook; it has a self-adhesive panel on one side and an adjustable chemical time fuse on the other.

To operate a charge, the user peels the sheet of protective plastic film from the adhesive panel, breaks the prescored fuse strip at the desired time delay (five to 60 seconds in five-second increments), pulls the primer, and dives for cover.

Fire departments and rescue units often have a few breaching charges, which are used in an effort to free people trapped in burning or collapsed buildings. Charges made for such "civilian" use are striped dazzle yellow and black, and they usually have a fixed 60-second delay. The breaching charge contains sufficient explosive to breach an armor factor 10, and it does 250 damage points, as discussed in the *Players' Manual*.

TL	*Vol*	*Weight*	*Price*
8	2 liters	2 kg	Cr100

Clothing, Cold Weather: At low Tech Levels cold weather clothing consists of boots, pants, hooded coat, mittens, and face mask, made from animal skins sewn together. These items may be manufactured from local materials provided several large furs, properly cured, are available. At higher Tech Levels, the protection is afforded by a head-to-toe garment made of several layers of fabric around an insulating layer of fluffy fibers. Below Tech Level 7, immersion in water renders cold weather clothing totally ineffective.

TL	Vol	Weight	Price
1	16 liters	4 kg	Cr200
6	12 liters	3 kg	Cr200
10	8 liters	2 kg	Cr800

Clothing, Desert: Rugged, lightweight clothing for use in the desert. Includes white, long-sleeved shirt; white, comfortable long pants, sturdy hiking boots, and a broad-brimmed, light colored hat. See also Suit, Desert Survival.

TL	Vol	Weight	Price
3	—	—	Cr95

Commdots: A commdot is most often found used as an adjunct to a communicator, although other uses are becoming more common. One commdot is temporarily affixed to the scalp just behind the ear; another commdot is stuck to the throat just above the Adam's apple. The microelectronics in the dots can transmit and receive for a distance of only about a meter, but this is far enough to put the dots in contact with a large, more powerful device. One can thus use a communicator or hand computer and still keep both hands free for other tasks. Commdots are powered by ultraminiature superbatteries and can be tuned by another device. Most communicators support this tuning capability.

When one desires to communicate over more than one frequency at a time or to operate more than one device, a commdot multiplexer is used. The multiplexer is a small box worn on the belt and coordinates activity between the commdot and several electronic devices. The operator can then receive or transmit only on the channels desired, and he can turn signals on or off at will.

	TL	Vol	Weight	Price
Set	10	—	—	Cr100
Multiplexer	10	.1 liters	.1 kg	Cr800

Communicator/Recorder: A miniaturized electronic device capable of receiving voice or radio input, recording it, and transmitting this information either on a given external signal or continuously. Reception and transmission is on the standard voice communication bands. Thus, the device can listen for signals and then retransmit them, or it can continuously transmit a prerecorded message. Tape length is 10 minutes; transmitter range is line of sight (it is blocked by buildings, mountains, and so on).

TL	Vol	Weight	Price	Range
11	0.1 liters	0.1 kg	Cr400	Very Distant (50 km)

Communicator: A communicator is defined as a radio transmitter/receiver combination capable of operating off an internal power source; it is portable in the sense that it need not be connected to a power supply. It may transmit and receive both voice and data. Communicators 0.2 liters and under can be worn as earpieces, which are unnoticeable to the casual observer.

TL	Volume	Weight	Price	Range
5	40 liters	20 kg	Cr225	Distant (5 km)
5	140 liters	70 kg	Cr750	Very Distant (50 km)
5	300 liters	150 kg	Cr1500	Regional (500 km)
5	600 liters	300 kg	Cr15,000	Continental (5000 km)
8	0.2 liters	0.1 kg	Cr75	Distant (5 km)
9	2.4 liters	1.2 kg	Cr500	Regional (500 km)
9	3.0 liters	1.5 kg	Cr5000	Continental (5000 km)
10	0.8 liters	0.4 kg	Cr250	Very Distant (50 km)
12	2.0 liters	1 kg	Cr1000	Continental (5000 km)
13	0.2 liters	0.1 kg	Cr250	Very Distant (50 km)
14	1.0 liter	0.5 kg	Cr500	Regional (500 km)

Communicator, Laser: The laser communicator is a line-of-sight device with a regional range (500 km). This distance is seldom needed on a world's surface since the distance to the horizon limits the range first, but this range often allows contact with an orbiting ship.

The laser communicator's main advantage is that it provides a tight beam and therefore a private means of communication. Sets of laser communicators are often set up in a "repeater" network. Spaced at a horizon-to-horizon distance, the units can instantly convey a message around a world by retransmitting it from station to station.

TL	Volume	Weight	Price	Range
10	5 liters	1.5 kg	Cr2500	Regional (500 km)

Communicator, Video: The video communicator transmits a voice and two-dimensional image over a range of 500 km (regional). The unit is small enough to be carried in a pocket or hung on a belt.

The communicator has a built-in microphone and video camera for input and a small speaker and a polylucent

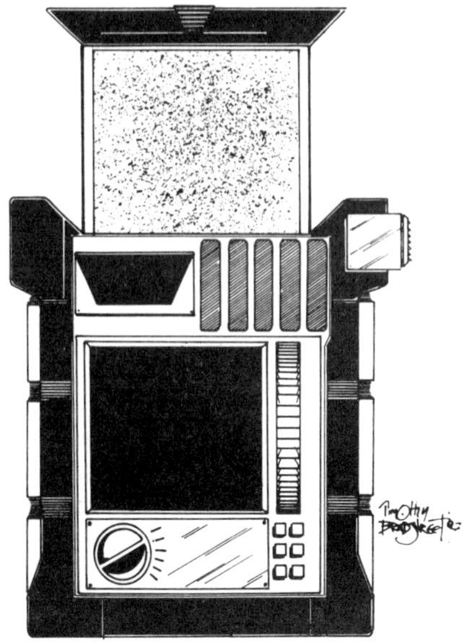

cuprothallium display for output. The cuprothallium display slides into the main housing when not in use, and the video camera can be switched off if desired. Commdots can be used to speak and listen if the device is attached to a belt.

By opening the unit up, interior controls can preselect five different frequencies for current use; one of these can then be chosen using the frequency selection knob on the front of the communicator. The communicator can transmit and receive simultaneously.

When used with commdots, the communicator can be used to set the commdot frequencies to itself; it will also automatically multiplex with a commdot for any of its five active frequencies.

TL	*Vol*	*Weight*	*Price*	*Range*
14	0.45 liters	0.2 kg	Cr500	Regional (500 km)

Compass, Magnetic: Indicates direction of local magnetic north, if the world has magnetic poles. May be influenced and give false readings in the vicinity of large masses of iron.

TL	*Vol*	*Weight*	*Price*
3	—	—	Cr10

Computer, Hand: Provides services of a supercomputer (equivalent to Model/1 in computing power), plus serves as a computer terminal when linked to a larger computer (such as on board a ship).

TL	*Vol*	*Weight*	*Price*
11	0.2 liters	0.5 kg	Cr1000

Counter, Radiation: Indicates presence and intensity of radioactivity in the immediate vicinity. Can be preset to give a warning signal if levels of radioactivity rise to dangerous levels. Readouts are given in specifics and in terms of danger to humans.

TL	*Vol*	*Weight*	*Price*
5	2 liters	1 kg	Cr250
10	—	—	Cr100

Crampons: Crampons are special spiked attachments strapped to boots to assist in climbs in icy conditions. Wearing crampons decreases the difficulty of crossing ice.

TL	*Vol*	*Weight*	*Price*
4	—	—	Cr20

D

Data-Display/Recorder Headpiece: This headpiece represents a significant breakthrough in holographic display technology at Tech Level 13. A small rectangle of polylucent cuprothallium provides a constant heads-up three-dimensional display for the wearer. Although useless by itself, the headpiece can be interfaced with virtually any number of Tech Level 13+ devices by using a multiplexer similar to that used with commdots. The multiplexer not only coordinates the information for the user but also synchronously records the multiple signals onto one standard holocrystal for later review.

Their use is common among bridge and engineering personnel on starships as well as smaller craft. For example, someone flying in a grav belt while using a neural activity sensor handset would find it inconvenient (to say the least) to refer to the readout on his backpack. Instead, the sensor's output is immediately displayed on his headpiece. At the same time, he can monitor his altitude, airspeed, position, and the operational status of his grav belt batteries and grav units. If he is also wearing a vacc suit, he can read off his oxygen supply and internal temperature besides.

When desired, the headpiece can be swung out of the way above the head; when the display is turned off, the cuprothallium is transparent. About three percent of the population find it difficult to focus properly on the headpiece and are unable to use the device.

TL	*Vol*	*Weight*	*Price*
13	0.1 liters	0.1 kg	Cr5000

Densitometer, Handheld: An outgrowth of gravitic technology, the remote densitometer uses an object's natural gravity to measure its density.

The densitometer records scan data in a three-dimensional matrix. The matrix is processed by the densitometer's computer to provide a 3-dimensional density map of the scanned object or region. Large massive objects (like starships) can be located out to planetary range, while smaller objects (vehicles, heavy metal deposits) can be located at very distant range or less.

TL	*Vol*	*Weight*	*Price*
14	15 liters	7 kg	Cr15,000
15	3 liters	2 kg	Cr25,000

Desert Survival Kit: A kit containing a variety of items useful in the desert. Includes a 1-liter canteen; first aid kit; salt tablets; folding shovel; plastic, watertraps, straws, and directions for building three solar stills; a knife and sheath; a signal mirror (for attracting the attention of searchers in the day-time); and a water purification kit (see below). The kit comes in a 30cm × 12cm × 12cm pack which can be worn on the back or hip or attached to a larger pack.

TL	*Vol*	*Weight*	*Price*
5	4.5 liters	1 kg	Cr450

Detector, Metal: Indicates presence of most metals, although degree of reaction depends on amount of metal present and on proximity. Weighs 1 kg.

TL	*Vol*	*Weight*	*Price*
6	2 liters	1 kg	Cr300

Detector, Stress: The linear descendant of the polygraph, the stress detector uses readings of a suspect's physical responses, voice stress, and similar phenomena to establish the individual's degree of truthfulness under questioning. It is not, however, necessarily accurate in its readings, and the interpretation of readings is a complex matter.

TL	Vol	Weight	Price
14	2 liters	6 kg	Cr1500

Disguise Kit: Allows change of personal appearance on a temporary basis.

TL	Vol	Weight	Price
7	8 liters	5 kg	Cr1000

Dye, Water: A tube of liquid dye which can be used to highlight a patch of water (around a raft at sea or in a lake near a crash site) with a bright, easily spotted color visible from the air. The primary drawbacks of this form of signalling are the short duration of the colored patch (it lasts no more than 15 minutes in still water and much less if the water is rough or there is any form of precipitation to break it up), and the fact that it cannot be used at night.

The latter problem is offset by dyes available at Tech Level 9. These contain a phosphorescent dye equally visible in day or night. Generally, water dyes are useful only when searchers are aware of the presence of the distressed travellers and are more in need of an exact location than some signal to draw their attention in the first place. A tube provides a single dye patch of standard dimensions.

TL	Vol	Weight	Price
4	0.3 liters	0.2 kg	Cr25
9	0.1 liters	0.1 kg	Cr50

E

Echo Sounder: A device which sends out a a pulse of high-frequency sound and then reads returning echoes to give a range between the sounder and any obstruction. Low-cost models are usually effective to no more than 80 meters, and at ranges of over 40 meters they have little accuracy. More sophisticated models (available at Tech Level 7) are capable of showing a fairly detailed display of the area at which they are aimed, including animal life and other details.

Echo sounders are usually mounted aboard boats and submersibles, where they serve as depth finders. Portable models, however, can be mounted in waterproof camera housings and used by divers. They not only determine depth but also can be used to find horizontal ranges.

TL	Vol	Weight	Price
6	2.5 liters	1 kg	Cr300
10	0.4 liters	0.2 kg	Cr150

Electronic Tool Set: Necessary tools for basic assembly and repair of electronic devices such as communicators, detectors, sensors, and control instruments.

TL	Vol	Weight	Price
7	10 liters	5 kg	Cr2000

F

Filter Respirator Combination: A combination filter mask and respirator which allows breathing of very thin, tainted atmospheres.

TL	Vol	Weight	Price
5	1 liter	0.5 kg	Cr150

Flare, Smoke: These flares emit both a bright light and a pillar of colored smoke for 15 minutes after ignition. Once set off, they burn constantly and cannot be shut off. Sighting in either day or night is nearly automatic in line-of-sight. Smoke flares are specifically designed to be hand-held or implanted in the ground.

TL	Vol	Weight	Price
6	0.5 liters	0.25 kg	Cr12

Flare Gun: A flare gun is used for long-range signalling, and it has a number of applications, both civil and military. It consists of a pistol-like launcher which can fire any of several types of flares up to 50 meters. In addition to being used for signals, it can fire illuminating flares which can be used for spotting purposes at night.

A signal flare is a standard type which provides an easily noticed trail of light (but no real illumination).

An illuminating flare for 30 seconds lights up everything in a radius of 50 meters around the firing character. Such flares are always noticed at night but have little effect by day.

	TL	Vol	Weight	Price
Flare Gun	5	1.5 liter	1 kg	Cr75
Signal Flare	5	0.1 liter	.25 kg	Cr10
Illum Flare	5	0.1 liter	.25 kg	Cr25

G

Gauge, Depth: A device for registering the pressure of water

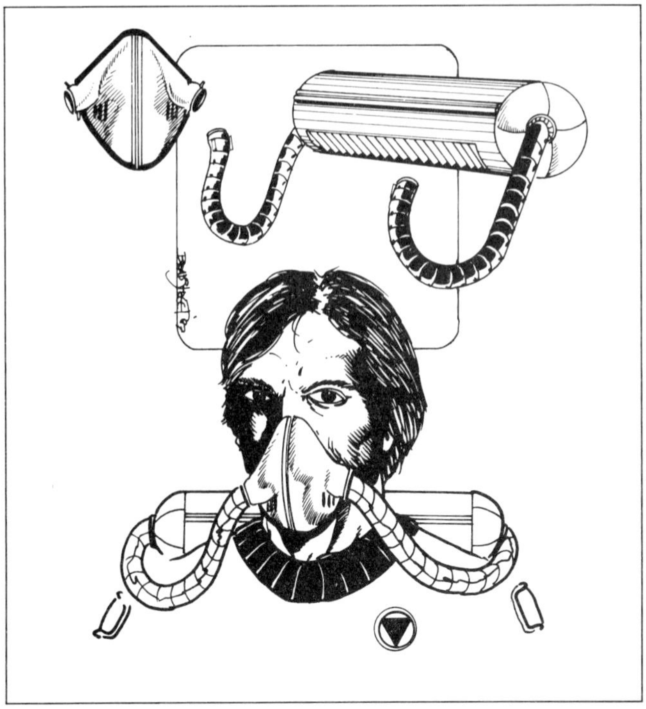

around a diver. Several models are available, which vary in accuracy and in special features. The simplest types register pressure only (forcing the diver to be familiar with the pressure/depth relationship for the specific planet). Of similar quality and price are gauges manufactured for diving on a specific world, which calibrate depth in meters (or other local measurement) rather than by pressure. In addition to concerns over reliability, characters should be aware of the danger of diving with a depth gauge calibrated for a different planet.

At Tech Level 8, a more elaborate model of depth gauge is a digital unit that records time as well as pressure and specifically processes information on decompression stops and durations.

Most sophisticated of all—at Tech Level 9—is a device which can be programmed to show pressure, decompression data, and depth in meters for any world merely by making some simple entries before diving.

Depth gauges are worn on a wrist mounting and usually require occasional battery charges for power.

TL	*Vol*	*Weight*	*Price*
6	—	—	Cr25
8	—	—	Cr150
9	—	—	Cr250

Gauge, Tank Pressure: A gauge showing the available air supply left in air tanks. A basic model shows this information in terms of one atm air supply (forcing the diver to convert for current depth); an advanced version can be tied in with a programmable pressure/depth gauge to give readouts of actual air supplies at specific depths.

TL	*Vol*	*Weight*	*Price*
6	—	—	Cr25

Gill, Artificial: Designed to extract oxygen from water, the artificial gill is a complex device which allows a virtually unlimited time underwater. A tank included in the mechanism carries a charge of nitrogen or helium, which is mixed with extracted oxygen. Exhaled carbon dioxide is eliminated, with the helium or nitrogen being recirculated. Some models have CO_2-absorbent chemicals, like a rebreather, to eliminate bubbles for covert dives.

The two chief dangers involved in using the artificial gill are anoxia and hypoxia.

Anoxia occurs in some layers of water where oxygen content is too low to allow extraction. This is normally a rare occurrence but should be watched for. Victims of anoxia must be given air within five minutes, or they will probably die.

Hypoxia occurs when a fault in the mechanism delivers an insufficient volume of the mixed gas (nitrogen or helium) to the diver. Shots of pure oxygen have an intoxicating effect and should be treated much like nitrogen narcosis. Hypoxia is based on the reliability of the gill.

The artificial gill functions only in thin, standard, and dense atmospheres.

TL	*Vol*	*Weight*	*Price*
8	6 liters	4 kg	Cr4000

Gill, Bionic: A surgical implanted device which enables the human body to function freely in the undersea environment. The individual breathes water as freely as air using a small intake device which is tied to the implant when a dive is made. The lungs are filled with water to equalize pressure, but water is not actually "breathed" through the lungs.

The chief danger of the bionic gill is a problem in adjusting from one environment to another; water trapped in the lungs upon resumption of air breathing can be a threat, which is primarily controlled through experience.

TL	*Vol*	*Weight*	*Price*
14	—	—	Cr35,000

Gill, Powered: A variant of the artificial gill, the powered gill is similar in function but quite different in actual design. Using a power pack to provide the high levels of energy required, the powered gill converts water to hydrogen and oxygen; it expels the hydrogen and combining the oxygen with a carried nitrogen supply. The powered gill has all of the same basic limitations as the artificial gill, but it is lighter. Power supply is good for 36 hours of use between recharges. Bubbles (from hydrogen, broken down by the unit) cannot be masked.

At Tech Level 13, a miniaturized refinement of the standard powered gill employs the same principles but is much smaller. It consists of a lightweight, mouthpiece-type breathing device with a small battery and a container of pressurized nitrogen attached to the unit. The unit will not accept helium, and thus it is limited by the threat of nitrogen narcosis to pressures of 3 atm or less. Total operating time is no more than 1 hour.

TL	*Vol*	*Weight*	*Price*
12	4 liters	3 kg	Cr5000
13	1.5 liters	0.5 kg	Cr7500

Goggles: Lightweight, plastic eye goggles which provide protection against both windblown sand or dust and sun glare.

TL	*Vol*	*Weight*	*Price*
5	—	—	Cr15

Goggles, Combination IR/LI: These goggles combine light intensification and infrared radiation detection in one unit and are worn like eyeglasses. They allow vision in anything more than total darkness and can detect heat sources up to 50 meters away. Most types have automatic sensitivity control in the LI mode to prevent blinding by a bright light source, and they can be adjusted manually in both the LI and IR mode by a knob mounted on the earpiece.

TL	*Vol*	*Weight*	*Price*
9	0.3 liters	0.2 kg	Cr1250

Goggles, Infrared: Allow wearer to see exothermic (heat-emitting) sources in the dark such as animals, fires, or hot engines. The quality of vision is necessarily distorted as heat sources and not reflected light images, are being viewed. IR goggles also provide protection from windblown particles.

TL	Vol	Weight	Price
6	0.5 liters	0.25 kg	Cr500

Goggles, Light Intensifier: Allow vision by intensifying ambient light and are usable in anything less than total darkness. LI goggles may allow darkness penalties in night or combat situations to be reduced or ignored. LI goggles also provide protection from windblown particles.

TL	Vol	Weight	Price
7	0.5 liters	0.25 kg	Cr500
10	0.5 liters	—	Cr400

Grapnel: A grapnel is a hook at the end of a line, which is used for attempting climbs up sheer pitches. Maximum range to throw a grapnel is about 30 meters; thus, seven separate climbs would complete a 200 meter pitch (planting the grapnel on a ledge or projection, climbing to it, then repeating). Grapnel climbing bypasses the procedure of sending up a lead climber; each climb is equivalent to a regular climb up emplaced ropes.

TL	Vol	Weight	Price
2	4 liters	2 kg + rope	Cr15

Grapnel Gun: At Tech Level 7, a grapnel launcher becomes available which doubles the range of a grapnel to 60 meters.

TL	Vol	Weight	Price
7	6 liters	10 kg	Cr100

Grav Belt: A standard-issue Tech Level 12 grav belt looks like a parachute harness with a "stiffener" that runs down the back and has a series of artificial gravity modules around the waist. The grav belt weighs about 10 kg, but once it is turned on, a neutral control setting eliminates this weight.

This configuration provides 300 kg of thrust for four hours between charges. The grav belt has a maximum speed in an atmosphere of 300 kph, a cruising speed of 225 kph, and a nap-of-earth speed of 40 kph.

TL	Vol	Weight	Price
12	25 liters	10 kg*	Cr100,000 (4 hours per charge)
15	15 liters	10 kg*	Cr110,000 (8 hours per charge)

* When not activated

H

Hammer, Rock: A rock hammer is required to set a Tech 4 or Tech 7 piton.

TL	Vol	Weight	Price
2	1 liter	1 kg	Cr10

Heatsuit: A skin-tight, head-to-toe covering which provides protection against extreme cold. A power source drives a network of heating filaments in the fabric. An internal thermostat allows any apparent temperature, negating the effects of low temperatures and wind chill.

TL	Vol	Weight	Price
8	—	—	Cr300

Heatsuit Battery: Disposable battery capable of powering a heatsuit's filaments for a period of 72 hours.

TL	Vol	Weight	Price
8	—	0.5 kg	Cr40

Heatsuit Power Pack: An energy source designed to replace the battery for a heatsuit. It powers the suit for up to 144 hours without recharging, and it is capable of recharging in one hour from any standard power source.

TL	Vol	Weight	Price
10	1 liter	2 kg	Cr500

Helmet, Transparent: A "goldfish bowl" type of helmet, this protective device has certain advantages over the protective mask. It is lighter, offers more complete protection against irritant atmospheres, and does not hamper the wearer as much as the clumsier mask. The helmet can also be worn with a protective suit or vacc suit in corrosive atmospheres.

TL	Vol	Weight	Price
8	6 liters	0.75 kg	Cr30

Hoist, Climbing: This hoist is a battery-powered motor which drives a reel with 25 meters of cable. It has a hook on one side for attachment to a belt or harness and another hook on the opposite side for the cable. A rocker switch in the handle controls direction and an adjustable clutch controls speed; the reel can also freewheel. Power lasts for about one hour before the batteries need replacing. A hand brake can lock the cable in position and a centrifugal brake keeps the cable from un-

winding too rapidly.

TL	*Vol*	*Weight*	*Price*	*Capacity*
8	0.5 liters	1.5 kg	Cr175	125 kg

Hoist, Jumar: A jumar is a personal hoist which makes roped ascents and descents much easier to undertake. Jumars do nothing to increase speed; they merely make the climb easier.

TL	*Vol*	*Weight*	*Price*
6	2 liters	1 kg	Cr50

Hoist, Mechanical: A mechanical hoist is used to haul heavy weights (supplies, people, etc.) up walls and steep slopes. Hoists of this type rely on people to furnish the lift. A mechanical hoist can be built to almost any specifications, and the size of the load is limited only by the breaking point of the rope.

TL	*Vol*	*Weight*	*Price*	*Capacity*
1	20 liters+	10 kg+	Cr50+	500 kg+

Hoist, Powered: A powered hoist replaces the mechanical hoist around Tech Level 5-7. A power source (generator, engine, etc.) is required; this replaces the need for individuals to haul a load up by brute strength.

TL	*Vol*	*Weight*	*Price*	*Capacity*
8	40 liters+	25 kg+	Cr100+	1000 kg+

L

Lamp, Gas or Oil: Provides about 6 hours of light (and heat) and weighs 500 grams. Refills of oil or gas cost Cr2 each.

TL	*Vol*	*Weight*	*Price*
2	1 liter	0.5 kg	Cr10

Lantern, Cold Light: The flashlight provides three days of light (no heat) in continuous use.

TL	*Vol*	*Weight*	*Price*
6	0.5 liters	0.25 kg	Cr20

Locator, Inertial: Indicates direction and distance travelled from any pre-set starting location. Accurate to within one-tenth of the total distance travelled; may be carried on a belt or sling.

TL	*Vol*	*Weight*	*Price*
9	0.5 liters	1.5 kg	Cr1200

Lockpick Set: Allows picking of ordinary locks by a dexterous and skilled user. Lockpicks are illegal on most worlds; on such worlds the cost rises to Cr100 or more.

A lockpick set of a given Tech Level cannot be used against types of locks of higher Tech Levels, but it may be used against a lock of a higher Tech Level if it is equipped to deal with that type of lock. For example, a TL 6 kit cannot be used against electronic locks since these begin to appear at TL 7. However, the same kit could be used against a TL 7 deadbolt lock, albeit at a slight disadvantage; the difference in Tech Levels could be used as a DM to the success roll.

TL	*Vol*	*Weight*	*Price*
5	0.5 liters	0.25 kg	Cr10-100

Locks, Combination: A nested series of notched disks are rotated by a numbered out disk to points where a tumbler falls into each notch. These locks depend upon the large number of possible combinations for security. These are also available as padlocks.

TL	*Vol*	*Weight*	*Price*
5	0.05 liters	0.25 kg	Cr30

Locks, Electronic: Any of several types of locks that depend upon solid state circuitry to arm and disarm them. Most have an automatic locking device in the event of power failure; more expensive versions have their own power sources (either primary or backup). All electronic locks can be set to give selective access (that is to limit access of certain individuals to certain times of day, etc.).

Keypads are similar to combination locks in that a series of numbers or letters must be entered in order to open them. This lock usually takes the form of a terminal-like keyboard next to a door.

Magnetic readers recognize the coding imprinted on a magnetized strip. This coding is usually sealed in a plastic card.

Fingerprint readers contain a small sensor that recognizes the distinctive markings on the skin of a thumb pressed against a glass or plastic plate.

Voiceprint readers identify the distinctive tones of individual voices.

Retinal scanners identify the distinctive pattern of blood vessels in the retina of the eye.

Metabolic scanners are a sophisticated network of scanners and sensors which distinguish individuals by various physical and chemical characteristics (size, mass, retinal patterns, voice patterns, brainwaves, blood analysis, and so on). Some models may require a small sample of tissue (such as a hair or a drop of blood) to be deposited into the lock. More advanced versions require the user only to be near them.

	TL	Price
Keypad	7	Cr40
Magnetic reader	8	Cr50
Fingerprint reader	8	Cr50
Voiceprint reader	8	Cr75
Retinal scanner	9	Cr75
Metabolic scanner	9	Cr200

Locks, Tumbler: The first true locks, these work by moving small metal or plastic pins into sleeves measured to precise lengths. When the tumblers are moved the proper distances by a properly-shaped piece of metal, the latch is free to move. Two keys generally come with each lock; duplicates can be made for a few credits. Tumbler locks can be keyed to work for several different keys, allowing some keys to open a series of locks, others only one. Padlocks (small, readily portable versions of the tumbler lock) appear at Tech Level 5.

TL	Vol	Weight	Price
4	0.1 liters	0.25 kg	Cr25

M

Machete: Blade used in cutting vegetation to clear a path, campsite, etc.

TL	Vol	Weight	Price
4	2 liters	1 kg	Cr125

Map, Electronic: The "map box" is a compact (250 × 250 × 10mm, which expand to 1000 × 1000 × 10mm when opened) display system for computerized maps of a world. Scale may be adjusted. Most inhabited planets have mapclips (diskettes until Tech Level 13, holocrystals at higher levels) available for Cr150. When not available, two orbital sweeps of the world are required to obtain the necessary photographs to construct a map chip. Blank mapclips are available for Cr30.

TL	Vol	Weight	Price
9	1 liter	1 kg	Cr2500

Mask, Face: Various types of masks are available; they permit clear vision underwater. In addition, if chemicals in the water are particularly irritating or dangerous (by the effect of pollutants, an atmospheric taint, or some other condition imposed by the referee), a mask is necessary to prevent damage to the eyes.

The simplest types of face mask appear at Tech 5; more sophisticated models, ones that are rigged for full head coverage to permit the use of radio or other special gear, appear at Tech Level 7.

TL	Vol	Weight	Price
5	0.5 liters	0.25 kg	Cr20
7	0.75 liters	0.5 kg	Cr75

Mask, Filter: A filter set which allows an individual to breathe tainted atmospheres.

TL	Vol	Weight	Price
3	1 liter	0.5 kg	Cr10

Mask, Protective: For use in irritant atmospheres, the protective mask covers the wearer's mouth, nose, and eyes, and it hooks up to an oxygen supply, which makes it ideal for use in atmospheres containing mild amounts of ammonia, sulfur compounds, or minimal amounts of chlorine.

TL	Vol	Weight	Price
6	1 liter	0.5 kg	Cr25

Mechanical Tool Set: Includes basic tools necessary to repair and alter mechanical devices, including vehicles and guns.

TL	Vol	Weight	Price
5	30 liters	20 kg	Cr1000

Medical Kit: A modern first aid and medical treatment kit containing drugs, surgical supplies, and diagnostic materials for use by doctors and emergency medical technicians. This medical kit is sufficient for both minor and serious wounds, and it can be used for the treatment of animal injuries, radiation burns, chemical burns, poisoning, and drug overdoses.

TL	Vol	Weight	Price
7	20 liters	10 kg	Cr1000

Medical Scanner, Computer: This larger, handheld version of the pocket med scanner (below) takes rapid readings just like its smaller cousin, and thus it greatly reduces the time spent on a medical diagnosis task. The larger scanner differs from the pocket version in that this handheld model includes a complete expert system diagnosis computer, which allows individuals with little or no medical skill to diagnose and treat illness and injury.

TL	Vol	Weight	Price
12	2 liters	1 kg	Cr25,000

Medical Scanner, Pocket: The pocket med scanner is an indispensable device in the satchel of any physician. Medical skill is not needed to operate the scanner, but the skill is necessary to properly interpret the readings. A doctor or nurse needs only to press against the patient's chest with the small disk-shaped probe. In five to ten seconds, the scanner accurately determines body temperature, blood pressure, pulse rate, respiration rate, level of neural activity, and fluid balance. This useful device greatly reduces the time needed to make a medical diagnosis task. The scanner probe can actually be used anywhere on the subject's body, but no respiration rate is available apart from the chest site.

Once the reading is made, pressing a small button on the

device records the values in the scanner's memory. These records can be called up later for review. Setpoints on the scanner can be keyed in, so if readings reach a certain level (either high or low), the scanner beeps to alert the attending physician. Small adhesive pads are used to attach the scanner temporarily to the chest for this purpose.

The med scanner is optimized for use on a given race, so using it on members of another alien race does not work. An individual skilled in electronics and medicine could, however, try to modify a particular device to work accurately for another species. (One exception to this rule does exist: the same device can be used for humans and Vargr.)

Vacc suits at Tech Level 12 and above are designed with special contact points to allow a med scanner to be used without requiring removal of the suit.

TL	*Vol*	*Weight*	*Price*
12	0.2 liters	0.1 kg	Cr10,500

Metalwork Tool Set: Includes basic tools necessary for metalworking, welding, and shaping. Metalwork may include the construction and repair of shelters, vehicle bodywork, and alteration of metal structural items.

TL	*Vol*	*Weight*	*Price*
4	50 liters	50 kg	Cr1500

Mirror, Return: A device consisting of several mirrors in combination such that they will reflect any incoming beam exactly 180 degrees within a field of 15 degrees. Largely a curiosity, the mirror is used in laser surveying.

TL	*Vol*	*Weight*	*Price*
9	15 liters	20 kg	Cr500

Mirror, Signal: A simple hand-held mirror which can be used to reflect sunlight and thus catch the attention of a distant observer. Signal mirrors can be improvised out of any reflective material; purchased mirrors will include a small sighting hole that enables the signaller to direct the flashes of light from the mirror at a particular target such as a passing aircraft.

TL	*Vol*	*Weight*	*Price*
2	0.2 liters	0.25 kg	Cr10

Mountaineer's Kit: A general collection of useful gear applicable to most mountaineering situations. It includes any type of equipment not specifically described elsewhere which would customarily be used by climbers in sufficient quantities to be used on a climb of average difficulty.

TL	*Vol*	*Weight*	*Price*
4	4 liters	2 kg	Cr100

N

Navigator, Inertial: A small (10cm × 6 cm × 1 cm) inertial navigation computer which allows the user to backtrack on his path by "remembering" movements and turns. Switched on at the point from which the user sets out, it will allow him to find his way back later from any distance. A simple math function can also allow the user to determine a straight line distance and direction to his starting point no matter where he is.

TL	*Vol*	*Weight*	*Price*
8	0.2 liters	0.15 kg	Cr1500
10			Cr750

O

Oxygen Rebreather: A closed-circuit SCUBA system which uses a chemical charge to absorb exhaled carbon dioxide and reclaim oxygen. The system functions for 6-8 hours before a fresh charge of chemicals is required. There is little advanced warning of exhaustion of the chemicals, so dives of longer than 6 hours are risky. A charge of chemicals costs Cr100.

TL	*Vol*	*Weight*	*Price*
8	8 liters	4 kg	Cr2000

P

Parachute: The parachute is a large canopy of cloth or other material held to the jumper's body by lines attached to a harness. The simple parachute affords only a small degree of control of the direction and rate of descent, for it is largely at the mercy of wind and drift effects.

Parachutes can use either static cord release (the chute is tripped automatically as the individual jumps) or ripcord release (either activated by the individual or by an automatic device preset for a given altitude). A static cord jump must be made from a minimum of 100 meters altitude and results in immediate deployment of the chute. The ripcord deployment requires 200 meters minimum altitude, but it also permits jumps from much greater altitudes with the chute opening delayed until the 200 meter level is reached.

A basic parachute weighs 10-15 kilograms; when packed, it fits into a pack worn either on the back or the front of the jumper's body. Many parachute packs incorporate a reserve parachute for use in case of faulty deployment of the main chute.

TL	*Vol*	*Weight*	*Price*
4	20 liters	15 kg	Cr250

Parachute, Grav: Utilizing a basic grav technology, the grav chute is a compromise between the expense of grav equipment and the basic problems of regular parachutes. A simple grav module capable of nullifying a portion of the individual's body weight (but not of providing motive power, as with the grav belt) is worn as part of the chute harness; a conventional parawing is also deployed. Because the grav module can alter the effective weight of the jumper, it can be used to reduce the distance required for chute deployment by a factor of roughly three-fourths (thus chute deployment is not necessary until an altitude of about 50 meters). Varying the grav setting can also be used to alter the rate of descent, which is a particularly useful ability when staging a military raid.

The grav chute cannot fully offset body weight (normally) and certainly cannot provide lift; the small size of the power pack and the nature of the grav module itself will not permit this.

The parawing is used for steering, to back up the module in case of failure, and is necessary to check the final portion of the descent. It is virtually impossible for a jumper to miss a given target area using a grav chute.

The power pack is capable of operation for a total of five minutes. Power packs can be recharged from the usual power services or replaced at a cost of Cr500.

TL	*Vol*	*Weight*	*Price*
10	15 liters	15 kg	Cr2500

Parawing: More sophisticated than the parachute, the parawing is an airfoil-shaped chute which permits much more control of the descent. Hitting a given target area is easier with a parawing; other performance characteristics are as for the parachute.

Parawings are lighter but somewhat more expensive than standard parachutes. A ripcord release is standard for parawing chutes.

TL	*Vol*	*Weight*	*Price*
7	5 liters	5 kg	Cr400

Pitons: Pitons are metal spikes fitted with a ring at one end with (to pass a rope through), which are used in mountain climbing as a hold. Several specific types are available.

The simplest pitons (Tech Level 4) are soft iron spikes driven into rock. An advanced version, available at Tech Level 7, is of similar design but uses superior alloys.

At Tech 8, pitons have a radical design: they are not driven into rock at all, but use a quick-setting superglue to attach themselves to rock faces. Once set, they cannot be removed without using special solvents; however, use of these pitons doubles ascent speeds. The solvent weighs 0.5kg (500 applications) and costs Cr20.

The ultimate in pitons, the sophisticated devices at Tech Level 10 include a small battery pack and a powerful heating element in the tip. When activated, a sudden white-hot burst of heat helps set the piton with a minimum of effort (just steady pressure by the climber).

TL	*Vol*	*Weight*	*Price*
4	0.1 liters	0.3 kg	Cr5
7	0.1 liters	0.2 kg	Cr6
8	0.1 liters	0.2 kg	Cr6
10	0.1 liters	0.3 kg	Cr10

Psionic Shield Helmet: Battery powered helmet creating a weak electrical field at human brainwave frequencies; psionic-talented individuals perceive this as static, which prevents undesirable telepathic influences or psionic assaults. The helmet gives little physical protection, but it gives the wearer and automatic psionic strength rating of 15 (for purposes of defense against psionic assault only). Shielded individuals cannot be detected by characters possessing life detection, nor can they receive telempathic or telepathic suggestions, nor can they be probed or have their thoughts read. The electronics of a psionic shield helmet are relatively simple, but one can break down or be sabotaged; a small meter on the unit allows testing of the helmet's effectiveness.

TL	*Vol*	*Weight*	*Price*
12	0.5 liters	1 kg	Cr4000
13	0.5 liters	—	Cr4000

R

Respirator: A small compressor which allows an individual to breathe in very thin atmospheres.

TL	*Vol*	*Weight*	*Price*
5	1 liter	0.5 kg	Cr100

Rope: Rope is a versatile tool that has no real replacement even at higher tech levels. It is the single most important element of a climber's equipment; it can be used to bind prisoners; it can add safety to water or ravine crossings. A variety of types and sizes are available; in general, however, they are all similar in reliability and price within any given tech level.

TL	*Size*	*Weight*	*Price*
5	10 meters	3 kg	Cr20
10	10 meters	1 kg	Cr10
15	10 meters	0.5 kg	Cr10

S

Satellite, Navigational: A small satellite placed in synchronous orbit over the hemisphere where exploration is taking place. It provides moment-by-moment information on the precise location of a tracking unit on the ground with an accuracy of 1 meter or less. For twice the size and price listed below, the satellite can relay the tracking unit (which would then include a TV-like viewscreen) to a plot projected on an accurate map of the region, which is created by the satellite through a combination of laser and radar mapping techniques.

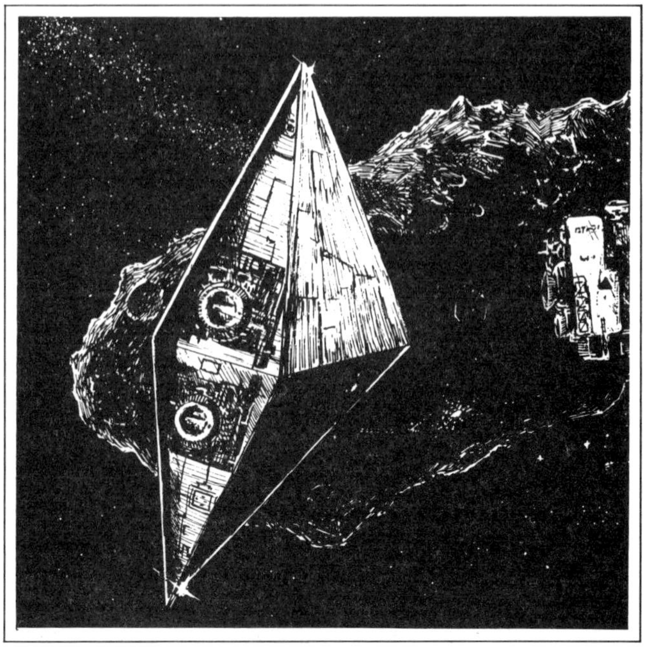

A small nuclear power plant provides over a year of operation without servicing, and the satellite can be retrieved and used over and over.

TL	Vol	Weight	Price
9	300 liters	100 kg	Cr35,000

Sensor, NAS, Portable, and NAS Handset: Developed from Tech Level 12 psionic helmet theory, the neural activity sensor (NAS) was first used medically. It remotely detects the electrical activity of a life form's central nervous system and classifies it according to amount and complexity. The data system compares the activity pattern to known types of life, especially intelligent life.

The portable unit has a range of 500 meters (very long). It consists of a backpack and a handset with a retractable parabolic dish focuser. The handset in fact is not attached to the backpack, and it can be operated up to 100 m distant, which further extends the range.

	TL	Vol	Weight	Price
NAS Backpack	15	20 liters	10 kg	Cr15,000
NAS Handset	15	.5 liters	0.3 kg	Cr20,000

Shoes, Rock: Lightweight, sturdy shoes specifically designed for stability, these are very useful to lead climbers ascending walls and steep slopes where toeholds must be constantly sought.

TL	Vol	Weight	Price
4	—	0.5 kg	Cr10

"Sniffer" Bioscanner: The bioscanner "sniffer" scans for evidence of biological/metabolic activity in the area. It is a highly advanced combination sampler/analyzer. The Tech Level 15 sniffer is a breakthrough in molecular analysis the device: provides both improved analysis speed and a cheaper price than sniffers of Tech Level 14 and less. Not only is the bioscanner useful for biological studies, but it also helps with regular chemical analysis. (A cheaper and smaller Tech Level 15 chemical analyzer is available, but it is not very useful for biological scanning).

The portable Tech Level 15 unit listed here incorporates both analyzer and collector into one. It has two modes and corresponding equipment: one mode for mass sampling of atmospheric content and the other for minute sampling.

The evidence of biological activity must be within short range of the scanner, for anything beyond short range is undetectable. The bioscanner helps a user to recognize or categorize evidence of familiar and unfamiliar organisms, which allows ecological classification, determination of potential hazards to other life forms, and estimation of potential uses (form of food, commercially valuable).

TL	Vol	Weight	Price
15	8 liters	3.5 kg	Cr350,000

Snorkel: A snorkel is a small tube which permits the diver to submerge completely but continue to breathe as long as the end of the snorkel is above water. There are many sizes of snorkels, but since these are all under 40 cm tall, once a snorkel gets past that length, the air exchange is not sufficient to support the diver.

TL	Vol	Weight	Price
5	0.5 liters	0.1 kg	Cr5

Snowshoes: Large, somewhat awkward, but highly effective, snowshoes permit a character to increase speed over snow by 50 percent.

TL	Vol	Weight	Price
1	4 liters	1 kg	Cr60

Solar 'Vaporator: A device which collects moisture from the air, especially at night. Yield is 2 liters per 24 hours in standard or dense atmospheres, 1 liter per 24 hours in thin atmospheres, and .5 liter per 24 hours in very thin atmospheres. The 'vaporator is stored in a compact (50 cm × 20 cm × 20 cm) package, but it unfolds (an operation requiring 5 minutes) to 200 cm × 10 cm × 50 cm and stands on a tripod which takes up 1 square meter.

If the 'vaporator is not running throughout an entire 24 hour period, partial yields can be calculated by assuming that 3 times as much water can be collected at night as during the day (0.5 liter during the day on a standard on a standard atmosphere planet, 1.5 liter at night).

Solar panels provide power directly during the day and accumulate and store power for operation at night.

TL	Vol	Weight	Price
10	See above	8 kg	Cr1250

Still, Fusion: A bulky device which breaks water molecules free from material placed within it. The amount of water delivered will vary with the type of material fed to the still, but ranges from 1% for very dry sand to 70% for organic material such as wood, plants, or bodies. This percentage of weight in kilograms gives a one-to-one yield of water in liters (thus, 100 kg of sand will yield 1 liter of water). The still requires 1 hour to set up, and 30 minutes for each 10 kg of material processed; the hopper must be cleaned out after each load, which requires another 30 minutes.

TL	Vol	Weight	Price
13	150 liters	60 kg	Cr4500

Suit Air Conditioner: A cooling unit designed to function in hot atmospheres like the suit heater functions in cold.

TL	Vol	Weight	Price
8	6 liters	3 kg	Cr200

Suit, Desert Survival: Cover-all garment with shiny outer surface which prevents major water loss in the desert. The wearer is cooled through evaporation of perspiration, but a series of traps and chemical filters condenses and purifies lost body liquid and stores it as pure water in pouches within the suit. A hood, goggles, and breathing mask (which traps moisture exhaled through the nose and mouth) are included. The chemical filters must be changed once a month, at a cost of Cr50.

Besides keeping the wearer comfortable in sweltering conditions, the suit supplies one liter of water every three daytime hours, and one liter every night.

The suit has certain disadvantages. At Tech Level 11 and lower, the bulkiness of the suit causes a loss to Dexterity. Also, the suit is extremely shiny, which makes it almost impossible for the wearer to sneak up on anyone, even in rocky terrain. (This last disadvantage could be an advantage for characters lost in the desert who are hoping to be spotted by aircraft.)

Note that vacc suits and combat armor will also, by their very nature, provide complete protection for desert travellers, at least as long as their air supply holds out.

TL	*Vol*	*Weight*	*Price*
9	20 liters	5 kg	Cr7000
13	5 liters	—	Cr9000

Suit, Dry: The dry suit, unlike the wet suit, is a completely watertight garment. Because of this, the dry suit is considerably warmer since cold water is not circulating through the suit. Wearing clothing under the dry suit is possible and will improve the insulation value, but doing so will also further reduce movement. If the suit is ever torn, the insulation value is reduced to that of a poor wet suit within minutes. The dry suit has one additional advantage in that a buoyancy control device is not needed since the entire suit can be used as one.

TL	*Vol*	*Weight*	*Price*
7	3 liters	3 kg	Cr300

Suit, Heated: See Heatsuit.

Suit, Heated Dry: An advanced-exposure diving suit, the heated dry suit utilizes heating coils built into the suit proper to heat the diver in extremely cold temperatures. (If it's warm enough not to be frozen, it's warm enough to swim in wearing a heated dry suit.)

Disadvantages of the suit include the extreme infrared signature, which makes detection of a diver extremely easy, and the possibility of a short circuit if the suit is damaged. Batteries, worn in a belt pouch, provide six hours of operation before recharge or replacement becomes necessary. Available at Tech Level 8, the suit is of negligible weight. An improved model, available at Tech Level 10, does not short circuit when penetrated, and the batteries last 12 hours.

TL	*Vol*	*Weight*	*Price*
8	3 liters	—	Cr650
10	1 liter	—	Cr800

Suit Heater: A suit heating unit to combat the effects of low-temperature corrosive and insidious atmospheres. Without a heater, a protective suit is worthless in these conditions.

TL	*Vol*	*Weight*	*Price*
8	6 liters	3 kg	Cr250

Suit, Protective: Protects against corrosive atmospheres. The protective suit is sealed, air-conditioned, and has its own air supply (good for six hours). The suit has no water supply of its own, nor will it protect the wearer once the air supply gives out, but so long as it works, the wearer will not suffer the ill effects of the outside environment.

TL	*Vol*	*Weight*	*Price*
6	8 liters	7 kg	Cr1000

Suit, Protective, Heavy: Protects against insidious atmospheres. In other respects, it is similar to the protective suit.

TL	*Vol*	*Weight*	*Price*
7	10 liters	7 kg	Cr1400

Suit, Wet: A nylon-lined, foam-insulated neoprene outfit designed to reduce the effects of cold water. Water is permitted to soak into the suit, but the insulation is designed to keep heat loss from becoming a problem. Several types are available, which are listed here in decreasing order of protection against extreme cold conditions. See also Dry Suit.

	TL	*Vol*	*Weight*	*Price*
Cold Water	8	—	—	Cr100
Advanced	8	—	—	Cr75
Light	7	—	—	Cr40
Standard	6	—	—	Cr60

Survival Bubble: A large (2m diameter) plastic sphere with alternating clear and opaque panels, and a small oxygen tank (capable of supporting one person for two hours) for inflation. Access to the interior is through a conforming plastic seal which functions similarly to an air lock. The bubble can be used for life support in a vacuum (it can be moved by walking on the

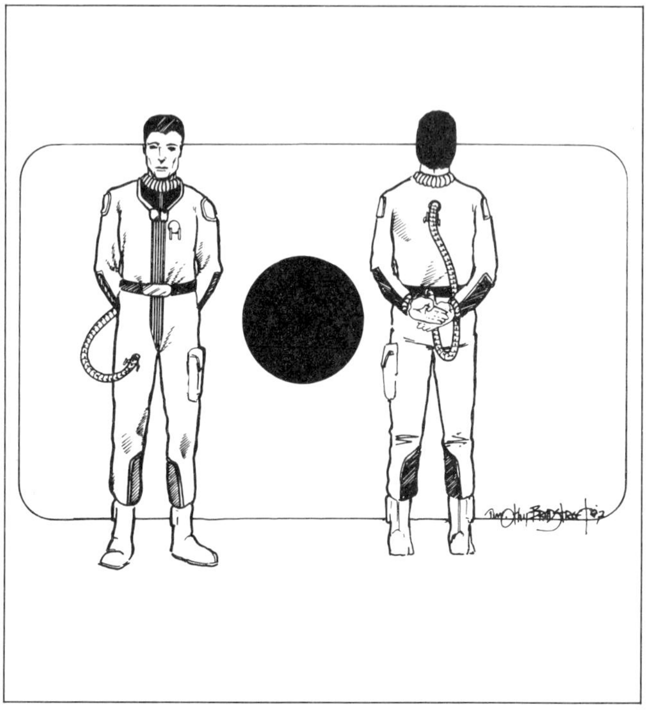

inside, treadmill fashion), and it can also be used for protection against weather or as a lifeboat on a sea surface.

TL	*Vol*	*Weight*	*Price*
9	3000 liters	3 kg	Cr600

Swim Fins: Fins increase a diver's speed in the water without exerting extra effort.

TL	*Vol*	*Weight*	*Price*
3	1 liter	0.5 kg	Cr15

Swimming Equipment: Includes swim fins, wet suit, face mask.

TL	*Vol*	*Weight*	*Price*
3	3 liters	1 kg	Cr200

T

Tarpaulin: A canvas or waterproof cloth sheet used for temporary shelter, measuring 2 by 4 meters.

TL	*Vol*	*Weight*	*Price*
1	4 liters	2 kg	Cr10

Tarpaulin, Reflectorized: An aluminized sheet which reduces incoming radiation by reflection, measuring 5 by 10 meters.

TL	*Vol*	*Weight*	*Price*
7	2 liters	1 kg	Cr400

Tent: Basic shelter for two persons. Tent: Larger, more elaborate tents weigh and cost more.

TL	*Vol*	*Weight*	*Price*
2	6 liters	3 kg	Cr200

Tent, Pressure: Basic shelter for two persons, which provides standard atmosphere. There is no airlock: the tent must be depressurized to enter or leave.

TL	*Vol*	*Weight*	*Price*
7	30 liters	25 kg	Cr2,000

Torches: Each lasts about 20 minutes.

TL	*Vol*	*Weight*	*Price*
1	1 liter	0.25 kg	Cr1

Torches, Electric: Each lasts about six hours in continuous use.

TL	*Vol*	*Weight*	*Price*
5	1 liter	0.5 kg	Cr10

Translators, Language: With the incredible diversity of cultures and languages found throughout the Imperium and neighboring regions, computer language translators (CLTs) have become a fundamental element of interstellar trade and communication. Dozens of models of various abilities, complexity, and price can be purchased on worlds throughout the Imperium of Tech Level 9 or better.

The basis of all portable CLTs is a program package called a memclip. Each memclip contains programming for one language. Typically, these clips can be purchased with preloaded language programs for between Cr100 and Cr150. Blank memclip can be bought for Cr10 and programmed by duplicating a preloaded program.

All CLTs work in the same manner. Two entities, each with a CLT and memclips for both his own and the other's language, adjust their units until they share a common radio frequency. Each speaks in his own language and his words are translated by the other's CLT and relayed to a detachable remote speaker worn in the receiving entity's ear. With practice, anyone can learn to follow the translation as the other individual speaks.

More than 700 languages are on memclips. Programs even exist for non-aural languages. The CLT can be carried in a hip pouch or by hand. CLTs have two to eight receptacles for memclips, plus the remote speaker. Prices vary. A standard CLT can be purchased for Cr2000. More expensive units have program correction features, more complete handling of idiomatic phrases, smaller size, bone implant speakers, greater durability, and a large capacity for multilanguage conversations.

TL	*Vol*	*Weight*	*Price*
12	1 liter	0.5 kg	Cr2000

W

Wall Patches: Steel-backed plastic patches faced with adhesive, activated by peeling off a backing and placing the patch over a hole or leak. These will serve for several days.

TL	*Vol*	*Weight*	*Price*
10	1 liter	4 kg	Cr150

Water Filtration/Distillation Unit: Purifies water for drinking. The unit includes a distilling plant, filters, and purification tablets.

TL	*Vol*	*Weight*	*Price*
7	4 liter	1 kg	Cr75

Water Purification Kit: A bottle of 250 tablets to make contaminated water safe. One tablet in 1 liter will render water safe in 30 minutes. Tech Level = 5+. Reliability: NA at Tech Level 7 of higher; reliability equals Tech Level if tablets are over 6 months old at Tech Level 5 or 6. Weight: Negligible. Price: Cr5.

TL	*Vol*	*Weight*	*Price*
5	—	—	Cr5

Weight Belt: A weight belt compensates for buoyancy. The weight of the belt itself is negligible.

TL	*Vol*	*Weight*	*Price*
5	—	See above	Cr25

DRUGS

A variety of pharmacological developments are available to travellers for medicinal (and other) purposes.

Drug availability, reliability, and price vary considerably from world to world depending upon the local law and Tech Levels.

Medicinal Drugs: Four types of drugs are useful in preventing or treating contagious diseases: vaccines, antitoxins, antibiotics and metabolics. They can generally be obtained only from a physician or with a physician's prescription on worlds with high law levels, but they are generally available at retail on worlds with low law levels. Since all are administered by injection, they must be given by a character with some skill in medicine.

Vaccines: First appearing at Tech Level 5, these help prevent illness if administered once per year by reducing both the chance of contracting a disease and the severity of any disease caught. Vaccines against a single disease are available for Cr15 per inoculation. Vaccines that prevent several similar diseases on the world where they are produced are available at Tech Level of 10 or above for Cr20 per inoculation. A separate vaccine must be taken for each disease. Antiviral vaccines are available at Tech Level 10 as well.

Antitoxins: At Tech Level 6, antitoxins hasten recovery by combating poisons generated by microorganisms which have infected the patient, again by reducing both the severity and duration of illness. Antitoxins can also help if the patient is in a coma. Antitoxins must be administered once a day throughout the duration of the illness at a cost of Cr20 per injection. Antitoxins are disease-specific, and each affects only one disease.

Antibiotics: At Tech Level 6, these drugs attack the microorganisms that have invaded the body and thus hasten recovery while lessening severity. While generally effective, antibiotics have drawbacks: they may not be effective against the specific microorganisms in a patient's body, and they sometimes cause allergic reactions. Antibiotics have a cost of Cr50 per injection, and they must be taken once per day during illness.

Metabolics: First used at Tech Level 8, these are extremely expensive drugs similar to interferon, which are effective against a wide spectrum of diseases. They function by altering the metabolism of the patient, and they enable the patient's body to resist the disease by reducing both the severity and duration of illness. They are always effective, but they are not always available, even on high tech worlds. Metabolics must be taken once per day of illness at Cr1000 per injection.

Nonmedicinal Drugs: Each of the following drugs has its own advantages and disadvantages; users should be aware of the effects. For the sake of uniformity and ease of use, all are available in consistent, one-dose pill form. Other drugs not listed here may be available in a variety of forms and dosages.

If more than one drug is taken at a time, the combination may cause an adverse reaction in the individual and result in injury or death. The use or possession of certain drugs may be restricted by local law.

Slow Drug: So named because it makes the universe (from the user's viewpoint) appear to move more slowly, the drug achieves the effect by accelerating the user's metabolism. In effect, the user lives approximately twice as fast as normal.

Slow drug takes effect 45 seconds after ingestion and continues to function for about 10 minutes. At the end of its effect, the user receives 1D in wounds. The person is extremely fatigued, is treated as if all available combat swings have been taken, and must recover from that fatigue. A person under slow drug (because he or she is living at twice the normal rate) can make twice as many actions or move twice as far as normal.

A medical slow drug is also available, which is used to hasten recovery from wounds or illness. One dose causes unconsciousness and the passage of thirty days equivalent recovery time in one day. During this period, ordinary healing takes place. No wounds are received from the use of medical slow drug, but the individual is unconscious or semi-conscious while under its influence.

Fast Drug: So named because it makes the universe (to its user) appear to move much more quickly, the drug slows down personal metabolism at a ratio of approximately 60 to 1. Users are extremely vulnerable while living at such a slow rate, but physical aging is also slowed, and the need for consumable supplies is reduced which thus allows conservation of air and food. Fast drug takes effect immediately upon ingestion; one dose lasts for 60 days, making that time appear to be only one day.

Combat Drug: Taken by fighters (usually military personnel) prior to combat, this drug increases personal strength and endurance. The effect begins 30 seconds after being taken and lasts for about 10 minutes. When the effect wears off, the user suffers 1D in wounds.

Anagathics: Drugs which counteract the aging process: supposedly, a regimen of regular monthly doses enables an individual to ignore the debilitating effects of advancing years. Because of the rarity and demand for anagathics, they are quite expensive and are often unavailable at any price. More details on the use of anagathics can be found in the *Players' Manual*.

Truth Drug: Used to compel individuals to answer interrogation truthfully, one dose is sufficient to assure truthful answers for approximately two minutes, after which the user experiences one hour of unconsciousness, and suffers 2D in wounds.

Antidotes: Available for both slow and fast drugs, these immediately cancel their major effects: the individual is returned to the normal rate of living, but still suffers any indicated recovery requirements.

DRUGS TABLE

Drug	*Per Dose*
Slow Drug	Cr500
Medical Slow	Cr100
Fast Drug	Cr200
Combat Drug	Cr750
Anagathics	Cr20,000
Truth Drug	Cr5000
Slow Drug Antidote	Cr600
Fast Drug Antidote	Cr900

VACC SUITS

The rigors of alien environments contrast with shipboard conditions. When people face extremes of temperature, pressure, and atmospheric composition, a vacc suit is the principal survival tool. At lower Tech Levels, these are unwieldy and uncomfortable, but they become lighter and more flexible with each technological advance. At the higher Tech Levels, the suits provide improved armor protection. At an additional cost, suits may be made self-sealing at Tech Level 13. At Tech Level 15, all suits are self-sealing. Vacc suits consist of suit, gloves, boot, and standard helmet; they protect against temperatures from +100° C to -110° C and pressures of up to 5 atm.

At Tech Level 14, tailored vacc suits become available. These include a soft helmet which is more comfortable but is wasteful of air supply: PLSS air supply duration is divided by two. Other advantages of a tailored suit are style and status.

At Tech Level 10, holographic heads-up displays become common in hard-helmet suits. The display shows the condition of the suit and the current battery level and air supply.

GENERAL PURPOSE VACC SUITS

TL	*Armor*	*Volume*	*Weight*	*Price*	*Encumbrance to Dexterity*
9	Cloth	3.6 kliters	8 kg	Cr7000	-3
10	Cloth	2.7 kliters	6 kg	Cr7000	-3
11	Cloth	1.8 kliters	4 kg	Cr7000	-2
12	Cloth-1	0.9 kliters	2 kg	Cr7000	-1
13	Cloth-1	0.5 kliters	—	Cr7000	
Self-Seal Option			1 kg	+Cr6000	-1
14	Cloth-2	0.2 kliters	—	Cr7000	
Self-Seal Option			0.5 kg	Cr5000	
15	Cloth-2	0.2 kliters	—	Cr9000	

TAILORED VACC SUITS

TL	*Armor*	*Volume*	*Weight*	*Price*	*Encumbrance to Dexterity*
14	Cloth-2	0.2 kliters	—	Cr9000	—
Self-Seal Option			0.5 kg	+Cr5000	—
15	Cloth-2	0.1 kliters	—	Cr10,000	—

HOSTILE ENVIRONMENT VACC SUITS

TL	*Armor*	*Volume*	*Weight*	*Price*	*Encumbrance to Dexterity*
8	Cloth-2	3.8 kliters	35 kg	Cr12,000	-3
9	Cloth-1	3.8 kliters	40 kg	Cr16,000	-3
12	Cbt armor-2	3.0 kliters	40 kg	Cr18,000	-3
13	Cbt armor-1	2.0 kliters	10 kg	Cr20,000	-3
14	Cbt armor	2.6 kliters	25 kg	Cr150,000	-2

ACCESSORIES

Portable life support systems (PLSS) are a necessity; they can be purchased with different supplies of air. Batteries power the air supply recycler achieve capacity; a recharge lasts as long as the PLSS oxygen supply. Lighter tanks with greater pressure are available at higher Tech Levels.

PORTABLE LIFE SUPPORT SYSTEMS

TL	*Type*	*Tanks*	*Duration*	*Volume*	*Weight*	*Price*
9	A	2 std	4 hours	11	7 kg	Cr3000
9	B	3 std	24 hrs (recycle)	20	14.5 kg	Cr5000
9	C	6 std	48 hrs (recycle)	55	29 kg	Cr8000
12	A	1 HP	4 hours	7	4 kg	Cr3000
12	B	1 HP	24 hrs (recycle)	16	11 kg	Cr5000
12	C	2 HP	48 hrs (recycle)	30	18 kg	Cr8000
14	A	1 UHP	12 hrs (recycle)	1.5	0.5 kg	Cr3000
14	B	2 UHP	24 hrs (recycle)	3.5	2 kg	Cr5000
14	C	4 UHP	48 hrs (recycle)	7	3.5 kg	Cr8000

OXYGEN TANKS

TL	*Type*	*Volume*	*Weight*	*Price*	*Refill*
5	Standard	5	2.5 kg	Cr500	Cr10
12	High-Pressure	4	2.0 kg	Cr400	Cr10
14	Ultra High-Pressure	1	0.5 kg	Cr200	Cr10

HARD BUBBLE HELMETS

TL	*Special Features*	*Volume*	*Weight*	*Price*
8	None	14	2 kg	Cr800
14	Integral Heads-Up Display	10	1 kg	Cr1200

Miscellaneous Accessories

Magnetic grips, handheld or fastened on boots, can make movement easier in low-gravity situations.

Suit patches come in handy in the event of a vacc suit breach. They are unnecessary for small holes on self-sealing suits.

The thermal-meteoroid garment is a hooded, coverall-like garment added over the top of a regular vacc suit. It lessens the risk from micrometeoroids, and can be used to temporarily "harden" a soft suit. It protects from +130° to -160°C.

The long range thruster pack (LRTP) is heavy, but it provides 2G acceleration for up to 48 hours, using standard starship fuel.

MISCELLANEOUS ACCESSORIES TABLE

TL	*Special Features*	*Volume*	*Weight*	*Price*
5	Magnetic Grips	0.5 liter	—	Cr20
7	Suit Patches (pack of 5)	0.2 liter	—	Cr2
8	Thermal-Meteoroid Garment (armor 6, cloth-1)	1 liter	—	Cr400
12	Long Range Thruster Pack	65 liters	38	Cr14,000

SPECIAL PURPOSE VACC SUITS

The body pressure suit is light and comfortable (no encumbrance to Dexterity) to work in for short periods of time under mildly hostile atmospheric conditions. It can be worn under clothes but is of no benefit in pressures less than 0.43 atm (thin atmosphere) without the vacuum belt. The suit protects against temperatures +50° C to -40° C and pressures up to 2.5 atm.

BODY PRESSURE SUIT

TL	*Special Features*	*Volume*	*Weight*	*Price*
10	Armor as Jack	0.2	—	Cr12,500
10	Gloves, Helmet	16		
	Air Charge (20 min)	0.75	—	Cr250
10	Vacuum Belt	2	1.5	Cr2500

Combat Equipment

All reasonable people agree that persuasion and negotiation are the preferable means of reaching agreement and compromise. Once logic and persuasion fail, however, those same reasonable people find that weapons and armor constitute their primary means of achieving goals. Weapons are also essential for self-defense. Commonly available weapons, weapon accessories, and armor are described in detail here. Specific characteristics (price, Tech Level, weight) for this equipment are contained in the weapons chart.

HAND-TO-HAND WEAPONS

The following hand weapons are generally available on most worlds; their availability may be restricted, however, on higher Law Level worlds.

Natural Weapons: Natural weapons (such as hands or teeth) are an intrinsic part of the fighting individual. In addition, clubs are typically freely available.

Club: Clubs cost nothing, generally weigh from 0.5 to 3 kg, and can be found in the area where hand-to-hand combat takes place. For example, a bottle may be used as a club (only once, however—after one use it becomes a dagger minus one).

Small Blades: The following edged weapons cover the range of small blades which are available. Small blade weapons are effective only at close and short range, but they may also be thrown.

Dagger: A small knife weapon with a flat, two-edged blade approximately 200 mm in length. Daggers are usually carried in a belt sheath and less frequently are concealed in a boot sheath or strapped to the forearm. Daggers are usually the last weapon of defense, and they are worn constantly. The weight of a dagger does not count against the weight load of the character.

Blade: A hybrid knife weapon with a heavy, flat two-edged blade and a semibasket handguard. Because of the bulk of the handguard, it is generally carried in a belt scabbard.

Large Blades: The following edged weapons cover the range of large blades which are available. Large blade weapons are effective only at close and short range. Large blades may not be thrown.

Sword: The standard long-edged weapon, with a flat, two-edged blade. It may have a basket hilt or hand protector. A scabbard to carry the sword may be attached to the belt or to straps (or a sash) over the shoulder.

Cutlass: A heavy, flat-bladed, single-edged weapon featuring a full basket hilt to protect the hand. The cutlass is the standard shipboard blade weapon and is usually kept in brackets on the bulkhead near important locations; when worn, a belt scabbard is used.

Broadsword: The largest of the sword weapons, also called the two-handed sword because it requires both hands to swing. The blade is extremely heavy and two-edged. The hilt is relatively simple, generally only a crosspiece with little basketwork or protection. When carried, the broadsword is worn in a scabbard attached to the belt; less frequently, the scabbard is worn on the back, and the broadsword is drawn over the shoulder.

Foil: The foil is a specific duelling weapon designed for fighting others also armed with foils. Also called the rapier, this weapon is a light, sword-like weapon with a pointed, edged blade and a basket or cup hilt to protect the hand. A foil is worn in a belt scabbard. (A foil is effective only at close and short range. A foil may not be thrown.)

Axes: Below are the special edged weapons known as axes, which are generally available. Axes are effective only at close and short range, but they may also be thrown.

Hand Axe: A weapon with a flat-bladed head mounted on a handle. The flat head is blunt on one edge and has a sharp-bladed edge on the other. An axe is worn on the belt.

Battle Axe: A weapon with a large, flat-bladed head mounted on a hefty handle. The flat head has two sharp-bladed edges.

A battle axe is worn on the belt in a special sling made for that purpose.

Polearms: The following polearms are generally available. In most cases, they will be in the hands of non-player characters encountered in the process of an adventure. Polearms are effective at close and short range.

Bayonet: A knife-like weapon similar to a dagger or blade. When not attached to a rifle, a bayonet is treated as a dagger (or blade) and can carried in a belt scabbard. When attached to the muzzle of a rifle (not a carbine or autorifle), it transforms the gun into a polearm.

Spear: A long polearm with a pointed tip, usually of metal. Often made by the soldier himself, the spear is quite inexpensive. A spear may be thrown.

Halberd: A quite elaborate polearm featuring a pointed, bladed tip. This weapon may be considered to be a combination of a battle axe and a spear. Halberds are often carried by Tech Level 2 guards.

Pike: A long polearm with some form of flat-bladed tip. Pikes are commonly carried as weapons by Tech Level 1 troops.

Staff/Cudgel: A basic stick which is used as a weapon. Staff/cudgels are easily obtained from standing trees or through the use of an unloaded long gun such as a rifle or carbine (laser weapons are too delicate to be used as cudgels more than once).

PERSONAL SLUG THROWERS

The following slug throwers are generally available on worlds of sufficient Tech Level; their availability is restricted, however, by the Law Level of the specific world. Slug throwers vary in effective range depending on their specific type; range limitations are shown in the combat charts.

All of the guns shown in this list (with the exception of the revolver) are autoloading weapons. Each automatically reloads the gun's chamber with a new cartridge after each shot. Only when the weapon's total capacity is exhausted must the shooter reload the gun with a new magazine. Although the revolver is not autoloading, it also contains a quantity of ammunition and need not be reloaded until its ammunition capacity is exhausted.

Unless noted otherwise, the weapons are semiautomatic; each fires one bullet or shot with each pull of the trigger. Automatic rifles and submachineguns are fully automatic with a burst control which allows the firing of four shots with each pull of the trigger. Fully automatic fire allows special effects with higher hit probabilities and a potential for group hits as detailed in the section on special considerations.

The section on special considerations also provides details on reloading weapons which have run out of ammunition.

Weights and prices for ammunition are for loaded magazines.

Revolver: An older variety of handgun, the revolver fires bullets with characteristics which are similar to those fired by the automatic pistol but not interchangeable with them. The revolver is a repeating handgun; it fires one shot with each pull of the trigger. It is not, however, semiautomatic, which depends on finger pressure to do the reloading. No magazine is used: six cartridges are inserted into the revolver individually. Reloading takes 30 seconds.

A revolver can be fitted with a silencer and a detachable shoulder stock.

Snub Pistol: The snub pistol is a low-velocity revolver designed for use on shipboard and in a zero-G environment. It fires 10mm, 7-gram bullets at velocities of 100 to 150 meters per second. No magazine is used: six individual cartridges are inserted into the revolver separately. Reloading takes one combat round, or two combat rounds if the firer is evading. Standard rounds include a tranquilizer round, gas round, high explosive round, and a high explosive-shaped charge round to defeat personal armor. The snub pistol is a standard shipboard security weapon generally loaded with five tranquilizers and one gas round.

More expensive pure combat versions of the snub pistol are available, generally in the automatic pistol configuration with extended magazines holding up to 20 rounds.

Body Pistol: A small, nonmetallic semiautomatic pistol designed to evade detection by most weapon detectors, including metal detectors and densitometers. It fires 5g projectiles at a velocity of 500 to 600 meters per second. A magazine containing six cartridges is located in the pistol handle. Body pistol ammunition is not interchangeable with the ammunition for any other types of guns.

A body pistol can be fitted with a silencer.

Autopistol: The basic semiautomatic handgun, which fires bullets at velocities of 400 to 500 meters per second. A magazine containing 15 cartridges fits into the handle of the pistol. Automatic pistol ammunition is interchangeable with submachinegun ammunition (although magazines are not).

An automatic pistol can be fitted with a silencer or a detachable shoulder stock.

Gauss Pistol: The gauss pistol is a popular weapon because of its silence and its deadliness. The gauss pistol is based on the same principle as the gauss rifle and the VRF gauss gun: an electromagnetic field accelerates the needle-like bullet down the barrel while a bias in the field imparts spin.

The gauss pistol may fire either single-round shots or four shot bursts. The pistol uses the same 4mm ammunition as the gauss rifle; however, the magazines are not interchangeable.

Carbine: A short type of semiautomatic rifle which fires a small caliber round at a velocity of 900 meters per second. A magazine containing 10 rounds is inserted into the underside of the carbine ahead of the trigger guard. Carbine ammunition is not interchangeable with any other type of ammunition.

In essence, a carbine is a short rifle which fires a cartridge of a smaller, lighter caliber. The carbine is a preferred weapon for individuals who otherwise do not handle firearms. Its light weight makes it convenient and efficient. A sling usually allows the carbine to be carried on the shoulder, where it is out of the way.

A carbine may be fitted with telescopic or electronic sight and with a folding stock.

Rifle: The standard semiautomatic military arm, which fires a bullet at a velocity of approximately 900 meters per second. Longer and heavier than a carbine, it is also more effective. Standard equipment includes provisions for attaching a bayonet, telescopic sight, and a shoulder sling.

A 20-round magazine is attached to the front of the rifle's trigger guard. Rifle ammunition may also be used in automatic rifles; rifle and autorifle magazines are interchangeable and weigh the same.

A rifle can be fitted with either telescopic or electronic sights or with a folding stock.

Autorifle: A highly refined and tuned version of the rifle, capable of fully automatic fire as well as semiautomatic shots. Normally, the automatic rifle fires in bursts of four bullets for each pull of the trigger. It may be switched to semiautomatic fire any time after firing, in which case it is treated as a rifle until switched back. Ammunition and magazines are identical to those used for the rifle.

The automatic rifle is equipped with a sling (which allows the weapon to be slung from an individual's shoulder while he carries it in the ready-to-fire position), a bipod, and a muzzle brake to steady the gun while firing. (See also the ammo belt below).

Gauss Rifle: The ultimate development of the slug thrower, the gauss rifle generates an electromagnetic field along the length of the barrel, which accelerates a 4mm, 4-gram needle bullet to velocities of 1500 meters per second. The round itself consists of a dense armor-piercing core surrounded by a softer metal covering that ends in a hollow point; this combination gives the round both high stopping power and a good armor-piercing capability. Flight along the barrel is nearly frictionless, for spin stabilization is imparted in this weapon through magnetic bias.

A 40-round magazine is attached behind the pistol grip, and each pull of the trigger fires one, four, or 10 rounds. The firing setting may be changed at the end of each combat round.

Standard equipment on the gauss rifle includes a battlefield sight similar to that used on the ACR, a RAM grenade adapter, gyrostabilization, and a sling. Reloading by replacement of an empty magazine or RAM grenade takes one combat round, during which the player is considered to be evading. Power is provided by a disposable power pack included in each magazine.

Shotgun: The basic weapon for maximum shock effect without regard to accuracy. The shotgun has an 18mm diameter barrel and fires shells containing either six 7mm bullets, or 130 3mm pellets. In each case, velocity for the projectiles is about 350 meters per second. A cylindrical magazine containing 10 shells is inserted under the barrel and parallel to it; cartridges are then fed automatically into the shotgun for firing. Reloading consists of replacing the cylindrical magazine and takes 30 seconds. One shot is fired for each pull of the trigger.

Magazines measure approximately 0.35 meters long by 0.02 meters in diameter and are quite clumsy to carry.

Shotguns are equipped with a sling for carrying. They may be fitted with a folding stock.

Autoshotgun: A fully automatic version of the shotgun.

SMG: A small automatic weapon designed to fire pistol ammunition. Magazines holding 30 cartridges are inserted into the weapon in a location forward of the trigger guard or in the pistol grip, depending on the design. The gun fires four rounds per pull of the trigger. Submachinegun ammunition (but not a submachinegun magazine) is interchangeable with automatic pistol ammunition.

Assault Rifle: A lighter and less-expensive military version of the automatic rifle, the assault rifle fires a bullet at velocities of 900 meters per second. A magazine containing 30 rounds is inserted into the underside of the assault rifle directly ahead of the trigger guard. Reloading the assault rifle takes one combat round, during which the firer is treated as evading. The weapon may either be fired automatically (four rounds per pull of the trigger) or semiautomatically (one round per pull of the trigger). The fire setting may be changed at the end of each combat round.

The assault rifle has an integral carrying grip/sight and is generally provided with a sling as well. Belt-fed versions are not available, and special sights may not be attached without considerable modification of the basic design.

Accelerator Rifle: Designed specifically for zero-G combat, the accelerator rifle fires a small bullet at an initial muzzle velocity of 100 to 150 meters per second, and upon leaving the barrel is accelerated by a secondary propelling charge to velocities of 700 to 800 meters per second. Normally the rifle fires bursts of three rounds per pull of the trigger, but it may be adjusted to fire single rounds at the end of any firing round. A 15-round magazine is inserted in the bottom of the weapon in front of the trigger guard, and reloading takes one combat round.

Advanced Combat Rifle: A progressive development of the assault rifle, the advanced combat rifle (ACR) fires either a high explosive (HE) bullet at 900 meters per second or a discarding sabot (DS) at 1,200 meters per second. A magazine containing 20 rounds is inserted into the underside of the weapon behind the pistol grip. Reloading takes one combat round, during which the firer is treated as evading. The weapon may be fired either automatically or semiautomatically (as with the assault rifle).

Standard equipment includes an electronic battlefield sight, which incorporates both light amplification and passive IR, visual magnification, and a laser rangefinder which may also

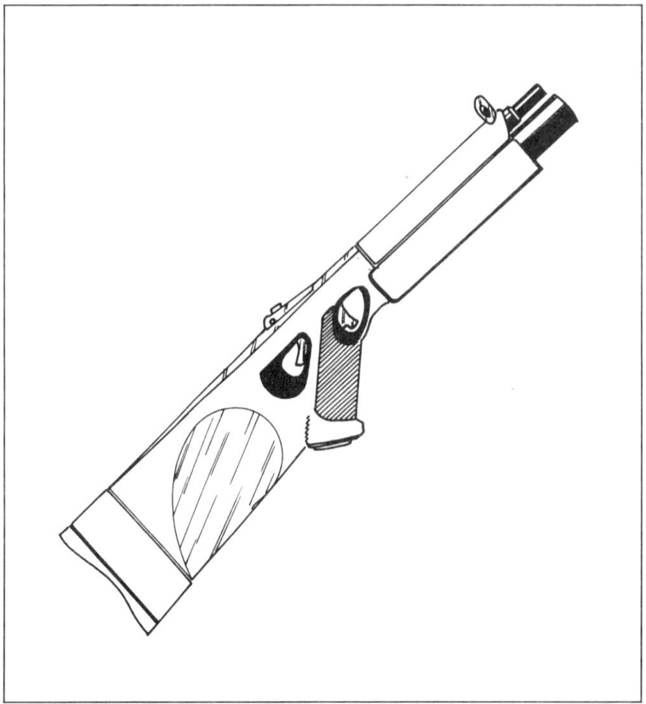

be used as a target painting device. The weapon is also gyroscopically stabilized during firing. A sling is provided along with the weapon, and the muzzle of the rifle includes an integral flash suppressor and an adaptor for launching a RAM shoot-through grenade.

Assault Rocket Launcher (ARL): Related to the advanced combat rifle (ACR), the assault rocket launcher's barrel is merely a launch tube for the ammunition. Like the ACR, the ARL is gyrostabilized when the trigger is pulled.

The ARL fires 10mm solid fuel rocket slugs. Each slug has four pinhole-sized nozzles angled to imitate rifling and "burns" for 5 meters before momentum takes over. The use of rocket slugs provides many advantages. For example, no cartridge ejection system is needed, so the weapon can be sealed from dirt. The action and barrel do not have to withstand high pressures. The weapon's chief disadvantage is its high signature.

The ARL can be fired in both automatic mode and semiautomatic mode, with each automatic burst consisting of four rounds.

Light Assault Gun (LAG): Essentially a heavy rifle, the LAG fires a 20mm, 30-gram bullet at velocities of 400 to 500 meters per second. A magazine containing five rounds is inserted into the underside of the weapon ahead of the trigger guard. Reloading takes one combat round, during which the firer is treated as evading. One round is fired per pull of the trigger. Ammunition includes HE, flechette, and 20/9mm discarding sabot rounds.

The LAG is provided with a sling to assist carrying.

PERSONAL ENERGY WEAPONS

The following personal energy weapons are sometimes available on worlds of sufficient Tech Level; their availability is restricted, however, by the Law Level of the specific world. Energy weapons, like slug throwers, vary in effective range depending on their specific type; range limitations are shown on the combat charts.

Laser Weapons: Laser weapons fire concentrated beams of energy at their targets and cause damage by their intense light and heat. All laser weapons require a power source either built into the weapon directly or carried in a separate pack. (At Tech Level 17, laser weapons are powered from internal matter-antimatter pods.) Laser weapons below Tech Level 13 use visible light so they can be seen by observers, while higher tech versions use invisible X-ray beams.

Laser Pistol: A pistol which functions much the same as a laser carbine or laser rifle but which has lighter weight and a much handier length. It still requires its own model of power pack (a laser carbine or laser rifle power pack cannot be used).

Laser Carbine: A lightweight version of the laser rifle, which fires high energy bolts using current from a backpack battery/power pack. The laser carbine fires a 2mm beam of energy aimed by integrated optic sights. The laser carbine is connected to the power pack by a heavy duty cable.

Laser Rifle: The standard high energy weapon, which fires high energy bolts in the same manner as the laser carbine. Heavier than the laser carbine, the laser rifle is also capable of longer sustained action and is constructed somewhat more sturdily. The power pack can provide 100 shots before recharging. As in the laser carbine, the laser rifle is connected to the power pack by a heavy duty cable. Power packs are not interchangeable between the two weapons.

High-Energy Weapons: High-energy weapons fire beams of super-heated plasma at their targets and cause damage by their intense heat and kinetic energy. All high-energy weapons require a power source.

PGMP (Plasma Gun-Man Portable): The PGMP consists of a power pack carried on the firer's back, the weapon itself, and a flexible power link. The power pack powers a laser ignition system in the weapon itself which heats hydrogen fuel to a plasma state. The plasma is contained in the ignition chamber briefly and is then released through a magnetically focused field along the weapon's barrel. The high initial velocity plasma jet is 2 centimeters in diameter, but it begins to dissipate immediately. Each power pack has sufficient energy to discharge 40 plasma bolts before recharging is necessary. Each pull of the trigger discharges one plasma bolt.

PGMP-13 is a high-gain, light plasma gun designed exclusively for use with battle dress. Of similar general configuration to the PGMP-12, the PGMP-13 may only be fired by an individual wearing battle dress and only when the firer is stationary and firmly braced in one of several standard firing positions. This condition allows the suit's normal strength enhancement units to function as a recoil carriage. Instead of a conventional stock, the PGMP-13 has a recoil cylinder terminating in a computer link to the battle dress. The computer link engages when placed in the PGMP socket integral to the battle dress (placed over the upper right or upper left chest/shoulder). The weapon may not be fired unless the socket is engaged. Engagement projects crosshairs on the faceplate for targetting. The weapon may be fired every combat round. The power pack is a small fusion reactor with effectively unlimited fuel for combat purposes (but it requires periodic refueling and routine maintainance every 24-36 hours, depending on amount of use).

PGMP-14 is the final development of the light plasma gun. The PGMP-14 incorporates a gravity field generator which enables personnel not in powered armor to both carry the weapon and to fire it. The weapon's computer system automatically biases the field to provide near total recoil compensation. It is otherwise similar to the PGMP-13 in performance.

FGMP (Fusion Gun-Man Portable): The FGMP-14 is similar in design and function to the PGMP-13. The FGMP-14 differs only in that it contains the plasma slightly longer until a fusion reaction begins to take place. The weapon is somewhat more powerful than a plasma gun, and it may only be used by individuals wearing battle dress.

The FGMP-15 incorporates a gravity field generator similar to that used on the PGMP-14 and a weapon system similar to that of the FGMP-14.

The FGMP-16 is an advanced, lighter-weight version of the FGMP-15 with all of its features.

Plasma Rifle: A highly advanced, very portable version of the earlier PGMP weapons.

Neural Guns: An advancement of remote neural activity sensing and psionic helmet technology, these guns remotely disrupt brain activity. Being hit by neural gun fire causes unconsciousness (i.e., a stun), but sometimes it has other random effects instead: disorientation, mind assault, or even death. Neural weapons are available only at very high Tech Levels.

Neural weapon fire can be detected at a distance by individuals with psionic life sense ability.

Referee's Note: Neural weapons are a very special type of weapon and as such are not on the regular weapon tables in the *Players' Manual*. A neural pistol has a "to hit" difficulty as a handgun, and a neural rifle has a "to hit" difficulty as a rifle—but in both cases, the maximum range is long. Neural weapons have a flat penetration of 10 over their entire range scale. If the weapon penetration is at least equal to the target armor value, handle hit damage based on the success level. On exceptional success, the target goes unconscious; on a normal success, implement a 2D mishap; on marginal success, implement a 3D mishap. Handle any mishaps as follows: **Superficial:** Disorientation of target for 1 combat round. **Minor:** Disorientation of target for 1D combat rounds. **Major:** Mind assault on target at a psionic strength of 2D. **Destroyed:** Death of target.

ARCHAIC WEAPONS

The following archaic weapons are generally available on very low-tech worlds. In most cases, they will be in the hands of non-player characters encountered in the process of an adventure.

Bola: Thrown weapon consisting of a cord with weights attached.

Blowgun: Long narrow pipe-like weapon through which darts or pellets are blown.

Boomerang: Aerodynamically designed throwing stick.

Sling: A simple loop of cord used to propel a stone or pellet over a relatively short distance.

Bows: A weapon consisting of a curved stave of a resilient material (usually wood) strung taunt from end to end and used to launch arrow bolts.

Crossbows: Crossbows consist of a bow fixed crosswise on a wooden stock with a groove for the arrow bolt.

Early Firearms: The following slug throwers are only available on low-tech worlds, and their availability, as with all firearms, is restricted by the Law Level of the specific world.

All these weapons require that the owner also carry gunpowder and properly sized lead balls; percussion weapons also require a supply of percussion caps.

Hand Cannon: Literally a small hand-held muzzle-loading cannon, it takes 30 seconds to load with powder and a ball and is fired by holding a flame to the touch hole.

Flintlock Pistol: A single-shot flint-lock pistol (with the same loading characteristics as described above).

Percussion Revolver: A six-shot revolver with each chamber individually loaded with powder ball and a percussion cap. The gun may be reloaded in two minutes or the cylinder may be detached and another previously loaded cylinder may be put on in 30 seconds.

Flintlock Musket: A long smoothbore weapon relying on sparks struck from a flint to ignite the powder. It requires 18 seconds to reload. When fired, the musket may misfire (using it is a hazardous task); if a misfire occurs the weapon will not fire but the firer may attempt to fire it in the next round.

Percussion Rifle: A muzzle-loading rifle relying on an explosive cap to ignite the powder. Loading is the same as for a musket, but there is no chance of a misfire.

ACCESSORIES

The following special accessories are generally available for the various weapons.

Telescopic Sight: High-quality telescopic sights for attachment to rifles and carbines, which are used to increase their accuracy, especially at longer ranges.

Telescopic sights are delicate, however, and may be jarred out of alignment by any violent action (such as being left untended in a moving truck, close to an explosion, or being dropped).

Electronic Sight: Electronic sights with image enhancement and low-light capabilities are available to provide the capability to see and hit in the dark. They can be damaged just as easily as a telescopic sight if handled carelessly.

Silencer: Devices are available which will muffle or eliminate the sound of guns firing, but so far they have proven practical only when applied to body pistols, revolvers, and automatic pistols. A silencer attaches to the muzzle of the pistol, which increases its total length and makes it impossible to holster until the silencer is removed. Silencers are not interchangeable; one must be purchased for each specific model of pistol used.

Shoulder Stock: It is possible to produce a shoulder stock which may be attached temporarily to a pistol or revolver, which results in a crude carbine arrangement and some greater accuracy at longer ranges. The overall length of the pistol is increased by the length of the stock, and the pistol cannot be holstered. Attaching the stock (or detaching it) requires one minute.

Folding Stock: Carbines, rifles, and shotguns can be equipped with folding stocks which make it possible to reduce

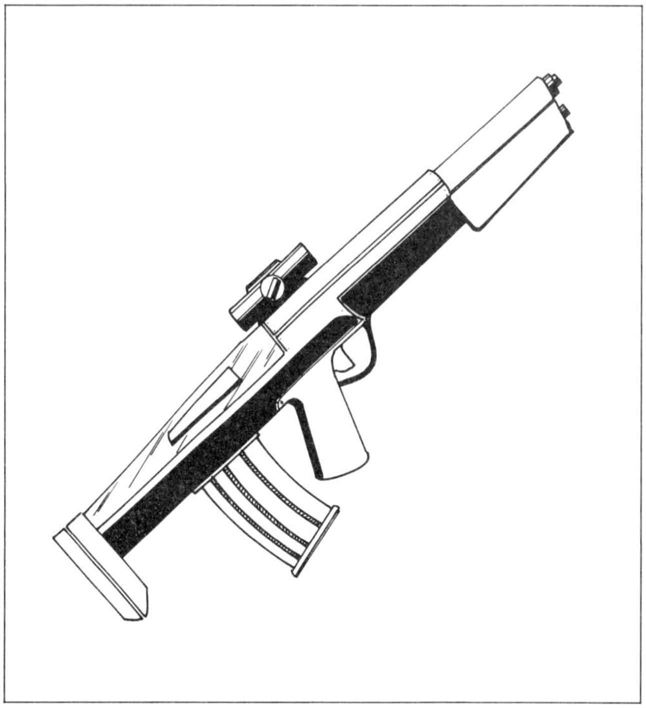

the overall length of the weapon by 0.3 meters.

Tangle Net: A small rope net intended to hamper or restrain animals (difficulty as thrown).

Tranq Spray: A small aerosol can which sprays a mist of tranquilizer (see the *Players' Manual* for the types of tranquilizers available). The spray can only be used at close range and must be aimed to allow the tranq to be breathed (difficulty as handgun). Each can contains four sprays.

Plastic Knife: Ordinary dagger fashioned of heavy duty hydrocarbon plastic. When subjected to microwave radiation (as in a microwave oven), the knife becomes a misshapen blob of plastic. When subjected to a series of sharp taps, it will gradually (over about two minutes) regain its shape. It cannot be detected by metal detectors, but treat as a knife in all other respects.

Machete: Blade used in cutting vegetation to clear a path, campsite, etc.; it can also be used as a weapon.

Integral Laser Pistol: The integral laser pistol contains a miniaturized, disposable power pack with enough energy for only three shots. The power pack cannot be recharged. The integral laser pistol is banned by the laws of most worlds.

Ammo Belt: Versions of some rifles are available which use 100-round belts of ammunition. Reloading with a new belt requires 45 seconds.

ARMOR AND PROTECTION

The following items of armor and personal protection are generally available. The weight of personal armor and clothing is assumed to be part of the character's clothing load. Only one form of personal armor may be worn, but reflec may always be worn under clothing or armor.

Jack: A natural or synthetic leather jacket or body suit covering the torso and upper arms and legs. Jack is somewhat better than ordinary clothing or bare skin when defending against blades; it is worthless against guns.

Mesh: A jacket or body suit made of natural or synthetic leather and reinforced with a lining of flexible metal mesh similar to chain mail but lighter and stronger. Mesh reduces or stops penetration by blades and has some effectiveness against guns; it is ineffective against laser fire.

Cloth: A heavy duty body suit tailored from ballistic cloth. The fabric absorbs impact energy and distributes the blow over the body, which possibly results in bruising. Nevertheless, cloth armor is almost the best and the most versatile available.

Flak Jacket: A less expensive version of ballistic cloth armor, generally covering only the torso and groin.

Reflec: Reflective material on a plastic base can be tailored into a body suit which is effective against laser fire but ineffective against most weapons. Reflec is worn under other clothing. Reflec is expensive and often difficult to obtain.

Ablat: Ablat is a cheap alternative to reflec fashioned from a material which will ablate (vaporize) when hit by laser fire. The ablation of the material carries away the energy of the laser and protects the wearer. Continued fire against ablat degrades its effectiveness, but the armor is cheap and easily replaceable. Ablat also has some value against other forms of attack.

Combat Armor: Combat armor is a complete vacc-suit-like array of metal and synthetic armor. Combat armor is strictly military and not available on the open market; it is issued to troop units and elite mercenary battalions.

Battle Dress: The ultimate in individual protection, battle dress is an advanced and powered version of combat armor. Battle dress enhances the strength and senses of individuals wearing it with variable feedback personal controls, servo-powered limbs, and various kinds of electronic assistance. The individual wearing battle dress is effectively doubled in strength and given unlimited endurance.

Combat Environment Suit: A neck to toe air-tight suit constructed of ballistic cloth. Generally worn open at the neck and wrists, the combat environment suit can be sealed by donning gauntlets and a clear flexible plastic headpiece. The suit is a military uniform which gives complete protection against most chemical agents, tainted atmospheres, biological agents, and a moderate defense against radiation. Heat buildup in the suit is handled by a simple, solid-state cooling system that is woven into the garment and that eliminates all infrared signature except on the exposed face, hands, and heat exhaust. The heat exhaust is a very pronounced IR source, but this can be dampened by inserting a chill can into the cooling system. The chill can eliminates the signature for 45 minutes to two hours; at the end of that time, the can is used up.

The combat environment suit is the preferred type of cold weather clothing for people who have any experience with it. Because it manages heat exhaust, it is effective insulation. Light in weight, the suit is very good cold weather clothing.

Chameleon Option: At Tech Level 12, a chameleon surface becomes available for the combat environment suit, combat armor, or battle dress, at an additional cost of Cr1000. It selectively bleeds heat to match background IR levels and effectively renders the wearer invisible to IR sensors.

Psionic Shield Option: Beginning at Tech Level 12, psionic shielding is available as an option for any armor at an additional cost of Cr4000. Psionic shielding protects the wearer from psionic mind reading and from psionic life sensing.

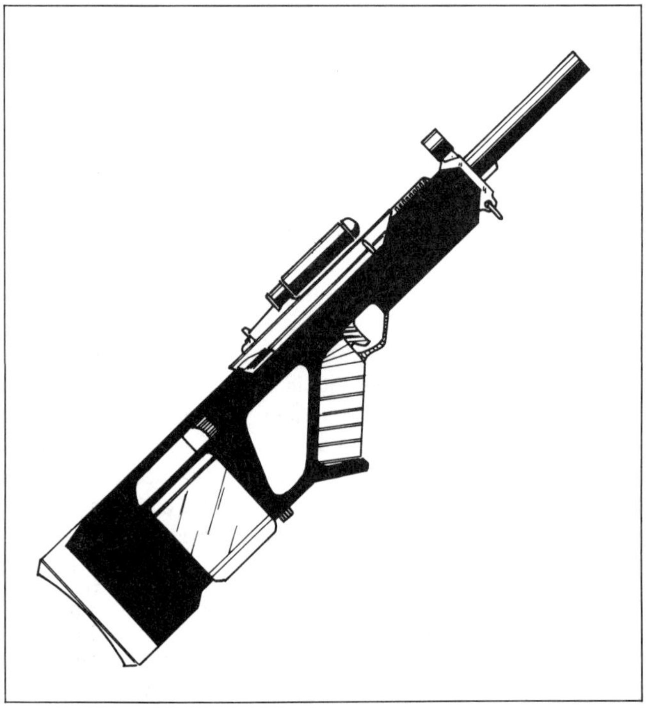

WEAPONS PRICES

Weapon	TL	Length	Volume	Unloaded Weight	Price	Ammo Weight	Ammo Price
Club	1	0.4 to 0.8	0.2 to 2.0	0.5 to 3.0	—		
Dagger	1	0.2	0.2	0.2	10		
Blade	3	0.3	0.2	0.3	50		
Sword	1	0.7 to 0.9	1.0	1.0	150		
Cutlass	3	0.6 to 0.9	1.0	1.2	100		
Broadsword	2	1.0 to 1.2	1.5	2.5	300		
Foil	3	0.8	0.6	0.5	100		
Hand Axe	1	0.3	0.5	0.5	50		
Battle Axe	2	0.6	2.0	3.0	200		
Bayonet	1	+0.2	0.2	0.2	10		
Spear	0	3.0	2.0	2.0	10		
Halberd	2	2.5	2.5	2.5	75		
Pike	1	3.0 to 4.0	2.5	3.0	40		
Staff/Cudgel	0	1.0 to 2.0	1.0	1.0	10		
Revolver 5mm	5	0.1	0.3	0.3	100	0.05	3
Revolver 7mm	5	0.1	0.6	0.6	125	0.07	4
Revolver 9mm	4	0.2	0.9	0.9	150	0.10	5
Revolver 9mm Magnum	5	0.1	1.2	1.2	300	0.12	8
Snub Pistol 10mm	8	0.05	0.2	0.2	150	0.03	10
Snub Pistol 10mm Auto	8	0.1	4.0	4.0	600	0.50	20
Body Pistol 5mm	8	0.1	0.2	0.2	500	0.05	20
Autopistol 7mm	6	0.1	0.5	0.5	150	0.20	8
Autopistol 9mm	5	0.2	0.7	0.7	200	0.25	10
Gauss Pistol 4mm	13	0.1	0.6	0.6	600	0.20	20
Carbine 7mm	5	0.8	3.0	3.0	200	0.12	10
Rifle 7mm	4	1.0	3.5	4.0	100	0.50	20
Rifle 7mm	5	1.0	3.5	4.0	200	0.50	20
Rifle 9mm	7	1.2	4.0	5.0	1,000	0.80	40
Hunting Rifle 13mm	5	1.0	4.5	6.0	2,000	1.50	60
Autorifle 7mm	6	1.0	5.0	5.0	1,000	0.50	20
Gauss Rifle 4mm	12	0.7	3.5	3.5	1,500	0.40	40
Shotgun 18mm	4	1.0	3.7	3.7	150	0.75	10
AutoShotgun 18mm	7	1.2	4.0	4.0	500	1.50	20
SMG 9mm	5	0.4	2.5	2.5	500	0.50	20
Assault Rifle 5mm	7	0.8	3.0	3.0	300	0.33	20
Assault Rifle 7mm	7	0.8	4.0	4.0	400	0.60	30
Accelerator Rifle 6mm	9	0.8	2.5	2.5	900	0.50	25
Adv Combat Rifle 7mm	10	0.7	3.0	3.0	800	0.40	10
Adv Combat Rifle 9mm	10	0.7	3.5	3.5	1,000	0.50	15
Assault Rocket Lnchr 10mm	10	0.7	3.5	3.0	800	0.50	35
Lt Assault Gun (LAG) 20mm	8	0.9	4.0	4.0	600	0.50	20
Laser Pistol-9	9	0.3	0.7	0.7	2,000	2.00	1,500
Laser Pistol-13	13	0.4	2.2	2.2	3,000	1.00	350
Laser Carbine-8	8	0.8	5.0	5.0	2,500	3.00	1,000
Laser Carbine-13	13	0.8	4.4	4.4	4,000	1.5	3,000
Laser Rifle-9	9	1.0	5.0	6.0	3,500	4.00	1,500
Laser Rifle-13	13	1.1	8.8	8.8	8,000	2.00	3,500
PGMP-12	12	0.8	6.0	6.0	10,000	3.00	2,500
PGMP-13	13	0.9	9.0	9.0	65,000	7.00	50,000
PGMP-14	14	0.8	1.0	1.0	100,000	1.60	250,000
FGMP-14	14	0.9	10.0	10.0	100,000	9.00	65,000
FGMP-15	15	0.8	1.0	1.0	400,000	2.00	300,000
FGMP-16	16	0.6	0.5	0.5	500,000	1.00	375,000
Plasma Rifle-16	16	0.7	0.8	0.5	125,000	0.50	300,000
Neural Pistol	16	0.3	0.6	0.5	225,000	0.50	30,000
Neural Rifle	16	0.5	0.8	1.5	125,000	1.00	50,000
Bola	0	1.0	—	—	10		
Blowgun Pellet	0	0.3 to 0.5	0.1	0.1	5.0	0.1	—
Boomerang Thrown	0	0.5	1.0	0.5	50		
Sling Stone	0	1.0	—	—	1.0	0.1	—
Short Bow	0	0.8	2.0	0.5	50	0.1	2
Long Bow	1	1.5	4.0	1.0	75	0.1	2
Light Crossbow	2	0.8	7.0	3.0	150	0.1	2
Heavy Crossbow	2	0.9	13.0	6.0	250	0.1	2
Repeating Crossbow	2	0.8	9.0	4.0	200	0.1	8
Hand Cannon Ball	2	0.3	5.0	5.0	50	0.2	5
Flintlock Pistol Ball	3	0.2	1.5	1.5	40	0.2	5
Percussion Revolver 6 Balls	4	0.2	1.0	1.0	150	0.3	15
Flintlock Musket Ball	3	1.5	4.0	4.0	60	0.3	2
Percussion Rifle Ball	4	1.0	4.0	4.0	100	0.3	2
Telescopic Sights	6	0.8	0.8	—	200		
Electronic Sights	9	1.5	1.5	—	2,000		
Silencer	6	0.1 to 0.3	0.5	0.5 to 0.7	200		
Shoulder Stocks	5	0.3	1.0	1.0	75		
Folding Stocks	6	—	—	0.5	100		
Tangle Net	1	0.5	0.5	—	20		
Tranq Spray	5	0.2	0.1	—	100		
Plastic Knife	9	0.2	0.3	0.35	300		
Machete	4	0.4 to 0.8	1.0	1.0	125		
Integral Laser Pistol-14	14	0.3	2.0	2.5	2,000	0.5	1,500
Ammo Belt	6	0.5	2.0	—	120		

ARMOR

Jack—
TL: 1.
Vol: 4.
Wt: 1.
Cr50

Mesh—
TL: 7.
Wt: 2 kg.
Cr150

Cloth—
TL: 6.
Vol: 4.5.
Wt: 2.
Cr250

Flak Jacket—
TL: 7.
Vol: 2.0.
Wt: 1.
Cr100

Reflec—
TL: 10.
Vol: 2.
Wt: 1.
Cr1,500

Ablat
TL: 9.
Vol: 4.5.
Wt: 2.
Cr75

Combat Armor-11—
TL: 11.
Vol: 2.9.
Wt: 18.
Cr20,000

Combat Armor-12—
TL: 12.
Vol: 1.8.
Wt: 10.
Cr30,000

Combat Armor-14—
TL: 14.
Vol: 0.7.
Wt: 6.
Cr60,000

Battle Dress-13—
TL: 13.
Vol: 3.8.
Wt: 26.
Cr200,000

Battle Dress-14—
TL: 14.
Vol: 2.7.
Wt: 12.
Cr350,000

Cbt Environment Suit—
TL: 10.
Vol: 6.
Wt: 2.0.
Cr1,000

Starships, Spacecraft, and Vehicles

While it's possible for someone to walk a considerable distance if properly outfitted and in good physical shape, the best way to become a "traveller" is to ride in an appropriate craft.

Craft Classifications: Powered craft can be organized in several different ways. Here, we make the broad distinction between starships, smaller spacecraft, and vehicles.

Starships have a displacement value of 100 or more and are usually equipped with jump drives for interstellar travel. Small spacecraft range in displacement from 20 to 100 and do not have jump capability. Vehicles travelling on land, water, and in a world's atmosphere, range up to 20 displacement.

The designs listed here are standard: that is, each ship type is mass-produced in shipyards throughout the Imperium, which provides economies of scale and saves the fees of a ship architect. All craft are described at Tech Level 15, the highest Tech Level commonly found in the Imperium. Such vessels are manufactured, of course, only on Tech Level 15 worlds and are normally purchased there.

The standard designs are also available at lower Tech Levels; use the craft design rules in the *Referee's Manual* to modify these vessels for the proper technology as needed.

GROUND CAR

CraftID: Ground Car, TL 5, Cr3100
Hull: 2/5, Disp = 2, Config = 4USL, Armor = 4B, Unloaded = 3.8tons, Loaded = 5.0tons
Power: 1/2, IntCombust = 0.1Mw, Duration = 6hours
Loco: 1/2, Wheels Road = 80kph, OffRoad = 25kph
Commo: None (some have a radio receiver)
Sensors: None
Off/Def: HardPoints = 1
Control: Panel = Mechanical, Environ = basic env
Accomm: Crew = 1 (Operator = 1), Seats = cramped × 6
Other: Cargo = 1.0kliters, Fuel = 0.072kliters ObjSize = small, EMLevel = moderate

The ground car is an ordinary self-powered vehicle suitable for use in civilized areas on low-tech worlds.

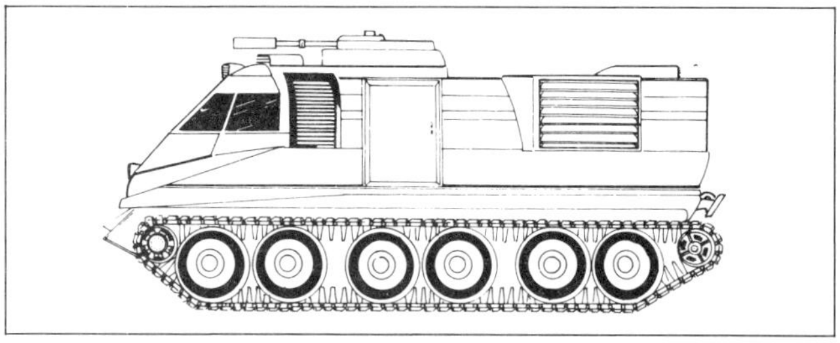

WHEELED ATV

CraftID: Wheeled ATV, TL 6, Cr46,380
Hull: 9/23, Disp = 10, Config = 4USL, Armor = 6B, Unloaded = 28tons, Loaded = 55tons
Power: 1/2, IntCombust = 2.0Mw, Duration = 4 /12
Loco: 1/2, Wheels Road = 100kph, OffRoad = 35kph
Commo: Radio = Regional
Sensors: None
Off/Def: HardPoints = 1
Control: Panel = Mechanical, Environ = basic env, basic ls
Accomm: Crew = 1 (Operator = 1), Seats = roomy × 17
Other: Cargo = 25kliters, Fuel = 18kliters ObjSize = small, EMLevel = moderate

The wheeled ATV is a wheeled vehicle used on low-tech worlds for exploration.

TRACKED ATV

CraftID: Tracked ATV, TL 6, Cr49,580
Hull: 9/23, Disp = 10, Config = 4USL, Armor = 6B, Unloaded = 47tons, Loaded = 74tons
Power: 1/2, IntCombust = 2.0Mw, Duration = 4 /12
Loco: 1/2, Tracks Road = 80kph, OffRoad = 50kph
Commo: Radio = Regional
Sensors: None
Off/Def: HardPoints = 1
Control: Panel = Mechanical, Environ = basicenv, basicls
Accomm: Crew = 1 (Operator = 1), Seats = roomy × 17
Other: Cargo = 25kliters, Fuel = 18kliters ObjSize = small, EMLevel = moderate

The tracked ATV is used on low-tech worlds for exploration.

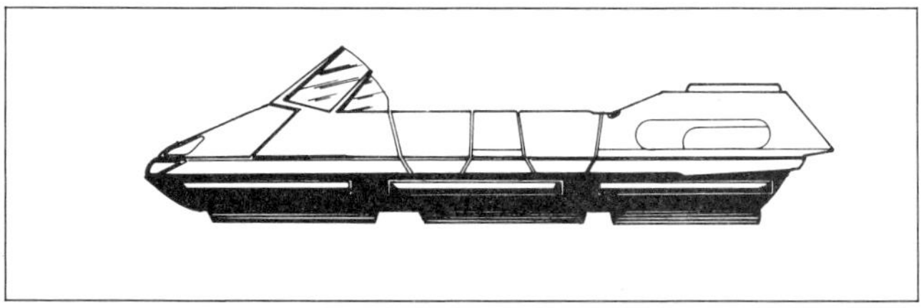

OPEN-TOP AIR/RAFT

CraftID: Open-Top Air/Raft, TL 15, Cr275,000
Hull: 1.8/4.5, Disp = 2, Config = 4SL, Armor = 4G, Unloaded = 1.6tons, Loaded = 7.2tons
Power: 1/2, Fusion = 1.5Mw, Duration = 60/180
Loco: 1/2, StdGravThrust = 8.0tons, NOE = 120kph, Cruise = 90kph, Top = 120kph
Commo: Radio = Planetary
Sensors: PassiveEMS = VDistant, ActiveEMS = VDistant, ActObjScan = Diff, ActObjPin = Diff, PasEngScan = Form
Off/Def: HardPoints = 1
Control: Computer = 0 × 2, Panel = holodynamic link × 5, Environ = basic env
Accomm: Crew = 1 (Operator = 1), Seats = roomy × 4
Other: Cargo = 5.4kliters, Fuel = 3.3kliters, ObjSize = small, EMLevel = moderate

Common on high-tech worlds, it is efficient and inexpensive.

ENCLOSED AIR/RAFT

CraftID: Enclosed Air/Raft, TL 15, Cr389,000
Hull: 3.6/9, Disp=4, Config=1USL, Armor=4G, Unloaded=4.6tons, Loaded=18.7tons
Power: 1/2, Fusion=0.25Mw, Duration=60/180
Loco: 1/2, StdGravThrust=20.6tons, NOE=120kph, Cruise=90kph, Top=120kph
Commo: Radio=Planetary
Sensors: PassiveEMS=VDistant, ActiveEMS=VDistant, ActObjScan=Diff, ActObjPin=Diff, PasEngScan=Form
Off/Def: HardPoints=1
Control: Computer=0×2, Panel=holodynamic link×1, Special=headsUp, Environ=basic env, basic ls, inertial comp
Accomm: Crew=1 (Operator=1), Seats=roomy×4
Other: Cargo=13.5kliters, Fuel=7.9kliters, ObjSize=small, EMLevel=moderate

The enclosed air/raft is another of the most common vehicles on high-tech worlds; it has a slightly higher cost but correspondingly more comfort than the open version.

GCARRIER

CraftID: GCarrier, TL 15, MCr14.44
Hull: 7.2/18, Disp=8, Config=1USL, Armor=10G, Unloaded=20.1tons, Loaded=48.1tons
Power: 1/2, Fusion=54Mw, Duration=10/30
Loco: 1/2, StdGravThrust=53tons, NOE=120kph, Cruise=90kph, Top=120kph
Commo: Radio=System
Sensors: PassiveEMS=VDistant, ActiveEMS=VDistant, ActObjScan=Diff, ActObjPin=Diff, PasEngScan=Rout
Off/Def: HardPoints=1,

	Ammo	*Rnd*	*Pen/ Attn*	*Dmg*	*Auto Tgt*	*Dngr Spc*	*Sig*	*Re-coil*
Fusion XRP-15	0	0	67/5	30	2	45	Hi	—

Control: Computer=0×2, Panel=holodynamic link×1, Special=headsUp, Environ=basic env, basic ls, inertial comp
Accomm: Crew=1 (Operator=1), Seats=roomy×14
Other: Cargo=27kliters, Fuel=13.1kliters, ObjSize=small, EMLevel=moderate

The GCarrier is an enclosed military or quasi-military grav vehicle. Similar in concept to an armored air/raft, the GCarrier has a gun mount and an armored rear hatch door.

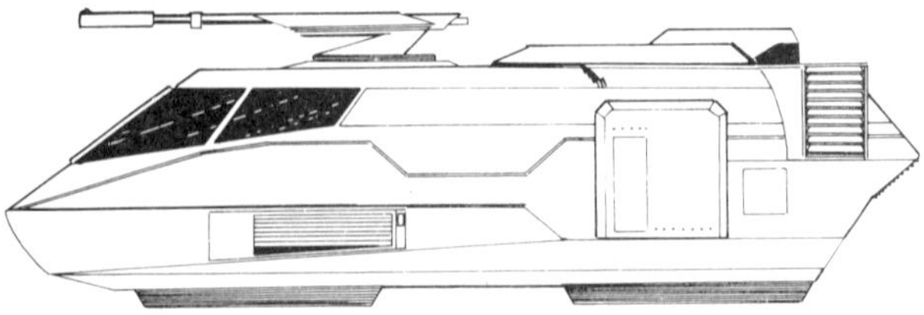

SPEEDER

CraftID: Speeder, TL 15, MCr1.36
Hull: 5.4/13.5, Disp=6, Config=1AF, Armor=4G, Unloaded=19.2tons, Loaded=25.4tons
Power: 1/2, Fusion=54Mw, Duration=45/135
Loco: 1/2, StdGravThrust=52tons, NOE=190kph, Cruise=810kph, Top=1080kph
Commo: Radio=System
Sensors: PassiveEMS=VDistant, ActiveEMS=VDistant, ActObjScan=Diff, ActObjPin=Diff, PasEngScan=Rout
Off/Def: HardPoints=1
Control: Computer=0×2, Panel=holodynamic link×1, Special=headsUp, Environ=basic env, basic ls, grav plates, inertial comp
Accomm: Crew=1 (Operator=1), Seats=roomy×2
Other: Cargo=2.0kliters, Fuel=58.4kliters, ObjSize=small, EMLevel=moderate

The speeder is a streamlined grav-powered craft intended for high-speed transport between points on a world surface.

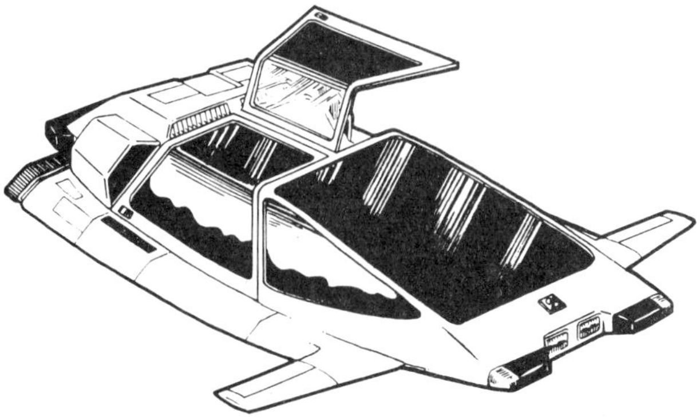

LAUNCH

CraftID: Launch, TL 15, MCr9.08
Hull: 18/45, Disp = 20, Config = 1SL, Armor = 40G, Unloaded = 120tons, Loaded = 180tons
Power: 1/2, Fusion = 200Mw, Duration = 30/90
Loco : 1/2, Maneuver = 1, Cruise = 750kph Top = 1000kph Agility = 6
Commo: Radio = System
Sensors: PassiveEMS = Interplanetary, ActiveEMS = Planetary, ActObjScan = Diff, ActObjPin = Diff, PasEngScan = Rout
Off/Def: HardPoints = 1, DefDM = +10
Control: Computer = 2 × 3, Panel = holodynamic link × 420, Special = headsUp, Environ = basic env, basic ls, extend ls, grav plates, inertial comp
Accomm: Crew = 2 (Bridge /Engineer = 1, Commander = 1), Seats = roomy × 20
Other: Cargo = 54kliters, Fuel = 70kliters, Scoops, ObjSize = small, EMLevel = faint

The launch is one of the smaller space-faring craft, and is often carried by another vessel to serve as a lifeboat.

SHIP'S BOAT

CraftID: Ship's Boat, TL 15, MCr20.12
Hull: 27/67.5, Disp = 30, Config = 1SL, Armor = 40G, Unloaded = 350tons, Loaded = 440tons
Power: 2/4, Fusion = 650Mw, Duration = 15/45
Loco: 5/10, Maneuver = 6, Cruise = 750kph Top = 1000kph Agility = 3
Commo: Radio = System
Sensors: PassiveEMS = Interplanetary, ActiveEMS = Planetary, ActObjScan = Diff, ActObjPin = Diff, PasEngScan = Rout
Off/Def: HardPoints = 1, DefDM = +8
Control: Computer = 3 × 3, Panel = holodynamic link × 25, Special = headsUp, Environ = basic env, basic ls, extend ls, grav plates, inertial comp
Accomm: Crew = 2 (Bridge /Engineer = 1, Commander = 1), Seats = adequate × 20
Other: Cargo = 81kliters, Fuel = 120kliters, Scoops, ObjSize = small, EMLevel = faint

The ship's boat is a small vessel ordinarily carried to perform odd jobs and minor operations for a larger ship.

SLOW BOAT

CraftID: Slow Boat, TL 15, MCr14.91
Hull: 27/67.5, Disp = 30, Config = 3AF, Armor = 40G, Unloaded = 220tons, Loaded = 300tons
Power: 2/4, Fusion = 450Mw, Duration = 15/45
Loco: 2/4, Maneuver = 3, NOE = 190kph, Cruise = 1925kph, Top = 2565kph, Agility = 6
Commo: Radio = System
Sensors: PassiveEMS = Interplanetary, ActiveEMS = Planetary, ActObjScan = Diff, ActObjPin = Diff, PasEngScan = Rout
Off/Def: HardPoints = 1, DefDM = +10
Control: Computer = 2 × 3, Panel = holodynamic link × 73, Special = headsUp, Environ = basic env, basic ls, extend ls, grav plates, inertial comp
Accomm: Crew = 2 (Bridge /Engineer = 1, Commander = 1), Seats = adequate × 30
Other: Cargo = 81kliters, Fuel = 80kliters, Scoops, ObjSize = small, EMLevel = faint

The slow boat is similar to the ship's boat but is optimized to allow convenient atmospheric travel.

PINNACE

CraftID: Pinnace, TL 15, MCr21.15
Hull: 36/90, Disp=40, Config=1SL, Armor=40G, Unloaded=410tons, Loaded=550tons
Power: 3/6, Fusion=680Mw, Duration=15/45
Loco: 5/10, Maneuver=5, Cruise=750kph Top=1000kph Agility=3
Commo: Radio=System
Sensors: PassiveEMS=Interplanetary, ActiveEMS=Planetary, ActObjScan=Diff, ActObjPin=Diff, PasEngScan=Rout
Off/Def: HardPoints=1, DefDM=+8
Control: Computer=3×3, Panel=holodynamic link×30, Special=headsUp, Environ=basic env, basic ls, extend ls, grav plates, inertial comp
Accomm: Crew=2 (Bridge /Engineer=1, Commander=1), Seats=adequate×30
Other: Cargo=135kliters, Fuel=120kliters, Scoops, ObjSize=small, EMLevel=faint

The pinnace is a larger, farther-ranging nonstarship capable of holding passengers and small vehicles.

SLOW PINNACE

CraftID: Slow Pinnace, TL 15, MCr15.88
Hull: 36/90, Disp=40, Config=1AF, Armor=40G, Unloaded=240tons, Loaded=450tons
Power: 2/4, Fusion=470Mw, Duration=15/45
Loco: 2/4, Maneuver=2, NOE=190kph, Cruise=1430kph, Top=1910kph, Agility=6
Commo: Radio=System
Sensors: PassiveEMS=Interplanetary, ActiveEMS=Planetary, ActObjScan=Diff, ActObjPin=Diff, PasEngScan=Rout
Off/Def: HardPoints=1, DefDM=+10
Control: Computer=2×3, Panel=holodynamic link×64, Special=headsUp, Environ=basic env, basic ls, extend ls, grav plates, inertial comp
Accomm: Crew=2 (Bridge /Engineer=1, Commander=1), Seats=adequate×50
Other: Cargo=202.5kliters, Fuel=80kliters, Scoops, ObjSize=small, EMLevel=faint

The slow pinnace is similar to a pinnace but is slower because more space is allocated for passengers and cargo, so less space is available for power plant and maneuver drives.

MODULAR CUTTER

CraftID: Modular Cutter, TL 15, MCr17.06
Hull: 45/113, Disp=50, Config=1SL, Armor=40G, Unloaded=430tons, Loaded=850tons
Power: 3/6, Fusion=700Mw, Duration=12/36
Loco: 5/10, Maneuver=4, NOE=190kph, Cruise=600kph, Top=800kph, Agility=3
Commo: Radio=System
Sensors: PassiveEMS=Interplanetary, ActiveEMS=Planetary, ActObjScan=Diff, ActObjPin=Diff, PasEngScan=Rout
Off/Def: HardPoints=1, DefDM=+7
Control: Computer=2×3, Panel=holodynamic link×76, Special=headsUp, Environ=basic env, basic ls, extend ls, grav plates, inertial comp
Accomm: Crew=2 (Bridge /Engineer=1, Commander=1), Seats=adequate×2
Other: Cargo=405kliters, Fuel=100kliters, Scoops, ObjSize=small, EMLevel=faint

The modular cutter is designed to carry one of many modules available. Three are the ATV module, which includes an operational ATV; the fuel module, which serves as a fuel skimming vehicle and storage tank; and the open module, which can be customized for passenger couches, fuel, cargo space, cabins, or staterooms.

SHUTTLE

CraftID: Shuttle, TL 15, MCr28.31
Hull: 86/214, Disp = 95, Config = 1AF, Armor = 40G, Unloaded = 630tons, Loaded = 1110tons
Power: 3/6, Fusion = 880Mw, Duration = 15/45
Loco: 7/14, Maneuver = 3, NOE = 190kph, Cruise = 1965kph, Top = 2565kph, Agility = 2
Commo: Radio = System
Sensors: PassiveEMS = Interplanetary, ActiveEMS = Planetary, ActObjScan = Diff, ActObjPin = Diff, PasEngScan = Rout
Off/Def: HardPoints = 1, DefDM = +6
Control: Computer = 2 x 3, Panel = holodynamic link x 168, Special = headsUp, Environ = basic env, basic ls, extend ls, grav plates, inertial comp
Accomm: Crew = 2 (Bridge /Engineer = 1, Commander = 1), Seats = roomy x 100
Other: Cargo = 472.5kliters, Fuel = 160kliters, Scoops, ObjSize = small, EMLevel = faint

The shuttle is a larger interplanetary passenger vessel.

FIGHTER

CraftID: Fighter, TL 15, MCr14.23
Hull: 9/22.5, Disp = 10, Config = 3AF, Armor = 40G, Unloaded = 4.6tons, Loaded = 18.7tons
Power: 1/2, Fusion = 186Mw, Duration = 5/15
Loco: 1/2, StdGravThrust = 1173tons, NOE = 120kph, Cruise = 2835kph, Top = 3780kph Agility = 6
Commo: Radio = System
Sensors: PassiveEMS = Interplanetary, ActiveEMS = Planetary, ActObjScan = Diff, ActObjPin = Diff, PasEngScan = Rout
Off: BeamLaser = x02
Batt 1
Bear 1
Def: DefDM = +10
Control: Computer = 2 x 3, Panel = holodynamic link x 47, Special = headsUp, Environ = basic env, basic ls, extend ls, grav plates, inertial comp
Accomm: Crew = 1 (Operator = 1), Seats = roomy x 1
Other: Cargo = 6.75kliters, Fuel = 33.6kliters, ObjSize = small, EMLevel = faint

The fighter is an armed, grav-powered space vehicle often carried on larger military vessels as a subordinate craft.

SCOUT/COURIER

CraftID: Scout/Courier, Type S, TL 15, MCr28.938
Hull: 90/225, Disp = 100, Config = 1SL, Armor = 40G, Unloaded = 840tons, Loaded = 916tons
Power: 3/6, Fusion = 864Mw, Duration = 30/90
Loco: 5/10, Maneuver = 2, 3/6, Jump = 2, NOE = 190kph, Cruise = 750kph, Top = 1000kph, Agility = 2
Commo: Radio = System
Sensors: PassiveEMS = Interstellar, ActiveEMS = FarOrbit, Densitometer = HighPen/1km, Neutrino = 10kw ActObjScan = Rout, ActObjPin = Rout, PasObjScan = Rout, PasObjPin = Rout, PasEngScan = Simp, PasEngPin = Rout
Off/Def: HardPoints = 1, DefDM = +4
Control: Computer = 1bis x 3, Panel = holodynamic link x 181, Special = headsUp, Environ = basic env, basic ls, extend ls, grav plates, inertial comp
Accomm: Crew = 1 (Bridge/Engineer = 1), Staterooms = 4, MidPsg = 7 (noncommercial), SubCraft = air/raft
Other: Cargo = 40.5kliters, Fuel = 515kliters, PurificationPlant, Scoops, ObjSize = average, EMLevel = faint

Built by the Imperial Interstellar Scout Service for exploration, survey, and courier duties, and many are in service throughout known space.

SEEKER

CraftID: Seeker, Type J, TL 15, MCr27.317
Hull: 90/225, Disp = 100, Config = 1SL, Armor = 40G, Unloaded = 815tons, Loaded = 895tons
Power: 3/6, Fusion = 720Mw, Duration = 30/90
Loco: 5/10, Maneuver = 2, 3/6, Jump = 2, NOE = 190kph, Cruise = 750kph, Top = 1000kph, Agility = 0
Commo: Radio = System
Sensors: PassiveEMS = Interstellar, ActiveEMS = FarOrbit, Densitometer = HighPen/1km ActObjScan = Rout, ActObjPin = Rout, PasObjScan = Rout, PasObjPin = Rout, PasEngScan = Rout
Off: PulseLaser = x02
Batt 1
Bear 1
Def: DefDM = +2
Control: Computer = 1bis × 3, Panel = holodynamic link × 167, Special = headsUp, Environ = basic env, basic ls, extend ls, grav plates, inertial comp
Accomm: Crew = 1 (Bridge/Engineer = 1), Staterooms = 2, MidPsg = 3 (noncommercial), SubCraft = air/buggy
Other: Cargo = 40kliters, OreBays = 270kliters, Fuel = 504kliters, PurificationPlant, Scoops, ObjSize = average, EMLevel = faint

A modified type S scout/courier vessel, it is popular with belters.

FREE TRADER

CraftID: Free Trader, Type A, TL 15, MCr36.915
Hull: 180/450, Disp = 200, Config = 1SL, Armor = 40G, Unloaded = 1130tons, Loaded = 2280tons
Power: 4/8, Fusion = 990Mw, Duration = 30/90
Loco: 4/8, Maneuver = 1, 4/8, Jump = 1, NOE = 190kph, Cruise = 600kph, Top = 800kph, Agility = 2
Commo: Radio = System
Sensors: PassiveEMS = Interstellar, ActiveEMS = FarOrbit, ActObjScan = Rout, ActObjPin = Rout, PasEngScan = Rout
Off/Def: Hardpoints = 2, DefDM = +4
Control: Computer = 1 × 3, Panel = holodynamic link × 354, Special = headsUp × 2, Environ = basic env, basic ls, extend ls, grav plates, inertial comp
Accomm: Crew = 4 (Bridge = 1, Engineer = 1, Steward = 1, Medical = 1), Staterooms = 8, LowBerths = 8,
Other: Cargo = 1107kliters, Fuel = 627kliters, PurificationPlant, Scoops, ObjSize = Average, EMLevel = Faint

An interstellar merchant ship, it carries cargo and passengers.

FAR TRADER

CraftID: Far Trader, Type A2, TL 15, MCr41.07
Hull: 180/450, Disp = 200, Config = 3SL, Armor = 40G, Unloaded = 1180tons, Loaded = 2050tons
Power: 3/6, Fusion = 738Mw, Duration = 30/90
Loco: 4/8, Maneuver = 1, 5/10, Jump = 2, NOE = 190kph, Cruise = 750kph, Top = 1000kph, Agility = 1
Commo: Radio = System
Sensors: PassiveEMS = Interstellar, ActiveEMS = FarOrbit, ActObjScan = Rout, ActObjPin- = Rout, PasEngScan = Rout
Off/Def: Hardpoints = 2, DefDM = +3
Control: Computer = 1bis × 3, Panel = holodynamic link × 233, Special = headsUp × 2, Environ = basic basic ls, extend ls, grav plates, inertial comp
Accomm: Crew = 3 (Bridge = 1, Engineer = 1, Steward/Medical = 1), Staterooms = 10, SubCraft = air/raft
Other: Cargo = 823.5kliters, Fuel = 671kliters, PurificationPlant, Scoops, ObjSize = Average, EMLevel = Faint

It can be found anywhere in the Imperium where goods are traded.

SUBSIDIZED MERCHANT

CraftID: Subsidized Merchant, Type R, TL 15, MCr67.50
Hull: 360/900, Disp = 400, Config = 1SL, Armor = 40G, Unloaded = 2060tons, Loaded = 4840tons
Power: 5/10, Fusion = 1476Mw, Duration = 30/90
Loco: 7/14, Maneuver = 1, 7/14, Jump = 1, NOE = 190kph, Cruise = 750kph, Top = 1000kph, Agility = 1
Commo: Radio = System
Sensors: PassiveEMS = Interstellar, ActiveEMS = FarOrbit, ActObjScan = Rout, ActObjPin = Rout, PasEngScan = Rout
Off/Def: HardPoints = 4, DefDM = +3
Control: Computer = 1bis × 3, Panel = holodynamic link × 403, Special = headsUp × 3, Environ = basic env, basic ls, extend ls, grav plates, inertial comp
Accomm: Crew = 5Bridge = 1, Engineer = 2, Steward = 1, Medical = 1, Stateroom = 13, LowBerth = 13, SubCraft = launch
Other: Cargo = 2700kliters, Fuel = 1071kliters ObjSize = Average, EMLevel = Moderate

This vessel meets the commercial needs of a cluster of worlds.

YACHT

CraftID: Yacht, Type Y, TL 15, MCr43.585
Hull: 180/450, Disp = 200, Config = 1USL, Armor = 40G, Unloaded = 1080tons, Loaded = 1320tons
Power: 3/6, Fusion = 738Mw, Duration = 30/90
Loco: 4/8, Maneuver = 4, 4/8, Jump = 4, Cruise = 2550kph (vacuum only), Top = 3400kph (vacuum only), Agility = 1
Commo: Radio = System
Sensors: PassiveEMS = Interstellar, ActiveEMS = FarOrbit, ActObjScan = Rout, ActObjPin = Rout, PasEngScan = Rout
Off/Def: Hardpoints = 2, DefDM = +3
Control: Computer = 1 × 3, Panel = holodynamic link × 307, Special = headsUp × 2, Environ = basic env, basic ls, extend ls, grav plates, inertial comp
Accomm: Crew = 4 (Bridge = 1, Engineer = 1, Steward = 1, Medical = 1), Staterooms = 13 (1 double stateroom suite) SubCraft = ship's boat, air/raft, ATV
Other: Cargo = 148.5kliters, Fuel = 536kliters, PurificationPlant, ExtraFuel = 54kliters, ObjSize = Average, EMLevel = Faint

The yacht is a noble's plaything, used to entertain friends and undertake political or commercial missions.

PATROL CRUISER

CraftID: Patrol Cruiser, Type T, TL 15, MCr163.53
Hull: 396/990, Disp = 440, Config = 1SL, Armor = 40G, Unloaded = 3540tons, Loaded = 4390tons
Power: 15/30, Fusion = 4032Mw, Duration = 30 /90
Loco: 40/80, Maneuver = 4, 14/28, Jump = 3, NOE = 190kph, Cruise = 750kph, Top = 1000kph, Agility = 0
Commo: Radio = System
Sensors: EMMask, PassiveEMS = Interstellar, ActiveEMS = FarOrbit, Densitometer = HighPen/1km, Neutrino = 10kw ActObjScan = Rout, ActObjPin = Rout, PasObjScan = Rout, PasObjPin = Rout, PasEngScan = Simp, PasEngPin = Rout
Off: Missiles = x02
Batt 2
Bear 2
BeamLaser = x02
Batt 2
Bear 2
Def: DefDM = +4
Control: Computer = 3 × 3, Panel = holodynamic link × 578, Special = headsUp × 5, Environ = basic env, basic ls, extend ls, grav plates, inertial comp
Accomm: Crew = 8(Bridge = 2, Engineer = 2, Gunnery = 2, Command = 1, Medical = 1), Staterooms = 10, LowBerths = 4, SubCraft = GCarrier, 30-tonship'sboat
Other: Cargo = 675kliters, Fuel = 2530kliters, Scoops ObjSize = Average, EMLevel = Faint

This military vessel is for customs, piracy suppression, and safety.

MERCENARY CRUISER

CraftID: Mercenary Cruiser, Type C, TL 15, MCr245.102
Hull: 792/1980, Disp=880, Config=5USL, Armor=40G, Unloaded=1130tons, Loaded=2280tons
Power: 20/40, Fusion=5382Mw, Duration=30 /90
Loco: 58/116, Maneuver=1, 29/58, Jump=1, Cruise=900kph(vacuum only), Top=1200kph (vacuum only), Agility=0
Commo: Radio=System
Sensors: PassiveEMS=Interstellar, ActiveEMS=FarOrbit, ActObjScan=Rout, ActObjPin=Rout, PasEngScan=Rout
Off/Def: Hardpoints=8, DefDM=+6
Control: Computer=5×3, Panel=holodynamic link×576, Special=headsUp×6, Environ=basic env, basic ls, extend ls, grav plates, inertial comp
Accomm: Crew=8 (Bridge=2, Engineer=3, Maintenance=1, Command=1, Medical=1), Staterooms=19 SubCraft=pinnace×2, extraModules×2, ATV×2, air/raft
Other: Cargo=1080kliters, Fuel=4097kliters, ExtraFuel=648kliters, ObjSize=Average, EMLevel=Moderate

**Note:* The price of subordinate craft is not included.

The merchant cruiser is built to carry small military (mercenary) units for corporate or government operations.

LABORATORY SHIP

CraftID: Laboratory Ship, Type L, TL 15, MCr72.13
Hull: 360/900, Disp=400, Config=1USL, Armor=40G, Unloaded=2230tons, Loaded=2640tons
Power: 5/10, Fusion=1480Mw, Duration=30/90
Loco: 7/14, Maneuver=1, 11/22, Jump=2, Cruise=900kph, Top=1200kph, Agility=1
Commo: Radio=System
Sensors: PassiveEMS=Interstellar, ActiveEMS=FarOrbit, Densitometer=HighPen/1km, Neutrino=10kw, ActObjScan=Rout, ActObjPin=Rout, PasObjScan=Rout, PasObjPin=Rout, PasEngScan=Simp
Off/Def: HardPoints=4, DefDM=+4
Control: Computer=2×3, Panel=holodynamic link×420, Special=headsUp×3, Environ=basic env, basic ls, extend ls, grav plates, inertial comp
Accomm: Crew=5(Bridge=1,Engineer=2,Stewards=1, Medical=1),Staterooms=20,SubCraft=pinnace, air/raft×2
Other: Cargo=310kliters, Laboratory=1150kliters, Fuel=1342kliters, PurificationPlant ObjSize=Average, EMLevel=Moderate

Note: The price of subordinate craft is not included.

A mobile base for scientific analysis, it includes a laboratory.

SAFARI SHIP

CraftID: Safari Ship, Type K, TL 15, MCr51.77
Hull: 180/450, Disp=200, Config=6SL, Armor=40G, Unloaded=1220tons, Loaded=1350tons
Power: 4/8, Fusion=1026Mw, Duration=30 /90
Loco: 4/8, Maneuver=1, 5/10, Jump=2, NOE=190kph, Cruise=750kph, Top=1000kph, Agility=2
Commo: Radio=System
Sensors: PassiveEMS=Interstellar, ActiveEMS=FarOrbit, Densitometer=HighPen/1km ActObjScan=Rout, ActObjPin=Rout, PasObjScan=Rout, PasObjPin=Rout, PasEngScan=Rout
Off/Def: Hardpoints=2, DefDM=+4
Control: Computer=1bis×3, Panel=holodynamic link×225, Special=headsUp×3, Environ=basic env, basic ls, extend ls, grav plates, inertial comp
Accomm: Crew=4 (Bridge=1, Engineer=1, Steward=1, Medical=1) Staterooms=11, TrophyLounge=95kliters SubCraft=launch, air/raft
Other: Cargo=81kliters, CaptureHold=189kliters, Fuel=775kliters, PurificationPlant, Scoops, ObjSize=Average, EMLevel=Moderate

This vessel is for trophy-taking (real or photographic) expeditions.

CLOSE ESCORT

CraftID: Close Escort, Type CE, TL 14, MCr301.37
Hull: 387/968, Disp=330, Config=1SL, Armor=49G, Unloaded=7080tons, Loaded=7340tons, DropTanks=1350kliters
Power: 55/110, Fusion=7400Mw, Duration=13 /39
Loco: 38/76, Maneuver=5, 16/32, Jump=5, NOE=190kph, Cruise=750kph, Top=1000kph, Agility=0
Commo: Radio=System
Sensors: EMMask, PassiveEMS=Interstellar, ActiveEMS=FarOrbit, EMSJammer=FarOrbit, Densitometer=HighPen/1km, Neutrino=10kw ActObjScan=Rout, ActObjPin=Rout, PasObjScan=Rout, PasObjPin=Rout, PasEngScan=Simp, PasEngPin=Rout
Off: BeamLaser=x04
Batt 2
Bear 2
ParticleAcel=x01
Batt 2
Bear 2
Def: DefDM= +5
Control: Computer=6 × 3, Panel=holodynamic link × 529, Special=headsUp × 5, Environ=basic env, basic ls, extend ls, grav plates, inertial comp
Accomm: Crew=10 (Bridge=2, Engineer=2, Gunnery=4, Command=1, Medical=1), Staterooms=8, SubCraft=gig
Other: Cargo=81kliters, Fuel=2500kliters, PurificationPlant, Scoops, ObjSize=Average, EMLevel=Faint

The close escort is a heavily armed ship used as a fighter aboard a larger ship or used as an independent vessel to escort convoys.

GIG

CraftID: Gig, TL 14, MCr13.78
Hull: 18/45, Disp=20, Config=1SL, Armor=40G, Unloaded=360tons, Loaded=400tons
Power: 4/8, Fusion=495Mw, Duration=5/15
Loco: 3/6, Maneuver=6, NOE=190kph, Cruise=750kph, Top=1000kph, Agility=0
Commo: Radio=System
Sensors: PassiveEMS=Interplanetary, ActiveEMS=Planetary, ActObjScan=Diff, ActObjPin=Diff, PasEngScan=Rout
Off: BeamLaser=x02
Batt 1
Bear 1
Def: DefDM= +2
Control: Computer=0 × 3, Panel=holodynamic link × 282, Special=headsUp, Environ=basic env, basic ls, extend ls, grav plates, inertial comp
Accomm: Crew=3 (Bridge=1, Commander=1, Gunner=1), Seats=roomy × 3, EmergLowBerth=2
Other: Cargo=40.5kliters, Fuel=33kliters, Scoops, ObjSize=small, EMLevel=faint

The gig is a small, armed space-faring craft and is often carried by another vessel to serve as a fighter/lifeboat.

SYSTEM DEFENSE BOAT

CraftID: System Defense Boat, Type SB, TL 15, MCr311.11
Hull: 360/900, Disp = 400, Config = 4SL, Armor = 67G, Unloaded = 10,980tons, Loaded = 11,150tons
Power: 32/64, Fusion = 8730Mw, Duration = 20/60
Loco: 61/122, Maneuver = 6, NOE = 190kph, Cruise = 750kph, Top = 1000kph, Agility = 1
Commo: Radio = System
Sensors: EMMask, PassiveEMS = Interstellar, ActiveEMS = FarOrbit, Densitometer = HighPen/1km, Neutrino = 10kw ActObjScan = Rout, ActObjPin = Rout, PasObjScan = Rout, PasObjPin = Rout, PasEngScan = Simp, PasEngPin = Rout
Off: Missiles = x03
Batt 2
Bear 2
BeamLaser = x04
Batt 2
Bear 2
Def: DefDM = +7
Control: Computer = 5 × 3, Panel = holodynamic link × 842, Special = headsUp × 5, Environ = basic env, basic ls, extend ls, grav plates, inertial comp
Accomm: Crew = 12 (Bridge = 2, Engineer = 2, Maintenance = 2, Gunnery = 4, Command = 1, Medical = 1), Staterooms = 10
Other: Cargo = 27kliters, Fuel = 2100kliters, PurificationPlant, Scoops ObjSize = Average, EMLevel = Faint

The SDB is a nonjump military vessel stationed in an important system and charged with its defense; it is used for customs inspections, piracy suppression, and normal safety patrols.

CORSAIR

CraftID: Corsair, Type P, TL 15, MCr138.74
Hull: 396/990, Disp = 440, Config = 4USL, Armor = 40G, Unloaded = 3090tons, Loaded = 5310tons
Power: 17/34, Fusion = 4590Mw, Duration = 20/60
Loco: 29/58, Maneuver = 3, 11/22, Jump = 2, Cruise = 2135kph (vacuum only), Top = 2850kph (vacuum only), Agility = 2
Commo: Radio = System
Sensors: EMMask, PassiveEMS = Interstellar, ActiveEMS = FarOrbit, EMSJammer = FarOrbit, Densitometer = HighPen/1km, Neutrino = 10kw ActObjScan = Rout, ActObjPin = Rout, PasObjScan = Rout, PasObjPin = Rout, PasEngScan = Simp, PasEngPin = Rout
Off: BeamLaser = x04
Batt 1
Bear 1
Def: DefDM = +5
Control: Computer = 2 × 3, Panel = holodynamic link × 905, Special = headsUp × 5, Environ = basic env, basic ls, extend ls, grav plates, inertial comp
Accomm: Crew = 11 (Bridge = 3, Engineer = 3, Gunnery = 3, Command = 1, Medical = 1), Staterooms = 10, EmergLowBerths = 5,
Other: Cargo = 2090kliters, Fuel = 1910kliters ObjSize = Average, EMLevel = Faint

The corsair is an armed ship, most commonly used by pirates or privateers to raid merchant spacecraft.

Travelling

Travellers do just that, they travel. Each interstellar jump places new worlds before the adventurers—exotic and far away settings for every conceivable activity from bold commercial ventures, to quests after fabled alien artifacts, to high-tech military expeditions.

Each new encounter on a world's surface can bring with it new challenges, new unsolved mysteries, or new information. Interchange with local personalities and the conflict in goals that inevitably occurs between the locals and the characters make for some memorable moments in adventuring.

Travel is fundamental to **Traveller**: both travel on the surface of a world and travel between worlds.

SURFACE TRAVEL

Travelling on a world's surface can involve everything from foot travel to high-speed grav vehicle travel. Travel can be on the ground, in the air, or over or underwater. The setting can be an urban one (from rural to densly populated) or remote wilderness (from lightly populated to vast empty expanses).

The Surface Travel tables provide the referee with the basic information she needs to administer surface travel. The Surface Travel Rates table provides information about how fast different modes of transporation move. The Surface Travel Movement Guide provides a quick reference relating world hex size to movement.

SPACE TRAVEL

Travel between worlds forms the most important type of travel to be undertaken by characters. Characters can purchase individual passages aboard a vessel, they can charter a ship, and those with sufficient resources may even elect to purchase a starship.

Space travel can be of two types: *interplanetary travel* to worlds within a star system, and *interstellar travel* between star systems.

Interplanetary Travel: Worlds orbiting the same star are accessible by interplanetary travel, on ships operated by local entrepreneurs, or with a variety of small craft.

Interplanetary travel takes time. The diagram of a typical interplanetary journey shows the procedure used for moving between worlds in the same star system. The travel formulae can be used to determine time required (if distance and acceleration are known), acceleration required (if distance and time are known), and distance travelled (if time and acceleration are known).

All of the formulae use the MKS (meters, kilograms, seconds) unit system, and they assume that the ship is undertaking a journey from a standing start, that it accelerates continuously to the midpoint of the trip, and then decelerates back to a stop again. In addition, several travel times and travel distances have been precalculated for ready reference.

Interstellar Travel: Worlds orbiting different stars are reached by interstellar travel, which makes use of the jump drive. Once a starship moves to a safe sdistance from a world, it may activate its jump drive. Jump drives are rated from 1 to 6, which are the number of parsecs which can be travelled in one week. Actually, making any jump takes about one week regardless of the distance travelled. Transit time to 100 diameters from a Size 8 world takes five hours at 1G.

Commercial starships usually make two jumps per month. They spend one week in jump, followed by one week in the star system, travelling from the jump point to the local world, refuelling, marketing cargo, finding passengers, leaving the starport, and proceeding to a jump point again. The week in the system usually provides some time for crew recreation and for wandering around the planet.

Noncommercial ships usually follow the same schedule of one week in jump and one week in a system. If haste is called for, a ship may refuel immediately and rejump right away. This allows the ship to make one jump per week but makes no provision for cargo, passengers, or local stops.

Interstellar travel is priced on the basis of accommodations; prices cover a trip from starport to starport, encompassing one jump regardless of length. There are four types of passage:

High Passage: The best method of travel is called high passage, which involves first class accommodations and cuisine. High passengers have the services of the ship's steward, entertainment, and complete attention to their comfort. There is a baggage allowance of up to 1000 kilograms. High passage costs Cr10,000.

Middle Passage: In order for starships to fill their staterooms with passengers, middle passage is offered on a standby basis, in the event that not enough high passages are sold. While middle passengers occupy staterooms normally similar to those occupied by high passengers, they do not receive the service or entertainment accorded the high paying passengers. In addition, the quality of the cuisine is mediocre. Baggage totalling 100 kilograms is allowed. Middle passage costs Cr8000.

A middle passenger may be "bumped" and the stateroom taken by a late arriving high passenger; the middle passenger's ticket is returned, but no other compensation is made. (The bumped individual could, of course, then buy a high passage

and in turn bump some other middle passenger if the extra cost seemed worth it.)

Working Passage: A starship captain with a crew shortage may hire an individual to fill the vacant position and pay not money but passage in return. Working passage may not continue for more than three jumps, or the individual is considered to have been hired for standard salary. In order to be hired for working passage, the individual must have some expertise in the position for which he or she is hired. Baggage totalling 1000 kilograms is allowed. Working passage costs nothing to the individual.

Low Passage: Transportation while in cryogenic sleep (suspended animation) is possible at relatively low cost to the passenger. The passenger is placed in a low passage berth before the ship takes off and travels the entire journey in a state of suspended animation. He does not age, and requires very little life support. Unfortunately, the low passage system involves some intrinsic dangers to the passenger, and he runs some risk of not surviving the voyage. Surviving uses the following UTP:

To survive a low passage voyage: Routine, Medical, Edu, 1 min. (fateful).

Referee: The Medical skill and Education characteristics used as modifiers to this task roll are those of the attending physician at the time of deberthing, not those of the character at risk. Various affects occur for any mishap (roll 2D): **Superficial Mishap:** The subject temporarily suffers 1D wounds for 1-6 days, after which healing is automatic; skin loses some of its tone and color for 1-6 weeks, having a gray, wrinkled appearance. **Minor Mishap:** The subject temporarily suffers 2D wounds for 1-6 days, after which healing is automatic; subject experiences motor function problems for 1-6 weeks with corresponding loss of 2 points of dexterity during that time. **Major Mishap:** The subject suffers 3D permanent wounds; the subject's internal organs are damaged; and the subject must undergo medical diagnosis and treatment to restore full health. **Destroyed Mishap:** This is not possible on a 2D mishap.

Commercial starship lines offering low berth passage typically guarantee that deberthing will be conducted by a physician of at least skill level 3; TAS advises all travellers to exercise caution when travelling low berth.

Stowaways: Stowing away on a starship is a fifth form of passage and the least advisable. Sneaking aboard a starship in order to gain passage to the next world is illegal on almost all worlds, if only because it operates to the detriment of the starship owner's economic standing. It is also often a violation of various customs regulations.

To discover a stowaway aboard a vessel:
Routine, Steward, Int, 2 min.

Referee: One attempt can be made per day. Various elaborate schemes on the part of the stowaway may allow DMs to this throw, based on the referee's judgment. Upon discovery, the stowaway must roll for the starship captain's reaction. A reaction of actively uncooperative or hostile behavior will result in spacing: the stowaway is forced out the air lock without a vacc suit. Other reactions are determined by the referee. Potential stowaways should realize that cargo holds are often depressurized during a trip.

LESSER KNOWN ASPECTS OF SPACE TRAVEL

As interstellar travel has developed, the field has developed its own dangers and customs. The following are just a few:

The Travellers' Aid Society: Individuals who have decided that they wish to pursue a life of travel and adventure may elect to join the Travellers' Aid Society in order to take advantage of its facilities and passage dividends. Members of the Travellers' Aid Society receive, as a dividend of membership, one high passage every two months. The high passage may be used, retained for later use, or sold for 90 percent of its cash value.

Membership in the Travellers' Aid Society may be acquired as a mustering out benefit using the benefits table in the navy and marine careers. Membership may also be purchased using the following task:

To be allowed to purchase a Travellers' Aid Society membership:

Routine, Admin, Int, 10 min (safe).

Referee: If a mishap occurs, the character has been "blackballed" and may not purchase a membership. Upon acceptance, the character must pay an initiation fee of Cr1,000,000. Only one application per person is allowed. Membership is for the life of the character and is not transferable.

Hijacking: Starships can be easy prey for hijackers. Starship crews maintain a constant guard against hijackers, and the ship's computer can run an antihijacking program which denies access to controlled areas to potential hijackers. Passengers are required to check all weapons (except blades and daggers) into the ship's locker; they are returned at the end of the voyage.

Nevertheless, there is a chance of an attempted hijacking, for ransom or to steal the multimillion credit vessel. Roll three dice for 18+ to indicate a hijacking attempt (this throw does not apply if all passengers are player characters). When an attempt occurs, randomly determine the number of hijackers, their identities, characteristics, and weapons, and implement their attempt at some point during the voyage. They will gain complete control of the ship only after defeating all other individuals on the ship. If the antihijacking program is functioning, gaining access to the bridge uses the following task:

To fool an antihijacking program and gain illegal access to a starship's bridge:

Formidable, Intrusion, Tactics, 2 min (fateful, uncertain).

Referee: The difficulty level on this task applies when an antihijacking program is running; otherwise the task becomes Difficult. If this task fails, an alarm has sounded on the bridge, warning the bridge crew. The hijacker(s) will know they have failed to achieve surprise only if their roll fails. Success at this task allows the hijackers to enter the bridge; subsequent combat may be called for.

The results of hijacking range from release of passengers without harm to marooning on uninhabited worlds to spacing and death.

Skipping: Most starships are purchased on credit, and the monthly payments required against the multimillion credit debt are staggering. The owner or captain may decide to steal the ship himself instead of remaining under that load. Passengers have no way themselves of determining if a specific ship is in such a status. Throw 12+ to determine whether a commercial ship is of this type.

Ships which have skipped are subject to repossession attempts if detected by the authorities. Such attempts may range from the formal service of papers, to legal injunctions, to armed boarding parties.

On each world's landing with a skipped ship, a repossession attempt will occur on 3+; apply a DM of -1 per 5 parsecs distance from the ship's homeworld, to a maximum of -9. If the ship has called on the same world twice within the last two months, apply a DM of +2.

Piracy: A starship may be attacked by pirates while entering or leaving a system. Similar encounters may involve customs agents or military vessels, including blockades. The ship encounter flowchart later in this book indicates the procedure.

Gas Giants: Most star systems include in their family of planets one or more gas giants, large worlds with hydrogen or methane atmospheres. These gas giants are a valuable source of fuel for starships.

In order to refuel from a gas giant, a ship must move into orbit around it and then dive deep into its atmosphere with open fuel scoops. The procedure (called skimming) takes approximately ten hours and results in fuel tanks filled with unrefined fuel. When skimming, perform the following task:

To skim a gas giant for starship fuel:

Routine, Pilot, Navigation, 1 hour (hazardous).

Referee: The upper reaches of a gas giant's atmosphere are dangerous. Mishaps can include simple turbulence, excessive radiation exposure, collision with debris, heat damage to the ship's hull, getting caught in a swirling cyclone storm, or getting caught in the gas giant's gravity well.

Ocean Refuelling: Ships can refuel from the water oceans of any world with a non-zero hydrographic percentage. Ocean refueling may require a permit on some worlds; roll Law Level or less on 2D to determine this. If the players wish to refuel their ship illegally, they should avoid populated areas, and they will have to circumvent the local world's sensors (if any).

The process calls for the ship to land in or near an ocean and fill its tanks from the local water supply. It takes approximately four hours and results in fuel tanks filled with unrefined fuel. When ocean refueling, perform the following task:

To refuel a starship from an ocean:

Routine, Pilot, Sensor Ops, 30 min.

Referee: Mishaps, when they occur, can include water leaks, corrosion damage from sea salts, running aground, sinking, or getting caught in a hurricane storm.

STARSHIP MALFUNCTIONS

A starship can malfunction. The two major malfunctions are drive failure and misjump. The primary influencing factors are unrefined fuel and lack of maintenance.

Refined fuel is available at starports at about Cr500 per ton; unrefined fuel is available at starports for Cr100 per ton, or it can be skimmed from gas giants for free. In addition, water can be taken from oceans or lakes (if there are any on the world) and used as unrefined fuel.

Military and quasimilitary starships often use unrefined fuel because it is more plentiful, and because their drives are specially built to use it. Commercial ships almost always use unrefined fuel because it is cheaper. (A fuel purification plant is necessary to safely use unrefined fuel.)

Starships require continuing maintenance as they operate and an annual maintenance overhaul to keep them in top running order. Ships which are undercrewed and do not carry enough dedicated or full-time skilled engineers and those which avoid or delay their annual maintenance run the risk of malfunction. See the Starship Operation Flowchart for details.

THE ECONOMICS OF STARSHIP OPERATION

Operating a starship in the interstellar market requires an understanding of how trade between the stars works. This includes an understanding of supply and demand control prices, as well as returns on effort and investment. Because starships are so expensive, many of the prices used when discussing them are expressed in megacredits (abbreviated MCr); a megacredit is one million credits.

STARSHIP PURCHASE

Bank financing is available to qualified individuals for the purchase of commercial startships. After the individual makes a down payment of 20 percent of the cash price of the starship, the shipyard will begin construction of a specific vessel.

Upon completion, the shipyard delivers the vessel to the buyer, and the bank pays the purchase price to the shipyard. Because the bank now holds title to the ship, the ship's purchase price must be paid off in a series of monthly payments to the bank. Standard terms involve the payment of 1/240th of the cash price each month for 480 months. In effect, interest and bank financing cost a simple 120 percent of the final cost of the ship, and the total financed price equals 220 percent of the cash purchase price, paid off over a period of 40 years.

The bank will insist that the purchaser submit an economic plan detailing the projected activity which will guarantee that monthly payments are made. Unless a character has some form of guaranteed income (perhaps large rents from some property he owns), this requirement generally rules out financed purchases of yachts, military vessels, or exploratory vessels.

Subsidies: The government may subsidize larger commercial vessels (built on type 600 hulls or larger), primarily to assure consistent service to specific worlds. These subsidized merchants are generally assigned a specific route connecting from 2 to 12 worlds of varying characteristics. The route will generally be determined before a subsidized merchant is purchased, to allow tailored design features as may be necessary.

When a subsidized merchant is ordered, the character himself must make the 20 percent down payment, with the government assuming responsibility for the payments upon delivery and taking 50 percent of the gross receipts of the ship while in service. The character is responsible for all expenses and costs of operation.

Subsidized merchants are also subject to mobilization (and use as auxiliaries) in the event of emergency or hostilities. At the end of 40 years, the vessel is completely paid off, and full title passes to the character, but the vessel remains subject to mobilization in case of government need.

STARSHIP EXPENSES

There are five basic expenses (in addition to the bank payment, if necessary) which are associated with starship operation:

1. Fuel. Starship fuel costs Cr500 per ton (refined) or Cr100 per ton (unrefined) at most starports. Fuel consumption is based on formulae related to the size of the starship power plant and the jump drive.

2. Life Support. Each occupied stateroom on a starship involves an overhead cost of Cr2000 per trip (two weeks) made. Each occupied low passage berth involves an overhead cost of Cr100 per usage. There is a normal limit of one person per stateroom, and travelling couples or groups usually take adjoining staterooms. Military vessels or chartered ships may be used with a double occupancy system (two persons per stateroom), but this requires twice the normal cost.

3. Routine Maintenance. Annually, a starship should be given a complete overhaul in order to insure that it is kept in good working order. Such maintenance costs 0.1 percent (1/1000th) of the cash price of the ship and requires two weeks at a class A or B starport. The owner must make provision for payment of the maintenance fee when it comes due. Crewmembers generally take their vacations at this time but must still receive their salaries. The ship owners must make provision for the expected loss of revenue while the ship is out of service.

4. Crew Salaries. Crewmembers must be paid monthly. Non-player characters must be paid using the standard crew salary schedule (with suitable modifications for expertise or seniority, generally +10 percent for each level of expertise above level 1). Player characters may bargain for better pay rates, or they may elect to accept worse. In addition, player characters may participate with the owner-captain and accept shares in the proceeds of the ship's activities.

Characters who take working passage are not paid, and receive passage, room, and board in lieu of salary (continuous working passage for more than three trips results in automatic

hiring and receipt of salary). The starship captain is usually the pilot or navigator and serves as owner-aboard, drawing his pay from the profits. Not all crew positions are required on all ships, and some ships will have more than one person performing the same function. For example, a large liner may have more than one steward.

5. Berthing Costs. Landing fees, handling costs, facilities use charges, and other starport fees are a common practice, and such costs must be paid as they occur. The average cost is Cr100 to land and remain for up to six days; thereafter, a Cr100 per day fee is imposed for each additional day spent in port. In some locations this fee will be higher, while at others local government subsidies will lower or eliminate it.

REVENUE

Ships generate revenue from cargo, passengers, and mail.

Cargo: Starships may inquire at a starport about the number, sizes, and destinations of cargos awaiting transportation. The referee should determine all worlds accessible to the starship (depending on jump number) and use the trade and commerce flowchart to determine available cargos.

Each cargo is a distinct shipment and cannot be subdivided, but the ship may accept or reject specific cargos based on the best fit within the cargo hold. All cargos are carried at Cr1000 per ton. Starship owners may purchase goods locally and ship them at their own expense, speculating that they can later sell at a profit. The trade and commerce flowchart illustrates the details of the speculative trading process.

Passengers: After a starship has accepted cargo for a specific destination, passengers will present themselves for transport to that particular destination. The procedure for locating passengers is illustrated on the trade and commerce flowchart.

Passengers will pay the standard fare for the class of transportation which they choose: standard fares are Cr10,000 for high passage, Cr8000 for middle passage, and Cr1000 for low passage. Passage is always sold to interested prospective passengers on the basis of transport to the announced destination rather than on the basis of jump distance. Differences in starship jump drive capacity have no specific effect on passage prices.

For example, a jump-3 starship charges the same passage price as a jump-1 starship. The difference between the two passages is that a jump-3 ship can reach a destination in one jump, while the jump-1 ship would take three separate jumps (through two intermediate destinations, which would require three separate tickets) to reach it. Higher jump numbers also may make otherwise inaccessible destinations within reach. But for two ships of differing jump numbers going to the same destination in one jump, each would charge the same cargo or passage price.

Mail and Incidentals: Subsidized merchants may receive mail delivery contracts, usually serving as an adjunct to their established routes. In order to receive mail delivery contracts, the ship must be able to dedicate five tons of ship cargo capacity to postal duty on a full-time basis; the ship must be armed; and a gunner must be a part of the crew at all times. The starship is paid Cr25,000 (which amounts to Cr5000 per ton of postal cargo area) for each trip which is made, regardless of the actual mail tonnage carried on any particular trip. The actual mail delivery tonnage will not exceed a total of five tons on each trip.

Other ships may, on occasion, be approached by an individual to deliver private messages, at times through the ship's owner or captain and at times clandestinely through a crewmember. Private mail is usually intended for delivery to a specific point (such as the Travellers' Aid society building or a tavern in startown), and is generally accompanied by a Cr20 to Cr120 honorarium. A private message can be handled by the referee as the motive for an encounter; see Encounters for details.

TRADE CUSTOMS

The following are standard procedures in interstellar commerce:

Delivery: Goods taken on in orbit are delivered when placed in orbit around the destination. Goods loaded on a planetary surface are delivered when off-loaded on the surface of the destination. This custom applies to cargo, passengers, and mail.

Shuttle Service: At any location with either a class A, B, or C starport, shuttles operate on a routine basis between orbit and world surface. Typical shuttle fares are sold to interested individuals for Cr10 per ton of cargo and Cr20 to Cr120 per passenger.

Charters: Nonstarships charter for Cr1 per displacement ton per hour, usually with a 12-hour minimum. Charter price for a starship is computed based on that particular starship's revenue-generating capacity. Starships are chartered in two-week blocks; the charge for chartering a starship is Cr900 per ton of cargo hold, plus Cr9000 per high passage berth and Cr900 per low passage berth. The owner of the starship being chartered pays all overhead expenses and supplies a crew for the trip.

STARSHIP ENCOUNTERS

1 Ship Type

Determine the ship type being encountered.

SHIP TYPE

Die	Type
1	Merchant (go to 2)
2	Civilian (go to 3)
3	Non-Starship (go to 4)
4	Xboat (go to 5)
5	Scout (go to 6)
6	Naval (go to 7)

2 Merchant Type Ship

Die	Type
2	Freighter (1000+ tons)
3	Subsidized Merchant
4	Nonstandard
5	Subsidized Merchant
6	Seeker
7	Free Trader
8	Subsidized Liner
9	Far Trader
10	Far Trader
11	Freighter (1000+ tons)
12	Freighter (5000+ tons)

DMs: If system only accessible by jump-2, DM+4.

Merchant Mission

Die	Type
2	Distress
3	Smuggling
4	Trade
5	Trade
6	Trade and Transport
7	Trade and Transport
8	Trade and Transport
9	Transport
10	Transport
11	Transport
12	Piracy

Note: If ship type is Seeker, replace Transport with Prospecting.

3 Civilian Type Ship

Die	Type
2	Liner (1000+ tons)
3	Yacht
4	Nonstandard
5	Yacht
6	Seeker
7	Detached Scout
8	Safari Ship
9	Mercenary Cruiser
10	Mercenary Cruiser
11	Lab Ship
12	Liner (5000+ tons)

DMs: If system only accessible by jump-2, DM+4.

Civilian Mission

Die	Type
2	Distress
3	Smuggling
4	Courier
5	Charter
6	Transport
7	Transport
8	Pleasure Tour
9	Business
10	Business
11	Business
12	Piracy

Note: If ship type is Lab Ship, replace Business with Research.

4 Non-Starship Type

Die	Type
2	Bulk Transport
3	Pinnace
4	Nonstandard
5	Launch
6	Shuttle
7	Shuttle
8	Cutter
9	Tug
10	Ship's Boat
11	System Defense Boat
12	System Defense Boat

Non-Starship Mission

Die	Type
2	Distress
3	Smuggling
4	Courier
5	Charter
6	Courier
7	Courier
8	Transport
9	Transport
10	Transport
11	Transport
12	Piracy

5 Xboat Type Ship

Die	Type
2	Scout Courier
3	Scout Courier
4	Nonstandard
5	Xboat
6	Xboat
7	Xboat
8	Xboat Tender
9	Xboat Tender
10	Xboat Tender
11	Xboat Tender
12	Xboat and Tender

XBoat Mission

Die	Type
2	Distress
3	Courier
4	Courier
5	Communciation
6	Communciation
7	Communciation
8	Communciation
9	Communciation
10	Communciation
11	Communciation
12	Piracy

6 Scout Type Ship

Die	Type
2	Xboat Tender
3	Scout Courier
4	Nonstandard
5	Scout Courier
6	Scout Courier
7	Scout Surveyor
8	Scout Surveyor
9	Scout Surveyor
10	Scout Surveyor
11	Scout Cruiser
12	Scout Cruiser

DMs: If system only accessible by jump-2, DM+4.

Scout Mission

Die	Type
2	Distress
3	Smuggling
4	Escort
5	Courier
6	Courier
7	Courier
8	Transfer
9	Patrol
10	Patrol
11	Patrol
12	Privateering

Note: If Scout Surveyor, replace Patrol with Survey.

7 Naval Type Ship

Die	Type
2	Fuel Shuttle
3	Fighter
4	Carrier (100,000 tons)
5	Escort (5000 tons)
6	Fast Courier
7	Patrol Escort
8	Escort (1000 tons)
9	Cruiser (20,000 tons)
10	Cruiser (50,000 tons)
11	Cruiser (100,000 tons)
12	Battleship

Naval Mission

Die	Mission
2	Distress
3	Escort
4	Escort
5	Courier
6	Courier
7	Patrol
8	Patrol
9	Transfer
10	Maneuvers
11	Transport
12	Privateering

8 Ship Disposition

Die	Disposition
2	Hasty Departure
3	Hasty Departure
4	Leaving
5	Leaving
6	Standing By
7	Standing By
8	Standing By
9	Arriving
10	Arriving
11	Hasty Arrival
12	Hasty Arrival

1 Starship Operations

Determine the ship type being operated, its capabilities, and the characteristics of the star system being travelled to.

This chart illustrates the procedures for travelling to another world with a jump-capable starship.

Annual Maintenance: If the ship is in need of annual maintenance and a mishap occurs on any task, roll 3D instead of 2D on the Mishap Table.

System Crosschecks: System crosschecks should be performed on all asterisked tasks. To do so, declare the task cautious. Otherwise, the task attempt becomes uncertain, with a *warning light* event to occur at a later time if **Some Truth** is a result of the task. The warning light situation produces a fateful task to avoid the problem becoming more serious.

2 Power Up

If the ship has been parked for less than 8 days, the power plant may be warm started; otherwise, it must be cold started.

To warm start a starship:
Routine*, Engineering, Edu, 30 sec.

To cold start a starship:
Routine*, Engineering, Edu, 5 min.

3 Prepare Maneuver Drive

The maneuver drive must be prepared.

To prepare maneuver drive:
Routine*, Engineering, Edu, 10 sec.
Referee: This task must succeed or the maneuver drive cannot be engaged.

Desperate Jump: A desperate jump can be attempted at this point; go to step 7.

4 Travel To Orbit

If the ship is not already in orbit, take it from the world's surface to orbit.

To pilot a ship from surface to orbit:
Routine, Pilot or Ship's Boat, Edu.
Referee: The Travel Time To Orbit table shows the expected travel times.

TRAVEL TIMES TO ORBIT

World	*Acceleration*					
Size	*1G*	*2G*	*3G*	*4G*	*5G*	*6G*
0	6m	5m	4m	3m	2m	1m
1	13m	9m	8m	7m	6m	5m
2	19m	13m	11m	9m	8m	8m
3	23m	16m	13m	12m	10m	9m
4	27m	19m	15m	13m	12m	11m
5	30m	21m	17m	15m	13m	12m
6	33m	23m	19m	16m	15m	13m
7	35m	25m	20m	18m	16m	14m
8	38m	27m	22m	19m	17m	15m
9	40m	28m	23m	20m	18m	16m
A	42m	30m	24m	21m	19m	17m

Starship Encounters: Check for a starship encounter during this journey.

Desperate Jump: A desperate jump can be attempted at this point; go to step 7.

5 Travel To Ten Diameters

Take the ship to ten diameters out from the world.

To pilot a ship to ten diameters:
Simple, Pilot or Ship's Boat, Edu.
Referee: The Travel Times to Ten Diameters Table shows the expected travel times.

TRAVEL TIMES TO TEN DIAMETERS

World	*Acceleration*					
Size	*1G*	*2G*	*3G*	*4G*	*5G*	*6G*
0	14m	10m	18m	7m	6m	5m
1	40m	28m	23m	20m	28m	16m
2	57m	40m	33m	28m	25m	23m
3	69m	49m	40m	35m	31m	28m
4	1.3h	57m	46m	40m	36m	33m
5	1.5h	63m	52m	45m	40m	37m
6	1.6h	69m	57m	49m	44m	40m
7	1.8h	1.2h	61m	53m	47m	43m
8	1.9h	1.3h	65m	57m	51m	46m
9	2.0h	1.4h	69m	60m	54m	49m
A	2.1h	1.5h	1.2h	63m	57m	52m
SGG	3.3h	2.4h	1.9h	1.7h	1.5h	1.4h
LGG	5.8h	4.1h	3.3h	2.9h	2.6	2.4h

Starship Encounters: Check for a starship encounter during this journey.

Dangerous Jump: A dangerous jump can be attempted at this point; go to step 7.

6 Travel To 100 Diameters

Take the ship to 100 diameters out from the world.

To pilot a ship to 100 diameters:
Simple, Pilot or Ship's Boat, Edu.
Referee: The Travel Times to 100 Diameters Table shows the expected travel times.

TRAVEL TIMES TO 100 DIAMETERS

World	*Acceleration*					
Size	*1G*	*2G*	*3G*	*4G*	*5G*	*6G*
0	45m	32m	26m	22m	20m	18m
1	45m	32m	26m	22m	20m	18m
2	3.0h	1.5h	1.2h	63m	57m	52m
3	3.7h	2.6h	2.1h	1.8h	1.6h	1.5h
4	4.2h	3.0h	2.4h	2.1h	1.9h	1.7h
5	4.7h	3.3h	2.7h	2.4h	2.1h	1.9h
6	5.2h	3.7h	3.0h	2.6h	2.3h	2.1h
7	5.6h	3.9h	3.2h	2.8h	2.5h	2.3h
8	6.0h	4.2h	3.4h	3.0h	2.7h	2.4h
9	6.3h	4.5h	3.7h	3.2h	2.8h	2.6h
A	6.7h	4.7h	3.8h	3.3h	3.0h	2.7h
SGG	10h	7.5h	6.1h	5.3h	4.7h	4.3h
LGG	18h	12h	10h	9.1h	8.2h	7.5h

Starship Encounters: Check for a starship encounter during this journey.

Safe Jump: A safe jump can be attempted at this point.

7 Prepare For Jump

Preparing for jump consists of computing the jump coordinates and preparing the jump drive.

To compute jump coordinates:
Routine, Navigation, Pilot, 2 min.
Referee: This task can begin any time after the ship powers up. The navigator also designates whether the destination in the system is the mainworld, a gas giant, or some other world.

To prepare jump drive for jump:
Routine*, Engineering, Edu, 2 min.
Referee: This task can begin any time after the ship powers up. This task must succeed or the jump drive cannot be engaged.

If the ship is using unrefined fuel (without a fuel purification plant), this task is hazardous.

If the ship is past annual maintenance, this task is hazardous. For every month past annual maintenance, increase the difficulty one level.

8 Engage Jump Drive

Engaging jump drive consists of a routine procedure.

To engage jump drive:
Routine, Engineering, Edu, 2 min.
Referee: This task can begin once a successful jump preparation has been accomplished.

If the ship is using unrefined fuel (without a fuel purification plant), this task is hazardous.

Safe Jump: A ship at least 100 diameters out from all massive bodies, using the proper fuel, and with properly maintained drives can make a safe jump with no chance of a mishap.

Dangerous Jump: If the ship is within 100 diameters of a massive body, this task is Difficult (hazardous).

Desperate Jump: If the ship is within 10 diameters of a massive body, this task is Formidable (hazardous).

Mishap: If a mishap occurs, go to step 15.

9 Jumpspace

The vessel enters jumpspace and travels to the world which the navigator designated. This ship remains in jumpspace for about one week (under normal circumstances).

Determine how much time the ship spent in jumpspace by rolling 1D: 1=6 days; 2 to 5=days; 6=8 days.

10 Emerge From Jumpspace

The ship emerges from jumpspace. The ship emerges at the limit of the gravity well (at about 100 diameters out) of the destination world that the navigator designated in jump preparation. The ship must be taken from 100 diameters in to ten diameters.

To pilot a ship in from 100 diameters: Simple, Pilot or Ship's Boat, Edu.
Referee: The Travel Times from 100 Diameters Table shows the expected travel times.

TRAVEL TIMES FROM 100 DIAMETERS

World Size	*Acceleration* 1G	2G	3G	4G	5G	6G
0	45m	32m	26m	22m	20m	18m
1	2.1h	1.4h	1.2h	63m	57m	52m
2	3.0h	2.1h	1.7h	1.5h	1.3h	1.2h
3	3.7h	2.6h	2.1h	1.8h	1.6h	1.5h
4	4.2h	3.0h	2.4h	2.1h	1.9h	1.7h
5	4.7h	3.3h	2.7h	2.4h	2.1h	1.9h
6	5.2h	3.7h	3.0h	2.6h	2.3h	2.1h
7	5.6h	3.9h	3.2h	2.8h	2.5h	2.3h
8	6.0h	4.2h	3.4h	3.0h	2.7h	2.4h
9	6.3h	4.5h	3.7h	3.2h	2.8h	2.6h
A	6.7h	4.7h	3.8h	3.3h	3.0h	2.7h
SGG	10h	7.5h	6.1h	5.3h	4.7h	4.3h
LGG	18h	12h	10h	9.1h	8.2h	7.5h

Starship Encounters: Check for a starship encounter during this journey.

11 Travel From Ten Diameters

Take the ship from ten diameters in to orbit.

To pilot a ship in from ten diameters: Simple, Pilot or Ship's Boat, Edu.
Referee: The Travel Times from Ten Diameters Table shows the expected travel times.

TRAVEL TIMES FROM TEN DIAMETERS

World Size	*Acceleration* 1G	2G	3G	4G	5G	6G
0	14m	10m	18m	7m	6m	5m
1	40m	28m	23m	20m	28m	16m
2	57m	40m	33m	28m	25m	23m
3	69m	49m	40m	35m	31m	28m
4	1.3h	57m	46m	40m	36m	33m
5	1.5h	63m	52m	45m	40m	37m
6	1.6h	69m	57m	49m	44m	40m
7	1.8h	1.2h	61m	53m	47m	43m
8	1.9h	1.3h	65m	57m	51m	46m
9	2.0h	1.4h	69m	60m	54m	49m
A	2.1h	1.5h	1.2h	63m	57m	52m
SGG	3.3h	2.4h	1.9h	1.7h	1.5h	1.4h
LGG	5.8h	4.1h	3.3h	2.9h	2.6	2.4h

Starship Encounters: Check for a starship encounter during this journey.

12 Travel From Orbit

The ship is in orbit. Unstreamlined ships deliver cargo to orbiting stations if the world has a type A or B starport. Small craft and streamlined ships can descend to the world surface.

To pilot a ship from surface to orbit: Routine, Pilot or Ship's Boat, Edu.
Referee: The Travel Times from Orbit table shows the expected travel times.

TRAVEL TIMES FROM ORBIT

World Size	*Acceleration* 1G	2G	3G	4G	5G	6G
0	6m	5m	4m	3m	2m	1m
1	13m	9m	8m	7m	6m	5m
2	19m	13m	11m	9m	8m	8m
3	23m	16m	13m	12m	10m	9m
4	27m	19m	15m	13m	12m	11m
5	30m	21m	17m	15m	13m	12m
6	33m	23m	19m	16m	15m	13m
7	35m	25m	20m	18m	16m	14m
8	38m	27m	22m	19m	17m	15m
9	40m	28m	23m	20m	18m	16m
A	42m	30m	24m	21m	19m	17m

Starship Encounters: Check for a starship encounter during this journey.

13 Refuelling

The ship may be refuelled when fuel is available.

Gas Giant Refuelling: If the ship is streamlined or airframe and is in orbit around a gas giant, it can skim the gas giant's atmosphere for fuel.

To skim a gas giant for starship fuel: Routine, Pilot, Navigation, 1 hour (hazardous).
Referee: Mishaps can include simple turbulence, excessive radiation exposure, collisions with debris, or heat damage to the hull.

Ocean Refuelling: If the ship has reached the surface of a world with a nonzero Hydrographics percentage, it can obtain fuel from an ocean.

To refuel a starship from an ocean: Routine, Pilot, Sensor Ops, 30 min.

Starport Refuelling: Starports offer refuelling services. Refined fuel (at type A and B starports) costs Cr500 per kiloliter; unrefined fuel (at type A, B, C, and D starports) costs Cr100 per kiloliter.

14 In System Transfer

A ship may need to move from a world to a gas giant or from a gas giant to a world. After moving out to 100 diameters, a ship can transfer within a system.

To transfer insystem: Simple, Pilot or Ship's Boat, Navig, 5 hrs.

15 Jump Mishaps

If a mishap occurs when the jump drive is engaged, handle it as follows.

Superficial: A jump relativity error occurs. The ship remains in jumpspace 1D+4 days (from 5 to 10 days) before emerging in the destination system, otherwise unharmed.

Minor: A jump relativity error occurs, but when the ship emerges in the destination system, it is 1D times 8 hours from the destination world.

Major: A jump relativity error occurs. When the ship emerges from jump, it discovers that it has misjumped.

Throw 1D for the number of dice to throw. Then throw that number of dice for the distance (in parsecs or map hexes) the ship travelled. Finally, throw 1D for the direction of the misjump.

Destroyed: The ship is destroyed.

16 Crew Settlement

The crew of the ship is paid every month. Assuming one week in jump and one week in system, they are paid approximately every two jumps.

The following are typical salary schedules:

Bridge Crew: Cr500 times BRN plus 10% for each level of Pilot or Navigation or Leader skill.

Engineering Crew: Cr500 times BRN plus 10% for each level of Engineering skill.

Maintenance Crew: Cr500 plus 10% for each level of Admin or Mechanical skill.

Command Crew: Cr1000 times BRN plus 10% for each level of Pilot or Leader.

Gunners: Cr500 plus 10% for each level of any applicable Gunnery skill.

Flight Crew: Cr1000 plus 10% for each level of Pilot or Ship's Boat skill.

Ship's Troops: Cr500.

Stewards: Cr500 times Steward skill.

Frozen Watch: Cr500.

Medical Crew: Cr500 times Medical skill.

Note: BRN is the Basic Rank Number from character generation: Merchant 4th Officer and Naval Ensign are Basic Rank Number 1.

Spinward Marches Data

This listing provides basic information about the worlds of the Spinward Marches. The text listing is divided into eight columns.

Hex: Hex indicates the hex number location of the system in the Spinward Marches. The first two digits indicate the column of hexes on the map; the second two digits indicate the row.

UWP: The Universal World Profile for the mainworld of the system.

B: The B column indicates bases which may be present in the system. The meanings for the base symbols are given in the notes at the end of the text.

Remarks: Trade classifications and remarks are given under Remarks.

Data: Data consists of three digits followed by a two letter allegiance code. The three digits may be preceded by a travel zone code (A for Amber; R for Red). The three digits indicate successively the population multiplier, the number of planetoid belts in the system, and the number of gas giants in the system.

Allegiance: The identification of the government which controls the system is provided by allegiance. The meanings of the abbreviations are given at the end of the text.

Stars: The spectral classes and sizes of the stars in the system are provided under the headings Star1, Star2, and Star3.

BASES

The following abbreviations are used for bases: A—Imperial Naval co-located with Imperial Scout. B—Imperial Naval co-located with Imperial Scout Way Station. G—Military Garrison. M—Non-Imperial Military. N—Imperial Naval. S—Imperial Scout. W—Imperial Scout Way Station. Z—Zhodani Naval.

REMARKS

The following abbreviations are used for trade classifications: Ag—Agricultural. As—Asteroid Belt. Ba—Barren. Desert World. Ic—Ice-Capped. In—Industrial. Hi—High Population. Lo—Low Population. Na—Non-Agricultural. Ni—Non-Industrial. Po—Poor. Ri—Rich. Va—Vacuum. Wa—Water World.

In addition, the following remarks are used: An—Ancient Site. Ex—Exile Camp. Pr—Prison. Re—Reserve. RsA—Research Station Alpha. RsB—Research Station Beta. RsG—Research Station Gamma. RsD—Research Station Delta. RsE—Research Station Epsilon. RsZ—Research Station Zeta. RsH—Research Station Eta. ☆—Subsector or Local Capital. ★—Imperial Sector Capital.

ALLEGIANCE

The following abbreviations are used for allegiances: As—Aslan New Lords. Bw—Border Worlds. Cs—Client State (of the Imperium). Da—Darrian Confederation. Dr—Droyne World. Fa—Federation of Arden. Im—Imperial. Na—Non-Aligned (Human). Sw—Sword World Confederation. Va—Vargr. Zh—Zhodani.

Hex	*UPP*	*B*	*Remarks*	*Data*	*Star1*	*Star2*	*Star3*
0101	C330698-9	A	Na Ni Po De	613Zh	M9 V		
0102	C1207B9-A		Na Po De	603Zh	G8 V	M1 D	
0103	B263664-B	Z	Ni Ri	910Zh	M1 V	M4 D	
0104	C366243-9		Lo Ni	520Zh	F1 III		
0108	D8B2889-5		Fl	824Na	A8 IV		
0111	B310598-8		Ni	933Na	K8 VI		
0114	C6B6431-A		Ni Fl	123Na	G4 V	M4 D	
0115	EA95124-4		Lo Ni	910Na	M0 III		
0122	D150441-4		Ni Po De	210Na	M3 V	M2 D	
0129	E62556B-4		Ni	210Na	K9 V	M9 D	
0130	A2008CB-A		Na Va	210Na	M1 V	M5 D	
0133	B564500-B	N	Ag Ni	A503Im	M0 V		
0139	B130300-B	N	Lo Ni Po De	A920Im	G3 V	M1 D	
0140	E687200-0		Lo Ni	702Na	K7 V		
0202	C868586-5		Ag Ni	801Zh	G5 V	M3 D	
0212	C436635-6		Ni	720Na	A9 V	K8 VI	
0215	E766674-4		Ag Ni Ri	903Va	A0 IV	M6 D	
0218	E200100-8		Lo Ni Va	812Na	K2 V		
0223	B321588-B		Ni Po	701Da	M0 V	M3 D	
0230	D833000-3		Lo Ba Ni Po	504Na	F8 V		
0231	EAA5543-7		Ni Fl	910Na	A2 V		
0236	C695735-9		Ag An	R603Dr	F3 V		
0240	E754401-8		Ni	924Na	G2 V		
0301	C686648-8		Ag Ni Ri	201Na	M1 V	M0 D	
0303	B21169B-C	Z	Na Ni Ic	801Zh	M9 D	M9 D	
0304	A6369A5-D	Z	Hi ☆	810Zh	M8 V		
0307	B4337CA-A	Z	Na Po An	810Zh	F7 V	M9 D	
0311	B46258A-8		Ni	323Na	F3 V		
0321	C233898-A	G	Na Po	623Na	G0 V		
0325	B354443-7	M	Ni	834Da	F0 V		
0326	C332652-9		Na Ni Po	423Da	M5 V		
0332	E22159B-6		Ni Po	310Im	F5 IV		
0333	B9998A6-A	B		A514Im	M6 V		
0336	C593634-8		Ni An	R920Dr	F6 V	M3 D	
0340	E88A46A-4		Ni Wa	210Na	M3 V	M1 D	
0412	B200310-A	Z	Lo Ni Va	701Zh	M3 V	M3 D	
0414	C400546-8		Ni Va	810Na	K1 VI	M6 D	
0416	E8C69AA-5		Hi Fl RsD	910Cs	M9 V		
0421	E897977-A		Hi In	223Da	M9 V		
0425	C554769-8		Ag	701Da	M1 V	M3 D	
0426	B444831-9	M		401Da	G3 V	M8 D	
0427	B566777-9		Ag Ri	420Da	K8 V	M9 D	
0429	E453123-6		Lo Ni Po An	410Na	F7 V		
0430	C774622-5		Ag Ni	310Cs	M5 V	M3 D	
0433	B792785-9	N		A810Im	M8 V	M5 D	
0440	D100133-7		Lo Ni Va	A202Na	G3IV	M6 D	
0503	D648500-8		Ag Ni	610Na	M8 V		
0511	C786342-9		Lo Ni	812Na	M7 D		

Hex	UPP	B	Remarks	Data	Star1	Star2	Star3
0512	E596400-4		Ni	205Zh	K8 V		
0518	D445436-3		Ni	810Cs	K9 V	M7 D	
0526	D765657-3		Ag Ni Ri	103Da	F4 V	M7 D	
0527	A665A95-B	M	Hi ☆	110Da	M6 V		
0528	E54779B-5		Ag	901Na	K3 V	M0 D	
0530	E42158A-8		Ni Po	510Na	K4 V		
0532	D574654-7		Ag Ni	A410Cs	F2 V	M6 D	
0533	C460642-4		Ni Ri De	323Im	F6 V	M7VI	
0534	A767768-C	A	Ag Ri	A410Im	M7 V		
0538	B455741-7	N	Ag	A910Im	M0 V	M1 D	
0539	C535225-9		Lo Ni RsZ	601Im	M7 V	M2 D	
0601	E975776-6		Ag	323Na	F1 V		
0605	C665658-9		Ag Ni Ri	410Na	M0 V	M1 D	
0607	E883401-7		Ni	910Na	F0 V		
0608	A211666-C	Z	Na Ni Ic	410Zh	A4 D		
0610	B756779-A	Z	Ag	111Zh	F4 V	M0 D	
0613	B869554-C		Ni	901Zh	G8 V	M5 D	
0614	B254788-9	Z	Ag ☆	804Zh	M6 V		
0618	EA8A799-6		Ri Wa	320Cs	M1 V		
0620	E887573-6		Ag Ni	501Da	K5 V	M9 D	
0622	D1405A7-9		Ni Po De	523Da	G0 V	M5 D	
0624	A333644-D		Na Ni Po	710Da	M6 V		
0625	X893000-0		Lo Ba Ni	R710Da	M1 V		
0627	A463955-G		Hi	225Da	G1 V	M1 D	
0632	C754766-7	S	Ag	523Im	F8 V		
0637	C31479B-9		Ic	210Im	M8 V		
0638	E779454-7		Ni	A601Im	M6 D		
0703	E334662-5		Ni	320Na	F6 V		
0704	E738475-7		Ni	820Na	K5 V		
0705	A886865-C	Z	Ri	121Zh	G2 V		
0710	E7667A8-2		Ag	801Na	M9 V	M2 D	
0712	C592320-8	Z	Lo Ni	402Zh	M5 V	M8VI	
0717	B243653-C		Ni Po	210Cs	M9 V	M1 D	
0720	E336AAA-C		Hi	110Da	G6 V	M1 D	
0721	X233231-4		Lo Ni Po Ex	R820Da	G1 V		
0723	C446556-9		Ag Ni	210Da	M5 II		
0724	B2326BB-C	N	Na Ni Po	620Da	G0 IV		
0727	C140200-A	M	Lo Ni Po De	434Da	M7 V		
0729	D326258-6		Lo Ni An	821Na	F7 V	M7 D	
0731	E224564-8		Ni	801Na	M8 V	M3 D	
0732	A887798-C	N	Ag Ri ☆	201Im	M9 V		
0739	E5136A7-4		Na Ni Ic	701Na	M8 V	M1 D	
0805	D525688-6	Z	Ni	A603Na	G4 V	M6VI	
0807	E845300-3		Lo Ni	910Na	G8 V	M7 D	
0808	B532720-B	N	Na Po	A401Im	M2 V		
0810	E9C3300-9		Lo Ni Fl	103Cs	F8 V		
0820	C110588-8		Ni	601Da	M6VI	M0 D	
0822	E65767A-3		Ag Ni	502Da	M0 V		
0830	B854123-9		Lo Ni	A822Cs	M2 V		
0834	E888421-7	S	Ni	A510Cs	M8 V	M7 D	
0837	E747569-7		Ag Ni	210Na	G8VI	M8 D	
0838	D786799-5		Ag Ri	701Na	M3 V	M3 D	
0840	E100316-9		Lo Ni Va	821Na	M0 V		
0901	E7A1522-8		Ni Fl	923Na	F8 III		
0902	C7B3386-9		Lo Ni Fl	502Na	K8 V	M4 D	
0904	B766766-A	Z	Ag Ri	A424Zh	M2 V		
0909	C372510-A		Ni	A420Cs	K2 V		
0911	C796746-5		Ag	510Na	G2 V	M4 D	
0912	E201300-8		Lo Ni Va Ic	520Na	F7 V		
0915	B200545-9		Ni Va	204fA	M3 V		
0919	X6B0000-0		Lo Ba Ni De	R020Na	M4 V		
0921	B463747-9	M	Ri	313Sw	M2 V		
0922	B386887-A	M	Ri	323Sw	K2IV	M3 D	
0927	B574A55-A	M	Hi In	224Sw	M0 II	M6 D	
0930	A623514-B	B	Ni Po	710Im	F8 V		
0931	B7A7402-A		Ni Fl	210Na	K7 V	M3 D	
0938	D12035C-A		Lo Ni Po De	823Na	F0 III		
0940	D553774-6		Po	901Na	M2 V	M2 D	
1004	C565673-8		Ag Ni Ri	A223Cs	F3 V	M5 D	
1005	B400445-B	S	Ni Va	201Im	M1 V	M3 D	
1006	B766555-B	S	Ag Ni	534Im	M1VI		
1010	D130546-7		Ni Po De	622fA	M8 D		
1011	C5549CB-8		Hi	810Fa	M4 V	M5 D	
1018	C200100-9		Lo Ni Va	101Im	M9 V	M4 D	
1020	C575677-6		Ag Ni	A910Im	M4 V	M7 D	
1022	B364685-B	M	Ag Ni Ri	A211Sw	K2 V	M8 D	
1026	B985855-B	M	Ri	222Sw	F2 V		
1031	E532000-8		Lo Ba Ni Po	310Na	M9 V	M1 D	
1037	C433520-A		Ni Po	724Na	M8VI		
1040	C503758-A		Na Va Ic	320Na	K3 V		
1102	C566A99-9		Hi	A214Zh	M7 III		
1103	B672899-A	Z		A901Zh	M8 V		
1106	A777999-C	A	Hi In ☆	623Im	G7 V		
1110	C792668-8	G	Ni	624Fa	F0 V		
1116	A200436-A	N	Ni Va ☆	110Im	M2III	M3 D	
1118	B978868-A	S		912Im	M3 V		
1119	A593943-A		Hi In	820Im	G5 V	M8 D	
1121	B530544-A	M	Ni Po De	522Sw	A5 V	G0 D	
1123	B464778-A	M	Ag Ri	A201Sw	M3 V	M9 D	
1126	B8A6733-A	M	Fl	401Sw	M7 V	M7 D	
1130	E25059B-4	G	Ni Po De	710Sw	M9 V		
1131	E5936A7-2		Ni	520Na	M7III		
1132	D000300-9	S	Lo Ni As	811Cs	M0 V		
1133	C438679-9		Ni	320Na	F0 V		
1138	B584620-A		Ag Ni	202Cs	K9 V		
1201	E410644-6		Na Ni	312Zh	K2 V	M3 D	
1204	A368685-A	A	Ag Ni Ri	603Im	M6III	M0 D	
1209	C473464-7		Ni	410Fa	M0 V		
1210	E5656B9-4		Ag Ni	710fA	M5 V		
1212	E53668A-5		Ni	920Na	M6III		
1213	E400220-5		Lo Ni Va	A401Cs	K6 V	M0 D	
1214	D955000-2		Lo Ba Ni	610Im	F1 V	M4 D	
1216	D5A4420-4		Ni Fl	210Im	M9III		
1217	E446845-6			402Im	M8 V		
1221	B444779-8	M	Ag	432Sw	G3IV	M4VI	
1223	A895957-B	M	Hi In ☆	603Sw	F2 D	M2 D	
1225	B324755-A	M		402Sw	M5 V		
1232	C544338-8	S	Lo Ni	302Cs	M5 V		
1233	E5A1422-6		Ni Fl	610Na	M8 V	M2 D	
1237	B628943-D	S	Hi In	101Cs	F1 V	M6 D	
1238	C6678D8-6			A701Cs	M7 V		
1305	D591314-2		Lo Ni	A501Im	M6 V	M0 D	
1307	B592655-A	S	Ni	623Im	M9 V		
1311	B511411-C		Ni Ic	201fA	K8 V	M5 D	
1315	E472300-8	N	Lo Ni	110Im	F5 V		
1320	D888588-7		Ag Ni	820Im	A8 V	M1VI	
1324	B637735-A	M		701Bw	M4 V		
1325	B775956-C	M	Hi In	801Bw	F9 V	M8 D	
1329	B365776-A	S	Ag Ri	710Im	F7 V	M0 D	M4 D
1331	E227633-8		Ni	801Na	M7 V		
1332	X600000-0		Lo Ba Ni Va	R011Na	K8 V		
1337	E9B2000-8		Lo Ba Ni Fl RsH	321As	M3III		
1339	B361851-C		Ri	923Na	M0 D		
1340	B68468B-5	N	Ag Ni Ri	710Cs	M2 V	M2 D	
1401	B638665-8		Ni	A910Zh	K0 V		
1402	A200400-B	Z	Ni Va	A415Zh	M3 II	M0 V	
1411	E67A612-7		Ni Wa	503Na	M8 V		
1413	B739573-A	N	Ni	324Im	M2 V		
1417	E567353-5		Lo Ni	910Im	M0 V	M1 D	
1424	B685686-A	M	Ag Ni Ri	610Bw	M4 V		
1429	E344110-8		Lo Ni	A602Im	M6 V		
1430	E000514-A		Ni As	924Im	M7VI		
1433	E7A5747-6		Fl	602Na	M5VI	M2 D	
1434	C466662-7	S	Ag Ni Ri	A310Cs	M0 V	M2 D	
1435	B8B5883-9		Fl	610As	F2 V		
1436	E333532-9		Ni Po	820As	F9 V	M1 D	
1510	E722000-8		Lo Ba Ni Po	801Na	M9 V	M8 D	
1511	C674321-8		Lo Ni	A210Cs	M9 V	M5 D	
1515	C334867-7			501Im	K9 V	M5 D	
1519	X3437C7-2		Po	R520Im	F5 II	M1 D	
1520	E567000-7		Lo Ba Ni	434Im	G6 II		
1522	B958412-A	M	Ni	201Bw	M4 V	M8 D	
1523	B687334-B	M	Lo Ni	714Bw	M1 V		
1524	B666553-A	M	Ag Ni	501Bw	M4 V	M9 D	
1525	B645896-A	M		302Bw	M0 V		
1526	B354623-A	M	Ag Ni	301Bw	M7 V	M1 D	
1529	E655000-7		Lo Ba Ni	324Bw	M8III		
1531	E885000-0		Lo Ba Ni	025Na	F8 D	M5 D	
1532	B426467-8	N	Ni	201Cs	M4 V	M5 D	
1533	D3129B8-A		Hi Na In Ic	610Na	M9 V		
1537	B262732-B	S	☆	610As	G1 V		
1604	D322A88-8		Hi Na In Po	110Im	M5 V		
1607	X664100-0		Lo Ni	R222Im	K6 V		
1611	C887624-8		Ag Ni	710Im	G5 V	M8 D	

Hex	UPP	B	Remarks	Data	Star1	Star2	Star3
1626	E529000-9		Lo Ba Ni	714Bw	F0 V		
1627	E201000-9		Lo Ba Ni Va Ic	510Bw	M3 V		
1628	E568000-0		Lo Ba Ni	301Bw	F4 D		
1631	C7B1462-5		Ni Fl	A601Cs	K8 V	M5VI	
1632	E21178A-7		Na Ic	920Cs	M2 V		
1634	C769873-4		Ri	913As	M0 V		
1635	A800231-A		Lo Ni Va	720As	F0 V		
1637	B9A2469-C	A	Ni Fl	301As	M6 V		
1705	A646930-D	B	Hi In	800Im	K4 V		
1706	B46789C-A		Ri	410Im	M7 V	M7 D	
1711	B45589A-A	N		110Im	M2 V	M4 D	
1719	A879533-B	A	Ni ☆	710Im	F5 IV	M9 D	
1721	C200200-C		Lo Ni Va	610Im	K2 V		
1727	B756486-B	S	Ni	A502Im	M2 V		
1728	C328342-7		Lo Ni	120Im	M6 V		
1729	C14078A-9		Po De	902Im	M1 V	M7 D	
1731	A400404-B		Ni Va	124Im	F8 V		
1733	E110430-6		Ni	902Im	M4III	M0VI	
1736	D140466-7		Ni Po De	A724As	G3 V		
1737	BAC6567-7	N	Ni Fl	521As	F8 V		
1739	C86A410-9		Ni Wa	401As	M9 V		
1802	BAC6773-7		Fl	335Im	G5 V		
1803	C652998-7		Hi Po	310Im	M5 II		
1805	B439598-D		Ni	320Im	M9 V		
1806	E676126-7		Lo Ni	224Im	A1 V	M1 D	
1807	E888787-2		Ag Ri	834Im	G3 V		
1808	E893614-4		Ni	312Im	G0 V		
1809	C776977-7		Hi In	A701Na	M5 V		
1810	C799663-9	S	Ni	323Im	M0 V		
1811	D100535-A		Ni Va	201Im	A4 III		
1815	B211455-A	N	Ni Ic	303Im	F8 V	M3 D	
1817	X697772-2		Ag	R112Im	M6 V		
1822	D5448BA-6	S		313Im	M5 D		
1824	A57189B-B	N		801Im	K8 V	M8 D	
1825	B000544-B		Ni As	512Im	G5 III		
1826	A774102-E		Lo Ni An	610Im	F7 V		
1836	E150852-6		Po De	810As	M7 V		
1903	A100103-D	N	Lo Ni Va	901Im	M1 V	M0 D	
1904	A8B3531-D	S	Ni Fl	601Im	M7 V		
1909	C200423-7	S	Ni Va	A320Im	K6 II	M6 D	
1910	A788899-C	A	Ri ☆	703Im	F7 V	M8 D	M6 V
1912	B674632-9	S	Ag Ni	204Im	M8VI		
1916	X587552-4		Ag Ni	R922Im	F9 V		
1918	X6266AB-3		Ni	R314Im	K6 V	M0 D	
1920	B120410-D	N	Ni Po De	312Im	M3 V	M0 D	
1924	E360697-5		Ni Ri De	924Im	M6 II	M9 D	
1927	C766846-8	S	Ri	715Im	M7 V		
1932	C8B5546-6		Ni Fl Pr	302As	M7 V		
1934	A626464-B		Ni	A703As	M0III	M2 D	
1935	C783511-9		Ni	210As	K9 V	M0 D	
1937	B45467A-9		Ag Ni	423As	G3 V		
1938	B837866-B	N		704As	F8 V	M0 D	
1939	C573645-3		Ni	923As	G7 V		
2005	B384879-B	S	Ri	620Im	G4 V	M3 D	
2007	C77A9A9-7	S	Hi In Wa	A323Im	F9 V		
2011	E9C4547-8		Ni Fl	A922Im	M3 V		
2024	C512799-8	S	Na Ic	901Im	M0 V	M7 D	
2035	B443987-9		Hi In Po	A214As	G6 V	M2 D	
2036	A000986-F	A	Hi Na In As ☆	821As	K9 V		
2038	C639422-B		Ni An	704As	F4 V	M3 D	
2106	X355423-1		Ni	R501Im	M5VI		
2110	C360757-A		Ri De RsB	713Im	F1 V		
2111	E459000-9		Lo Ba Ni	R822Im	K5 V		
2112	D9957AA-6		Ag	501Im	M0 V		
2124	A995984-D	A	Hi In ☆	810Im	M3 D	M7 D	
2125	B984510-B	S	Ag Ni	A723Im	G4 V	M1 D	M1 D
2128	X978310-1		Lo Ni	R320Im	M0 V		
2129	C330737-9		Na Po De	910Im	M7 D	M5 D	
2132	E222447-6		Ni Po	220As	K3 V		
2134	C541636-5		Ni Po	910As	M4III	M0 D	
2137	E48569A-2		Ag Ni Ri	921As	G3 V	M3 D	
2138	C3378A6-A	S		920As	F4 V		
2140	B450456-B	A	Ni Po De	112As	M5 V	M3 D	
2201	C979500-A	S	Ni	920Va	M2 V		
2202	A663659-8		Ni Ri	622Va	M7 V		
2204	D88349D-4		Ni	701Im	M0 V	M2 D	
2205	C411988-6		Hi Na In	600Im	M6 V	M5 D	
2207	EAC28CC-9		Fl	703Im	F0 V		
2212	CAA5345-8		Lo Ni Fl	102Im	M8 V		
2215	B150679-A		Ni Po De	A721Im	M3 V		
2224	C463325-9		Lo Ni	601Im	M8 V	M6 D	
2228	B775833-A	W		922Im	M2 V		
2231	D868772-5		Ag Ri Re	924As	M7 V		
2232	E4359CA-7		Hi	314As	M7 II	M9VI	
2233	C7B5975-B		Hi Fl	621As	K5 V		
2234	C100598-B		Ni Va	924As	K3 V		
2236	D120636-5		Na Ni Po De	A301As	M5 V	M2 D	
2237	C795300-A	S	Lo Ni	A510As	F8 V		
2303	C7C6503-7		Ni Fl	220Va	M8VI		
2306	X000742-8		Na As	R714Im	M4 V		
2308	X766977-4		Hi	R723Im	M9VI		
2309	E7B4643-5		Ni Fl	824Im	K9 V		
2311	D232866-8		Na Po	610Im	M1 V		
2313	C53A313-A		Lo Ni Wa	720Im	G4 V		
2314	D691142-5		Lo Ni	802Im	M4 V		
2317	C100576-A		Ni Va	A710Im	M7 V		
2319	B324659-A	A	Ni	112Im	A9 V		
2321	B365300-8		Lo Ni	323Im	M6 V		
2322	X554220-0		Lo Ni	R801Im	M8 V	M6VI	
2323	B310100-B	S	Lo Ni	501Im	M5 V	M8 D	
2324	B747748-A	N	Ag	610Im	M9 D		
2325	C575101-A		Lo Ni	503Im	K5 V		
2327	A745988-D	N	Hi In	920Im	M5 V	M4 D	
2331	E563576-2		Ni	210As	M0 V		
2334	A41489D-C		Ic	904As	F3 V	M3VI	
2336	A756656-C	A	Ag Ni	820As	A5 V		
2402	B687745-5		Ag Ri	734Va	K6 III	M8 D	
2405	E2718CA-3			812Im	G5 III	M9 D	
2406	CA5A588-B		Ni Wa	801Im	M9 V	M9 D	
2408	E230AA8-8		Hi Na Po De	323Im	G7 V		
2410	B575776-9	A	Ag	423Im	F8 V		
2411	C792348-7	S	Lo Ni	213Im	M3 III	M2 D	
2414	C465540-9		Ag Ni	614Im	M3 V		
2415	E481542-3		Ni RsE	901Im	M9 V		
2416	C564112-4		Lo Ni	701Im	F2 V	M3 D	
2417	B55A858-B	S	Wa	202Im	F6 V	M5 D	
2418	B5245A9-7	N	Ni	A301Im	M9 V	M8 D	
2419	CA6A643-9		Ni Ri Wa	432Im	M1 II		
2420	C2237C7-9	N	Na Po	601Im	M1 V	M0VI	
2425	E000347-8		Lo Ni As	813Im	M7 V		
2426	EAB6311-5		Lo Ni Fl	904Im	F1 V		
2509	A655241-9	N	Lo Ni	603Im	F3 V		
2510	C9A769D-4		Ni Fl	202Im	M5 V		
2512	C449433-9		Ni	502Im	A0 V	K9 D	
2514	C483103-6		Lo Ni	203Im	M9 V		
2519	E9C5677-7		Ni Fl	224Im	K5 V		
2520	B632520-7	S	Ni Po	410Im	M0 V	M7 D	
2521	B6449B9-8		Hi In	721Im	F3 V		
2523	B485697-6		Ag Ni Ri	812Im	M9 V		
2527	E500343-4		Lo Ni Va	903Im	K0 V		
2534	C462667-8		Ni Ri	402Im	M4 V		
2536	A300550-B		Ni Va	303As	F4 V	M7 D	
2537	A450457-A	S	Ni Po De	523As	G0 V		
2538	E566335-2		Lo Ni	214As	M6 V		
2539	E4305AD-5		Ni Po De	322As	F8 II		
2540	B659772-6			924As	M5 V		
2602	X895674-8		Ag Ni	R222Va	M0 V		
2607	EA88544-A		Ag Ni	724Va	F3 V		
2612	B000453-E	N	Ni As	911Im	G8 V	M8 D	
2613	A674210-D		Lo Ni	810Im	G3 V		
2620	C8879AB-9		Hi An	204Im	F4 V		
2621	A633656-A		Na Ni Po	620Im	M3 V		
2624	B658663-8	A	Ag Ni	304Im	F7 V		
2627	C534477-8		Ni	401Im	M3 V		
2632	X895674-8		Ag Ni An	R201Im	F3 V	M0 D	
2637	C00059C-C		Ni As	212As	M5 V		
2638	E75A798-5		Wa	910As	F4 IV		
2639	C525567-9		Ni	602As	M6 V		
2701	B646589-A		Ag Ni	503Va	M2 III	M4 D	
2706	E66A224-C		Lo Ni Wa	510Va	M5 V	M7 D	
2708	C669452-A		Ni	420Va	M0 V		
2712	A325579-A	N	Ni	401Im	M5 V	M3 D	
2715	A867A74-B		Hi	201Im	M1 V	M9 D	
2716	A434934-F	A	Hi ☆	810Im	M2VI		